Larry Harrison

GLIMPSES OF A FLOATING WORLD

Year Zero Writers
http://yearzerowriters.wordpress.com

First published in 2009 by Lulu.com
http://www.lulu.com

Larry Harrison is a member of the Year Zero writers' collective.

Year Zero Writers
http://yearzerowriters.wordpress.com

ISBN 978-1-4092-9338-5

Acknowledgements

Thanks are due to my wife, Mary, to Dan Holloway and Oliver Johns, and my colleagues in the Year Zero Writers group, and to all of my supporters on the Authonomy website. I also benefited from the advice of John Murray, Martyn Bedford and the Arvon group of 2007. Special thanks are due to my first readers: Andy Alaszewski, Hannah Davis, Bill Downs, David Fernbach and Robert Harris.

About the author

Larry Harrison started life as a cowman and yak keeper for the Tibetan Buddhist community at Karma Kagyu Samye Ling, in Dumfriesshire. After working his way up to the post of assistant dairyman on a commercial Ayrshire herd, he left Scotland in 1975 to work with disadvantaged children at London's Clapham Junction. Larry became surprisingly good at persuading children not to stand on the railway tracks at Earlsfield Station, and he was able to talk them down from rooftops in Battersea, without them bombarding passers-by with slates. To this day, Larry is relieved that he was able to negotiate the release of everyone held hostage by Barry in the school unit. The Parks Department should not have left an axe unattended within sight of the building, and had Barry not been so amenable, the outcome could have been a good deal worse. (Thanks, Baz. What fun we had! Sorry to hear you were done last year for kidnapping that Assistant Governor on D Wing.) During Larry's subsequent career, as a university researcher on alcohol and drug problems, he wrote *Tobacco Battered*, a BBC Radio 4 feature, and over fifty journal articles, academic books and book chapters. He was appointed Reader in Addiction Studies at the University of Hull, long a centre of excellence in problem drinking, before retiring to the East Yorkshire countryside to make cider and write fiction. *Glimpses of a Floating World* is his first novel.

Chapter One

The Sandman leaned against the balustrade and punched the stone until bright spots of blood appeared on his knuckles.

'This is turning out to be a bloody awful year.' He stared out across a rain-swept Trafalgar Square, as if searching for someone to blame. 'The beginning of June? More like non-stop bloody winter.'

'Yeah, and you're bringing me down,' Ronnie Jarvis said. It was bad enough having to wait all evening for a fix, without having to listen to some cunt moaning all the time. He took several short, impatient drags at his cigarette. A shred of tobacco found its way onto his tongue, and he wiped his mouth with the back of his hand. The act was hasty and ill-judged. His umbrella tilted and raindrops cascaded down, soaking the cigarette. Ronnie gazed at the sodden Woodbine in disgust, then hurled it into the gutter.

'Things are falling apart,' the Sandman whined. 'Weeks of snow, and then continual bloody rain. It's unnatural.' He looked distraught. 'Did you know that Nostradamus predicted the world would end this year?' Ronnie waved his hands dismissively, as if shooing pigeons, and the Sandman became insistent. 'It's true, man. Nostradamus predicted the world would end in 1963. *In the year of Our Lord One Thousand Nine Hundred and Sixty-three, the world by ice will cease to be.* They reckon it means there's going to be a new Ice Age.'

'You're junk-sick,' Ronnie said. 'You'd feel cold in the Turkish Baths.'

Ronnie looked at his watch and counted the minutes. As usual, he was conducting a mental countdown until the midnight hour, when the next day's prescriptions would be dispensed at the all-night chemist's in Piccadilly Circus. 'Not long to go,' Ronnie said, trying to sound upbeat. 'Twenty minutes to the witching hour.'

'Gypsy Dave owes me four fucking jacks.'

'How does it go?' Ronnie said. 'The witching time of night, when something-something? When graveyards yawn?'

'No idea!'

For fuck's sake, Ronnie thought, you're only nineteen. Only three years older than me, and you're whining like an old man. 'Don't you ever read Classic Comics?' Ronnie sighed. 'The world's greatest authors meet its finest cartoonists? *When graveyards yawn* is from number 99. Hamlet, by William Shakespeare. Artwork by Steve Grant.'

'Gypsy Dave sneaked out of the Three Tuns yesterday and thought I hadn't seen him,' the Sandman mumbled, from underneath his umbrella.

His flat, nasal voice hardly varied in tone; it made a low droning sound, like an engine stuck in first gear. 'People are always taking liberties.'

The Sandman had been pestering Ronnie since lunchtime, trying to score some H. The berk wasn't interested in a two quid ball of opium, he wanted to hold out for heroin. He would wait, he said, until Ronnie got his script at midnight. Then he fastened onto Ronnie like one of those toothless catfish that suck the life out of their prey.

Ronnie began walking slowly towards Pall Mall, and the Sandman lurched after him. 'You still in that Marshall Street squat?' the Sandman called out. 'I need to crash there tonight.'

'It was closed down weeks ago. I'm staying up in Archway, with Samantha and Guido. A Black chick I know from Swindon, and her feller.'

'Oh yes, I forgot. You're a country boy.'

'You keep saying that!' Ronnie snapped. 'I'm a Londoner, like you.'

'Nothing to be ashamed about, being from the sticks.'

'For fuck's sake!'

Eighteen minutes left. Ronnie hated these last few minutes when he was waiting for his script. If there was a God, you could offer Him a deal. God, take away the next eighteen minutes. Let it be midnight now. Take a quarter of an hour off the end of my life. I don't mind dying a bit earlier, if I can have my fix *right now.*

'Gypsy Dave's turned a lot of people over,' the Sandman was saying. 'I know exactly how I'm going to get even with him—'

'Can't you walk a bit faster?' Ronnie said. 'It's a long way up the Haymarket.'

Ronnie was aware that they looked an odd pair as they left Trafalgar Square. He was tall enough to be a guardsman, while the Sandman was only five foot four inches. Ronnie was proud of his classy walk: he bounced on the balls of his feet, ready to move in any direction, like a tennis player. The Sandman kicked his feet forward, sullenly, like a squaddie engaged on a route march. And Ronnie's blond hair reached his shoulders in ringlets, while the Sandman had his hair cropped short.

Growing his hair long had been one of Ronnie's big accomplishments in life. When he first saw a man with long hair, at the Anarchist Ball in 1962, the level of public hostility fascinated him. People stood in the street and stared; men's faces were contorted with rage. From that moment, Ronnie knew he had to grow his hair long. It was an act of defiance, and he often paid a heavy price. Sometimes, shop assistants refused to serve him, or bus conductors wouldn't allow him onboard. Once, as he walked along Brighton beach, the preacher at an open-air evangelical meeting interrupted his sermon to condemn longhaired men.

Today had been free of incident, but as they headed up the Haymarket, an ex-soldier screamed out, 'Get your hair cut!' The man was pacing to and fro, on the opposite side of the road, outside Her Majesty's Theatre. One sleeve of his regimental blazer was empty, pinned back across his chest, surplus to requirements since the day he'd lost his arm. His thin face was pink with anger.

'Get your throat cut!' Ronnie shouted back. He noticed disapproval in the Sandman's expression and grinned. 'That usually shuts them up,' he explained. 'You can't let the buggers get the upper hand.'

The Sandman frowned. 'You ought to get rid of your barnet. Long hair attracts too much attention.'

Ronnie shook his head, so that his hair spread out over his shoulders and could be seen to best effect. They turned into Piccadilly Circus, and Ronnie stood and stared across at the statue of Eros, silhouetted against the neon advertising displays behind: Coca Cola, Wrigley's Chewing Gum, Gordon's Gin. 'During the war,' Ronnie said, 'the Yanks called Piccadilly Circus the biggest open-air whorehouse in the world.'

'It still is,' the Sandman sniffed.

Ronnie thought of the wartime poster his doctor had never bothered to remove from the surgery wall. A woman was wearing a pink orchid on her hat, only her face was dissolving into a skull. *Hello boys, coming my way?* Venereal disease. She may look clean, but she's a carrier. She's as dangerous as a Panzer division. Doing Hitler's work for him.

Ronnie checked his watch. Seven minutes to go. Time seemed to slow down when he was waiting for a fix, each minute stretching, until the last few moments lasted for hours. Then, when he shot up, time ceased to have any importance. He would get up late tomorrow, have his morning fix, and watch children's telly, or take an hour or more over coffee and biscuits. But time always reasserted itself, gradually, and he ended every evening like this, waiting for the minute hand on his watch to edge forward.

Leaving the Sandman to wait on the corner, Ronnie walked back to the all-night chemist's. When the minute hand reached midnight, the pharmacist would begin calling out the names of people whose prescriptions carried the next day's date. Most were junkies, claiming a new day's supply. Like Ronnie, they were registered with one of a handful of private and NHS doctors who treated addicts.

Ronnie was prescribed four grains of heroin and two of cocaine every day. Last week he'd told his doctor it wasn't enough.

'Your tolerance is increasing, that's why,' the doctor said, peering over his half-moon glasses. 'We're going to have to get you in for a Cure.'

Better shut up. That's what they say when you start to hassle them. Gypsy Dave told him that private doctors like Lady Frankau were worse:

they sent you for a detox if you didn't pay your bill. When Dave hadn't paid for a while Lady Frankau said, 'I'm afraid I'm going to have to start cutting you down'. Dave took out his wallet and said, 'I'd like to settle my account'. (That's what you had to say, nothing crude like 'Do you want some loot?' or 'Here's some bread, man'. You had to keep up appearances with private doctors.) Dave said the doctor smiled as she wrote out the usual script: 'Pay the receptionist on your way out.'

Ronnie reckoned he could manage on four grains of Horse for now, even if it wasn't giving him the buzz it used to. Cocaine helped, but he didn't think of himself as a coke-head, even though he'd hassled to get coke on his script. He mainly used it to get out of bed in the mornings. When you had a big heroin habit you could get a bit lethargic. Coke helped kick-start the day. Fucked the brain into action. Made it move. He wasn't like the coke-heads, people who were mainly hooked on cocaine, who only used heroin for a soft landing. They almost always picked up their script at midnight, and injected coke continually, until it ran out in the wee small hours. You could often sell them some of your surplus coke, if you managed to hold some back.

Rain started to drip through a tear on one side of Ronnie's umbrella and he decided to wait inside the chemist's. Mr Spear, the Home Office civil servant responsible for inspecting the Dangerous Drugs Register, was standing near the pharmacy counter, chatting to three Canadian junkies. Ronnie met Spear's gaze, and felt uncomfortable. Although he had a genial manner, Spear kept every customer under surveillance; he had a mind like a card index, able to retrieve current intelligence about most addicts on the list. The Sandman reckoned that Spear knew every junky by name—all 360 of them. That may have been an exaggeration, but Spear knew all the big names, the old guys Ronnie respected because of their single-minded commitment to heroin, like Barry One-Leg and Tony Moss.

Spear joined the night-duty pharmacist, and started going through recent entries in the Dangerous Drugs Register, holding the book up at chest height, to make maximum use of the florescent light. Ronnie looked up at the clock, prominently sited on the wall above the dispensary counter, so that every customer could watch the minute hand crawl forward. Three minutes to midnight. Not much longer. Soon straighten out. Have a fag, and, by the time you've finished, it should be time.

As he lit up, he distinctly heard Spear say, 'You know, I'm a little concerned that *Our Mutual Friend* has taken on a youngster who's under seventeen.' They both looked in his direction. Bad news: they were talking about him. Although he refused to cut his hair, Ronnie hated attracting attention at times like this. He opened his paper and pretended to read, while observing Spear surreptitiously. The man glanced over several times.

Then all eyes turned towards him. The name Ronald Jarvis had been called, and he hadn't even noticed. The pharmacist was holding his prescription at arm's length, as though obliged to handle a parcel of dog shit.

Ronnie collected a paper bag containing two small medicine bottles—one with the pure white crystals of cocaine hydrochloride BP, the other with twenty-four white tablets of diacetyl-morphine hydrochloride BP. Spear was watching from his vantage point beside the counter as Ronnie rushed out, heading for the underground public toilets in Piccadilly, the Sandman in close pursuit. The Sandman handed over a ten shilling note as they trotted down the stairs, and Ronnie slipped half a grain of heroin into his friend's outstretched hand. Ronnie almost ran into the karzi and found the first available cubicle. Rather than risk attracting attention by taking water from a washbasin, he flushed the toilet and caught some water in a spare medicine bottle as it swirled around the lavatory pan. Then he cooked it up over a match, making sure it came to the boil. He added nearly a grain of heroin and half a grain of cocaine, and cooked the mixture again. That should give a nice rush. In just a few seconds that raw feeling would cease, and he would be flying high again.

As soon as he made the hit he knew that it was a dirty fix. The water hadn't boiled enough. Unsterile. He'd injected some nasty bug. Could do without that, he'd had a run of dirty fixes. Almost immediately, his stomach went into a spasm, and he started to retch. He knelt down and spewed into the toilet bowl, a thin, yellow, acidic jet, all that remained of the bacon sarney he'd had for lunch.

Still feeling queasy, Ronnie came out of the cubicle and washed his face at one of the sinks. The smell of carbolic soap always helped, he thought. Bloody witching hour. It's an unhealthy time. Fatal overdoses always happen at midnight.

Ronnie reached for a clean roller towel and started to dry his face, but the newly starched towel wouldn't absorb water easily. Bloodshot eyes stared back from the mirror as he patted his wet cheeks. Baron Samedhi prowling the graveyards, in *Tales from the Crypt*. Best comic ever. Artwork by Wally Wood.

'You scum!'

A searing pain flushed tears from Ronnie's eyes. It shot from his hair-roots, at the base of his skull, to the crown of his head. It tore at his scalp. His face was forced down into the sink, as someone seized his hair, wrapped it around their fist, and pulled.

'Cut my throat would you? Eh? Eh?' Each word was expelled through gritted teeth, like scraps forced through a meat grinder. 'Not-so-cocky-now!'

Ronnie forced his head up and saw the mirror image of the old git from the Haymarket. He had Ronnie's hair in a vice-like grip with his only hand.

'What? Get the fuck off!' Ronnie yelped like a dog, and tugged against the man's fist. 'You're mad!'

Pulled off balance, Ronnie was forced down on one knee, into a puddle. Dirty water soaked through the knee of his jeans. He held onto the washbasin to stop being dragged to the ground. He could see the ex-soldier looming above him in the mirror, the empty sleeve of the man's blazer pinned back across his chest with a safety pin, the regimental badge on his pocket, showing what looked like a lion and a crown above a red rose, and a motto that said something about *Loyalty*.

The man rammed Ronnie's head against the washbasin, opening a deep cut above his left eyebrow. Blood gushed out, running into his eyes and down his cheek, before dripping onto his green cord jacket.

'I'm sick!' Ronnie yelled. 'Let go!'

'Long hair? I'll pull the bugger out!'

A long shadow passed across the mirror, and then the Sandman came into view with an eight-inch lock knife, pointed at the assailant's back.

'Let the boy go or I'll fucking do you.'

'Want a fair fight?' the ex-serviceman shouted. 'I'll give you one! Only cowards use knives.' He pulled harder on the hair, forcing Ronnie to squeal.

'Let go,' the Sandman said, holding the man's shoulder and pressing the knife against his backbone. 'You started this. I'll do you!'

'You're dragging this country down, you scum!' The man's shoulders began to shake with convulsive sobs. 'This poor country. It's losing everything.' He let go of Ronnie's hair and knelt down in front of the washbasins, crying without restraint. 'Poor England! We gave our lives.'

Ronnie flushed with embarrassment. The man who had assaulted him looked pathetic, crouched on the floor, so frail that a breeze could knock him sideways, and hardly strong enough to threaten anyone. Ronnie exchanged a glance with the Sandman, and then walked backwards towards the exit.

'Scum!' the man called after him. 'Giving everything away. First India and now Kenya!'

The Sandman closed his lock knife and slipped it back into his pocket with one smooth hand movement, indicating, with a jerk of his head, that they should scarper. They climbed the stairs to the street level hurriedly, and then paused, gulping in the night air like men who had been confined underground for weeks.

'You are extremely lucky I was with you,' the Sandman said, putting an arm around Ronnie's shoulder, a gesture that would have been reassuring in a more trustworthy person. 'That could've been very nasty. What you got yourself into, back there.'

'Sure.'

'Well, don't get overcome with gratitude.' The Sandman displayed his narrow, crooked teeth in a sneer.

'I won't, man.'

'Only, I probably saved you from a real beating.'

Ronnie had no intention of thanking the Sandman for his assistance. Gratitude would encourage the Sandman to try to blag more junk. Besides, Ronnie didn't feel grateful; he felt resentment, because he'd been caught offguard, and the Sandman had seen him looking vulnerable, like a child.

Ronnie Fizz was on his knees in the bogs, the Sandman would say. *He was crying 'Oh! Don't touch my barnet!'—Just some old cripple! A one armed tosser! I put the frighteners on him. Fizz was shaking like a leaf, couldn't do nothing. Lost his bottle!*

Ronnie didn't want a story like that doing the rounds. Too many people on the scene treated him like a kid. People went by appearances, like the fact that he was unable to grow a beard yet. They underestimated him. Ronnie considered he'd grown-up at the age of twelve, when he stopped going to school. In the last few years, he'd gathered more worldly experience than others had in a lifetime. Ronnie had gone out and collected extreme experiences, in a conscious attempt to destroy childishness. Now, he felt so much older and wiser than the Sandman that he was almost sorry for him. The berk didn't understand that no one on the scene believed in violence. If anyone asked about the incident, Ronnie decided, he would say, 'The Sandman freaked out and started waving a chiv around.'

The Sandman was pretty uncool, actually. He was always running out of junk. Ronnie reckoned the idiot was too generous, insisting on sharing smack with every novice he met. That's how the Sandman, whose real name was Paul Alfred Spackman, acquired his nickname: he once initiated a roomful of kids, and every one of them went on the nod.

Funny how you got stuck with a nickname, Ronnie thought. He was known as Ronnie Fizz, because when he was fourteen he'd broken into the wine cellar of a country club, and only managed to come away with a single bottle of champagne. He'd hitched down the M1, trying to sell the bottle to lorry drivers along the way. When he received no takers, he drank the fizz on a street corner in Soho. This was before the Sandman turned him on to junk.

The one-armed man came into view at the foot of the stairs, and pointed them out to one of the lavatory attendants, an old bugger with bushy eyebrows like Rudolph Hess, who nodded his head continually, as if it was on springs. Both men started up the stairs towards them. Without saying goodbye, the Sandman dodged through the traffic and was soon lost in the crowds around Eros. Ronnie tucked his hair under his jacket collar and walked swiftly in the opposite direction, along Shaftesbury Avenue, until he felt that he, too, must be invisible in the late night throng.

Ronnie wondered whether to head for Leicester Square Tube. He needed to speak to Samantha urgently, tell her that Guido suspected they were screwing. Maybe they should cool it for a bit. Didn't want Guido getting heavy. He might start throwing his weight around. This wasn't cowardice, just common sense. Never put yourself in the firing line. If people accused him of being a coward, that's what he'd say: 'never put yourself in the firing line'.

If he was to be sure of getting to Samantha before Guido, he needed to catch the last Tube to Archway. On the other hand, he needed to get rid of the opium he'd been carrying all day. It was worth a couple of quid, and he wouldn't need to sell anything off his prescription for the rest of the week. Ronnie decided to go up Soho, to see if anyone wanted to score. He could skipper somewhere tonight, and speak to Samantha tomorrow. Surely she'd keep schtum if Guido confronted her?

Ronnie turned left into Dean Street, and then right into Old Compton Street. He hadn't gone more than twenty yards when he noticed that he was being followed. He walked faster. It wasn't the ex-serviceman. It was a woman, and whenever the crowd was particularly dense, she was there. He first noticed her on the same side of the street, some thirty yards away. She wore a black suit, the skirt just below knee length, and a black pillbox hat that belonged at Ascot, with a pink organza flower that seemed to float above the hat, like a halo.

He slowed down until she was almost close enough to touch. A silver grey fox fur stole was draped around her shoulders, the kind that looked as though it had been produced by a taxidermist, complete with dangling legs and a preserved fox head. The fox's beady eyes stared back at him, like a stuffed animal in a display case, frozen in a moment of rage. The woman's own eyes were lustrous, thick-lined with kohl, jet black behind the veil that half-covered her face. She was pale and aloof, aged about sixty, with her face heavily powdered and rouged to hide the decay.

Ronnie knew the woman from somewhere, but where? He could hear a loud humming sound, as if his ear was jammed up against a beehive. The noise burrowed down into the pit of his stomach, making him nauseous. The woman stood still and gazed at him. His breath stopped in his throat and he felt suffocated. She was choking the life out of him.

He had to get away.

Chapter Two

Ronnie cut through into Charing Cross Road, but she was still behind him. Who would tail him, he wondered. Guido? That was absurd, Guido couldn't afford a private eye. It must be the Old Bill. Was it because of the one-armed man? Or had Spear put the word out, told the law to go after him? No, if it was the law they would pull him over, give him some hassle. Just relax, stay cool. Easy to get paranoid.

Halfway up Charing Cross Road, Ronnie stopped and looked at his reflection in a music publisher's window, waiting for the image of her face to appear behind his shoulder. From the shop doorway came the smell of London dust: old mortar, soot, crumbling bones, dog-ends. His own pale face stared back from the dark glass, his pupils so small they were like two pinholes. The cut inflicted by the ex-serviceman had left a smear of blood across his forehead. He couldn't see any sign of the woman. He walked on slowly until he reached the public toilets at the junction with Tottenham Court Road, and stood surveying the crossroads, as though she might appear from any direction. Time for another fix. His mission to sell opium could wait for a few minutes, while he straightened himself out. And if she was still on his tail, she couldn't follow him into the bogs.

He let himself into a karzi, found a vein on the first attempt, and shot up. There was too much coke in the mix and, as the minutes ticked by, he sat looking at the toilet door, disinclined to move. His works remained lodged in his vein, and a thin trickle of blood reached down to his wrist.

Someone had carved a life-sized female nude in the paintwork, with a disembodied dick pointing towards her pubic hair, like a guided missile. The artist had added drops of dark-coloured blood, and the title, 'I shagged my brother's wife when she had the rags up.'

The artist's bold, angular strokes, and fury of execution, reminded him of an illustration he'd seen in *National Geographic*, a magazine he sometimes pinched from his doctor's waiting room. It was a carving called *The Sacrifice of Blood*, made in a country called Axtec, or Aztec, or something. One of the ancient Aztec gods extracted blood from a wound in his dick, and used it to give life to humanity. Maybe that's what this drawing was really about? There was the heavenly dick, and there was the sacred blood.

What would some future archaeologist make of it all, if London was overtaken by a catastrophe, as Pompeii had been? He imagined archaeologists digging out this underground cell, his own body perfectly preserved in volcanic ash, sat upright on the toilet seat, facing the artwork. A man ritually letting his own blood, contemplating the sacrifice of God.

An avalanche of sound descended, shaking the walls of his cubicle, and forcing his heart to thump wildly in his chest. He thought the catastrophe had begun, until he realised it was just someone hammering on a toilet door.

'Come on out. Now!'

A drunken baritone launched into song, and the words *Jesus Wants Me for a Sunbeam* rang out across the public convenience. The singer had locked himself in the next cubicle. As Ronnie looked up, a boot came over the top of his toilet door, and there was the Old Bill gazing down on him.

'What's this then, lad? Get this door open!'

'It's okay, I'm registered. It's all legit.'

They dragged Ronnie out and went through his pockets. The opium was found, squashed into a Swan Vestas matchbox. Plod's face lit up. He held the matchbox under Ronnie's nose, forcing his head back.

'What's this then, lad? This is *Hemp!*'

Indian Hemp. They're as thick as pig shit. Going to get away with it. They haven't seen opium or cannabis before. Make out it's a lump of toffee. It's brown and chewy, it's toffee. I'm saving it for later, my toffee. They're looking unsure. Going to walk away from this.

'Better take him down the nick for questioning,' said the second cop.

One cop held onto the drunk and marched him across the road, with Ronnie's syringe held aloft like a trophy; the other dragged Ronnie along. The drunk wrestled the cop to a halt in the middle of Charing Cross Road, extending his free arm towards the street crowd, like Sinatra singing an encore.

A sunbeam, a sunbeam,
I'll be a sunbeam for Him.

The crowd stared back accusingly. They thought the old guy was a junky. Ronnie had an odd feeling, as if he was acting in a film in which the script had been abandoned, and every scene improvised. Any outcome was possible.

At West End Central, a young Detective Constable led Ronnie into an interview room. The DC, whose name was Andrews, had a lumpy face, which meant he found it difficult to shave without nicking himself. There were several recent cuts, and from the powdery deposit on his cheeks they'd been treated with an alum pencil. Ronnie stared at the lumps and bumps on Andrews' neck and chin. Maybe they were cysts, or maybe it was a skin disease.

The detective's auburn hair swept straight back from his forehead, but because it was naturally wavy it had been flattened with Brylcream, to form a stiff, corrugated sheet. This gave him a dated, pre-war appearance, like the young Jerry Lee Lewis. It was out of keeping with his modern Italian suit, with its bum freezer jacket, as though a country boy had come down to London and been kitted out by fashion-following cousins. They hadn't been able to persuade him to style his hair, so he still looked like a hick from the Midlands.

'What were you doing with Indian Hemp in your pocket?' Andrews asked, in a broad Black Country accent. Ronnie repeated the story about toffee, and for a long time things seemed to be going his way. He was led from his cell towards the street door and was convinced, from the disappointed faces around him, that they were about to let him go. Then Andrews came down the corridor from the opposite direction, carrying a sheaf of papers. He reached the charge desk ahead of them and called out, 'It's okay—you can charge him! Opium prepared for smoking.'

Ronnie could hardly believe what he was hearing. He was going to be charged with possession of a dangerous drug—one that wasn't on his script. He was going to be banged up. The bastards looked jubilant. The thick Brummy had managed to identify opium. Sent it to a forensic lab or something. Ronnie wondered how Samantha would know what had happened. She might be standing at Archway station, waiting for him to arrive on the last Tube. He had to be there; he couldn't afford to spend a night in the cells.

'Tell us who's giving you this stuff, Ronald,' Andrews said. 'We're not interested in people like you. We're after Mr Big. If you help us out …'

Everyone on the scene knew there was no Mr Big. There were just a few junkies doing small deals to keep themselves going. But Ronnie knew the Old Bill would never believe that. They were convinced that the rise in drug use was due to organised crime. Then he thought of a Greek cafe near the Middlesex Hospital. He'd asked for a Turkish coffee, but this waiter started shouting something about only selling Greek coffee. When Ronnie made a little joke about Cyprus they threw him out. So he gave DC Andrews a detailed description of the waiter. In a moment of improvisation, he described him as Maltese. Wore a little pork pie hat. Scar on his boat. It was if an alarm had gone off in West End Central. Two more detectives joined them.

'This Maltese geezer who sold you the drugs, what was he called?' Andrews asked. 'What do you know about the Mejlak brothers? Are the Mejlak firm dealing in drugs now?'

'Are they? Everyone knows the Mejlaks are behind all the dope in the West End.'

DC Andrews consulted the others in the corridor. Ronnie could hear an older guy saying 'Well done,' and 'It's worth a punt'. Andrews came back looking pleased with himself.

'You can give yourself an injection out of your own prescription tonight. We just have to wait for the police surgeon to arrive, to supervise it.'

When the police surgeon arrived, they handed Ronnie his shit and allowed him to make up his own fix. He couldn't believe his luck, and shot up a really big fix of H&C, to last as long as possible. He almost floated back to the Flowery Dell, and decided he was going to walk straight out of court, once they realised he was a registered addict. And he'd helped the police; that must count in his favour.

In the morning there were no more smiles. DC Andrews was nowhere to be seen. The police surgeon said, 'I'll give you the injection this time.' It wasn't heroin. Some kind of sedative. Intra-muscular. By the time he got to Marlborough Street Magistrates' Court, he could hardly stand up in the dock. This made a bad impression, as the stipendiary magistrate assumed he was intoxicated.

'How do you plead?'

'Technically guilty, like, but not really, because I'm registered on heroin and cocaine. I'm a registered addict, you see, so it's all legit.'

'Three drugs!' The beak stared accusingly at the arresting officer, as though this was evidence that should have been presented in court. 'Remanded to Ashford for medical reports.'

And that was how it all began. They had him, bang to rights.

***

They ran Ronnie backwards along the dark corridor, a screw holding each arm, and reversed him into the padded cell. That way he couldn't drag his feet or brace them up against the doorjamb.

They made him wear a grey woollen dressing gown, but had taken away the cord, so that he wouldn't be able to hang himself. The gown fell open as they rushed him along, and he looked down at his own emaciated body. Each rib could be seen, as clearly as a chicken's when you ripped the meat off the bone. His long blond hair hung down in rats' tails. His cock and balls looked small, shrunken in the cold. He wanted to cover himself up, but couldn't, and he realised how defenceless he was. That was the first thing the screws had told him: 'You're in prison now, lad, and we can do anything we like to you!'

Ronnie was pinned face down on the padded floor, one screw kneeling on his back. His breath came in ragged gasps as he shouted at them to get off. Then, changing tack, he tried pleading with them.

'I just need my fix! Please!'

This seemed to provoke the man restraining him. The knee pressed harder into his back. He felt the warmth of the man's breath, first on the nape his neck, and then in his ear.

'We'll give you an injection, lad: a ruddy meat injection!'

'Right up your fucking arse,' added the second screw.

A third screw, who wore a white jacket, entered the cell, carrying a syringe in one of those kidney-shaped bowls, the kind made of white enamel, with a blue line painted around the rim.

'400 milligrams of Largactil,' White Jacket announced, 'equals one quiet night, for Yours Truly.' He said it with satisfaction, as though he'd just won an argument.

Ronnie fought to throw off his persecutors.

'He's getting his dander up now!' laughed the first screw.

'Oh dearie, dearie me!' said White Jacket. 'Should I be worried?'

Ronnie smelt an alcohol swab, and felt a large needle stab into his buttocks, the muscle slowly forced apart by the injection. Above him in the ceiling was a red light, behind a steel mesh. It would stay on night and day, so that he would soon lose all sense of time.

His jailors paused to look at him as they departed, swinging the heavy padded door closed. Ronnie heard the jangle of a key turning in the lock. He'd not had a fix for over fourteen hours. His feet felt as if they were immersed in icy water, and the chill was seeping up his legs, poised to invade the core of his body. His strength was ebbing away. Every limb felt flimsy, too weak to support his weight. He forced himself to stand. It was hard to walk on the padded floor; it bounced like a mattress and pitched him sideways, so that he swayed around like a gale-struck sapling, and lurched from one wall to another.

The ceiling and four walls were padded with the same material as the floor. Some kind of cream-coloured plastic had been used to cover dense foam rubber, so that you could throw yourself against a wall and simply rebound. And yet the cell didn't feel like a safe space. It had the aura of a death chamber, something to do with its airlessness, its red light, and its all-seeing spy-hole, squatting in the centre of the door. The cell felt like a pit into which animals were thrown, to fight to the death; a sleazy, night-time venue for badger baiting, or dog fighting.

Ronnie gave up trying to walk, and curled up in the corner. For nearly twelve months, ever since his sixteenth birthday, he'd lived with an uninterrupted supply of heroin. Every four hours or so, throughout the waking day, he'd been able to shoot up. The only withdrawal sickness he'd experienced was when he couldn't get to see his doctor, who prescribed heroin and cocaine for him, or when he'd over-slept, so that he was late for his morning fix. That had been a slight sickness, a bit like the onset of flu. He was scared that he was in for a complete physical breakdown this time.

The padded cell smelt like the inside of a car tyre. He longed for fresh air, and tried to stand up. The Largactil hit him, like a blow to the back of the skull. He was walking into the dentist's surgery as a child, the dentist and his nurse standing behind the chair, both very tall. They held his wrists down and the rubber mask enveloped his face. The surgery was near a railway goods yard and he could hear a train being shunted, see billowing steam through dim, grime-obscured window panes. The stench of rubber was blown down his nose by the dry, cold gas; his teeth clenched on a leather bit. A train whistle was blowing somewhere in the distance, while chilled blood rolled around his body. He heard the sound of the door banging in the dental surgery, and echoing again and again as he fought against unconsciousness.

Standing in a red, boulder-strewn desert under a hazy pink sky. He recognised it from the cards in tea packets that he'd collected as a child, a Brooke Bond series on the solar system. It was Mars, the Red Planet. Fourth planet from the sun. There are probably no canals on Mars—Oh shit!—Mars has two moons called Phobos and Demos—Oh shit! The sweat was rolling down his brow in the intense Martian heat. He couldn't walk. He looked down and his feet had grown roots that were reaching out into the sand. There were knobbly protrusions growing from his shoulders and elbows. His limbs ached; he was growing branches. He was turning into a plant. A cactus or something.

His heart skipped a beat. Why did it do that? It was as if it couldn't decide whether to carry on. His stomach was fucked too. Diarrhoea. And only a plastic piss pot in the cell. His bowels ached; his guts were knotted into tight strings. He stretched out, as far away from the spy-hole as possible. There was a crash of bolts, and a rattle of keys, and the cell door sprang open. White Jacket entered, carrying a stethoscope. Without speaking, he applied it to Ronnie's chest. And then the smell of surgical spirit as a swab sterilised the skin on Ronnie's buttocks. The fat hypodermic syringe was brought out of its kidney-shaped bowl, the thick needle pierced the muscle, and the foul liquid was squirted into his body. Another injection of Largactil.

Ronnie asked what day it was, but White Jacket walked out without speaking. It was like being trapped inside a soundproof bubble: no one could hear him.

The red light in the cell reminded him of the cellar in the Swindon Communist Party headquarters. The cellar had been fitted out with red and blue light bulbs in the 1950s, so that it could be used as a folk club. A lot of the singers were from the North East. They sang unaccompanied, finger in ear. And there was an Irish group, the Rebel Lads. *Tu-ra-lu-ra-lu.*

He filled his lungs and sang out against the suffocating silence:

Tu-ra-lu-ra-lu-ra-lu,
They're looking for monkeys in the zoo,
And if I had a face like you,
I'd join the Prison Service!

No reaction. No one could hear him. It was so quiet that it must be the middle of the night. But he'd thought that once before, and then a screw came in with his cocoa, which meant it was about six in the evening.

His eyes slowly closed. Hundreds of giant spiders were descending from the sky, on silver threads. 'The Daughters of Grace,' said a figure, just outside of his field of vision. 'They come to pick flesh off the bones of men. Then they return to the Great Mother. She is waiting in Her web at the centre of the Tree of Life, for them to return with your juices. She uses your lifeblood to weave the matrix that holds the stars in place. See, they come for you now.' Ronnie struggled to climb a slippery bank, but the Daughters of Grace were gaining on him.

What was that? His breakfast was on a tray by the cell door. Who'd brought it? How long had it been there? It was porridge, in a yellow plastic bowl. Cold. So was the tea. Tea in a soft blue plastic cup, weak as piss. No spoon: was he supposed to eat porridge with his fingers?

He forced himself awake. Although he felt cold, he was sweating as though lying in a sauna, and his nose and eyes were running, so that it was hard to see. There was something else wrong. His sweat didn't smell right. It wasn't his own smell. Must be the Largactil, giving him an acrid kind of smell. And it didn't work, didn't stop the dreams that lurked, waiting for his eyes to close. The dreams started when he needed a fix. Only an opiate would stop them. Morphine would help. Or opium. What about that patent medicine, Dr J. Collis Browne's Chlorodyne? It contained tincture of opium, morphine and chloroform. That would damp it all down, if you swallowed the whole bottle. A couple of bottles, anyway. Buy it over the counter, at the chemist's. Tell them you've got the runs, and ask for a couple of bottles.

Chlorodyne acts like a charm in diarrhoea, and is the only specific in cholera and dysentery. Beware of piracy and imitations.

That's weird: piracy and imitations. The pirate flag, the skull and crossbones, the Jolly Roger. Beware of imitations, sailing under false colours, running up the Jolly Roger at the last minute, unleashing the terror. *La Jolie Rouge.* Beware of methadone hydrochloride, fool's gold. His doctor, screwing up his nose in distaste: 'The Germans invented methadone when they couldn't get the opium to produce morphine, during the war. They had a lot of deaths with it.' No deadly imitations for me. Give me J. Collis Browne's.

A crash of bolts. They'd sent a prisoner to empty his piss-pot. Without moving from his crouched position, Ronnie called out, 'I can't get warm! It's freezing in here. Get us another cup of tea, mate? This one's cold.'

'What do you think this is, the bleeding Ritz?'

The prisoner spoke in a whisper, a finger held to his lips to indicate that talking was not allowed. A single scar made a long, white line across his shaven head, like a slug's trail, but it was the sunken eyes that made him look like a concentration camp victim: the darkness of their sockets resembled bruised fruit.

'Wish it was the Ritz. I'd get sugar with the sodding porridge,' Ronnie replied.

'If we gave you sugar with your porridge, or with your cocoa, there wouldn't be enough sugar for all your puddings, and all your jam tarts. We work to a budget.'

'Who's we?'

'The prison service.'

'So you're part of the prison service, are you?'

'I'm the Red Band in this hospital. See this red armband? That tells you I'm a trusted prisoner. That says I've got all the fucking privileges round here, and you've got none.'

The Red Band was the kind of idiot who identified with the screws. A collaborator. Stoolie, fink, squealer. James Cagney, pointing his gun at the Red Band: 'Come out and take it, you dirty yellow-bellied rat!' That rat with a swollen belly he'd seen on a bombsite once, and a bloke killed it with a brick. No animal should die like that. The bloke said, 'So what, they carry the plague.'

Ronnie asked what day it was. The Red Band answered, without moving his lips. Not the day Ronnie expected. He'd lost a day. How had that happened?

'Why won't the screws tell me what day it is?'

'Because you're down the Block, sunshine. They never speak when you're down the Block, except to give you an order.' The Red Band moved to the door, the piss-pot held at arm's length. 'You don't half pen and ink. Can't you bung a cork up your arse for a couple of days?'

The heavy padded door banged shut. Somewhere in the prison he could hear an altercation. When he was a child, he would lie in bed and listen to his parents argue; he could tell by the rhythm of the quarrel whether it was going to get nasty, or just peter out. Sometimes he could hear the warning signs long before his mother, could tell that she was going to say something foolhardy.

His father was a policeman. It was always a bad sign if his father came into his bedroom at night, especially if he was in uniform. The light snapped on, and Dad perched on the edge of the bed. He brought the friendly, public house smell of beer and cigarettes into the room, and he radiated good humour, but that could change in seconds if Ronnie said the wrong thing. Then it was a slapping.

'Bought you a present.'

His Dad never bought him presents but, after digging deep in his trouser pocket, he produced a toy spaceman and tossed it onto the counterpane. The figure was about two inches tall, grey plastic, with a Perspex helmet, and oxygen bottles worn on the back, like a diver.

'I want you to do something for me. You know how you're interested in police work?' His father put a comforting arm around Ronnie's shoulder. 'Well, I want you to help me out with an investigation. Observe someone for me. Tell me what you see. You're going to watch your mother for me.'

So that's why he'd been bought a spaceman. It was his prize for informing. You had to keep a secret from your Mum, that you were spying on her. That was the deal; that was the way you kept out of trouble. You had to show your loyalty to one side or the other. That's why he'd cried when a neighbour asked, 'Are you a Daddy's boy or a Mummy's boy'? He didn't want to take sides.

Ronnie gazed up at the red light in the ceiling, and could hear the distant rumble of the early morning traffic. The wind was gusting up to gale force, threatening to uproot the neighbourhood trees. Some strange god was concealed in the eye of the storm, lurking behind the tempest. Ronnie couldn't look into the light. The cold air was drilling holes in his body. His flesh was falling from his bones, like a waterlogged loaf of bread, dissolving in a lake. He screamed, but there was no sound.

Now he was sat in a pharmacy somewhere, preparing a fix. They'd left the drugs cupboard open, and it was full of morphine sulphate ampoules. Too mucking futch! All he had to do was break open a box of amps and draw the liquid into a large syringe, and he would be feeling good again. Everything would be peaceful. But somehow he couldn't open the amps. They were slipping through his fingers and breaking on the floor. There were tight manacles on his legs, deforming his knee joints, crippling him so that he could hardly stand. Then, when he finally got the shit into the works, and made a hit, the needle blocked. He pressed harder, but the needle exploded off the end of the syringe. Blood and morphine sprayed everywhere. He tried frantically to mop it up.

The rattle of a key in the cell door. He was not standing in the pharmacy; he had no morphine; he was still in prison. HMP Ashford

Remand Centre, to be precise. In a YP nick. Down the block. In the pads. White lights flared on in the cell, and two boots marched across the padded floor towards his face. Then the order was shouted: 'Stand up for the doctor, lad!' He tried to comply but was incapable. He sprawled, naked before them.

Two medical practitioners stood in the doorway: the prison doctor, a woman in her fifties in a tweed suit, which made her look as though she was judging pedigree Labradors at a dog show, and a man he understood later to be an NHS consultant. He heard the words *cardiac dysrhythmia.* The man asked the woman why she hadn't at least prescribed the synthetic opiate, methadone.

The woman replied slowly, enunciating each syllable with exaggerated care. She had the cold, impersonal tones of an executioner. Or maybe of a taxidermist—Ronnie could imagine she spent her days immersing dead animals in embalming fluid.

'They like drugs and they are not going to get them in prison.'

I'm going to have my say, he thought, but he remained in the crouching dog posture. He'd seen his father, in that posture, years before, when he was eight. Ronnie heard him fall over in the toilet when there was no one else in the house, and went to see if he needed help. Dad was drunk again. His body blocked the door, but Ronnie managed to push it open a few inches. Four of his father's expensive fountain pens, the ones with gold-plated nibs, had fallen from his jacket pocket, and were lying on the toilet floor.

'Do you need help, Dad?' he asked. 'Shall I get someone to help?'

'Get back to bed, you silly little sod!' His father punched the door shut.

An hour later, Ronnie woke when his bedroom light came on and his father, now friendly and jovial, asked if he fancied some liver casserole. Some banging around in the kitchen ensued, and then he appeared in the doorway with a tray.

'Sit up! Look at this! Better bloody grub than your mother makes.'

Dad went to sit on the edge of the bed. In a horrifying misjudgement, he missed and fell on the floor, the tray crashing down on top of him, food spilling over his copper's uniform. He had his mouth open, as though he couldn't understand what was happening.

'Who moved the bloody bed?' Dad asked, after what seemed like a long interval.

He wanted to help his father. He volunteered the information freely.

'Mum did, when she was cleaning this morning.'

'Bloody cow!'

It must have been after midnight when his mother came home, but his father was waiting for her. He was hiding behind the front door, so that when she stepped into the dark hallway he was able to hit her, before she had a chance to switch on the lights. She was knocked across the hall, and then kicked while she lay screaming on the floor.

Ronnie listened from his bedroom, and felt that he had betrayed his mother. He'd informed on her. Even now, he could hear Mum's screams. He tried to stand up in the cell. There really were screams. It wasn't his mother. It was in the next cell. He heard the sound of slapping, and then raised voices.

'Are you going to shut it? Are you?'

The doctors had gone, and the screws were beating someone in the neighbouring cell. Was he next? Would they give him a slapping? But he heard the cell door bang shut, and their footsteps fade down the corridor.

At home, he was sitting on the carpet, looking up at his Dad, who was wearing civvies. The radio was playing a familiar signature tune: *Ray's a Laugh.*

> *Come on and meet Ted Ray,*
> *He'll chase your troubles away,*
> *And raise a laugh!*

'Thank you, good evening, and hello, boys and girls. My solicitor's just called me. He said: "Your mother-in-law's just passed away in her sleep. Shall we order burial, embalming or cremation?" I said, take no chances—order all three!'

Prolonged applause. Dad smirked.

'My wife's mother was a very greedy woman. She was so greedy that when she had body lice, she made all the little fleas pay rent! My wife's just the same. My friend called round the other night, while I was out. My wife answered the door wearing just a towel. He said ten quid to drop that towel! My wife's so greedy, she dropped the towel and took the cash! When I came home I asked if my friend had called. She said yes. Then I asked her if he'd left the ten quid he owed me!'

Laughter. Dad was chuckling, and cradling a large tumbler of whisky in his hands. 'Just like a bloody woman,' he mused.

'What do you call a woman who has just lost 95 per cent of her intelligence? A divorcee!'

Dad roared with laughter. He looked very pleased with himself.

' … He said, "What do you tell a woman with two black eyes?" I said "Nothing. You've already told her twice!" '

'I don't get it, Daddy.'

'You don't want to bloody bother!' Dad said. He always said that.

On the radio, the dance band played a music hall song:

I'm following in father's footsteps,
Following my dear old Dad!

'I'll teach you how to bloody dance,' Dad said, leaping up from the armchair.

He let Ronnie stand on his feet, and held his hands, so that they glided around the room like ballroom professionals. Both of them laughed, as they whirled around the room, faster and faster. Then he flew off his father's feet and fell backwards, hitting his head against the sideboard.

'Watch out, you stupid little sod!' Dad shouted.

Ronnie cried. Dad picked him up, sat him on his knee, and jigged him up and down, saying comforting things. When he stopped crying, Dad moved the bottle of Scotch next to the chair, poured himself a large measure, and said in his ear:

'I'll teach you the words of a war-time song, *She'll Be Coming Round the Mountain.*'

He couldn't ever remember feeling closer to his father. That funny smell of whisky on the breath, mixed with the faint odour of unwashed socks. And he could feel the warmth of Dad's dark red pullover against his cheek. They sang together: '*She'll be wearing silk pyjamas when she comes.*'

His mother flopped down in an armchair. Her face looked tired and sad.

'Why do you have to teach the boy filth like that, Freddy?' she asked eventually.

Dad placed him carefully on the ground and reached into the fireplace for the poker. He whipped his wife twice across the side of the head, and she fell backwards in the armchair, stunned.

'There, there,' Dad comforted him, 'it's all your mother's fault.'

On the radio, the audience was applauding. The band played *Such Is Life (Life Is What You Make It).* Ronnie went out into the hall, where he could be alone. Near the front door, where Dad had waited for Mum to come home, was a print in a large, ornate frame. It showed two children being interrogated by a Parliamentary tribunal during the English civil war. It was called *When Did You Last See Your Father?* You always had to keep your father's secrets, however much they questioned you.

Chapter Three

A rattle of keys, and white light. He was so used to red light that it hurt his eyes when the door opened. How many days had he been here: was it four or even five?

'Right, lad, stand up! You're going up to A2 landing.'

Ronnie was slow to respond, so the screw dragged him to his feet, shouting as though they were on a parade ground. 'Come along, come along! Move yourself, you steaming shower of shit! You're not in a Soho sewer now!'

He was marched at the double to his new cell in the hospital wing, issued with the uniform of the convicted remand prisoner, and given his tobacco ration—one quarter ounce of *Black Beauty*, one packet of cigarette papers and one box of matches. The door slammed shut; prison doors never closed quietly, they banged or boomed shut, with a clatter of bolts and a rattle of keys. He sat on the bed and rolled a cigarette. Black Beauty was the strongest and foulest tobacco he'd ever tasted, like smoking horsehair out of a mattress.

The new cell was about nine foot square and had a barred window, out of which he could just about see, although it only looked onto the exercise yard below. The walls were brick, painted in gloss paint; the lower third was dark green, the remainder was yellow, with a one inch red line sandwiched between.

In his bedside locker was a Bible. Ronnie had heard that you could consult the Bible at times of personal danger, to obtain omens or advice. He stretched out on the bed and opened it at random.

> *Deuteronomy 23, 1. He that is wounded in the stones, or hath his privy member cut off, shall not enter into the congregation of the Lord.*

Not much consolation there. Bugger religion. Someone else had obviously felt the same, as the next page had been ripped out, probably to use as cigarette paper. A kid on reception had tried to blag some skins from him; they were always in short supply.

A shadow fell across the window in the door, and a screw shouted, 'Off the bed! You do not sit or lay on your bed in the daytime! Now get ready for exercise, before I put you on report!'

The exercise yard was on the ground floor. Prisoners walked in a circle, supervised by a landing officer and three other screws, until they were told to stop. Others who'd ended up in the hospital wing included a couple of Mods, caught with their pockets full of purple hearts; a kid charged with murder; one going up to the Quarter Sessions for rape; another rumoured to be a fire setter; and the usual tearaways. They trudged around for about twenty minutes before the landing officer called a halt. They came to attention in a square three rows deep.

'Step forward the Birthday Boy!'

The landing officer held a flimsy sheet of white paper in his hand, which fluttered in the breeze. The lads looked at each other warily. Whose birthday was it?

'Come along, Ronnie! It's your birthday, you lucky boy!'

Ronnie took one pace forward and came to attention.

The landing officer looked smug, like a gambler who knows a deck of cards is rigged in his favour. He read out: *Happy Birthday Ronnie. Love Mum. XXX*. 'There you are, at least his mother loves him! No other bugger does!'

There was a dutiful laugh from the prisoners.

He'd received a birthday telegram from his mother. He was seventeen, the age at which it was legal to detain him in a YP nick. But that meant it was the twelfth of June. He must have been in the padded cell for six days.

'Right, I want you all to line up and give Ronnie your tobacco as a birthday present,' said the landing officer, smiling as if he'd just delivered the best joke of the week.

Ronnie recognised the malicious humour from his schooldays. He was supposed to collect everyone's quarter ounce of rolling tobacco, and then, when they entered the dark interior of the boot room, where outdoor shoes were exchanged for gym shoes, he would be jumped. An assailant could take possession of several ounces of tobacco in one move. He was being set up, and it was necessary to take immediate avoidance action.

'Sir! I've given up smoking, Sir!'

The screws looked annoyed at this development.

'You won't be wanting your tobacco ration, then. Hand it over, Belsen Boy.'

The screws on Reception had nicknamed him 'Belsen Boy', because his skin was stretched so tightly over his ribs. The name was following him around the prison. Screws never wasted an opportunity to ridicule a prisoner. He offered up his tobacco to the landing officer, and the screws looked at each other and grinned. The bastards were trying to rile him, to provoke some kind of outburst so they could discipline him.

'Many happy returns of the day,' the landing officer said.

Keep a poker face. Give nothing away. Don't give them the satisfaction.

'Right-oh, A2 landing, lead off! At the double!'

The landing officer had a thin black moustache that quivered when he was agitated. It was quivering now. He marched over to the front row as the lads executed a right turn, and his voice rose by an octave.

'Come along, Belsen Boy, I want to see daylight under those heels! You may've broke your mother's heart but you're not going to break mine!'

Back in his cell, he decided to lie on his bed, but keep listening for footsteps, so he could jump up quickly if a screw came along. He shut his eyes and imagined a spike sliding into a vein on his left forearm. Just one hit, then nothing the screws could say would hurt him. He would be invulnerable. Super-cool.

Ronnie made a conscious effort to return to happier memories and reflections. There was the time he first spoke to Jack Fitt, the Irish anarchist and musician, at a shabeen in Swindon. Must've been almost two years ago, when he was fifteen. Jack was tall, late forties, with an unruly shock of grey hair. His hooked nose reminded Ronnie of a parrot's beak, and there was a long gap between his nose and upper lip, as if his face had been stretched downwards. His eyes, dark and beady like a teddy bear's, twinkled with secret mirth, as though there was a joke he wouldn't share.

Jack Fitt was standing in the darkness at the back of the room, sharing a joint with a group of Jamaicans. At one point, the Irishman stamped his foot and shouted '*Rasclaat!*' and his new friends doubled up with laughter. Then the Irishman became more expansive, like an actor taking centre stage, and produced a stream of invective, '*Pussyclaat, man! Bumbaclaat! To Raas!*' Ronnie wondered if the group were laughing at Jack, but decided that they were probably impressed to hear a white European speaking Jamaican patois.

No more bad talk,
In this land,
Because I'm king.

Two men jostled each other on the dance floor. The DJ called over his microphone, *No strife! No strife!* Ronnie took advantage of a pause in the music to push his way through the crowd, until he drew level with Jack.

'No more bad talk?' he said.

Jack grinned. 'Jamaicans know some of the foulest curses on earth.'

'So do you, by the sound of it.'

'Well, Jamaicans are second only to the Irish as world-class cursers.'

'Have you ever been to the West Indies?'

Jack looked as if the answer was obvious, as though it was a question that didn't need answering, but then he seemed to relent.

'I was there with the Art Blakey All-Stars.'

Jack lit a joint he'd been rolling. He held it so that he could draw a mixture of smoke and air into his lungs. Sucking down the air was such a noisy, conspicuous, process that every onlooker knew what he was doing, and Jack looked gratified to be centre stage. He passed the joint to Ronnie, with the air of a man who expected to be admired by others.

The ganga smoke, dim lighting, and bouncing beat combined to lift Ronnie's spirits and make him feel that this was a supreme moment in his life. He was smoking dope with someone who'd played with the Art Blakey All-Stars. *All Stars*: that meant every musician was famous in his own right. He was friends with a famous musician, someone who'd been to the West Indies; not only that, someone who could swear in Jamaican.

***

Ronnie looked out of his cell window. Grey light bore down upon the exercise yard, like a lead weight. The asphalt was wet with rain, and a bedraggled pigeon picked its way between puddles. Exhausted, and unable to fly, it walked around in tight circles, looking lost. Perhaps it would never get out, and would march around the yard until it died.

He felt the internal landscape of his mind becoming unrecognisable. A dark chasm opened up beneath him. His customary thoughts and feelings seemed fictitious, a story he'd told himself to hide the ugly truth about existence. You tried to make sense of life, you tried to weave events into patterns, but it was all meaningless.

Unzipping his trousers, he caressed his dick with the fingers of his right hand. Wanking would bring back a happier mood. He pictured Samantha standing naked, with her legs apart. He'd gone out with Samantha, briefly, over twelve months ago, when they were both living in Swindon. Awarded a place at the Slade art school, she moved to London, where she shacked up with Guido Roberts, a small-time dealer she met at Eel Pie Island. Ronnie met them both by chance near his Soho squat, and Samantha persuaded her partner to allow Ronnie to sleep on their sitting room floor. Then she started to come home early in the afternoon so that they could shag.

He imagined laying Samantha face down on the bed, while he kneeled behind her and placed the tip of his dick between her bum cheeks, and she shouted yes. Yes, yes, yes. Heavy boots marched down the corridor towards his cell. Ronnie threw himself off the bed and pulled up his zip, just before a man's face darkened the window in his cell door.

'Come along, Belsen Boy, I expect to see this cell cleaned out by now!'

'Sir!'

The landing officer's black moustache was clipped with great precision, so that a clear line of flesh could be seen above the upper lip. The topmost limit of the bristles was also shaved to an exact line, as if painted on his face. The maintenance of this moustache must have been undertaken on a daily basis, and represented a considerable investment of time.

'Mr Allcott: a broom for this prisoner, if you please!' the landing officer shouted. 'We don't want to encourage him in his habits of idleness, do we?'

A newly recruited screw arrived, carrying a broom, and had trouble unlocking the cell door. The landing officer paced around impatiently.

'Sorry sir,' the new recruit said, 'but I thought you were waiting for the medics to declare him A1.'

'Declare him A1?' the landing officer said, raising his eyebrows in mock surprise. 'That's beyond the power of medicine, Mr Allcott. We'd be waiting until doomsday for this reprobate to get a clean bill of health. No, put him to work!'

'Get this cell swept out, lad,' the new screw said, almost apologetically. He handed him the broom. 'And when you've finished in here you can sweep the corridor down as far as the kitchen.'

The screws departed, leaving his door open. The floors were highly polished and appeared dust-free. Ronnie leaned on the broom, and thought of happier times. Jack Fitt, standing at the back of a public meeting at the Baptist Tabernacle in Swindon, calling for opposition to the Bomb through "jazz consciousness". Bebop the Bomb. Super-fast, fluid notes, dissolving the structure of music, dismantling the pattern of thought that led to the H-Bomb.

'Bebop reverses nuclear technology. Bebop is life, vitality, spontaneity, Africa, a massive influx of solar energy that holds death at bay.'

Every head in the crowd craned round as Jack addressed them; the Chairman tried to intervene but went unheeded. In recent tests, Jack continued, the H-Bomb released thirty per cent more energy than physicists could account for. A pause for effect. 'It was flooding in from another space-time continuum!'

Jack had the gift of the gab, the blarney. He could be a persuasive speaker, as long as you kept him off his pet theme, something called fifth dimensional space-time curvature. For several weeks in 1962, Jack had addressed street meetings around England, claiming that the world would stumble into a nuclear conflagration over Cuba, not by design, but because the military machine was accident-prone. It turned out that much of Jack's information about military matters was correct, but just when he was needed most, at the height of the missile crisis, he took off for the west coast of Ireland. Better to die on holy Irish soil; and anyway it's the safest bloody hole in Europe.

If you ignored all that dodgy stuff about the fifth dimension, or whatever it was, Jack was right about most things. The conduct of the Cold War wasn't rational; it was an absurd game of chance. Ronnie read everything he could find on nuclear weapons. He couldn't understand people's complacency, their failure to grasp the magnitude of the threat, their acceptance of government rhetoric. He was convinced that even a limited nuclear exchange would end European civilization. The civil defence precautions—making a bomb shelter in a broom cupboard under the stairs—were so much bollocks. How could people believe the politicians?

> *Please send back issues of* Youth Against the Bomb. *Also one copy of the Mershon Report on accidental war, for one shilling, and one hundred leaflets for the Ministry of Aviation demo. I enclose a postal order for twenty-five shillings and sixpence. I am/ ~~am not~~ willing to be a local convenor.*

***

Ronnie could hear a disturbance, not far from his cell: delighted shouts, punctuated by splashes of water, like children playing in a paddling pool. It was coming from the hospital kitchen, where food, brought over from the main prison kitchen in aluminium containers, was dished up for hospital inmates.

He stepped into the corridor. The lads on washing-up duty were having a water fight. A bowl of water was thrown across the kitchen, another out the window. A few moments later, the Principal Officer came up the stairs, water dripping off his cap, his jacket sopping wet. He must've been in the yard outside, and caught the lot. The PO walked into the kitchen, and total silence followed.

Ronnie wondered whether throwing water at a PO counted as a flogging offence. You were flogged for assaulting a screw; tied to the Gunner's Daughter, as they used to say in the Navy. Tied to an execution triangle, and whipped with the birch, or the cat'o'nine tails. The prison doctor looked on, able to stop the proceedings if there was any risk of death or disability. The dregs of the medical profession. Not only did they supervise the punishment beatings, they checked that the condemned man's heart had stopped before he was cut down from the gallows. No surprise that the bastards forced you to undergo a cold turkey, when it was possible to withdraw drugs gradually, like they did in NHS hospitals.

Ronnie moved back into his cell, and gave it a quick sweep so that he could say it had been done. He heard footsteps in the corridor and swung the broom backwards and forwards over the floor, in an attempt to look busy. The landing officer arrived in the doorway, and gazed at his efforts with a sour expression. Then he dropped to his haunches and ran a finger under the bed, holding it up for inspection.

'What do you call this?' he barked. 'Dust! I want to see this floor dust-free. If we make you eat your dinner off the floor, we don't want you blaming us if you get ill. Now get out here and sweep this corridor, you long-haired streak of piss!'

The landing officer marched off, and Ronnie ambled slowly along the corridor, nudging the broom ahead with two hands clasped in front of his stomach. He thought back to the time of his first fix, taken a year before, some time after the Cuban Missile Crisis, and just before his sixteenth birthday. It was in a bleak, unfurnished room, on the top floor of a tumbledown Georgian terrace in Bristol. An old Dansette record player, plugged into an adaptor plug in the light socket, was playing a Charlie Mingus LP. He remembered the track: *Don't Let Them Drop That Atomic Bomb On Me.* Don't let them drop it, Stop it, bebop it!

He was standing by the window, gazing down on the street. It was late afternoon and raining steadily. Fallen leaves were turning slippery on the autumn pavements. He licked one side of the joint, to stop it burning unevenly, and then took a deep draw. Some seeds cracked and popped, giving off a pungent, oily smell that made the throat constrict. It was Jamaican bush; a half-ounce of dried leaves piled onto a sheet of newspaper, spread over the table. It had just arrived at the Bristol docks. He wondered if the growers celebrated Harvest Festival when they cut down the ganja. Did they have someone like his old primary school teacher, thumping the piano keys, and looking over her shoulder with joy in her heart:

We plough the fields, and scatter
the good seed on the land.

If anything was a gift from heaven above, it was ganja. He turned to the Sandman and said, 'The spades call ganja the "holy herb". It's sent from heaven above.'

The Sandman's pale face was immobile, like a wax effigy, with only his eyes alive, intense, animated. He looked like that when he was about to accuse someone of bullshit. *You're full of shit, Ronnie.* Or, *That's fucking bullshit, man.* The Sandman was a master of denunciation, always condemning someone for misrepresentation or falsehood: 'That fucking Gypsy Dave is so full of shit. He tried to make out he knew Ginsberg. I really put him down. The closest he's ever been to America is Weston-super-Mare.'

Ronnie went to great lengths to avoid the Sandman's put-downs. But after a moment's silence, all the Sandman said was, 'Do you want to try a fix, Ronnie? I can let you have half-a-jack. Half of one of these tablets. That's one twelfth of a grain. Should be okay for a first fix.'

The Sandman watched him intently, his eyes squinting against smoke from a cigarette, held in the corner of his mouth. Ronnie took another deep draw on the joint before passing it to the Sandman; when you're holding down a lungful of smoke you have time to reflect. *You're not scared of this. If you don't do it now, you may not get the chance again. You won't have tried it.* As always, he took a major decision as casually as tossing a coin; anything was better than prevarication. A moment of hesitation, but not long enough for the Sandman to notice.

For the first time in his life, Ronnie performed the solemn ritual. He dropped the half-tablet of heroin into a small bottle of water and held it over a match until it bubbled. The tablet dissolved. He took up the eyedropper, a hypodermic needle wedged onto the end with a twist of tissue paper. He expelled the air from the rubber bulb of the eyedropper and then watched it suck the clear liquid up the glass tube. He'd tied a belt around his upper arm for a tourniquet, and now the veins in his forearm were bulging. This was the most holy moment in the ceremony, a moment of quiet contemplation, like the Elevation of the Host during Mass. Taking a deep breath, he pressed the needle into a vein. A plume of blood rose up the tube, tingeing the fluid rose-red.

'Squeeze it all in, Ronnie. But don't let any air go in your vein. It might give you an embolism.'

Ronnie was about to ask 'What's an embolism?' but thought better of it. It would sound naïve. It's got to be some kind of blood clot. He squeezed the rubber bulb, and then released it, letting his blood flush back into the tube, before squeezing again, the way that the Sandman always did. He counted two, three, four, and then felt a heavy, languorous warmth in his nose which spread throughout his throat and then down into the rest of his body. Diamorphine hydrochloride, British Pharmacopoeia; one twelfth of a grain by intravenous injection.

The Sandman was explaining a complicated deal involving a shooter he'd obtained for Moxey, a local student, who'd been planning an armed robbery on a Bristol jewellery store. The Sandman, who helped by putting Moxey in touch with two London villains, liked talking about 'the blag'. Although only nineteen, it meant he was someone with an intimate knowledge of the underworld, and it reminded Ronnie that he'd been told he was too young to be involved. The Sandman enjoyed putting him in his place. Offering a fix was all part of this game; if it looked like he couldn't handle it, the Sandman would put him down.

'Two old geezers,' the Sandman said, 'in their seventies. Jumped on him! *This is a stick-up*, Moxey says, and they jumped him.' The Sandman shook his head in disbelief. 'What a pillock! Imagine saying "This is a stick-up"? The guys from town just turned and ran. He got five years ... You okay?'

A dark shutter had come down.

'I thought it would be a high, like hash, but it sort of closes you down,' Ronnie mumbled. He thought: five years? But you helped set the job up. A success and you'd be claiming the credit.

'Heroin is slippers-by-the-fireside,' the Sandman observed. 'Total comfort.'

As the heroin infiltrated his brain cells, Ronnie felt strange. He was warm and comfortable, but nausea seeped into the pit of his stomach, like the time he'd travelled by coach as a child. He'd been sick, and his father had moved to a different seat, leaving his mother to deal with the problem. His father, who hated to be shown up, ignored them for the rest of the journey.

Kneeling in front of the toilet bowl that day in Bristol, Ronnie vomited, but without any trace of discomfort. Being sick was a natural activity. No need to be brought down by it. He spent the next two hours on his knees.

'I'm fine, Sandman. Yeah, it's a great buzz. Yeah, I'll be okay in a minute.' *Why do you turn everyone on? It must make you feel better. Everyone has to be the same as you. Share your vices. At least I'll never get hooked. I don't like Horse that much. I don't see what people go on about.*

'It's the greatest buzz in the world,' the Sandman said. 'You see why you've got to get out of Swindon. Provincial dump! Stop hanging around with idiots like Jack Fitt. Get on the scene, and stay stoned for the rest of your life.'

'Jack's not an idiot, he's a jazz musician. He smokes pot and everything. He used to fix, too.'

'It's all moody with Jack Fitt!'

***

In the morning they gave out the razor blades. The screw held a board covered in hooks, each with a number painted above it. A razor blade hung on every hook. Each prisoner was asked the number of his cell, and then carefully handed his own used razor blade. At the end of the session it was checked in again; each razor blade had to last several days.

'Number twenty-eight,' Ronnie said.

'Twenty-eight? Do you qualify for a razor blade, Belsen Boy? Nothing to shave, is there? Little bit of blond peach fuzz, like a girl's bum?' The razor blade was placed in his out-stretched palm, like a penny being given to a beggar. 'Don't do anything silly now. I've had enough suicides this year.'

After shaving Ronnie returned to his cell. Making himself comfortable on his bed, he wondered if he had any means of retaliation. He always felt better if he could figure out a way to hit back. He remembered the first time he had taken direct action against the State. It was a Saturday afternoon, and Jack Fitt was playing a new LP. Jack sprawled across the sofa, his feet higher than his head, reading the lead story in *Freedom*, the anarchist weekly. Protestors had taken to canoes to disrupt the operation of the American submarine base at Holy Loch. He told Jack he was thinking of hitch-hiking to Scotland, to join the protest. 'Su-i-cide, to base them on the Clyde—.'

'There is a better tactic,' Jack said, tossing his paper to one side.

'The mayor of Dunoon, he wants his half-a-croon—.'

'You strike a blow where the enemy least expects. It's a matter of guerilla tactics. That's the anarchist way: guerilla tactics. An army that melts into the fields.' Jack had risen to his feet, and was looking at the horizon, as if addressing a vast crowd. 'The spontaneous action of the masses!'

'Where would they least expect it?'

'Here, of course!' Jack became irritated whenever anyone failed to comprehend one of his strategic visions. 'The best place for a battle is on your home territory: here in Swindon!'

'But we don't have any Polaris submarines in Swindon.'

'Do we not have an American air base right on our doorstep? Burderop Park, just outside Wroughton village?'

'Burderop's not really an air base, Jack. It's an American forces hospital.'

'And is that not a military installation? Strike where the enemy least expects.' Jack was scornful and Ronnie fell silent.

An hour later, a cold wind nipped in across the fields as they headed up a bleak country road. Jack, who worked as a postman, walked briskly, and periodically Ronnie had to run to catch up. As always with Jack, he had a sense of great power held in reserve, like a greyhound being walked on a lead, when it would rather sprint.

'My Mum used to come here for dances during the war,' Ronnie said. 'They called it Bird Drop.'

Jack didn't reply. After a while, he launched into a briefing, in preparation for the demonstration ahead.

'What we are doing is direct action. When I give the word, we lay down on the ground. Let them carry us out. If they use force, we do nothing. It doesn't matter how violent they are, we don't retaliate. Passive resistance, like Gandhi.'

The two demonstrators remained unnoticed as they marched up to the entrance, passed a large notice welcoming them to the 7505 USAF Hospital, Burderop Park. The sentry remained seated in the guardroom, together with two other airmen, huddled over a one-bar electric fire. Jack seized the initiative. With his duffle coat slung over his shoulders like a cloak, he strode into the guardroom to confront the military. Ronnie followed close behind.

'I am seizing this air base on behalf of the people!' Jack said, his fist raised in a revolutionary salute.

The airmen looked perplexed. 'Sir, this base is owned by the RAF and leased to the United States Air Force,' said the sentry.

'This land belongs to the people,' Jack said, 'not the war-mongers! We shall sit here until we regain possession.'

'In that case, sir, I can't allow you to leave this guardroom. You'll have to wait here until the British police arrive.'

'No Polaris!' Jack shouted.

'There's a monster in the Loch!' Ronnie added.

The airmen stared at the two prone figures on the guardroom floor, and then the sentry went into an adjacent room to make a phone call. The two remaining airmen looked at each other in bemusement.

'We're engaging in passive resistance, like Mahatma Gandhi. Satyagraha it's called,' Jack said.

One of the airmen knelt down, so he could speak quietly in Jack's ear. He produced three packs of Lucky Strikes from his jacket pocket.

'You boys like some cigarettes? A shilling a pack. Plenty more where these came from. And Camels. How about Bourbon? I can get you two bottles for ten bob. Superman comics for the kids?'

Ronnie waited for Jack to denounce the airman for bourgeois black marketeering. Instead Jack looked thoughtful, as though buying illicit tobacco could be a blow against the State.

After his eviction from Bird Drop, Ronnie canvassed for the Campaign for Nuclear Disarmament for nearly a year. He followed Jack's example. He would stand on the doorstep and, without any preamble, present one fact to householders: if a hydrogen bomb landed on the centre of London, the firestorm would reach Reading, a distance of over thirty miles. This rarely had the desired effect; some looked blank, others smiled enigmatically as they closed their front doors. Bollocks to it. If that was the level of understanding, there was no point in political campaigning.

The Cuban missile crisis was the last straw. Every day, Ronnie asked himself how he would like to spend his last hours. Not banging on bloody door-knockers, that's for sure. Not looking for a job, either. You had to live like Kerouac, in *On the Road.* Ramble from town to town. Live for the moment, like the Beat Generation in America. You couldn't live for some imaginary future. You had to embrace the present, whether it was ugly or beautiful. That's what the Beat poets did.

***

After lunch, the landing officer unlocked his cell door, shouting, 'Stand by your bed! Governor's inspection!'

The prison governor had semi horn-rimmed glasses like his old headmaster, and the same air of self-righteousness. Probably prided himself on 'Muscular Christianity'. The governor peered into Ronnie's cell and frowned at his unkempt appearance. Three screws stood alongside the governor, to provide security.

'Any complaints?'

As if I'm going to complain with that mob standing beside you. 'No sir.'

'Get this lad's hair cut!'

An hour later, he was led to a chair placed in the centre of the dining hall. He'd nurtured his hair for over a year, trimming out any split ends and using special conditioners. When his hair reached his shoulders, he adopted the use of coconut butter after every shampoo, because he'd heard it replaced lost oils and encouraged the formation of ringlets. Now, one of the screws brandished the hair clippers. Two others gathered round to watch the ceremonial hair cutting.

'How do we want our hair, sir? Short back and sides? Or would you rather have a perm?'

Ronnie didn't reply. He was determined to show no emotion, to give them no satisfaction.

'I'll take that as a yes, shall I? Yes, shave the bloody lot off? Yes, stop me looking like a bloody pansy?'

Hair fell to the floor in long tendrils as the clippers shaved close to his head.

'There you are, you almost look like a boy now. Be careful, you might not get that lovely cock up your arse tonight.'

'Spoken like a true Bertie Woofter,' one of the onlookers said.

'Bertie Woofter? Not me, mate. My views on poofters are well known. I'd string the lot of them up.'

The screws reminded him of his father, who was always offering to hang someone. Ronnie decided it was safest to remain silent, and pretend to be indifferent to the loss of hair. But it was hard to hide his feelings. The screws had made him look unrecognisable, with a schoolboy's hairstyle. In the mirror, he looked about fourteen years old. It was so uncool.

His hairdresser called out to the Principal Officer, who was watching from the doorway, 'Do you think I'm worth my tip, sir?'

'I think my old mother could've done better with a pudding basin!'

'Yes, but look at the amount of hair I've had to deal with. You could sell all that hair to a blinking furniture maker. They'd use it to stuff a sofa … I think I've halved your weight, Belsen Boy. Not that you could afford to lose any.'

He was marched back to his cell by the hairdresser screw, while the Red Band swept up the hair. White Jacket was standing at the top of the corridor and called out, 'What's this then, a new admission?'

'Don't you recognise him?' laughed the hairdresser. 'Goldilocks! I've cleaned him up for you. Taken away his sissy curls.'

He was banged up again. At six, there was a clattering noise as the Red Band came along the corridor, pushing a stainless steel urn on a trolley. He stopped outside Ronnie's door and poured a mug of watery cocoa.

'It took me half an hour to sweep up that blasted hair,' the Red Band murmured. 'What did you do, grow it for a bet?'

Ronnie shrugged. 'The Rolling Stones are trying to grow their hair. Everyone wants to look like me.'

'Keep your voice down!' the Red Band hissed. 'You'll get us all fucking nicked.'

The Red Band passed the cocoa through the barred window in the door, and moved on to the next cell. Cells in the main prison were arranged along one side of a corridor, so they faced a brick wall, but those in the hospital block looked out onto another cell, immediately opposite. Ronnie's neighbour opposite, a Glaswegian, complained about the quality of his cocoa, and this gave the Red Band an opportunity to explain Prison Service policy on the allocation of the sugar ration.

The Red Band's conspiratorial whisper reminded him of Lawrence McShane, a boy he'd known in his block of flats. They'd played on the bombsites together when he was eight. Lawrence had a mop of blond hair and a slow, lazy smile. He once climbed onto the roof of the public baths and said he'd seen a woman having a bath, through a skylight.

'She was frigging herself.'

'She wasn't!'

'She was. I got my knob out and waved it at her through the glass.'

'You're a bloody liar, McShane!'

'God's honest truth! I saw her minge and everything. She begged me not to tell anyone.'

'You bloody make it all up.'

If you saw a gold chain around a woman's ankle, Lawrence said, it meant she was a whore. It was a secret sign, everyone knew that. Ever seen a pro straightening the seams of her stockings, after she's been doing it? A fur coat on a bombsite, how odd's that? There's a knotted Durex, full of spunk. And that sleek, glossy rat, its head and belly split open by a brick.

They got onto the factory roofs at Waterloo, and sneaked down the fire escapes, by the railway lines. Lawrence knew a special way to climb the drainpipes, and get over the barbed wire. Lawrence McShane couldn't be penned in. He would've found a way out of this piss-hole.

Coke was good for climbing. It let Ronnie shin up walls like a mountain goat, and walk on narrow ledges, placing his feet with great accuracy and precision. He could walk a tightrope over the Niagara Falls on coke. A few months ago, he'd broken into a house, at dusk, so that he could help set up a squat. He shuffled along a narrow ledge, one storey up. He was coked up. His back was to the wall, his movements careful and controlled. Lucy Frankish, who lived in the basement flat, came out into her backyard, smoking a joint. She was wearing a light green summer dress, an insubstantial hazy leaf of a dress that floated over her thighs. In a gesture that was familiar to him, she licked her finger and carefully wet one side of the joint, to stop it burning unevenly. She looked up and saw him. He said 'Good Evening', as though it was natural to see someone fifteen feet above your head, pinned to the wall of your house. She giggled. The brickwork was rotten and his right foot rocked on a loose brick, mortar falling into the yard below. He recovered his balance, every sense as sharp as the day he was born. One slip and you're dead. It was only when you took such risks that you really came alive, when each action had a life-or-death significance.

One slip and you're dead, man. Look how coke crystals pack down when it's damp. Easy to misjudge when you're mainlining. That much is a buzz; that's an OD. Goodnight Nurse, eh? Goodnight Nurse!

Ronnie remembered old John the Road, one of the regulars in the Duke of York, shooting up too much coke and falling backwards on his bed, the works still in his arm, eyes staring straight ahead. The worst of a coke OD was that you might die in full consciousness, John reckoned. You felt your heart speed up and you thought, 'I've done too much,' and then you waited to see if you'd survive. It was like standing on a railway line and watching a train speed towards you: could it brake in time?

A few weeks before he was busted, he'd been staying in a room in Ladbroke Grove with two coke-heads, who always wanted to buy a couple of grains to augment their own scripts. These guys shot up coke in turn, because the amount they were using took each of them close to a fatal overdose. The first guy shot up and fell forward on the table, his breath coming in ragged gasps. His friend wrapped a wet towel around his head and revived him, walking him around the room until his heart rate steadied. The second guy then shot up, and it was his turn to be revived. There followed a few minutes of animated conversation while they prepared the next fix. They carried on like this until the cocaine supply was exhausted, and then slept fitfully through the daylight hours.

The day before he left, the two guys from Ladbroke Grove discovered coke bugs crawling under their skin. They could feel, and then on close inspection they could see, these little burrowing insects, about the size of body lice. They started to gouge them out with the tip of a hypodermic needle. There's nothing there, Ronnie said, it's an illusion, a hallucination. It's coke poisoning. But his companions insisted they could see the bugs wriggling through each other's flesh, like maggots, and soon their arms were lacerated.

'Look, there's one—quick! They're laying eggs, man! Dig them out! Dig them out!'

The last time he'd seen the two coke-heads, the cuts they'd inflicted on their arms were going septic. They were still lousy with coke bugs. And they'd become convinced that the police were sat in a tree outside the house, keeping them under surveillance. They began boarding up the windows. Give Ladbroke Grove a miss, everyone was saying. The scene's got really uncool. Ronnie moved out, and found a squat in Marshall Street with a couple of pavement artists.

***

Without warning, the lights went out. Ronnie whispered across the darkened corridor, to attract the attention of the Glaswegian in the cell opposite; he wanted to know how his neighbour came to be in prison. The Glaswegian told him he'd razored a rival gang member and jumped on the train to London, only to be arrested when he reached Kings Cross. He now believed he should've ripped out the kid's windpipe. The kid had cheated him, and 'most people' would've killed him. Ronnie agreed, although actually he was rather mystified. Why did an offence to your sense of honour justify murder? Junkies didn't usually adhere to a code of conduct.

'What are you in for?' asked the Glaswegian.

Ronnie told him about the bust and the remand. After a few minutes, they heard the screw on night duty reach the end of their corridor, and they both moved away from their cell doors. If the screw heard them talking after lights-out they would be sedated with Largactil, or chloral hydrate.

When the footsteps faded, they returned to their doors. The Glaswegian's whisper sounded surprisingly loud and sonorous, like floodwater rushing through a storm drain. 'Listen, they'll probably try to put you on probation when you come up for sentencing. That'll tie you down for maybe two years. *Refuse probation!* Okay? *Refuse probation!* They'll have to send you to detention centre, and that way you'll be out in three months, all bright-eyed and bushy-tailed. Unless the Mejlak brothers decide you've grassed them up, that is!'

That sounded like good advice. He didn't want to be forced to live in Swindon for two years. Towns like Swindon were uncool. They didn't have a scene, a community of users, a place to score. The Sandman was always reminding everyone about Ronnie's links to Swindon, and he was forced to deny any close connection with the town.

Long after lights out, Ronnie lay down to sleep. He was tied to a table in the dining hall and the god with the head of a black dog cut through his breast bone, reached into his chest cavity, and tore out his living, beating heart. The Dog-headed One held the heart aloft and watched it die and shrivel, until it looked like a dried fungus, a giant puffball. It was blown off an outstretched hand, like so much dust. Ronnie felt nauseous and struggled to turn his head, so that he could see what was happening behind him. Crouched in the shadows, in the corner of the hall, was the female doctor, wearing sunglasses. She was dressed in a gold lamé ball gown, and, under her full skirt, not two but eight long nylon-clad legs splayed out, in a circle. She began to creep towards him; soon he would glimpse the deadly fangs. He was about to be consumed by one of the Daughters of Grace. 'Your blood goes to Our Mother in the sky,' she explained. 'Without Her web, all things fall apart. We must nourish Her to renew the universe.'

***

The next morning, the prison doctor came to his cell to conduct a diagnostic interview. He could read the first sentence of her notes: *On admission, the patient was exhibiting tachycardia and hypertension, and initial signs of severe heroin withdrawal.* She went through a list of predictable questions, in her peculiar, strangulated Oxford accent, and, standing to attention, he gave yes-or-no answers.

She arrived at a key question on her checklist: 'You realise if you carry on like this you're going to die?'

'We're all going to die,' he replied. 'You're going to die a lot sooner than I am.'

All the rage submerged beneath a thick, inert layer of depression bubbled to the surface. The Spider Woman. The person responsible for his cold turkey. He wanted to get back at the old crone. She couldn't expect to live that much longer, so she shouldn't lecture him. He would tell her what an ancient, decrepit whore she was. As he moved closer, however, she moved back, until she was half out of the cell door. She gripped the door handle on the outside, so that she could pull it shut.

'That's it!' she said, raising her voice in fear. 'Don't come any closer!'

He caught the edge of the door and tried to pull it open again, but she prised his fingers loose and stepped backwards into the corridor. A screw, who'd been waiting a few feet away, shoved him out of the doorway and banged the door shut.

A long time afterwards, he managed to read his file and see the interpretation that had been placed on his words. Apparently, he had threatened the life of a prison doctor. He was inconsequent, and a danger to himself and others. He was diagnosed as a psychopath, and it was recommended he should be transferred from the court to a mental hospital, under Section 60 of the Mental Health Act 1959.

A second interview followed later that day, with Dr Joseph Weiss, a world authority on alcohol dependence and editor of the British Journal of Addiction. Ronnie told Weiss that he intended to refuse probation, in order to be sent to detention centre. That way, he would be out on the street in three months' time. He thought that he would come off junk by himself. Weiss replied, a little tetchily, that he didn't think he could.

In his court report, Weiss supported the use of Section 60. While the patient might have a personality disorder, he felt it secondary to the disease of drug addiction, which should be the focus of treatment. He would have taken the patient at his own alcoholism unit at Southall, but for a shortage of beds.

A few days later, when Ronnie appeared in court, expecting to be sentenced to detention centre, he was surprised when the magistrate said: 'You are going to be sent to a mental hospital. You will not be allowed to escape!'

You just try and stop me, shitface, Ronnie said, under his breath.

Chapter Four

It took two buses for Ronnie's mother to get to the central post office in Swindon, so that she could send him a birthday telegram. Florence Jarvis—Flo to her family and friends—was obliged to give the clerk the address as HMP Ashford Remand Centre. She felt ashamed. It was the way he looked at her, like she was one of those tarts from the Morden bungalows, whose children were always in trouble with the police.

As she caught the bus back home, she started to think of another day when she'd felt shame and regret, during the war. She'd been to a dance at the American base at Burderop Park with two old school friends. A local band, Johnny Stiles, was playing. One of the GIs offered to see her home; there was no harm in it, he was a real gentleman.

She remembered the excitement of that wild, wind-blown jeep-ride to the town centre, squealing in delight at the speed, her hair streaming out behind her, and the driver laughing and doing a U-turn in Regent's Street, before dropping them both on the corner by Stead and Simpson's. A group of GIs, watching her jump out, shouted *'Hey! There's Veronica Lake!'* and she felt really glamorous. It was the first time she'd been in a motorcar, let alone an open-top jeep. She'd been in buses, and plenty of trams, but never in a car.

It was about 10 p.m. and there was a full moon in a cloudless sky, which made up for the lack of street lighting in the blackout. As they walked through the deserted streets, she started to sing a Glenn Miller number that she'd asked the band to play, *Don't go walking down lovers' lane with anyone else but me.* Her escort joined in.

He had a good voice. His name was Chuck Wiebner, and he came from just outside Cedar Rapids, Iowa. It was the Midwest, he said; the prairie. She wondered if that meant he was a cowboy, but he said it was all arable where he lived, with just one or two pig farms nearby.

'Old blooming Lord Haw-Haw mentioned Swindon in his broadcast the other night,' Flo said.

'Lord *who*?' He sounded irritable. He'd already told her she kept using words or expressions he'd never heard before.

'Lord Haw-Haw. William Joyce is his real name. He's a Blackshirt—a traitor who went over to the Jerries. He makes propaganda broadcasts for Hitler now.' She pinched her nose and imitated a sinister, nasal voice with an upper class drawl, 'Germany Calling, Germany Calling'.

She watched his face for a sign of recognition, but there was none. She continued, 'I know you're not supposed to listen to the German broadcasts, but you wonder what they're saying don't you? Haw-Haw said, how's everyone in *Swindon* tonight? Blooming cheek! He said the clock on Swindon town hall is five minutes slow. And it is! How do the Jerries know that? Is that fifth columnists?'

'Probably seen it from the air.'

He had a dimpled chin like Cary Grant, and when he smiled his face lit up. Fair-haired though; Cary Grant had black hair.

They started out along the dried-out, disused canal that led from Swindon town centre to Rodbourne Road, past the three storey Communist Party headquarters with the message facing the canal side, in letters four foot high: *Read the Daily Worker.*

'My husband thinks all the communists should be rounded up and dumped on a desert island.'

'Oh yeah? Where's he going to find an island big enough? Might be easier to round up the remaining anti-communists. Put them on an island.'

'That's an idea. You could send them to join my husband on Gibraltar!'

'Yeah, then the rest of us could get on with winning the war.' He held her hand, and she worried that he might get the wrong idea. This was strictly platonic; she didn't want to get talked about like Maisie Drummond, or some of those loose girls you saw at all the dances.

'There's a lot of communists in the railway works in Swindon.' Her words came in a rush, as though there wasn't time for all the things she needed to say. 'Loads of people are backing the commies now, aren't they? Old Uncle Joe's pinning down the Jerries at Stalingrad, isn't he?'

'Certainly is. My father's in the American Communist Party.'

They came to a narrow section of the canal, where they were hemmed in by tall factory buildings on both sides. She felt worried, and a bit puzzled by his last remark. 'Wiebner, isn't that a Jerry name?' she asked.

'Yeah. So's Eisenhower. So are the names of half the generals in the US army.'

'Your family were Jerries, then?' She had stopped walking and was looking down into the canal. He walked on a few paces, impatiently.

'A lot of people in the Midwest are of German or Scandinavian origin,' he said. 'Did you know that German nearly became our national language? Why do you think it took us so long to enter the war?'

'Blooming hell. You'd be interned over here.'

A long, awkward silence intervened. She looked across at his face in profile; he was frowning, and he reminded her of Cary Grant in that Hitchcock film, *Suspicion.* She decided to say something more positive about the Germans.

'You know that hatcheck boy at the dance, the German PoW? He said to me, "You look like a proper German Fraulein." A proper German Fraulein!'

He turned to face her and the frown disappeared. 'Must be your blond hair, long and wavy,' he said. 'And those blue eyes. Would you like to be my little Fraulein?'

'Don't be silly, I'm a married woman.'

'You're much more glamorous than most of the local girls, who—quite frankly—look a bit dowdy. You've got style. You could be a movie star. You're just like Veronica Lake in *This Gun for Hire*. You even peep out from under your hair like Veronica Lake.'

She beamed. 'I'm not really local. I don't live in Swindon anymore, I just came to stay with my Mum during the Blitz.'

'Everyone I meet here tells me they don't really belong to Swindon. It must be the kind of town no one owns up to coming from. Like Buffalo, New York.'

They had just drawn level with some isolated railway workshops that had been occupied by Shorts, the aircraft manufacturer. In the soft, deceptive moonlight, she could imagine the canal as it had been, when the water was still flowing.

'It's beautiful in the moonlight,' she said. 'It reminds me of the time I went boating on the river at Lechlade, by the light of a full moon.'

'Beautiful? There's no water in the canal. Just some old rubbish. It's a tip.'

'Don't spoil it, Chuck,' she laughed. 'Why do men have to be so unromantic?'

'Why do women want make-believe?'

'You've got to dream of something,' she said. He might be nice and he was clever, but he didn't understand basic philosophy: keep to the sunny side of the street. Life had a dark side, but if you didn't dwell on miserable thoughts they held no power over you.

The towpath had been made of hard-packed ash and cinders, but here and there clumps of yellow ragwort had forced their way through. They were ailing and tattered, their sickly hue darkened by a thin film of soot. He bent down and carefully picked a bunch, and presented it with a flourish: 'Beautiful flowers!'

'You daft bugger!' she laughed, hitting him over the shoulders with them. 'Rotten old weeds! Is that what you think of me?'

She danced along ahead of him and sang *Don't sit under the apple tree with anyone else but me.* He joined in the chorus. She waited for him to catch up and asked, 'Why do they call that dance the Jitterbug?'

Before he could answer, the air-raid sirens began their melancholy wail.

'Oh God, it's a raid!' she said. 'You leave London to get away from the Blitz and they blooming follow you here.'

They could see searchlights dredging through the night sky just behind the gasometers, and they could already hear the throbbing sound of enemy aircraft overhead. Anti-aircraft guns, far away on the other side of the railway lines, began firing at the stars.

'Look Chuck, here they come!'

'Heinkel one-elevens. They're going after Shorts' aircraft factory.'

Factory railings were to their left and right. Just ahead, there was a patch of open ground, known as Ferndale Road Rec, in front of long, low factory buildings. They started to run towards the safety of the open space. They reached a bridge over the canal and instinctively stopped under it, just as the first bombs fell less than thirty yards away on the Rec. The earth shook, and they were showered with mud.

Chuck put his coat over her head, and held her tenderly in his arms against one of the bridge's brick pillars. Hundreds of fireflies danced along the path towards them. As they drew nearer, she saw they weren't fireflies. Moonlight was reflected in the eyes of dozens of rats, fleeing the canal-side in alarm. At any other time she would have screamed as the rats scurried past their ankles, but she was so preoccupied that she didn't react.

The explosions were deafening. Not one bomb hit the aircraft factory. When they looked out, the grass had been churned up and cratered like a battlefield. Five or six dismembered bodies lay less than twenty yards from the canal.

'That Rec was full of courting couples,' she whispered. Death sneaked up, when couples thought they were alone, while they lay happily in each other's arms.

The all-clear sounded as they made their way slowly past the debris, and out of the Rec, into the road leading to her mother's terraced house. She said nothing, aware of the proximity of death. *Yea, though I walk in death's dark vale.* She had to walk through the parlour when Uncle Bob was laid out there, his face looking like a wax model. His coffin was lowered into the ground, while Mum bit her lip. English elm, with best brass handles. Elm doesn't rot; even in wet ground it'll last for centuries. The best for him, Dad's youngest brother. *He leadeth me, the quiet waters by.* That horrible funeral tea, when she was chided for allowing the tears to fall.

'Now, now; let's not start all that, our Flo. There's too much weeping in the world as it is.'

You had to be strong. It had been in the Sunday papers for all the neighbours to see. Her uncle had murdered his sweetheart, and then killed himself with a cut-throat razor. Dad never got over it. In the end, they came and took Dad away to the asylum at Devizes. Mum got a job and carried on, and went to visit him each month, and kept herself respectable. Never owed a penny to nobody nor nothing.

Flo began trying to clean the mud off her dress with a handkerchief.

'We'll have to say goodnight here, Chuck. I can't ask you in, my Mum's waiting up.'

He kissed her goodnight. She pulled away. There was no pleasure in a kiss tonight. Her knees were shaking from the shock of seeing young bodies torn open and tossed aside, as if gored by a rampaging bull. Anyway, she didn't want the neighbours to see her kissing a GI. They'd get the wrong idea. They wouldn't understand that he was just walking her home. It was all platonic. She wasn't going out with him.

She inserted her key in the lock and opened the door very quietly, almost colliding with her mother, who was waiting in the darkened hallway.

'Where have you been?' her mother snapped. 'What time do you call this? Freddy's here!'

'Freddy? He can't be. He's on Gibraltar.'

'He's in the front room.'

'I'm not going to see him.'

'Don't start that again! You'll make us a laughing stock. You married him and you're going to do your duty. Get in there!'

She could smell the booze as soon as she entered the room. Freddy sat with his Lee-Enfield rifle over his lap, as though he was going pigeon shooting. His army forage cap was worn at a jaunty angle. He held a packet of Senior Service in one hand, and an unlit cigarette between the fingers of the other. He was sat sideways, so she could see his left profile, which she'd always told him was his best side. He was posing, she thought, as if he was waiting for someone to take his photo.

'They've given me compassionate leave. I've got forty-eight hours.' He struggled to his feet and thrust his face forward, until they were almost touching noses. 'I told them my wife was going with all the bloody Yanks in Swindon. She's the biggest bloody whore in town.'

His speech was slurred. He must have been drinking all day.

'Don't be daft. Who told you that? I've just been to a dance with some girl friends. I've been caught in the raid down—'

'You've been bloody seen, you stupid whore!' He screwed his face into a devilish mask and stamped his foot, like an infant having a tantrum. 'Seen taking your knickers down for bloody Yanks! They're all talking about you.'

He was becoming incomprehensible.

'Don't wave that gun at me. I was caught in the air raid over Ferndale–'

'Take your knickers down!'

'Get off me!'

'What's the matter, don't you do it for Englishmen?'

'You disgust me.'

That was when it all started to go wrong. It was the first time he'd ever hit her: he pummelled her head and upper body until she fell back across the sofa and slid down onto the floor. Her lips swelled and bled; bruising closed her right eye. The next day he was contrite, and he apologised, but he also warned her never to say anything like that again.

She hadn't always been unhappily married. When they started courting, Freddy was very romantic. He could play the piano: all the old Noel Coward songs. He would play, while she stood by the piano and sang. Other girls envied her. But little by little the drinking increased, and so did the jealous rages. When he was posted to Gibraltar, he asked one of his brothers, who lived in Swindon, for regular reports on her conduct. Who did she talk to? Had she been to a dance? Who did she dance with? Then he would write these long letters accusing her of being unfaithful. In the end she decided she might as well go dancing regularly; he got more suspicious if she said she was staying in.

Immediately after the war, they were living in two upstairs rooms in his brother's house in Kilburn, and she was getting desperate. She gave birth to a little boy and Freddy used to go mad if the baby cried at night. Once he held the baby out of the window and said he was going to drop the brat if it didn't stop. He came back from the war with this terrible temper.

He didn't talk about the war very much, but he'd shot a German in a face-to-face confrontation. 'It was him or bloody me,' he said, 'and they'd already killed five of my mates.' He said he didn't give a toss, and he'd do the same again, but sometimes he woke in the night, sweating. He had nightmares in which he saw his pals killed again and again, blown apart by grenades. And his drinking got heavier.

Living in two rooms was beginning to get to them, and there were constant arguments. He began to hit her more frequently. Once she hid in his brother's flat downstairs, because he started to smash up the furniture. She thought he'd gone mad. Then, just when she was thinking of running away, Freddy joined the Metropolitan police, and they were given one of the new council flats in Hampstead. Freddy was in his element. It was the sort of address he thought he should have. Bit of a snob really. A Tory and a snob. He had no reason to be. His father was just a joiner from the Rodbourne Road.

Things seemed to improve for a while. Freddy seemed to do well in the police force, but he was becoming more moody. Sometimes he would walk past his family in the street without speaking, as though he didn't know them. Sometimes he would fly into uncontrollable rages. He used to buy liver sausage for his own use. One day he thought someone had been stealing slices, so he threw it on the floor and stamped on it. He was getting a bit odd; a real little Hitler. She couldn't carry on like this.

***

'I've got a Section 60.'

Ronnie could hear two screws in the corridor outside his cell in Marlborough Street Magistrates' Court.

'What is he, round the twist?'

'Psychopath.'

'Oh? Where are you taking him? Broadmoor?

'No, Devizes in Wiltshire.'

Bloody hell. They were taking him to Devizes. Roundway Hospital. The local Loony Bin. As a child in Swindon, anyone who behaved in an eccentric way had been warned 'You'll get taken to Devizes.' It's where his Granddad had ended up, after going to a police station and confessing to robbing all the shops in Swindon Old Town.

He'd visited his Granddad in 1952, around the time that the old King died. He knew when it was, because he remembered hearing funereal music over the wireless, and then the announcer saying 'the King is dead', and his mother sitting up and gazing into space for a long time, in silence.

Grandfather was a frail old man, confined to bed. He had grey hair, and an even greyer face, which looked like it had never seen fresh air. And he had a black eye. As Ronnie sat with his Gran at the bedside, Granddad claimed that one of the nurses had hit him.

'That one gave me a black eye!'

Gran lowered her voice, 'Shush, Bill. Don't take on so.'

Granddad raised his voice, 'Gave me a black eye!'

'Everything all right, Mrs Foxton?' a nurse enquired, moving towards his Grandfather's bed.

'If I need your help I'll ask for it, thank you very much,' his Gran said. 'He'll be fine in a minute.'

Granddad said nothing, but hauled himself upright in bed and sang as loudly as he could: *Two lovely black eyes!*

'Bill, we have to be going now!' Gran announced. 'Stop that! Bill, we're going! I'll see you next month. Say goodbye to the boy, Bill.'

But Granddad wasn't listening. He sang in a loud, lusty voice:

Two lovely black eyes!
Oh! what a surprise!
Only for telling a man he was wrong,
Two lovely black eyes!

When they were walking to the bus stop, Gran said, 'He fancies things are happening when they're not. He's been like that since 1933.'

'Yes, but who gave him that black eye, Gran?'

'The nurses said he did it to himself. He fell against a door or something.'

The bastards had given his Granddad a black eye and lied about it. And now he was going to the same Loony Bin, instead of a detention centre, where he could've been out in a couple of weeks.

Ronnie was handcuffed to the escort, and they sat together in the back seat of a large, black saloon car. 'More comfortable than a Sweatbox, anyway,' Ronnie said, thinking of how tightly he'd been wedged into a locked compartment on the way to court.

He hadn't anticipated the sheer excitement of being able to look out of the car windows, after a month of incarceration. Every sight, from women's fashionable clothes, to street flower sellers, and even Tube stations, seemed fresh and full of life. The sounds of the city were exhilarating: car horns, snatches of music, street vendors' cries.

The escort was in an affable mood and chatted to the driver about lack of progress in the hunt for the Great Train Robbers.

'They've got clean away, if you ask me. That was a professional job. They're never going to catch them.' At one point, he turned to Ronnie and added, almost as an afterthought: 'You'll be kept in some special unit. You won't be kept with all the people who think they're Napoleon and that.'

After several hours' drive, the saloon edged down a narrow country road called Pan's Lane, towards the Lodge that guarded the entrance to Roundway Hospital. *Pan's Lane.* What perverse joke lay behind the naming of that road? What kind of sanctuary would you expect to find at the end of a lane dedicated to Pan? The bestial god Pan had a shout that drove men mad, didn't he? It was in that comic where the Greek gods came back as modern super heroes and super villains. Pan was the Lord of Panic, and Hercules had to silence him by smashing a giant tree trunk over his head.

Roundway was built in Bath stone. The buildings were squat and heavy, like a Victorian prison or workhouse. As they drove under an archway he saw the legend carved above, *Wiltshire County Lunatic Asylum 1851*. He was filled with a sense of foreboding.

They came to a halt in a courtyard, outside what appeared to be a butcher's shop—perhaps it was, the asylum had its own farm. The quarry-tiled floor, seen through the open door, was sprinkled with sawdust. A man with the stigmata of Down's syndrome was wiping blood off his hands, onto a blue and white striped apron. An iron grating set into the flagstones outside was slippery with blood, and there was a dark pool of ox blood on the floor. For some reason it reminded him of the time he'd gone to see the blood staining the pavement outside the Magdala tavern.

Still handcuffed, he was led up some narrow stone stairs, as if entering a castle keep. On the first floor, a side door led to Larch ward. Waiting for their party was the charge nurse, Don Butler, a bald man, who must have weighed eighteen stone. Built like a brick shithouse. As the group made its way to his office, Butler stood with the key ready to lock the door, but appeared lost in thought. A small, dark-haired man, standing in the shadows, threw himself towards the open door, in a frantic dash for freedom. At the last minute, Butler swung his body in front of the open doorway, executing a perfect body check. The patient fell to the floor, winded. It was like watching wrestling on television.

'Do mind where you're going, John. You'll hurt yourself in a minute,' said Butler, joining the crowd in the office. This seemed to be an in-joke, because several male nurses, perched on the office windowsill, started giggling.

'What have we got here?' Butler enquired, of nobody in particular. 'A Section 60. Not to be released without the Home Secretary's consent, eh lad? Well, you'll see the doctor tomorrow and he'll decide what to do with you. Just find a chair out there while we do the paperwork.'

The handcuffs removed, Ronnie walked into the day room, a long, narrow corridor, the walls painted a dismal cream, the woodwork picked out in chocolate brown. The Georgian windows looked down on a courtyard, which never received sunlight. Enclosed in the courtyard were two lofty trees, which despite their height had a stunted appearance. Although it was still summer, they had already lost some of their leaves.

Armchairs were spaced at regular intervals, facing a blank wall. A few patients were seated and appeared to be contemplating the wall in front of them. The atmosphere was as sedate as a crematorium getting ready for the morning service.

What had they meant about Section 60, he wondered, and not being released without the Home Secretary's consent. Was that true? Did it mean it would be hard to get out? How long would he have to stay before his release?

When Ronnie met the consultant, Dr Fitzgerald, at ten the next morning, he was disappointed. He was called into the office and asked to stand by the door, while the psychiatrist stood near the window, keeping the maximum distance between them, as if Ronnie was highly infectious.

'You're with us because Dr Weiss's unit, at St Benedicts, didn't have any beds at the moment. We used to have someone with an interest in alcoholism, but I'm afraid she left. Anyway, we can keep you here until St Benedicts are able to free up some space. Can't say how long that will be, I'm afraid. Shouldn't be more than twelve months. You'll have to stay on Larch until then, because of your, um, your legal status.'

Fitzgerald was a tall man with a stoop and a vague, distracted air. He didn't look at people when he spoke to them.

'Twelve months? How long before I'm going to be released then?' Ronnie asked.

'Released? Well, you're being held under a section of the Mental Health Act, and we'll continue to hold you until we think you're better.'

'When will that be?'

'When you've stopped wanting to take drugs, I should imagine. Okay, that's it: I've prescribed some vitamin B to help build you up, and something to calm you down a bit. Duty calls. Onward and upward.'

Six nurses formed a human square around Dr Fitzgerald as he hurried down the ward, and physically prevented any patient accosting him. The small, dark-haired patient, seen running for the exit on the previous day, pursued the pack, and tried to attract the doctor's attention from a safe distance.

'Excuse me. Excuse me, Dr Fitzgerald? Could I see you, Dr Fitzgerald?'

Dr Fitzgerald ignored him. When the psychiatrist reached the exit, he performed a strange contortion, opening the door with his key, and turning the door handle, while keeping both hands in the pockets of his white coat. No part of his anatomy touched the door or the surrounding doorframe.

'Why does he do that?' Ronnie asked the nearest nurse.

'Dr Fitzgerald's a very clever man, Ronald. Very clever. He has this theory about schizophrenia and germs.'

He scrutinised the nurse's expression to see if there was any trace of a smile, any twinkle in his eyes, to show that they both understood the absurdity of the situation. There was not.

Twelve months. And how long after that before they decided he was cured? Instead of being released in three months, as he'd hoped, it looked as if he was going to be incarcerated for the maximum Borstal sentence, two years. The hopelessness of his predicament started to dawn on him. He needed to keep in touch with people on the scene, or he'd be forgotten by the time he came out. He'd be a nobody.

He went to the office and asked the deputy charge nurse, Mr Blake, for some writing paper. He was given twenty sheets of lined foolscap. Sitting in a corner of the dayroom, he began a long letter to the Sandman, telling him about conditions at Roundway, asking whether it would be possible to visit, and including a full page drawing of the charge nurse, Don Butler, as Frankenstein's monster. Ronnie was rather pleased with this, particularly the way he'd drawn Butler's arms, which were longer than the sleeves of his white coat.

When Ronnie asked about stamps and post boxes, he was told to leave any letters in the office; the nursing staff would see that they caught the evening post. Ronnie deposited a bulky envelope addressed to Paul Spackman, a.k.a. the Sandman, and started another letter to Jack Fitt, and a brief note to his mother, asking if she could bring some spare clothes and some horror comics when she visited.

He finished both at teatime, and took them to the office. The door was ajar. He paused, about to knock, when he heard raucous laughter. Through the gap in the door he could see four nurses, gathered around Mr Blake, who was known to the others as Snakey Blakey, possibly because of his cold, reptilian eyes. Blakey was pinning Ronnie's drawing of Don Butler onto the office notice-board.

'Wait till old ruddy Don Butler sees this!' one of the nurses cackled. 'He'll go bleeding mental.'

'It's a bloody good likeness!' Snakey Blakey said. 'Look how he's got old Don's big nose. The Monster Mash!'

Ronnie went back to the dayroom, took his two letters, tore them into small pieces, and threw them in the wastepaper bin.

***

'You've got a visit, Leonardo.'

The charge nurse, Don Butler, was standing over Ronnie with his head jutting forward, and his arms akimbo, as though he was about to seize him in a head lock. Snakey Blakey hovered behind Butler's shoulder, like a wrestler in a tag team, keen to enter the ring.

'A visit? Who?'

'A young lady to see you. And the next time you leave a letter for posting, you're not to stick down the envelope.'

'That letter was private.'

'Nothing you do is private. You're on a section. My nurses have the right to read anything you write, in case you're trying to get hold of drugs. Or slandering members of the hospital staff … Now go and speak to your visitor in the dormitory. I've put some chairs out.'

They wouldn't want to bring visitors into the dayroom. Most of the patients were sent out during the day to labour on the farm, or around the hospital grounds. Those who remained were too disturbed to be allowed out. A man who'd suffered meningitis as a child stood all day in the same spot, examining his fingernails. At the far end sat two or three East Europeans, who spoke no English, and had been brought to England as displaced persons, after the war. One of them had a deep indent in the centre of his forehead; presumably a war wound. Another, a Ukrainian patient, paced up and down the length of the corridor, sometimes shouting *Raus! Raus!* at invisible assailants.

‘I wouldn’t feel sorry for him,’ one of the nurses advised, when the Ukrainian became agitated and started shaking his fist at the shadows. ‘Waffen SS. He’s one of the Ukrainian nationalists who joined the SS when Hitler invaded.’

Two kitchen chairs had been placed facing each other in the centre of the dormitory. On either side were long rows of neatly made beds—‘Should be able to bounce a penny on the counterpane,’ a nurse explained—but the dormitory was otherwise empty. There were no personal possessions in evidence. The patients all wore the same clothes, a tweed suit which seemed to come in one size only, so that for many it was extremely ill fitting.

Ronnie couldn’t think who his visitor could be. He wondered if it was one of the female patients, Longtown Lil. On fine days, Lil wandered aimlessly around the hospital grounds, while Ronnie, who hadn’t seen a woman for weeks, stood silently at the window and watched, and wondered what it would be like to embrace her. Once, Lil looked up at his vantage point and waved, and he imagined slipping a hand down her panties and cupping his fingers around her warm cunt.

Longtown Lil was anaemic-white, and wore a long, scarlet, lacey gown, like a nightdress, her head tipped back in ribald laughter. Her beauty was marred by bad teeth. When Lil opened her mouth, she showed a row of blackened stumps where her front teeth should have been. Oddly, the horror that was Lil’s smile, the flaw in her beauty, made her more rather than less attractive to him, and he dreamed of meeting her in the courtyard one night, and fucking her up against a lime tree. The bark would graze his knees, and scratch her buttocks, and she would grunt as he piled into her wetness, and they would cling together, panting in the night air, yowling like two cats.

Snakey Blakey unlocked a door at the far end of the dormitory. A dark figure, waiting in the shadows of an unlit stairwell, took three cautious steps forwards and stood blinking in the daylight. Ronnie was surprised to see Samantha Ojukwu, the girl he’d been staying with when he was busted.

Samantha was the sun to Lil’s moon. Samantha’s beauty didn’t need to be highlighted by any blemish, indeed her appearance was flawless. She had immaculate teeth, her skin was golden brown, the colour of molasses, and she radiated healthy energy. Today, Samantha was wearing tight jeans and a man’s striped shirt, and her wild and luxuriant hair, usually free to surround her head like a halo, was tucked into a large, floppy, baker boy’s cap. She’d made the cap to her own design, out of red corduroy.

‘Jesus! What have they done to you?’ Samantha called out, as she advanced towards him across the polished wooden floor.

‘I’m putting on weight?’

'No, your hair. What do you call that haircut?'

As Blakey left the room, Ronnie saw him grin. Ronnie frowned, annoyed at being the butt of a joke. He was very conscious of the institutional haircut he'd been given, ashamed of his short back and sides. He hated the way it made him look so young. It was a haircut for school kids, designed to signify servitude and obedience. Shaven heads belonged in orphanages, prisons and asylums.

'They've left a long bit here and then shaved the back right up to the top of your head. Looks like they did it with a lawnmower,' Samantha said, putting both arms around his neck and kissing him on the lips. 'You look years younger. It's that pretty boy face of yours. And your skinny frame, crying out for nourishment. You'll have all the girls here chasing after you. They'll want to mother you.'

'Sod off.'

'We ought to call you Baby Face Jarvis.'

Ronnie adopted a tough expression, designed to show that he was not a baby, that he was older and more experienced than his chronological age of seventeen years. He was Brando in *On the Waterfront.* The bit where he argues with Rod Steiger: "You was my brother, Charlie. You should've looked after me a little bit." Tough but sensitive.

'Had to visit my Mum and Dad in Swindon, and your Mum told me you were here. So I thought I'd come down to see you,' Samantha said, in a special, frivolous voice she only adopted when she wanted to sound less confrontational. He hoped she realised she had gone too far, saying he was baby faced, and now she going to make it up to him. He needed her to make him feel good. That's what a guy wanted from a chick: a little bit of affection, her fingers through his hair, a little bit of friendliness, a little respect.

'You're the first person I've known who's been in the nick,' she continued. 'Better not tell my Dad.'

'No. Better not.'

'You know, I waited for you at Archway station that night.' A note of accusation crept into her voice. 'You said you'd be on the last Tube.'

Ronnie began to wish she hadn't come. 'I didn't know I was going to get busted,' he said.

Ronnie felt increasingly uncomfortable sitting on the hard wooden chair. He tried putting both feet on the seat and squatting on his haunches. That didn't seem a lot better, so he reverted to sitting with his feet on the floor, but with the chair rocking on its back legs. He wondered how Brando would've played this scene. A bit tougher, perhaps, like Stanley Kowalski in *Streetcar.*

'Well, I was about to leave Guido,' she continued, 'and I'd just packed my case.'

She sounded annoyed by his disappearance, as though he'd engineered the whole thing to evade some commitment to her. Everything was about *her*. It was ridiculous. He said, 'Sorry about that. A bit careless of me, getting myself banged up in West End Central.'

It was Samantha's turn to wrestle with the chair. She turned it around so she could straddle it, and Ronnie was reminded of a nude picture of Christine Keeler, the model in the Profumo affair. He wondered if Samantha had adopted the pose deliberately.

'Did you have a bad time?' Samantha asked, her lowered voice signifying a definite change of mood. 'How did you cope?'

Her expression of concern triggered a wave of sadness. They'd shorn his hair. They'd starved him of junk. He was confined to the back ward of a West Country asylum, without a release date, by people who believed in zapping brain cells with electric shocks. Things couldn't get much worse. Tears blurred his vision. He shook his head, scared he would start crying if he started to speak. His gaze wandered around the room, until she seized his face in both her hands, so that he was obliged to look at her directly.

'Most people feel like shit, you know, when they've been fucked around,' she said.

A hot tear ran down his face. He stiffled a sob by gulping air and, taking out a handkerchief, blowing his nose. Oh God, if he cried in front of her she really would think him baby faced. When Brando cried in *Streetcar* he'd said to Kim Hunter, 'Never leave me, baby.' That wasn't the right message somehow. Not when you're being accused of disappearing at a convenient time.

Before Ronnie could decide what would sound right, she asked, 'Was it a cold turkey? How did they treat you?'

Not for the first time, he thought that her eyes were capable of conveying a thousand meanings without a word being spoken. They could be warm, and sensual, and mournful, and compassionate at the same time.

He shrugged. 'Actually it's worse here than in the nick. At least you can speak to other prisoners in the nick. Here you can only speak to the staff, and they're all a bit odd … Talking of oddballs, how's Guido?'

'He's a fucking creep. He spends all day in the betting shop. I could just about cope with it when you were staying with us. We could meet up in the daytime and screw,' she laughed. 'He'd kill you if he knew … Here, brought you some chewing gum, Ronaldo.'

He felt overwhelmed by the allure of Samantha's warm flesh, her scent, her deep brown eyes. It was strange to be in such close proximity to an attractive woman again. 'Cheers,' he said, digging into the packaging and extracting a slab of gum. 'How are your ears?' He'd pierced her ears for her, pressing a darning needle into a leather knife scabbard held behind each ear lobe, so that she could wear gold earrings, like the ones he wore.

'Okay, actually. Look.' She rotated the earrings. 'All healed up … I've left college. I got fed up with it. Got a job instead, designing clothes.'

'Fashion? What do you want to do that for?'

'Because I'm good at it. It's what I've always wanted to do. Any objections?' She seemed ill at ease and looked away, gazing around the austere, comfortless dormitory. He decided against telling her that fashion was a hollow, parasitic industry, based on the manipulation of desire.

'That's my bed, over there,' he said, nodding to the bed opposite. 'When the day shift comes on, they all march in through that door. Snakey Blakey shouts, "Hands off cocks, hands on socks!" Sometimes he tips someone out of bed as he goes past.'

'Sounds like the ruddy army. What do you do all day, in this place?'

'I sleep a lot. *Only trouble is …*' He knew she would be able to complete the words of a Buddy Holly song.

'Gee Whiz! …' She waited for him to join her on the next line.

'I'm dreaming my life away!'

'I cried all the way to school the day Buddy Holly died,' she volunteered.

'And Ritchie Valens. He was on the same plane. And the Big Bopper. Remember *Chantilly Lace*?'

'The best die young—.' She was diverted by loud birdsong, a complex melody that rang out like a carillon, invigorating the drab surroundings. 'It's a nightingale, I think,' she said.

They went to the window and looked across to the mortuary chapel and the yew trees in the asylum graveyard. They could hear a nightingale singing nearby, but it was just out of sight.

'It's very close,' he said. He leaned towards her and kissed the nape of her neck.

She unzipped his jeans and felt for his dick. 'Would you like me to give you a wank?'

He couldn't believe that she found him attractive, with a haircut that made him look like one of the patients. Maybe she was offering him sex as an act of kindness, like taking fruit to people in hospital. Maybe it was a consolation. He felt confused and awkward. Snatching her hat, he placed it on his own head, covering his lack of hair.

'It suits you,' she said, grabbing it back. 'I'll make you one.'

He lunged after the hat again, but she held him off and they wrestled each other to the floor, laughing. After a long pause, he said, 'I thought you were going to give me a J. Arthur Rank?'

They were unaware, although Ronnie was soon to learn, that Snakey Blakey and two other nurses were taking turns to watch through the keyhole, in order to monitor their patient's behaviour.

'Dirty bastard, he's got his cock out! She's tossing him off!'

'What, that coloured bint? Let me see.'

'Dirty little bastard!'

'Here, she can give me a wank any time.'

'Hey, should we enter this in his casenotes? *Got a bint to come in and give him a wank.*'

'Well, they say psychopaths are all sexual perverts, don't they? He'll probably get up to some real fun and games in a minute.'

'I bet he bloody shags her up the arse! He looks like a little arsehole bandit to me.'

In the dormitory, the couple said their goodbyes, and Ronnie called for Mr Blake to escort the visitor down the circular stone staircase. Reaching the door to the outside world, she stood behind Blake in the gloom, waiting to be let out. The nurse turned and grabbed at her crotch with his left hand, rubbing her pubic mound briskly. She recoiled as if stung by a wasp.

'Go on, you love it,' Mr Blake said.

'Piss off, you old tosser!'

On the bus home, her anger rising, she rehearsed other things she could've said. She hadn't been prepared for an assault on the hospital stairs, she later told Ronnie. She ought to have kicked the old git in the balls.

Back in the day room, one of the nurses made an obscure reference to a handjob, and the others giggled.

'It's what you might call covert surveillance,' said Blake, 'or *What the Butler Saw.*' He turned to Ronnie. 'You dirty little bastard,' he sniggered. 'Making that bint toss you off.'

Snakey Blakey took obvious delight in confronting Ronnie with everything the staff had seen and heard. Rather than feeling humiliated, Ronnie felt proud. The staff seemed envious of him. He was not in the role of helpless psychiatric patient, he was Don Juan. He'd only been in the Loony Bin for a week, and Samantha had taken the trouble to travel down to see him, and she still fancied him. He'd been worried that admission to the Bin would be such a disgrace that none of his friends would speak to him, but her actions demonstrated that he was still acceptable, to her at least. It meant that escaping from the Bin was a practical proposition. Once out, his friends would help him stay at liberty. If only he could find a way out.

Chapter Five

Florence Jarvis could remember the day when she decided to leave her husband. It was the morning of Wednesday 13 July, 1955. She had gone with her neighbour, Doris Milbright, for a walk on Hampstead Heath. Doris's husband was also a copper, a colleague of Freddy's at Rosslyn Hill. It was the school holidays, so they'd taken Ronnie with them. A stiff breeze ruffled the Vale of Health, and the boy watched and waited while the two women stood still, looking out across the lake, their backs to the wind, as the bells at Christ Church tolled 9 a.m.

'That's Ruth Ellis gone,' Flo said. 'We're still able to breathe and she's not.'

'Yes, that's it,' Doris said. 'She's dead now. Hanging on the end of a rope. And she was only defending herself, something she had every right to do. He'd punched her in the stomach, you know. Given her a miscarriage.'

Flo lowered her voice, aware that her son was trying to listen. 'None of the police in Hampstead thought she deserved to die.' She walked over to her son and gave him a gentle push in the back. 'See if you can find some tadpoles, in the lake.'

'It's too late for them,' Ronnie said. 'They've all turned into frogs.'

'No it isn't, there's some over there,' Doris said, gesturing vaguely in the direction of the water's edge.

He walked to the lake reluctantly and stood peering into the water. He looked small for his age, Flo thought; too skinny, with his short trousers reaching down to his knees, and two thin white legs sticking out below.

'They all said it was wrong to hang her,' Flo said. 'Apart from Freddy. He blooming wanted her dead. He says everyone who commits murder should be executed.'

'It could've been any of us. I'd have done the same. If a man treated me like that, I'd bloody kill him. Brian blacked my eye once, but I threw a vase at him. I brained him. And I hit him with the bloody iron. He was out for the count. Give as good as you get, that's my motto. You should hit that Freddy back. He'd soon lay off you.'

Flo's eyes filled with tears. 'You don't know what he's like, Doris.'

'I know what he's like—he's a bloody man!'

Flo was aware that Doris didn't have children. If Doris had kids, she'd understand that you couldn't get into stand-up fights in front of them. Ronnie was always distressed if there was any violence, and she did everything to avoid it. It pained her to hear him crying in his bedroom, or hiding under his bed. She even lied about Ronnie's misdeeds, like climbing over the ruins of bombed-out houses, so Freddy wouldn't find out and punish him.

'I can't hit Freddy, he'd kill me,' Flo said, dabbing at her eyes with a handkerchief. 'He gets into terrible tempers. But if he lifts a hand to me again, I'm going. That's it, I shall be off. I'm only staying now because of Ronnie. He's only nine; I'm stuck there till Ronnie's older.' She paused, and then added, 'I've only just decided to leave Freddy. I realised it was the answer when I heard myself saying it. Isn't that funny?'

'Bleeding obvious to everyone else,' said Doris. 'Do you know your problem, Flo? You're always pretending. You pretend things are nicer than they are. You pretend things are improving, when they're not. You're always looking for the silver lining to every cloud. When you find out there isn't one, it's too late.'

***

Ronnie knew about Ruth Ellis. He'd been playing in the cellars of the bombed houses up New End when Lawrence McShane came up and said, 'There's been a murder'. They ran down to South Hill Park, and joined a group of kids looking at the dark red stain on the pavement, outside the Magdala Tavern. If they'd been a bit earlier they'd have seen the body, Lawrence said.

When he got home, Ronnie asked his Dad about it. A woman called Ruth Ellis had shot her boyfriend in the street. The police had caught her and, after a fair trial, she would be hanged, at Holloway prison. Women murderers were the worst, Dad said. He'd seen all types of killers, and some were worse than others, but the females were always evil. 'Always remember, the female of the species is more deadly than the male.'

A few months before, there had been another murder in Hampstead. The mother of one of the boys in his class had been killed by her mother-in-law. The boy's Gran had strangled his mother, and then doused the body with paraffin and set it alight. This kid was off school for weeks, and when he came back they were all told to say nothing about it by the headmaster. But Ronnie told his mates, in secret, that his Dad had been to the scene of the crime, and that the body had shrunk in the heat of the flames, until it was tiny. His Dad said the Grandmother was a wicked old woman, who deserved the noose.

Murder was something that happened in families when people got really cross with each other, but you weren't supposed to talk about it. It was a secret, like condoms. He went to the seaside with the school once, and the headmaster made one of the teachers go round and bury these condoms that were being washed ashore, because children weren't supposed to see them. The teacher pushed each one under the sand with his foot, as if he was stubbing out a cigarette, and then he covered them with more sand for good measure. You buried secrets.

Condoms were really called Durex, and they came in a purple paper packet. His father had some in the dressing table drawer. He wondered if his father would ever murder anyone with the heavy service revolver that he kept hidden in the same dressing table drawer, just above the condoms. His Dad might shoot his Mum if she kept on arguing.

After an uncertain start to October, there was a Michaelmas summer, and autumn was held at bay by blue skies and warm sunshine. On Saturday, the eighth of October, Ronnie's Dad, who was on nights, took him out for a walk, which ended with a lunchtime session in the local boozer. Ronnie had a glass of lemonade, and sat with his Dad, at a table outside the saloon bar. Freddy was wearing a green open-necked shirt and tweed sports jacket, and sat with his back to the wall, where he could get the sun on his square, blunt face. He closed his eyes and tilted his face heavenwards. His bushy eyebrows nearly met in the middle. They were like those dark, hairy caterpillars, Ronnie thought; at any minute they would crawl off his face.

They sat in silence; Dad never chatted much. Around about 12.45, an ex-army colleague, Sammy Carmichael, spotted Freddy as he walked by, and stopped in front of them. He came to attention, and gave an elaborate military salute, in slow motion.

'Good morning, sir!' Sammy said, giving Ronnie a conspiratorial wink. 'That's sir spelled c-u-r.'

Freddy's eyes opened, and the two hairy caterpillars jumped skywards. 'Sammy, you old scoundrel! You can usually be persuaded to join in a serious drinking session.'

'Don't mind if I do, Freddy. No, put that away, Freddy; won't hear of it. Next round's on me. No, no, it's my shout, Freddy. Have a whisky chaser this time? Good man! Down the hatch!'

The two men had a mutual interest. At a certain point in the conversation, Sammy could be relied upon to lean forward, a glint in his eye, and say, 'That's bloody women for you, Freddy'. And Freddy would launch into his thesis on female psychology.

'Women don't actually think, Sammy. They can't conceptualise things the way a man can. They don't actually have a mind, in the way a man does.'

Sammy would nod, and say that women were just animals. Like the beasts of the field, they did not possess reason. Sammy was one of the few men who really understood women, Freddy said. He'd developed ways of managing the female's fundamental lack of logic. But sometimes Sammy seemed to treat the whole idea as a jest. He said things that were so outrageous that the other men in the saloon bar would burst out laughing. Then Freddy would get cross.

'Never forget, Sammy, *the female of the species is more deadly than the male!*'

Today, however, Sammy lacked his usual air of hail-fellow-well-met. Lowering his voice, so that it was hard for Ronnie to hear, Sammy spoke in a confidential tone.

'I say Freddy, old chap. None of my damned business, I know—and tell me to mind my own business if you like—but you did once ask me to tell you if I ever saw your wife—you know.'

'What's she been up to, Sammy? Spit it out.'

'Well, there's no easy way to put this, Freddy. I've just been over to Battersea Funfair and I saw your wife with another man.'

'Are you sure? What did he look like?'

'Yes, as sure as I can be. I was as close to them as I am to you now, old chap.' Sammy mimed someone preening a moustache. 'Tall, with a handlebar moustache. *RAF type.*' The two men exchanged a knowing look.

'Right. That's just what I've been waiting for. A bloody Brylcream Boy! Always the bloody RAF behind any mischief! Thanks, Sammy. What's your poison?'

Freddy downed his pint, bought one for Sammy, and told his son it was time to go. They walked the short distance to their council flat, at a fast pace. His father seemed almost elated. 'I've got the evidence now,' he said, 'after years of searching. This time she won't get away with it. Infidelity. It was all true. She's been unfaithful all along, the cow, and now I've got her!'

Ronnie said, 'Will you give her a slap?' but his father didn't reply.

Flo was in the kitchen, pulling wet sheets out of the boiler, her face flushed red with exertion. Freddy walked straight up to her and, before she could look round, grabbed her by the hair and yanked her head down, so that she was looking into the boiling water.

'Enjoy the Funfair, did you? Cow!'

Instead of pleading with him, she said in a firm voice, 'Freddy, let go of my hair. Let go of my hair.'

He released his grip and pushed her backwards at the same time, but without his usual force. Flo staggered, but didn't fall.

She turned to Ronnie and said, in a very composed, level voice, 'Mummy wants you to go to the shops. Go to Barney's and get a tin of beans.' And she handed him a shilling.

Ronnie ran all the way to the shops, and all the way back. When he entered the flat, his mother had locked herself in his bedroom. He could hear her crying. His father, who had been pacing up and down in the hall, went into the front room to pour a Scotch. And then, before Ronnie had time to ask what was going on, his mother emerged with a suitcase in her hand, took him by the arm, and led him silently through the front door. They walked quickly up the street, without speaking.

There was only half-a-minute's delay before his father realised they had gone, and ran after them. As he drew level, he saw the Davenports on the balcony of their second floor flat. They held him in their gaze. Daphne Davenport nodded, as though she was directing her husband's attention to something. Old man Davenport was smoking his pipe, and staring accusingly at Freddy. A curtain twitched in the window of one of the other flats.

'A bloody audience!' Freddy muttered, walking alongside Flo. 'You planned this, didn't you? Planned to make a spectacle of me in front of the neighbours, you silly, daft cow! You know I can't afford to be shown up like this, to be talked about! Davenport's on the local council. He's the sort to complain to my senior officers!' Flo didn't reply. Then Freddy's manner changed, and he asked, calmly and gently, 'Where are you going? I need to know, Flo. Need to check that you're all right, love. And the boy, I need to watch out for him.'

Flo still wouldn't say, and kept her eyes looking straight ahead, like a soldier on parade. She kept marching forwards without looking back. After a few minutes, Ronnie realised that Dad was no longer in sight.

They went to his mother's friends in Frognal, Mary and Wally Jones. Mary had a servant's job in one of the big houses in Oak Hill Park, and the couple lived in the basement. Wally was a lorry driver, a stout Welshman with a florid complexion and fair hair. Mary was petite and dark, and a Londoner. When the couple had first married they'd lived in the Welsh valleys, and for some reason this hadn't been a very happy experience for Mary, and she never lost any opportunity to disparage Welsh people. Wally always listened to this invective as though it didn't apply to him; no one had ever heard him defend Wales from his wife's onslaughts.

Mary was telling his Mum that the boy would be all right staying by himself, while they went to the pub.

'Come on, girl,' Mary said, 'you've got to start thinking of yourself, putting yourself first. Don't be a doormat. You've had a terrible time, and you deserve a bit of fun.'

Flo was soon persuaded. 'Look, Mary and Wally have got a television,' she said to her son. 'You've never seen television before, have you? You can watch it while we're out, but you're not to touch any of the controls, do you understand? And don't let anyone in while we're out.'

As soon as the adults left, Ronnie thought he heard a noise in the hall, as though the basement door was being forced. He turned off the sitting room light and tiptoed into the hall, but there was nobody there. On three more occasions, he thought he heard the creak of the basement door opening, only to find the hall silent. Then, half an hour later, there was a loud, authoritative knock at the door. This time, he saw his father's green short-sleeved shirt through the frosted glass door panels.

'Ronnie, open this bloody door! It's your Dad!' His father sounded angry and in no mood for any delay. 'Let me in! Open the door now!'

Ronnie had never wanted to take sides in his parents' battles. Now he was forced to. You were supposed to do what your parents told you, but what if they wanted you to do different things? Whose side should you take? Would you lose your Mum or your Dad?

'I'm not allowed to.'

His father turned his back, leaned against the door, and settled down to wait.

***

In Hampstead High Street, the friends set out on a pub crawl, from the King of Bohemia to the Horse and Groom. They'd got as far as the Bird in Hand, gathering more friends into their party along the way. Two sailors on shore-leave joined them, and several of Wally's regular drinking companions. A group of Welsh rugby fans, in London for a match, came into the public bar just behind them.

Mary climbed onto one of the pub tables and screamed defiance, in a voice that rasped like a chainsaw: 'Down with the bleeding, bloody Welsh! Down with the sheep shaggers!'

Violence erupted. A big man in a rugby shirt was being held back by his friends.

'She's just a stupid woman, Trev! Leave it!'

'Nobody says that about Wales!'

Wally squared up to the man being restrained and announced, 'I'll bloody say it. Welsh bastards! You'll have to get past me first.'

'You're bloody Welsh yourself, man! What are you doing sticking up for her, you daft prat?'

Mary continued unabated, '*Sosban* bloody *Fach*! God's hypocrites! Sheep shaggers!'

The landlord interposed himself between the two groups, and ushered Mary and her friends out into the street: 'That's it—out! Wally—out! If you don't go now, you're barred.'

Mary cheered as they spilled out onto the street. Within the pub, the rugby fans struck up a chorus of *Sosban Fach*. It was exhilarating to be involved in a fight in which no one had lost face, no one had been defeated. Triumphant laughter rang out over Hampstead High Street.

'Appy 'Ampstead, Mary!' Flo shrieked.

'Sod the bleeding, bloody Welsh! Let's go home and have a knees-up!—What are you staring at, you daft sods? Haven't you ever seen people enjoying themselves?'

***

Ronnie heard the party returning long before it reached the big house, set back from the avenue in its own grounds. They were singing the Lambeth Walk. Wally was prancing along the centre of the road, with a crate of beer balanced precariously on his head. Outside the house, he turned to face the others, running on the spot, his beer belly bouncing up and down.

One of the sailors called out, 'Oi Wally—watch that brown ale! You're shaking it up!'

Wally continued his high stepping jig, whirling one arm while the other clutched at the crate, and swaggering as though he was an overweight drum majorette.

'Wally, you bugger, you better not drop that! That's a week's wages in the navy.'

Looking through the kitchen window, Ronnie saw his father hiding behind a tree in the garden. In a minute he's going to jump out on them. My Dad's going to bash them all up. He'll give them all a good hiding. But the group reached the front door unmolested and, when he looked out a little later, his father couldn't be seen.

Wally was standing in the centre of the hall, his face red from the exertion, singing *Won't You Please Oblige Us With a Bren Gun (Or Maybe With a Hand Grenade Or Two)?* When he finished, everyone applauded.

Flo said, 'Hasn't Wally got a lovely voice?' His Mum's eyes sparkled as she laughed, threw her head back, and danced around the room. She looked years younger.

'We're going to have a good old sing-song,' Mary announced as the first bottle tops came flying off. 'We're going to celebrate Flo leaving her old man!'

'What you going to sing, Mary? *We'll Keep a Welcome in the Hillside, When You Come Home Again to Wales*?'

'You'll get a bloody thick ear in a minute. No, a good old music hall song: *Make Yourself at Home.*'

Come round any old time,
Make yourself at home.

Wally, who had collapsed in an armchair, lurched to his feet and began to mime the actions in the song.

Put your feet on the mantelshelf,
Go to the cupboard and help yourself.

Ronnie joined in the singing.

I don't care if your friends,
Have left you all alone.
Rich or poor,
Knock at the door,
And make yourself at home.

'He knows all the words, Flo. Shame about the tune,' one of the sailors said. 'Do you want a shandy, little 'un?'

'I'd like one of those brown ales.'

'No, you can't have that, that's too strong for little boys. Have a shandy.'

'When I grow up I'll drink you under the table.'

'Will you, by God? You'll have a bloody job. You'll have to join the Navy like me.'

The sailor held up a pack of Players Navy Cut cigarettes and pointed to the picture. It showed the profile of a sailor with a full beard, framed by a life-belt, set against the backdrop of a choppy sea. The sun had just sunk below the western ocean, and the sky glowed red and gold. On the horizon were two ships of the line, and a lighthouse.

'Do you know who this is?' The sailor adopted a portentous tone, as though he was about to impart the accumulated wisdom of the ages.

'No.'

'It's Jack Tar. When he's not drinking, he's fighting. And when he's not fighting, he's drinking. And he's the best bloody sailor on the seven seas. You'll never drink more than jolly Jack Tar.'

'Where's that harbour?' Ronnie asked, pointing to the lighthouse.

'Where? The port of Bristol, I expect. Where all the best sailors come from.'

'Okay, I'll be a sailor like you and I'll sail out of Bristol.'

'Good boy. I'll let you have some brown ale now, and you can start practising! Don't tell your Mum.'

The second sailor appeared in the doorway, dressed not in his uniform but in a set of Mary's old clothes. He was wearing lipstick, mascara and a blond wig.

'Is he trying to recruit you to the navy?' asked the sailor in fancy dress. 'Don't listen to a word of it. Silly old tart! You stay on dry land.' He grabbed his shipmate's hand. 'Come on. If you have any more to drink you'll be getting up to your favourite party trick—lighting your own blinking farts!'

They waltzed into the sitting room, singing *All the Nice Girls Love a Sailor.* There were gales of laughter.

When Ronnie went to bed, his Mum was leading everyone in a chorus of *Knees Up Mother Brown,* and one of Wally's mates was accompanying her on the spoons.

If I catch you bending,
Ra-ra-ra-ra-ra,
Knees up, Knees up!
Don't get the breeze up,
Knees up Mother Brown!
—How's your father? All right!

Ronnie thought, how is my father? Has he gone home, or is he still hiding? Will he jump out and arrest everyone? It was frightening how much trouble they were going to get when his Dad caught up with them. They'd all get a good hiding. And that wasn't fair, because he'd done nothing wrong. It was his Mum who made him run away. Ronnie just wanted to go home and sleep in his own bed. He wanted everything to go back to the way it had been, before his Mum left his Dad.

***

Mary awoke around 6 a.m., as usual. Ronnie was asleep on the camp bed; most of the others had fallen asleep in chairs. She wanted to catch the milkman before breakfast, but there was a pint on the doorstep, so she'd missed him. She set off in hot pursuit, still wearing her dressing gown and slippers, and chain-smoking NAFFI cigarettes donated by the sailors. She didn't catch up with the milk float until she reached the elegant, early Georgian façade of Church Row, which was about five minutes away.

'John—give us two pints. I've got a lot of people staying over. Party last night. Pity you don't sell booze, they're all going to need a hair of the dog this morning.'

'Champagne's what you want, Mary, that's what the rich drink for a hang-over. Champagne. They're all at it round here, the filthy rich. Champagne drinking is the game. You should see the bloody things I see.'

She tucked two pints under one arm. Since she was right next to the graveyard, and everything was quiet in the early morning mist, she thought she'd go in for a quick browse. She had a long-standing interest in commemorative texts. She lit another fag and read aloud:

Sacred to the memory of Samuel Perrow ... Also sacred to the memory of Joanna, his beloved wife ... With her it was light at eventide, and she died resting in the arms of her Saviour.

Blooming heck. They all died young. She was only twenty-three. Died in childbirth. 'Jesus called her.' Poor bloody bitch. Hope he doesn't call me. Look at this: 'Anna, beloved daughter of Charles Fortune, aged eight years ... his son, aged six years ... Susan three years ... the year of our Lord 1840'. He bloody lost his wife and all his kids in the same year. 'Suffer ye the little children to come unto Me.' No thanks!

Out of the corner of her eye, a movement attracted her attention, and she looked up. About twenty yards away, a dishevelled man in a green shirt, coming from the direction of her flat, passed the cemetery gates heading towards the High Street. She recognised Flo's husband. She called out as loudly as she could, 'What do you want, you horrible bugger?' He either didn't hear, or he chose to ignore her.

***

The day following Samantha's visit, and feeling strangely confident and outgoing in his new role as a successful womaniser, Ronnie allowed himself to chat to one of the nurses. Ben Wheeler was more approachable than the others. He'd once played clarinet in a dance band, and wore rimless spectacles like Glenn Miller's. He wasn't cool, like the jazz musicians on the scene, but he seemed friendly enough.

'Do you know Jack Fitt?' Ronnie asked. 'He's a famous trumpet player. Jammed with Charlie Parker. He used to play with Art Blakey, and with the Lew Stone Orchestra. And he played with the Johnny Stiles band in Swindon.'

'Fitt? Can't say I've ever heard of him. I know Johnny Stiles though. Good old Johnny.'

Ben Wheeler was keen to explain mental illness, and went into considerable detail when Ronnie showed interest. He recounted at length the difference between hebephrenic and catatonic schizophrenia, and the benefits of ECT and the major tranquillizers. Pausing, he asked if Ronnie would like to see a demonstration of symptomatology.

Wheeler explained, 'The staff have a bit of fun sometimes; you've got to. The patients appreciate it. Larch is a happy ward. It's a bit like an old soldiers' home. Now, you see old Jim over there?'

Anyone would have noticed Jim, because he had a strange, simian gait, and he always had a vacant smile.

'Yes, what's wrong with him? Has he always looked like a monkey? Well, a bit like one. Not being nasty.'

'You'd never believe it, but Jim used to be a fighter pilot in the last war. Spitfires. He was in the Battle of Britain. But he went mad, see. You used to hear Jim screaming when you came on duty, right from the top of Pan's Lane up there. You wouldn't think so now. He's a happy man now. He's had the Big Chop.'

'The what?'

'The Big Chop we call it. A complete frontal lobotomy. We used to have a surgeon come over from America once a year, to do all our patients in one big batch. Psychosurgery. They sever the frontal lobe of the brain, so that the patient isn't troubled by strong emotion any more.'

'He doesn't walk properly now.'

'The latest techniques are much more precise. We don't cut through all the neural pathways now, we can just target one set of functions. We could even help someone like you—just take away the drive and the motivation, so you wouldn't go chasing after drugs all the time. Really, psychosurgery is the way of the future. We can shape people the way we want them.' He turned to face Ronnie. His eyes looked very big behind his Glenn Miller spectacles. Making a scissors motion with two fingers, he said, 'Snip! Snip!'

Ronnie stepped back, putting some distance between the nurse and himself. Wheeler moved closer, so that his face was only inches away.

'See, they didn't use surgical scissors in the early days. They had an instrument like an ice-pick. They knocked the patient out with an electric shock, slipped the pick into the eye socket and then tapped it through the thin bone at the back. Then they wiggled it about, to destroy the pre-frontal lobe. It was all over in a few seconds.'

'Okay, I get the picture.' Ronnie stepped further away again. 'I can see why he's lost all human feeling.'

'There has to be some sacrifice if you're going to be free from mental suffering. Jim's lost some of the higher functions, such as empathy and abstract reasoning, but he's happy enough. I was on the rehab ward with him. After the operation I had to teach him how to do everything all over again, even how to tie his shoelaces. It was like being reborn. He'll do anything I tell him now.'

To demonstrate compliance, Wheeler handed Jim a glass of water, with the injunction: 'Throw this in old Bert's face.'

Old Bert was an epileptic who'd served in the Royal Navy during the war. He'd been on board a ship that was torpedoed and sunk in mid-Atlantic, and he became distressed whenever water splashed over him.

Jim ambled slowly across the room and threw the water over the old sailor's head. Bert grabbed him by the throat, threw him to the ground and started to throttle him. Jim was growing purple in the face as his breath was choked off, but still he smiled. There was no sign of alarm or fear. Five nurses standing in a circle, watching, were convulsed with laughter. Then, at a signal from Wheeler, they waded in and separated the two men, dragging Bert to the other end of the ward and holding him until he calmed down.

The charge nurse, who had been watching from his office doorway, called out in his broad Wiltshire accent, 'If I don't have a disturbed ward at nine o'clock, I've got one by ten past nine!' Everyone laughed.

Ronnie took himself off to a corner of the ward, where he could sit and think. Poor buggers were put through their paces every day, just like the days when aristocrats paid to view the lunatics at London's Bethlem Hospital. *Bonny mad boys, Bedlam boys, Bedlam boys are bonny.* It was all in the tradition of Bedlam: using the insane for entertainment. No wonder his Grandfather never came home to his family again. It would drive anyone mad to stay here. Come to that, it would drive him mad, especially if he had to stay for another year.

One other possibility: what if they were lining him up for the Big Chop? *We can shape people the way we want them.* That was their vision for England: take all the awkward buggers and reshape their minds. Make everything safe and secure. Take away messy freedom of choice and replace it with absolute obedience. Take away the personality. He would become a vegetable, sat in the back ward of a country mental hospital. He remembered the magistrate's parting shot, 'You will not be allowed to escape.' He must get out.

Several weeks passed before he was allowed to wear his own clothes instead of a hospital dressing gown, but the day finally came when Snakey Blakey brought his corduroy jacket and Levis out of storage, and laid them across his bed. Ronnie dressed and went into the day room. Charge nurse Butler was standing by the heavy oak door, which was open; was it possible to rush him? Ronnie had seen how Butler was able to body-check an escaping patient. What if he head-butted the charge nurse—ran at him hard, and rammed him in the guts? Would it be possible to snatch his keys, run down the stairs, and open the outside door, all before they caught him? Probably not, he decided.

Perhaps Butler expected him to try something desperate? Ronnie walked slowly in the direction of the door and, just as slowly, the charge nurse pushed it shut and turned the key in the lock.

'Did you want something, Jarvis?' Butler said, with a knowing smile.

Ronnie shook his head, and carried on walking, as if intending to go for a stroll around the dayroom. He would only get one chance, he decided, and couldn't afford to take a silly risk. It would be better to steal someone's keys, and try to unlock the door without being seen. He needed to see if there was a hook or a drawer in the office, with a spare set of keys. He sat opposite the office and watched nurses enter and leave, but by the end of the day he was no wiser. He went to bed in a state of agitation; he had wasted an entire day, and was no nearer getting out.

Two or three hours passed without sleep, and he got up twice to visit the dormitory toilet. The second time, as he stood in front of the toilet bowl, gazing through the window at a crescent moon, he cursed himself for being so stupid. He was standing in front of a Georgian sash window with wooden blocks screwed into the frame, to prevent it being opened more than two inches. It was the only window that wasn't overlooked during the day. Unlike the latrine block, the dormitory toilet was hardly used in the daytime. This window had to be his escape route.

Next day, he stole a knife from the table when lunch was served, and hid it in the dormitory toilet. He hadn't realised they would count the knives, and was surprised when a full-scale search was announced that afternoon. Fortunately, no one searched in the lavatory cistern, where it was hidden.

Every lunchtime, while the nurses were playing snooker in the dayroom, he slipped into the dormitory toilet and hacked at the wood blocks in the window frame. He flushed the wood chips down the toilet, or carried them out in his pockets to dispose of in the kitchen dustbin.

After three days of steady work, he got to the stage where he'd carved the blocks away and could force the window open. His heart raced in his chest. It was near the end of the lunch hour, when his absence would be noticed, so it would make sense to postpone his exit until night-time. After a moment's hesitation he decided that he couldn't wait, even though it wouldn't allow much time to escape before they came looking for him. He climbed out of the window and down the cast iron drainpipe. He was outside! No bastard was going to stop him now. He found himself on a path that led to the central administration block; beyond that lay the gatehouse, the outside world and freedom. As he hurried forward, Snakey Blakey and Ben Wheeler came out of the side exit to the administration block. They were heading his way, deep in conversation. They had not looked up yet, but they would soon spot him.

He looked around in desperation. On his left was the drainpipe he'd climbed down; on his right the morgue, and then the hospital chapel. The chapel had its own graveyard, shaded by gloomy yew trees. It was his only chance. He hurried forward, each step taking him closer to the two nurses, hoping that neither man would raise his head. The two nurses were only thirty yards ahead when he dodged into the shadow of the graveyard, and walked slowly between the trees, taking care to make no sudden movement that might attract attention. He could hear Snakey Blakey's voice quite clearly, complaining about the way the charge nurse undermined his authority as deputy.

Ronnie crouched behind a gravestone. His heart was pounding so hard that he thought the nurses might hear it. He looked around. On the other side of the graveyard, past a high hedge, was open country, in the shape of a high hill, newly ploughed. He ventured onto the ploughed field and looked around. No one was pursuing him. Go now! He ran like the wind, stumbling over the deep-ploughed earth, his shoes weighed down with thick clods of mud sticking to the soles, his breath coming in ragged gasps as he headed uphill.

Halfway up, he paused and looked down on the stately asylum buildings, spread out across the valley below. Still no sign of any pursuers. He hadn't been missed yet, but it wouldn't be long. He carried on running, more slowly now as his legs were tiring, and his breathing laboured.

At the top of the hill, he came to the village of Potterne. He had to get as far as he could from Devizes, so he turned his back on the village and started walking along the country road in the direction of Salisbury. The realisation that he was free brought a sudden release of tension. To his shame, tears streamed down his face, and he snuffled like a little boy. He longed for a fix, to put the lid back on his emotions.

After a few minutes, he dried his eyes, and composed himself enough to hitchhike. He was lucky enough to get a lift almost immediately, to Andover, a nearby town, and from there he picked up another lift, in the cab of an old lorry, bound for London.

It was warm in the cab, and he stretched out and tried to relax, but the engine was so loud that conversations had to be conducted by shouting. The driver asked, at the top of his voice, if he'd heard about the assassination of President Kennedy.

'It was a lone bloody gunman. Shot the bastard as he drove past. In an open-topped car. In bloody Texas, of all places; the Lone Star State. He was a bloody lone star, wasn't he, the gunman? Trained by the Russians. I'll tell you what—'

Ronnie suggested that a few more politicians ought to be shot, but the driver had no real interest in his passenger's political philosophy; he just wanted an opportunity to air his own. This seemed to involve reclaiming the British Empire and extending the use of capital punishment. Ronnie gave up the attempt to conduct a conversation after this. The wagon took two more hours to reach central London, and Ronnie had time to think about his next move. He'd not had a fix in over a month and was not aware of any craving. Physically he felt fine, better than he had for months. He would exercise his free choice now, and score some heroin. He would go straight to his GP and see if he could get a script. Nothing to lose. Could only say no.

He was relieved to find his GP knew nothing of his arrest. Ronnie gave an account of how he'd spent time in the country trying to kick his habit, but had failed, and he walked out of the surgery with his full heroin prescription. For some reason, the GP had been reluctant to prescribe cocaine, going on about it not being physically addictive. As a concession, Ronnie agreed to try to forego it. In return, he received a script for barbiturates, because he had trouble sleeping, and a new syringe. Less than four hours after wriggling out of a window in Devizes, he was stoned on heroin again. The familiar sense of solidity, comfort and warmth spread throughout his being. It was like coming home after a long absence.

He needed to find a safe place to stay, somewhere the law wouldn't think of checking. He couldn't go to his mother's, it was the first place the police would look. If only he could still stay with Jack and Ruby Fitt, in Swindon Old Town. Jack and Ruby, who always left their door unlocked, used to let him wander in during the night, help himself to food, and crash out in the back room. Liberty Hall, Jack used to say.

'While I've got it, you can share it.'

Although they were inseparable for a while, like master and disciple, the friendship had ended when Ronnie started fixing. He'd let himself in one night, while Jack and Ruby were asleep, and fixed up in their kitchen. In the process, he'd squirted blood over the dinner plates in the sink, and not thought to rinse it off.

'And you can fuck off!' were Jack's first words in the morning.

When Ronnie asked what they were getting so uptight about, he was left in no doubt. 'You fixing, and blood all over the sink!' This was completely illogical, Ronnie reasoned, given that Jack loved Charlie Parker, who was famous for the size of his heroin habit. Ruby was already escorting him to the door when Jack exploded in rage. Charlie Parker was a giant, he shouted, not a leech.

Ronnie felt he'd been thrown out of his own home. Jack had been a guide, a mentor, and now he wouldn't speak to him. It was like losing his father all over again. A few weeks later he saw Ruby in the town centre, and asked after Jack, hoping for signs of a rapprochement.

'You should not have brought heroin into our home,' she said. 'Jack has used it before. He's scared of it ... He's a good man. He deserved better than this.'

Ronnie headed for the Duke of York in Rathbone Street, a haunt of Beats, buskers and pavement artists. As he reached the short alleyway known as Charlotte Place, Tony Moss came down Rathbone Street. Leaning backwards, the collar of his donkey jacket turned up, hands thrust into his pockets, Moss walked quickly, but with his body immobile above the knees. Moss was in his mid-thirties, but could have been fifty.

His black hair was greased straight back, like Bella Lugosi's, and he looked as if the light hurt his eyes. He needed a fix. His whole being was focused on his need. Ronnie watched as, at a distance of fifty yards, Moss registered him as another user, someone who could be holding. Old junkies employed a cerebral location device which scanned the horizon for signs of heroin, and Moss homed in on the signal.

'Hey man! You got some shit? I'm as sick as a pig, man.'

Moss was in a bad way. He was agitated, and in such a hurry there was a danger he would spill the fix, or fail to find a vein. Tracks of blue scar tissue traced the line of Moss's veins, and on a bad day it could be hard to make a hit. Ronnie helped him into a telephone booth and made up the fix for him, keeping watch outside while Moss made the hit. The relief was immediate. The man's health was restored. The mind, which had been as taut and unbending as a leopard stalking its prey, became playful and floppy.

'Tony, do you know anywhere to kip? I've just got out. Been in for a Cure.'

Moss was admitted to London hospitals periodically for 'Cures' and came back rejuvenated, with his tolerance reduced. There was never any question of abstaining from heroin; no one expected it any longer, least of all Moss. He'd been fixing for over ten years.

'You can stay with me, man,' Moss said, after a few moments' reflection. 'I've found a new place. Just don't tell anyone else, right? And can I blag another half-grain until tomorrow, when I get my script?'

Ronnie knew that he would never be repaid. He decided to think of it as rent. He handed over another three tablets, and they set off in the direction of Moss's new place.

'Perhaps I should take you on as an apprentice?' Moss said. 'Every tradesman needs an apprentice. You could walk behind me and carry my works.' He seemed pleased with the idea, and kept returning to it. 'After six years, you'll be a time-served junky … Teach the next generation how to fix … I should get a fee, man, for taking you on: thirty grains!' Then Moss fell silent, lost in thought. After a few minutes, he asked, 'How are you doing for Charlie?'

'He's taken it off my script,' Ronnie explained. 'Said cocaine wasn't physically addictive, so I should be able to manage without. But he's prescribed some Nembutal, to help me cope.'

'You shouldn't have let him get away with that,' Moss said, in horrified tones. 'You're going to make it bad for other people, if they get the idea that they can just take Charlie away. They'll be trying it on.'

'Well, I didn't want to make a fuss about it, in case he didn't give me a script. I just wanted to get my H again. I figured I could hassle for coke later on.'

'Yes, you'd better,' Moss said, shaking his head in disapproval.

Moss's new place was in a mews off Eastcastle Street, at the bottom of a lift-shaft. You had to slip in a fire door at the side of a garment factory, and follow some service stairs down one flight, to where another door led into the lift-shaft. Cables hung down below the lift, but they didn't reach the bottom of the shaft, and Moss had spread newspapers on the concrete floor to make it more comfortable.

'This is a good find,' Moss announced. 'It's dry. There's even a little service light here. Home from home.'

They both sat on the floor and made up a fix. Moss rolled up his shirtsleeves, to inspect and assess the veins in his arms.

'I can usually get in here … and here,' he said, stroking two veins on his left forearm. 'Try not to use the veins in your feet. They balloon up and you can't get your shoes back on.'

Whenever Ronnie worried about his health, he thought of the way Moss had kept going for over a decade, using record quantities of heroin. His doctor explained that opiates were quite benign, in many ways; people could live into their seventies on morphine or heroin, provided they followed a sterile procedure and avoided overdose. It was not opiates that damaged health so much as blood-borne diseases, like hepatitis. But Moss had picked up most of these diseases along the way, and he'd lived a hard life, eating badly and sleeping rough. He seemed indestructible.

Moss was saying, 'You'll be okay as long as you keep to four grains a day. No one really has a habit under about five grains. Six or seven grains a day—now that's a different story. That's more difficult to come off. When you get up to fifteen grains—a gram a day—you can really call it a habit. It's got you for life then.'

Every conversation with Moss revolved around quantities of heroin: how much different people were using; what different doctors were prepared to prescribe; what it took to straighten out, and what it took to get really high.

Just above their heads, the lift jolted into action. The cables swayed around as it ascended. Ronnie held his breath, scared that they might carry a live current, but they didn't come any closer.

Moss had called him an apprentice, and he felt proud. Moss was the top man, and not only could Ronnie say that he knew him, he had been appointed as some kind of junior partner. Soon, everyone on the scene would respect him.

Ronnie shot up half a grain. Ephemeral thoughts seemed to be stripped away by his fix, leaving only that which was essential. The confusing feelings that had dominated his mind during his flight from Devizes were replaced by a sense of unity. Ronnie felt he had achieved psychic wholeness again. Junk suppressed doubt, and lack of confidence, and angst—it stripped away accretions so that the essential self, or its shadow, came to the fore.

Moss blagged a handful of barbiturates and made them up into a fix, so that he would get what he called a 'proper kip'. Ronnie increased the amount of H he'd been using, and fell asleep sitting upright.

As always, he entered a darkened space, the yellow half-light before the storm. A whirlwind blew through the forest, driving fallen leaves before it. Out of the storm stepped a man eight foot tall, with the head of a black dog. His eyes shone with the light of the stars. He limped forward, supported by an oak staff. There was a stump where one foot should be. It was the Lord of the Dead, the Forest Dweller. *He is searching for someone. Hide in that thick carpet of leaves. If he touches you with his staff, you must follow him forever.* A tap-tapping sound, as the lame figure made its way down the stairs towards the basement. *He must take one in two. Seek the protection of flowers, of Wolves' Bane, of Feverfew. He is sniffing at the door to the lift-shaft. Don't let him in.*

He stared at the door in the darkness, until he could see that it had a striated texture; he was looking at the old blackout curtain that hung over an alcove in his childhood bedroom. It always looked as though someone was hiding behind it. He spotted a long sliver of light, a crack opening up in the centre. It was turning into a heavy theatre curtain. A dark figure slipped through the gap. Spotlights picked out the figure of the comedian, Ted Ray.

'Hello and good evening, boys and girls! This blonde got into the lift ahead of me—'

For fuck's sake! Turn him off!

'Turn him off? Is there no gratitude? We live in a cruel, and heartless world nowadays, boys and girls, a cruel and heartless world. Did you hear about the two junkies who were trying to take the lift? They couldn't figure out how it worked. Eventually, they forced the door open and fell into the lift-shaft. They fell five floors. They're lying broken and battered on the ground, and one says to the other, "Damn, we wanted to go up!"

I won't listen to any more.

'You've got to laugh, haven't you? Anyway, I must be going. It's cold enough in here to freeze the balls off a brass junky. And I'll pass on that message to your mother. Don't send me any more ear-muffs, mother; that's not where I'm feeling cold!'

Chapter Six

Early afternoon, and bloody Moss was *sparko.* After taking his first fix of the day, Ronnie headed down to Rathbone Street, wrapped in a cocoon of heroin. Nothing was going to bring him down today. Heroin cuddled up to him, soothed him, made him impervious to the outside world. It was like watching a storm beat upon the window pane, while curled up in an easy chair, in front of a blazing coal fire.

As he passed the Newman Arms, he noticed someone lurking in the poorly lit alleyway that ran alongside the pub. A solitary, pale-faced man stepped backwards, into the shadows, but not before Ronnie had seen a familiar, rotund belly, bursting out of a plum-coloured waistcoat, like a latter day John Bull. He glimpsed shoulder-length, rust-coloured hair, with the texture of wire wool. Guido Roberts, Samantha's boyfriend, who'd given Ronnie a place to kip, stared back at him. Ronnie had used Guido's address to register at the doctor's, and Guido's address appeared on Ronnie's prescriptions.

'You cunt!' Guido didn't look pleased to see him.

'What? Who's upset you?' For a moment, Ronnie wondered whether Guido had found out that he'd been screwing Samantha.

'We had the Flying Squad round last night! They nearly kicked the fucking door in. They pulled Samantha out of bed. Wouldn't believe you weren't staying with us. Said you were an escaped psychopath. Luckily for you we were out of dope—we'd have been busted!'

Guido's face was a doughy mound, the contours blurred by rising, swelling flesh, the sweat glistening on his nose. His eyes looked up and down the street continually, as though he could be busted for talking to an escaped mental patient. He cupped his cigarette inside his hand, as though he needed to hide the fact that he was smoking. His whole demeanour suggested someone who was uncomfortable at being under surveillance, who had something to hide. If Ronnie hadn't known better he'd have worried, but Guido was one of those dope dealers known for paranoia. Sometimes he would disappear for days at a time, convinced that the net was closing in, just because of the way someone had looked at him.

Ronnie tried to reassure him. 'I'm sorry, man, I didn't know. It's just because I've done a runner from the nuthouse, that's all. I was in for a Cure. Here, you'd think the Sweeny would have something better to do, wouldn't you? Why don't they go and chase the Great Train Robbers?'

Guido's eyes continued to scan the street and didn't return Ronnie's gaze for some time. Instead, he sucked on his cigarette and blew the smoke back down his nose.

'Well, they said you're a dangerous psychopath, and people are to contact the police if you show up. Anyway, we don't want you coming round no more.'

Guido pushed past him and headed for the Duke. He walked heavily, his cowboy boots worn down at the heels, because of the way he slapped his feet down on the pavement. There was nothing elegant about him; he reminded Ronnie of a slow and ponderous bullmastiff.

Still, Guido wasn't the only person who would give him the cold shoulder. When others learned he was being called a psychopath, they were going to react in the same way. Even his mates might not take a risk, when they were told he was dangerous and untrustworthy. Being labelled a psychopath was going to make life difficult. And he couldn't work or claim National Assistance while he was on the run. He had no income apart from dealing, and that meant he had to stay around Soho and Fitzrovia, which was precisely where the Old Bill was going to look for him.

At least he could make a living by selling a little Horse. Ronnie didn't have a problem with selling junk to casual users. They were getting a good deal. Heroin was cheaper than beer, as long as the punters were only using one jack at a time, and it was their lookout if they developed a habit and needed more. The market for heroin was a steady one; there were a number of weekend ravers and small-time users who would pay at least a pound a grain. The market for cocaine was much more volatile. Sometimes you couldn't give it away at a pound a grain; sometimes everyone wanted it. Coke was just the icing on the cake. You couldn't live off it, but it brought in some cash occasionally, and let you make a couple of speedballs in the wee small hours. As long as he could sell enough heroin to make a few bob each day, he would have cash enough for food. And provided he slept rough, and kept moving around, it would be hard for the Old Bill to trace him.

Ronnie parked himself in the doorway of a boozer in Goodge Street. People often tried to score here in the afternoon and early evening. He'd been outside the pub for about ten minutes when a female soldier accosted him.

'Here,' she said, 'I know you.'

It was a chick he'd known in Swindon, Jane Clark. She'd joined the army. He couldn't imagine why anyone would want to join up, and she wasn't able to explain. It just seemed to be a wild, impulsive act.

'Everyone said you went on drugs,' Jane said.

'What?'

'Are you taking drugs and that?'

She wasn't going to give up on this. 'I've got a bit of a habit,' he conceded. 'Horse.'

'I want to try that.'

She surprised him. Very few young people were willing to take any substance other than amphetamine. June was obviously someone who lived for risk.

'Can you get me some?' she continued, in the wheedling voice of a little girl who could always command her Daddy's affections. Her head was tilted on one side, her smile coquettish. He wondered if she fancied him. The Sandman had been offered a fuck-for-a-fix once. Ronnie wondered whether Jane was looking for a way to offer him a similar deal. He placed his hand on her arm and asked, 'What's it worth?'

She looked down at his hand as coldly as if it was a horse-fly that had landed on her sleeve.

'No more than ten bob,' she said, stepping backwards until she was beyond the range of his hands.

He felt clumsy, like the time he'd fallen off his bike in front of a group of girls and they'd burst out laughing. He pretended he'd not been interested.

'I suppose I could let you have a few jacks … You could snort it. You know, sniff it up your nose. Be easier, if you've never fixed before. Don't use more than half a jack.'

She scored half a grain for ten shillings. Taking her army cap off, she stuffed the shit in the hatband, and then marched off down the street, as if going on parade. As he watched her disappear into the distance, he wondered if she was the sort of kid who would develop a habit. Not his problem, he hadn't forced her to score. He'd even warned her not to use too much.

Now that he had some cash, he went over to the Duke of York. The public bar was small, the size of a front room, and, although it was usually busy, there were relatively few customers that lunchtime. Two dykes with greased-back hair and motorcycle gear sat by the door, drinking pints of bitter. He could tell they weren't users. Hardly anyone on the junk scene drank alcohol. Booze had a bad reaction with heroin; it made you throw up. Anyway, he hated the loss of coordination and the stupidity that came with drunkenness.

Ronnie ordered a glass of orange squash. The landlord, known as the Major, was in a taciturn mood, and served him without speaking, simply holding out his hand in a silent demand for cash. The coins were given a perfunctory inspection and tossed in the till. A glass of squash was plonked down, and a beer mat propelled along the counter in the general direction of the glass. The landlord returned to gazing through the open street door, while chomping on a cigar. Ronnie placed his squash on the beer mat. 'Proprietor: Major Alf Klein,' it read. 'Motto: Service, Civility and Courtesy.'

Ronnie tipped the synthetic-tasting liquid down his throat and was about to leave, when Graham's wife Pam strode into the public bar. Graham was a friend of the Sandman's, and Ronnie had only ever heard the woman referred to as *Graham's wife Pam*, as though she had no independent existence. She was a tall, rangy woman, with ruddy cheeks and a weather-beaten face, who looked as though she would be more at home riding to a point-to-point than marching around Fitzrovia. Her long, blonde hair was fastened back in a ponytail, and she was wearing jeans and high leather boots. She headed straight towards him.

'Ronnie Fizz! Can you let us have a grain of Horse?' she asked when she drew level.

'I can do you half-a-G.'

'Cheers,' she said, slipping a ten shilling note into his hand. 'Have you seen Moss?'

'You're speaking to Tony Moss's apprentice. We've got a gaff together. He'll be around later,' Ronnie said, handing over three tablets. 'There you go, love.'

'Don't call me love!' she snapped.

She perched on a bar stool next to him, stashed the heroin in her cigarette packet and extracted two cigarettes, one of which she passed to Ronnie.

'Has Graham got a habit now?' he asked.

'Sod Graham, this is for me!' Pam replied, giving him a straight look. 'I don't go out to work so he can stay at home and fix all day!'

Ronnie couldn't prevent surprise showing on his face. 'I thought you had some kind of understanding? You handled the external world and he handled the domestic side of life?'

He didn't really know Graham. He'd met the bloke once or twice, and the Sandman had held him up for approval, as an example of a man who knew how to handle women. He'd got his wife to go on the game, the Sandman said, while he stayed at home and got stoned all day.

Pam lit her cigarette with a lighter, and then offered the flame to him. 'Yeah, well, pity he forgot that.' She smiled beatifically. 'He's going to have to do a lot better, otherwise he'll get what the punters get.'

'What?' asked Ronnie, blankly.

She shook her fist as if beating a drum, and her upturned, smiling face reminded him of a Catholic devotional image of Saint Teresa of Avila.

'A dose of *Flage*,' she said. 'A dusting down with the cat'o'nine tails.'

Ronnie grimaced. 'Who'd pay for that? You can get that for free in the nick.'

'You'd be surprised. The English desire for flagellation pays for all the little luxuries in my life, including Horse.'

'You should've become a screw, instead of a brass. Or a schoolteacher. Then you could've caned people all day long.'

'Who are you calling a brass? I'm a professional dominatrix. Domination is not prostitution. No punter gets near my pussy.'

A group of Mods, standing at the bar, burst into song. It was a recent hit by Freddy and the Dreamers, *If You Gotta Make a Fool of Somebody.*

'It's Rod the Mod,' Pam said, glancing over her shoulder. 'They look like a group of Regency beaux, don't they?'

The Mods had long, backcombed hair, and their clothes were immaculate: crocodile skin Cuban-heeled boots, straight-leg trousers, and long, round-collared leather jackets.

'Rod the Mod? He never sits down, because it would spoil the look,' Ronnie said, 'He's a tailor's dummy.'

'Just because he's not a Grot Pot like you. He's a better singer than most of them in the Top Ten.'

'Well that's not difficult.'

'You're just jealous because he's always surrounded by girls.'

Ronnie shrugged, as if being irresistible to women was not something he coveted.

'I'm going to have to take you in hand, I think. You're becoming a bit of a sulky boy.'

The street door swung open. A strikingly attractive young woman called out, 'You ready, Pam?'

Ronnie felt a jolt at the base of his brain, like a hit of speed. 'Who's the mystery woman?' he asked.

'My new co-worker, Mistress Elara. Watch your Ps and Qs. She's a proper lady.'

Ronnie gazed at an angel, clad in a black leather skirt and coat. Her dyed black hair, splayed out across her shoulders, was the colour of Indian ink, black with a hint of Prussian blue in the highlights. She stood with her hands on her hips, chewing gum in a determined fashion.

'For fuck's sake, Pam!' the angel said, 'I ain't got all day!'

Pam jumped to her feet. 'When you see Moss, tell him I'm looking for him. He owes me two grains.'

As Pam made for the street door, Rod the Mod launched into the chorus of *If you gotta make a fool of somebody.* Pam turned back. 'See? And Freddy and the Dreamers got to number two? Freddy Garrity dances like a puppet, and he sings like one as well! Rod makes this sound like a rock'n'roll classic!'

Elara shouted, '*Pam!* I'll be late!'

Reaching the door again, Pam paused and called over to Rod, 'Hey there, Woody, how you been?' Elara grabbed her arm and tugged her through the entrance.

Pam's comment seemed to be some kind of in-joke. Ronnie didn't catch the reply, but he found himself envying the respect accorded the Mod. Why didn't Pam treat him with equal respect, for being registered, or for dealing? Ronnie didn't know how to respond to women who were assertive or confrontational. He was used to chicks who deferred to his ideas on music. He wondered if he wasn't forceful enough. His father would never let a woman sound off like this.

He left the pub and strolled towards Wigmore Street, in case anyone was trying to score outside John Bell and Croyden's, the classy chemist's used by Lady Frankau's private patients. As he crossed Cavendish Square, and looked towards the junction with Harley Street, he saw a familiar face, although strangely aged, and bone-white.

Jack Fitt had already seen him and was waving. There was no sign of his former hostility. When he got nearer, Jack called out, 'Well now, they say that if you stand on a street corner in Piccadilly, eventually everyone you know will pass you by, so maybe it's a bit like that in Cavendish Square.'

Pinpoint pupils. Jack was using. His face was carved out of ivory, like the head of a walking stick, or some strange mineral, like those Meerschaum pipe bowls. Deep lines etched into his face. *Marks of weakness, marks of woe.* That comic where Sherlock Holmes tracked down a vampire, and its face became hundreds of years old when the detective brandished a crucifix.

'I'm staying in town,' Jack said. 'I've a couple of auditions to do and a few people to see. I'm back in the music business now, having a blast.'

Always knew he'd play in a band again. Bound for glory.

'How's Ruby?'

'Grand. She's holding the fort in Swindon. The sweetest girl that ever came out of Cork.'

'Are you well?'

What's wrong with you, Jack? Bilious. Shrunken into yourself. Whiskers turning silvery white. Those thick hairs peeping out of your nostrils are white, where they used to be black. You're dying by degrees. Bones show through your skin.

'I'm fine. I've a habit now, but I've just signed on with Lady Frankau, in Wimpole Street. I'm on my way to the chemist's, with this private prescription.'

Another one down. It's like a plague, someone was saying in yesterday's *Daily Herald.* A social plague.

'But you wanted to stay away from Horse, Jack.'

Bone white. A carved opium pipe, or a white casket for laudanum. No, a Meerschaum pipe bowl, in the shape of a skull. A present from Turkey. The skull and crossbones. All that was preserved of medieval monks: the skull, and the crossed thigh bones. Memento mori. That issue of *Tales from the Crypt* with thousands of bones stacked against the walls of a vault, under the streets of Paris. Venerate the bones, don't bury them where we can't see them.

'Everyone on the scene is using. Everyone is registered …' Jack began. He coughed into a handkerchief. Phlegm. *Egungun*, the Bones of the Dead, walking the streets by day and night, in the bumper issue of *Voodoo Nights*. Don't let *Egungun* touch you.

'It's because of infiltration from a parallel universe, you see. People don't understand where the pressure is coming from. It's from another universe …'

Jack's eyes glittered. He'd launched into metaphysics. Ronnie said he'd have to be going.

'The next time you see me, I'll be in a band,' Jack interrupted. 'I'm meeting Tubby Hayes tonight.'

Brilliant. Ronnie was sure that Jack was a great musician, although he'd never heard him play. He could see the biography on display in a shop window, *Jamming with Bird.* On the cover would be a photo of Jack, playing alongside Bird Parker. Perhaps the biographer would want to interview Jack's friends.

'What was it like, knowing him in those early days, in Swindon?'

'You always knew he would be famous one day. He was a cut above the rest.'

On the scene. Part of an elite. The best people all know one another. *This train is bound for glory. Don't carry nothing but the righteous and the holy.* It's like the Israelites in the Bible, chosen people. Until a plague takes all the first born, that is. He'll end up dying, like so many others. I'll tell you what he was like, Mr Biographer: he betrayed his fucking talent. Sold out to heroin. He lost his authority. Became corrupt. Became a plague carrier. The Bones of the Dead stalking Cavendish Square.

Ronnie's mood had taken a sudden downturn, as his morning fix began to wear off. He half-turned, and spotted the woman who was following him, on the far side of the Square. She was standing by the kerb with one foot in front of the other, as if posing for a photograph. This time, she was carrying a bunch of ivory-white chrysanthemums, held in front of the lower part of her face. The same demure hat and veil obscured her upper face, except he could just glimpse some hair, and she was blonde. She wore a black suit, as before, and her fox fur stole. It was as if she was going to a funeral. A blonde widow, taking flowers to a grave. He decided against accompanying Jack. Instead, he headed down Cavendish Place and walked fast, to give the Widow the slip.

As he reached Mortimer Street, the crowd thickened, and he couldn't maintain his pace. He paused, feeling jubilant because couldn't see the Widow, before he realised she might be hidden from view by the throng. To his dismay she reappeared, not far behind, on his side of the street, one claw-like hand clutching at her fox fur. She placed her heels down with difficulty, walking determinedly with a slight limp. He set off again, pushing his way through the crowd, waving his arms like a windmill so people would give him a wide berth. He didn't stop until he reached Charlotte Place, by which time she was no longer in sight.

Outside the Duke, a kid known as Freddy the Fly wanted pot. Ronnie was about to send him in Guido's direction, when he realised he could turn him over. He offered the Fly an ounce of kif for a fiver. Ronnie produced a packet of crisps that he'd bought for lunch, and improvised: 'Screw up the fiver. Take a crisp and drop the note in the crisp packet.' The Fly was intrigued, and did exactly as he was told. Ronnie did an impersonation of Guido surveying the street and said, 'Okay, wait here.'

At this point the Fly became alarmed, but he was too slow to react. Ronnie had slipped around the corner, through an alleyway, along the next street, and was soon heading north along Tottenham Court Road.

Ronnie was walking in the opposite direction to the crowd, which was heading for the theatre, and for the strip-clubs and bars of Soho. The faces that floated towards him were either elated and jubilant, or haggard, dejected, and lined with suffering. Jack Fitt told him that the Japanese called their eighteenth century red light districts the *Ukiyo,* the Floating World. *Ukiyo* was the transitory world of sense-pleasure; illusory, devoid of lasting satisfaction. Soho was an *Ukiyo,* a floating, insubstantial domain of cinemas, erotic dancers and street prostitutes. It was the secret territory of heroin and cocaine, where you could float through the city in the night, drifting through the crowds in a post-orgasmic, weightless state. But, like the Japanese *Ukiyo,* it was also the world of suffering, when the illusion of gratification slipped away and the raw flesh screamed for solace.

His own flesh was clamouring for the solace that only heroin would bring. He found a phone box and made a fix. He set out his precious bottles on top of the telephone directories: the bottle of tablets, with its label from Boots the Chemist (Dia-morphine hydrochloride, take as directed); the bottle of clean tap water, carried for occasions like this; and the soot-stained bottle that he held over a match while he cooked the mixture. He loved his new syringe, and the smooth way the piston slid up and down inside the glass barrel. So much better than an eye-dropper. It was a precision instrument. And he loved the relief that came flooding in when he made a hit, when the heavy, bitter taste of heroin saturated the back of his face.

Leaving the phone box, he was aware that he was moving to a different time-rhythm to passers-by. It was like being the only person on the dance floor who could hear the band; everyone else was out of step. He was moving to the beat, his body was at ease and everything felt harmonious. Even the feel of the pavement beneath his feet was warm and comfortable. This was home: Fitzrovia, the place where he was one of the locals. This was the neighbourhood frequented by everyone on junk. He could stand on the street most days and, sooner or later, meet everyone who was using, or who wanted to score. He placed himself in the centre of the pavement, gazing north towards Warren Street Tube station, letting the crowd surge past him. There was no sign of the Blonde Widow, but he spotted a face he knew, in the crowds streaming out of the Tube station exit. It swirled towards him, bobbing up and down, vanishing and reappearing, like a paper cup swept along by the river. It was the Sandman.

When they'd both lived in Bristol, Ronnie had argued that theft was generated by capitalism, and that in an anarchist society, with people living together on the basis of mutual aid and voluntary cooperation, such behaviour would become irrelevant. Now, a year later, he was almost embarrassed by his former idealism. He remembered how the Sandman had taken the piss: 'The only person in history who is too naïve to survive as a bum.'

He resolved to tell the Sandman about the way he'd stolen the fiver. Ripping people off was a sign of his growing maturity and self-confidence, and he wanted approval of his quick thinking. 'He used to be dead naïve,' the Sandman would say, 'but he's come on a lot lately. He knows the score now.' He might even let the Sandman have a fix. The Sandman would respect him then.

The Sandman spotted him and raised a hand in salute. His jacket collar was turned up, and he was holding the lapels together at the neck. He looked cold, and unshaven.

'Sandman! How you doing, man? How's things?'

'You got any shit, Fizz?'

'I can let you have a couple of jacks, Sandman. I know you're not registered yet, and there's not much on the street.'

'I need a grain, man. Can you give us a grain?' A desperate gleam came into the Sandman's eyes.

Ronnie looked away. His tone became impersonal, disinterested. 'No. Sorry, man. Two jacks.'

'Don't fuck me around, man! I'm *sick!* I'm at the end of the line! This is *me* you're talking to! This is Paul Spackman! *Your friend!* You must have a grain; you're fucking registered!' The Sandman grasped his arm and gripped tightly.

'No, man. Calm down. This is getting uncool.'

Instead of calming down, the Sandman became incensed. 'Give me a grain, you fuck-pig! The times I turned you on, in Bristol! You were just a runaway kid! I looked after you! Who saved your life down the Dilly, when that one-armed git had you by the hair?'

'Okay, forget it.' Ronnie turned and started to walk back down the street.

'No, wait! Come back. Give me two jacks! Come back. I'm sorry, I'm strung out! Have a heart, man!'

Ronnie turned back to face the Sandman. 'Just don't raise your voice like that, man. It's uncool,' he chided. 'Here, two jacks.'

The Sandman sounded contrite, as two small tablets rolled onto the palm of his hand. 'Cheers, thank you. Cheers. Yeah, I'm sorry. A bit strung out. You know how it can get to you?' As he stepped into the phone box, the Sandman mumbled, 'Can you do the honours? Give us a shout if you see the fuzz.'

The Sandman lifted the telephone receiver and held it against his ear, as if he was on a call, while he made up a fix with his free hand. He was growing his hair long, Ronnie noted. It was below the nape of his neck, and, although it was mostly blond, it looked dark at the roots as though it had been dyed at some stage and was now growing out. Beneath the well-cut jacket with its upturned collar, the Sandman was wearing an old vest, rather than a shirt; it gave him the slightly seedy look of someone who had once taken pride in his appearance, and was now neglecting everything.

Ronnie stepped away from the phone box and glanced up and down the street. No sign of the police, only a group of nine or ten crew-cut yobs, marching across the road towards them. They were clapping their hands and singing the Beatles' hit *I Wanna Hold Your Hand* at full pitch. They made it sound as menacing as the Nazi *Horst Wessel Lied.* People with short hair shouldn't be allowed to be Beatles fans. John the Road knew the Beatles from Liverpool. He'd bummed cups of tea off them, and reckoned they were okay.

One of the yobs looked in the phone box as they passed. The Sandman was hunched over, with his naked left arm held between his knees. Blood ran down his arm, as he stood flushing the syringe, trying to get every last trace of heroin into his veins. The yob's eyes opened wide in disgust.

'Oi, there's a fucking drug addict, injecting his self. That's fucking sick!'

They gathered in a semi-circle on the pavement and conferred. Ronnie wondered whether he should try to talk them out of violence. They didn't look as though they were in the listening mood. He moved away and pretended to be looking in a shop window. One of the yobs stepped towards the phone booth. A good kicking, that's how they'd describe it in the pub afterwards. *We gave this drug addict a really good kicking.*

***

Freddy went to the dressing table and felt in the top drawer for his Webley 38. In the top of the wardrobe, he found a cardboard box containing live rounds. The gun had been issued to him when he'd been involved in intelligence work in the Signals Corps, and he'd managed to hang on to it on demob. Now he had a use for it.

He sat on the bed and loaded eight rounds into the clip. He hefted the Webley in his hand. It was a heavy, bulky gun, but accurate and reliable. He always felt reassured by its presence. It had saved his life once, in the Pas de Calais. A Wehrmacht officer was four feet away with a Walther P38 in his hand, and Freddy shot first. Blew the man's brains out. You don't have time to think, he always explained, you just do what you're trained to do. Except they didn't train you what to do with the rest of your life. And they didn't tell you that brains spill out of a shattered skull like porridge.

He didn't have a holster, and he supposed he wouldn't get far carrying a handgun down the High Street, so he searched in the back of the wardrobe for his briefcase, and carefully placed the gun and spare ammunition in the front pocket. He knew where she'd gone. Over to those bloody friends of hers in Frognal.

The night before demob everyone sang, '*When I get my civvy suit on, oh how happy I shall be*'. Happy? He was happier in the bloody army. He had a wife he couldn't trust. She'd spent the war on her back, with Yanks queuing up to shag her. She must have thought he was bloody stupid. And it wasn't long after the boy was born that she started getting up to her old tricks again. Wanted to go Square Dancing on Wednesday nights. He used to follow her to check where she was going, and to see who she was dancing with. She couldn't leave men alone.

The first time he ever saw her, he thought she was the most beautiful woman in town. A natural honey blonde, with big knockers. She was leaving a dance hall, with a girlfriend, just as he arrived. He told her she needn't hurry off: now that he'd arrived there was someone worth dancing with. She laughed, but said they had to go. The next time he saw her, he asked her to dance, and that was the beginning of their courtship. He was determined that she would marry him, and wouldn't take 'no' for an answer. And when they married, a year later, every other man was envious. He'd bagged the most glamorous woman in Swindon.

Yes, she was glamorous all right. Men admired her, until she opened her mouth. She had this broad Wiltshire accent. He told her to get rid of it. He'd got rid of his own accent. You were never taken seriously in London if you talked like a country bumpkin. The other coppers would call you a swede-basher. But she was too thick to change. When he got his sergeant's exam, he had Inspector Charles Cornish and some of his colleagues round for dinner, and he overheard Cornish saying to the other guests, 'Has Flo got hayseeds in her hair?' Bloody hayseeds. In the end, he took the guests into the front room while she cleared up. Kept them away from her, before she said something stupid.

Over the next few years, Freddy tried to have dinner parties, but she couldn't cook anything fancy, and she'd sit there saying silly things. Well, they must be laughing at him now. Thinks he's clever, but that silly cow out-witted him. He's been cuckolded by half the American army. And some RAF johnnies, some slimy bloody Brylcreem Boys. Well they wouldn't bloody laugh by the time he'd finished. He would settle the score. It didn't matter what happened to him afterwards, because she'd ruined his life anyway.

He walked briskly to Frognal, a little over one and a half miles from his flat. The servant's quarters took a bit of finding, especially as Freddy was anxious not to alert the family upstairs, owners of the elegant, white stucco, Regency house. Eventually he spotted the servants' door, in a basement at the side. He peered through the frosted glass. The boy was in there, but it looked like the others were out. Freddy told him to open up; it would be better to be waiting inside when they came back. Element of surprise. For some reason, his son wouldn't open the door. Bit of a nervous child. Took after his bloody mother. Same blond hair.

Freddy had been so pleased when the nurse told him that the baby was a boy. He'd looked forward to playing football on Hampstead Heath, when the bambino was old enough. Now the boy was eight, and showed no interest in sport. He preferred to sit with a book or a comic. Reading was an unnatural bloody interest in boys; Freddy sometimes lost his temper, told him to put the ruddy comic down and get out in the fresh air.

He realised there was a problem when he called on Peter Drake, a Masonic brother who was an ENT surgeon. They left his son in the sitting room while they talked, only for about two minutes, but when they returned the boy was reading a textbook on surgery. The book was open at these colour plates of a dissected thorax. Freddy assumed he was just looking at the pictures, but then his son asked Peter what an abdomen was. Read the word out: abdomen!

You've got a right one there, Peter said, and grinned. He'll become a doctor, mark my words. And then Peter just stood there, smiling and playing with his watch chain, and looking from Freddy to the boy, and back again. Freddy knew what he was really thinking. Who did the boy get it from? Peter knew Freddy's view of intellectuals, and he knew that Flo had never opened a book in her life. He's not one of yours, my old darling. Did a Yank put her up the spout? Or was it some Hampstead prima donna? A bi-sexual sculptor or a sissy violin player?

Whatever they thought, Freddy knew that he was the biological father. These things were instinctual, like the way animals always knew their offspring. His wife had been a bad influence, and she'd bloody turned the boy against him. Some sort of revenge. Freddy began collecting evidence of her malign influence, starting with one small fact, the sort of thing that, while it wasn't conclusive, had set the old alarm bells ringing. Freddy had asked the boy about Flo and her carryings-on. Any normal boy would've told his father the truth, willingly. But this little sod had to be bloody bribed. And even then it was like getting blood out of a stone.

Freddy remembered coming home to an unlit flat, one misty, autumnal evening. His wife was off gallivanting. The boy had gone to bed, and Freddy looked in to say goodnight, not something he usually bothered with. Seeing the boy wide awake, he took the opportunity to ask a direct question: 'Who's she seeing, son?'

'Just a man.'

'What do you mean, just a man?'

'Dunno, an ordinary man.'

'What does he look like?'

'Ordinary.'

'What do they do together?'

'They talk.'

'Well, the last time you heard them talking, what was it about?' Freddy took a deep breath. The boy was close to getting the biggest hiding of his life. 'Listen to me, Ronnie. I'm not stupid. In fact, I'm a lot brighter than you are. I know when you're going to tell a lie, even before you know it yourself.'

'This man said Mum could get a lot of pleasure from reading books. She should read *The Mill on the Floss* by George Elliott.'

Freddy gave the boy a handful of change: 'Buy yourself another ruddy spaceman!' He watched the boy's eyes grow big. One and six. Three weeks' pocket money. 'See—it always pays to help your old Dad.' He patted Ronnie on the back, as though they were colleagues, and scoffed, 'Mill on the ruddy Floss! He'll soon be disappointed in her. Your mother's never read a blooming book in her life.'

You'd think the little sod would've learned something, but he never volunteered any more information. Clammed up. She must've got to him. Freddy thought he was probably the last person to find out she'd been carrying on. Peter Drake and the others must've known all along. No one would be surprised when he settled her account. Just have to wait out here until the pubs turned out, and she'd be back soon enough, along with lover boy. He'd deal with both of them out here. He undid the straps on the briefcase, so he wouldn't fumble getting the gun out. He checked the gun again, to make sure that everything was in order. Leave the safety catch on until nearer the time.

He would be handing out justice, nothing more. He'd done everything for her and she'd been unfaithful. And disloyal. She'd tried to tell lies about him to anyone who would listen. She'd tried to make out he was an alcoholic to the neighbours. No one was taken in. Betty Carmichael said, 'Freddy, I just laughed at her. I laughed in her face.' And she'd told everyone he mistreated her, which was totally untrue. He'd never been violent towards her. It's true he gave her a bit of a slap sometimes, but he'd never hit her with his closed fist. Maybe he should. Maybe she'd behave herself if he did.

He could do with a drink. Was there time to slip down to the Fiddlers for a quick one, before they came back? Probably not. Better just wait. And then? Was he seeking revenge? Yes—he deserved revenge after being betrayed. He imagined his wife in bed with another man and felt almost a physical pain.

He could hear some drunken idiots singing in the street. This must be them. He moved behind one of the trees to get a better view. About ten of them were coming up Oak Hill Park, carrying crates of beer. There were too many of them. He wouldn't confront her here, something might go wrong. He watched the raucous, noisy group filing into the servants' quarters, like a gaggle of geese. Which one was lover boy? He couldn't see anyone with a handlebar moustache.

He looked at his watch. It wasn't closing time yet. He could pop down to the Fiddlers for a stiffener, while he sorted out his plan of campaign. Walking briskly down the road, he decided there was just time for a pint of bitter with a whisky chaser.

The landlord rolled his eyes, as if accustomed to customers making impossible demands. 'No whisky until next Thursday,' he sighed. 'It's still under ration, Freddy. It's all supposed to go for export. That means it ends up in the pockets of those dirty little spivs in the City. I can do you a gin, or an arak?'

'Arak,' said Freddy. 'Make that a treble, Jack.'

'Treble arak? Did you serve in North Africa, by any chance? No? It's the national drink of Syria, arak. We get some ex-desert rats in here and they like to drink it. Milk of Arabia: I could call it something else, but I won't … There you go, a pint of special and a treble arak. That'll be three shillings and nine pence. And you don't have to rush, Freddy.' The landlord winked. 'I'm going to have a bit of a lock-in tonight. I've got the Hampstead CID in the saloon bar, and they want to make a night of it. Landlord's private party.'

Freddy looked through to the other bar, to where a group of five revellers had their arms draped around each other's shoulders. It was DS Dick Clements and the local CID. Strange. Perhaps I ought to buy them all a drink, Freddy thought, and he smiled at the incongruity of it all. Detectives drinking with him, a uniformed officer, hours before he committed a double murder? That might raise a few bloody eyebrows, especially when he turned himself in at Rosslyn Hill nick. Still, discretion is the better part of valour. No point in drawing attention to yourself when you're carrying a loaded gun in your briefcase.

'What's your poison?' Freddy said, taking out his gold cigarette case and offering a Craven A to the landlord. Jack had a glass eye which always looked away from you. It was a bit disconcerting, as though you never really had his full attention.

The saloon bar revellers launched into:

Drunk last night!
Drunk the night before!
And I'm gonna get drunk
Like I've never been drunk before!

'I'll have a G&T, Fred. But I'll show you a dodge. If you can pick out the real G&T from this line-up, the round's on me.'

Three glasses were placed on the bar. They all tasted similar. Freddy guessed, and for once he was wrong.

'It's a clever dodge, Fred. You pour a glass of tonic. Then you dip your finger in the gin, like this—look—and you wipe it round the rim. The customer gets a whiff of gin when they lift the glass to their mouth, the taste of tonic, and—Bob's your uncle! They'll pick that ahead of a real G&T every time. That's why you should never drink gin in those clubs where they bring your drinks on a tray.'

'I never touch the stuff anyway. Bloody woman's drink.'

Freddy didn't want to enter into a conversation with the publican, or anyone else for that matter. He preferred to brood, to come face to face with his pain, to caress it. It was like using his tongue to probe the wound where a tooth had been extracted. Here it was just sore, here a jolt of pain. Get used to it, it was real.

When we're drunk,
We're as happy as can be,
Cos we are the men of
The Hampstead CID!

A roar of laughter from the saloon bar. Blimey O'Reilly, what a bunch of berks. Why don't they just shut up?

All day I've faced a barren waste,
Without the taste of water, cool water.

Very funny. Ha bloody ha. My drink is water bright, from the crystal stream. When did those piss-artists last drink water? Freddy sank his pint and signalled for another by pointing into the empty glass impatiently. He looked around the public bar with its tattered wooden furniture, and bare floorboards, impregnated with the smell of hops from stale, spilled beer. The lack of comfort suited his mood.

He was concerned that he was beginning to lose conviction, like a balloon slowly deflating, and that if he tarried too long he might change his mind. He wanted to sit quietly and go over all the lies, the deception, the betrayal, until his anger swept all before it, until he could form an unshakeable resolution to exact revenge. *Immortal hate and study of revenge*—wasn't that how Milton put it, in *Paradise Lost*? He might not be a bloody intellectual but he knew his Milton better than most of the Hampstead nancy boys, because he'd been to a decent school. He'd been given a copy of *Paradise Lost* when he matriculated. Still had it at home. Inside the front cover it said 'For outstanding merit' and the year, 1929. That was when the future looked bright. Before marriage and before the war, when all seemed promise and potential. Before a bloody woman had to ruin it all. Just like in *Paradise Lost.*

He mustn't weaken. People got it all wrong, they thought killing someone was like opening a door in the mind to some evil force. Evil wasn't a mystical force, it was an effort of will. What had Milton made Satan say to the rebel archangels after their expulsion? *Awake, arise or be forever fallen.* You had to make a supreme effort of will to rise above your fate. Otherwise you were eternally defeated. He was going to rise above his fate by the act of killing, by a conscious act of will.

'Come along gents, there's a free drink for the winner of this game.'

There were four other customers in the public bar, all single men, all staring into their beer. The landlord was working hard to sell the maximum quantity of booze and had no intention of allowing his guests to sit in peace. Before long, he'd managed to involve everyone in a drinking game. Freddy had played it before. You threw dice and the highest score named a drink—usually some odd concoction like Drambuie and gin. You threw the dice again, and the person with the lowest score paid the bill. On the third throw, the lowest score had to down the potion in one. Jack warned the other customers that this game would sort the men from the boys, and he wasn't joking. One by one his customers left for home, the worse for wear, until only Freddy and Jack were left in the pub, the CID having finished their private celebration about an hour before.

The victors saluted each other. Freddy noticed that Jack had the ability to reach to the optics behind his head and pour himself a double gin, without looking, and without a break in the conversation.

'Shall I tell you something, Jack? And I don't want you to take offence. Don't take this amiss. You're what I call a serious drinker. And that's an accolade. An *accolade*. Serious drinkers always recognise each other.'

Jack leaned forward confidentially. 'I want you to know this is a drinker's pub, Fred; a genuine, one hundred per cent, no-frills, drinker's pub. And if you ever need a drink first thing in the morning, Freddy, my old china, just come and tap on my side door. I usually have a few mates in.'

It was 5 a.m. before Freddy moved on. He stepped out into the early morning mist on feeble, unsteady legs, struggling to light a cigarette with a gold lighter that had gone on the blink.

Feeling his briefcase under his arm reminded him that he was a man on a mission. He realised he had hardly thought about revenge for three or four hours, and had only decided on a provisional strategy. He would see if he could break-in without making much noise. Didn't want to wake the whole house; not before that was inevitable, of course.

At one point along the way Freddy got lost and found himself in an unknown street, and had to retrace his steps. When he eventually reached Oak Hill Park, the house seemed fairly secure. He tried all the basement and ground floor windows, in case any were unlocked. He tried the basement door, which seemed to be bolted as well as locked.

While he was testing the door he heard the bolts being drawn and a petite figure loomed up behind the opaque glass panel like a pale, dark-haired ghost. Someone was coming out. He tip-toed quickly up the basement steps and around the corner. There he waited, forcing his breath into a slow and steady rhythm. It was that bloody friend of Flo's, in her dressing gown. She locked the door behind her and stomped off down the drive.

Only the lock now secured the door. He put his shoulder to it and was surprised at the lack of give. It was a solid oak door with a stout, five-lever mortise lock. It would take some shifting.

He was desperate for a piss and went behind a sycamore tree to relieve himself. Urine splashed down the fissures in the bark, and ran in narrow rivulets between the roots, sending up a small cloud of steam, before sinking into the parched earth. He shook his cock. *No matter how much you shake your peg, the last few drops run down your leg.* Some idiot had written that on the toilet wall at work. Bet it was bloody Milbright. A bit like his writing. Catch him at it one day. He buttoned up his fly, taking care not to miss a button. Adjust your dress, and wait for the last few drops to run down your leg. True, though. The body always let you down at times like this. The sly drop of piss that leaked out, after you'd shaken it carefully. Shaken hands with John Thomas.

As he looked out over the wooded copse and down towards the road, he was overcome by a sense of futility. A few hours ago he would have shot her without hesitation, but how much better off would he be? What was the bloody point? Wouldn't his revenge feel a bit meaningless after a day or so? Besides, if he got the chance to speak to her, alone, she might agree to come back. She wouldn't want to throw away fifteen years of marriage. She wouldn't want to become a divorcee and have people talk about her. He'd kicked her out, and she'd come back on his terms. Be a darned sight tougher on her in future.

He arrived at a new plan of action. Meet up with her for a private chat. Give her one last chance. With that resolved, he felt a measure of tranquillity. If he caught an early morning Tube from Hampstead, he could breakfast in one of the taverns that opened at dawn for the porters at Billingsgate. Then he could move on to the Cheshire Cheese for lunch, and maybe on to the free vintners near Charing Cross, when the Cheese closed for the afternoon. If you knew your way around London, you could drink around the clock, and that's what he intended to do. He'd go sick for a couple of days. Go on a bit of a bender.

***

It was late afternoon before Mary came clumping down the stairs to the servant's quarters, after cleaning the big house. Her expression was grim as she paused halfway, took a cigarette, lit up, and inhaled deeply. She pulled her pinafore over her head, and threw it in the general direction of the sofa.

'Home is the hunter!' Flo called out. 'I've just made a pot of tea. Are you going to take the weight off your feet?'

Flo sat in her dressing gown at the kitchen table, her hands spread palm downwards on the green oil-cloth, as if trying to steady herself in a fast-moving world. Her son sat in the corner drawing, with a set of coloured pencils she'd found in a drawer. He no longer clung to her, like he had a few years ago; now, he occupied his time in reading or drawing, pastimes that made no demands on adults, although he would always watch them for signs of anger or alarm.

Mary nodded, but remained standing on the bottom stair, leaning against the banister. The copper glow from the cigarette illuminated her face in the gloom. Her eyebrows had been plucked out, and reinstated with an eyebrow pencil, as two thin black lines.

Flo said, 'You look just like Hedy Lamarr, standing there.'

'I wish I had tits like Hedy Lamarr,' Mary replied, after a long pause. 'Mine are too ruddy big.'

'I wish I had smaller tits. Yours are just right. I hate it when men stare at my tits. Or when they make comments.'

'She can bloody think again if she thinks she's going to talk to me like that.'

'Who, Lady Askwyth?'

'Lady Arsewipe, I call her. All fur coat and no knickers. She said, oh, there was an outrageous noise last night. She said, noise in the street and noise down here. I said it's once in a blue moon. I said it's not as if we have a party every week. Oh no, she said, and you won't have one again. So I said to her, quick as a flash: if it doesn't suit, just say the word. I said there's plenty of service jobs out there, I can be gone as soon as you like. She soon bloody shut up!'

'I hope you're not going to lose your job!'

Mary's lips had compressed into a thin line. 'I'd bloody walk out tomorrow. I'm not having Arsewipe tell me when I can have a party.'

'Mary, you don't give a damn!'

'I'm a bloody bohemian, me! I don't give a sod!'

Their laughter was too hard, forced.

'Well, you're a long time dead, aren't you?' Flo said. 'Eat, drink and be merry, that's what they say.'

'Here, Flo …' Mary jumped to her feet and did a little shuffling dance, her cigarette held away from her body.

Back to back, belly to belly,
I don't give a damn cos I'm damn dead already!

Flo joined in. They swayed their hips as they danced around each other.

Oh back to back, belly to belly,
At the Zombie Jamboree!

'Mary, when those two sailors danced together last night! Laugh? I could've cried! I didn't know where to look!'

'Vic and Tony. Generous! Gave me a load of free ciggies when they left this morning. Both queer as a nine bob note, of course.'

Flo's hand covered her mouth in alarm. 'Oh no. Were they really queer boys?'

'Couldn't you tell? Still, that's Hampstead for you. Everyone's shagging everyone else. It's like a bloody barnyard on heat.'

Flo's face fell. 'I'm not sleeping with Georgie,' she said, stiffly. Seeing Mary's blank expression she continued, 'Georgie boy: my boyfriend … He just took me to the funfair because I was lonely … We're just friends. It's platonic.'

Mary stared at her friend for a several moments. Then she said, 'What if you had slept with him? The way you've been treated? Anyway, everyone else is at it. Everything's changed since the war.'

'Well I didn't, that's all. I've never committed adultery. I'm Church of England.'

Flo looked as if she was going to cry. Mary caught her up in her arms, and gave her a hug.

'But I can't remember when I last had such a good sing-song,' Flo sniffed. 'Can't imagine old blooming Freddy letting his hair down like that, can you?'

'Here, I saw your old man this morning, when I went for the milk. In Church Row.' Mary's face darkened.

'He's been round here, Mary. Ronnie saw him last night. He tried to get in while we were out. I don't know how he knew we were here.'

'Let him come round. What's he going to do? Wally would flatten him.'

'No, I don't want to see him. I don't know how I got out of that flat without Freddy bashing me up. I can feel it building up, like a storm. He's working himself up to something. He always does. I just want to find somewhere to live where he can't find me.'

Mary took another deep draw on her cigarette. 'Well, what are we waiting for? Let's go and find that fellow you met. Where are his digs?'

'Georgie? He's staying over the Bird in Hand. Always in there.'

'Let's get round there. We'll have a swift half, and we'll catch him when he gets in from work. Georgie Porgie, pudding and pie. Ronnie will be all right here.'

Ronnie seemed to stiffen as Mary said this, and his brow creased into a frown. He pressed harder on his pencil, until his knuckles went white and the lead snapped.

***

Within the hour, the two women had left the basement flat and were heading for Hampstead High Street. They were unaware that, a few minutes' walk away from the Bird in Hand, Freddy sat slumped on a chair in the corridor of New End Hospital. He held his head in his hands. His left hand was covered in a mass of bloody bandages. He'd been drinking hard all night, and that morning he'd fallen while going up the escalator in a Tube station, somewhere in central London. As he tried to get to his feet, the escalator reached the top of the incline and levelled out, and he was pitched forward. He caught his hand between the side of the escalator and a metal grille, breaking two fingers.

He seethed with anger at the injustice of it all. His wife had set this whole train of events in motion. As always, she'd introduced confusion and disharmony into his life. He had to see her, to sort this nonsense out. There was no time to hang around a hospital. He picked up his briefcase, still containing his Webley 38 from the night before, and jumped to his feet. He pushed past the nurse who came to check on him, and headed for Oak Hill Park.

A gentle drizzle started as he turned into the driveway of the big house, and the rain began to soak into his shirt, sticking it to his back. The overcast sky was as dark as dusk, and lights were on in the basement. He hammered on the basement door with his good right hand. The boy appeared in the hall, his mouth gaping open in surprise. Just like his bloody mother.

'Get this door open!' Freddy shouted.

There was no reply. Lifting his leg, Freddy kicked the centre of the door with force. The sound exploded around the hallway. The boy started crying.

'I'll give you something to cry about in a minute,' Freddy snapped. 'Now get this bloody door open, before I kick it down!'

There was no response, and so Freddy beat on the door with his fist. He heard an adult voice cry out in exasperation. Through the basement window he saw a grey-haired woman coming down the staircase that led into the servant's quarters, tottering on a pair of very high heels.

'What is going on?' she demanded.

'It's my Dad,' he heard the boy reply. 'He won't go away.'

She went back upstairs. Opening a window, she leaned out and shouted, in imperious tones, 'If you don't go away immediately, I shall call the police!'

'I want to speak to my son.'

'I'm calling the police now!'

Ronnie called out, 'He is the police, Lady Arsewipe!' but there was no reply; she'd gone to dial 999.

Freddy decided on a tactical retreat. He didn't want police colleagues turning up. They wouldn't take any action over a 'domestic', of course, but it would be all round the canteen by tomorrow night.

'You bloody wait until I catch you,' he shouted through the door as he departed, 'you daft little sod!'

Freddy couldn't see the boy, who'd crawled under the kitchen table to hide.

Chapter Seven

The Sandman was trying to hold the door closed with his one free hand. He'd removed his works from the vein in his arm, but still had one end of his leather belt in his teeth, and the other wrapped around his upper arm as a tourniquet. Ronnie watched the door swing open as the yobs pulled out the Sandman. He heard boot studs scraping on the tarmac. There was a scuffle, and the Sandman went sprawling in the gutter. A dull thud, and a hob-nailed boot slammed into his friend's stomach. It looked like a football match, with each member of the team taking turns to kick an invisible ball. Another boot connected with the victim's head. The Sandman was up on his knees, struggling to pull down his shirtsleeve, as if the rolled-up sleeve made him feel exposed, but a kick in his back sent him down again. One youth stamped on his hand, and another kicked him in the chest. Ronnie stared at the scene in disbelief. He'd had the same feeling of paralysis whenever he'd watched his father beating his mother.

A Black Maria swerved to a halt by the kerb, and five coppers jumped out. The youths stood around in confusion, not sure whether to fight or run. One of the coppers approached them with his hands held wide apart, as if herding cows. He said to the nearest, 'Run along home, sonny.' The Bill were letting the assailants go. That was weird, they must've seen what was going on.

Then they pulled the Sandman out of the gutter and run him backwards to the phone box, where he was pinned by his shoulders. 'You can't tell the boys from the girls,' said one copper.

'You must be fucking blind, then,' the Sandman mumbled, as though moving his mouth was painful.

'Right! You want us to finish where they left off?'

One of the Bill looked over his shoulder and saw Ronnie watching. Without waiting another second, Ronnie turned the corner into Maple Street and kept walking. He headed down Fitzroy Street and along Charlotte Street. No point hanging around, inviting questions from the law.

Ronnie turned into Charlotte Place, pausing outside the Greek. He couldn't see through the steamed-up window, so he opened the door to peer inside. The owner, Dimitri, was leaning on his chromium-plated coffee machine with an air of unrelieved boredom, his chin resting on folded arms. Ten regulars, all elderly Greek Cypriot men, sat hunched over their coffees, their talk animated, their voices raised. They were meeting in the village cafe, just as they had back in Cyprus. Ronnie spotted Guido in a window seat, his long, wiry, ginger hair scraped back into a bushy ponytail. The *Sporting Life* was open on the table in front of him.

Guido spent a lot of time studying the form. Ronnie had heard that Guido used to be a bookie's runner, when he was about fourteen. He'd sat around in cafes, just as he did now, waiting for people to sidle up to him with their money tight-wrapped in little paper packets. The instructions were scrawled inside: *Doncaster 2.30. 1/6d on Laughing Cavalier please, Gweeder — To WIN*. At intervals, Guido took these illegal bets round to the local bookie, earning his own stake money by the end of the day. One lucky morning, he invested the winnings from an accumulator bet on several ounces of North African kif, and made the natural progression from bookie's runner to dope dealer.

Guido was sitting with a pavement artist known as Dave the Pave. Ronnie knew Dave from the squat in Marshall Street. Dave had a pitch on a broad stretch of pavement near the National Portrait Gallery, where he specialised in copying Raphael's *Madonna and Child* in pastels. Raphael and Bellini went down best with tourists, Dave reckoned.

Ronnie had heard that Dave was using heroin, but hadn't seen him for a few weeks. He was surprised at how quickly a deathly white pallor had descended over the man. Dave looked like a cadaver. Ronnie went in and joined them. Guido ignored his greeting but Dave the Pave nodded in recognition.

'You know the Sandman? Paul Spackman?' Ronnie asked. There were no spare chairs where they were sitting, so Ronnie fetched one from an unoccupied table, pushed it into the narrow space next to Dave, and squeezed himself into the gap. 'Short kid, uses junk?' Ronnie continued. 'Just got beaten up by some yobs. He was having a fix in a phone box, up Tottenham Court Road.'

'Is he badly hurt?' Dave asked, his voice reduced to a tremulous whine, like an old man's.

'Don't know. I had to split. The Old Bill turned up.'

'People get very nasty about fixing in phone boxes,' Dave said, with a sigh. 'It's the blood.'

'Probably shagging someone else's woman, your mate,' Guido said. 'He picked on the wrong man, and got what was coming to him.'

Ronnie felt his throat being squeezed, as if someone was tightening a noose around his neck. His heart started to pound. What did Guido know? Had Samantha told him? Was Guido trying to be clever? Ronnie decided he ought to confront him. He adopted a cool and level gaze, like Brando staring down the sheriff in *The Wild One*. He wanted to say, 'What do you mean by that?' but his voice faltered, and then failed, so that he only managed 'What?'

'Were you with him?' Guido asked, narrowing his eyes. 'Did you get stuck in?'

'I was too far away,' Ronnie said, shaking his head firmly, 'otherwise I'd have stepped in, naturally.' His voice came out as a thin croak.

'Probably ran a mile in the opposite direction,' Guido sneered.

'I don't run away from trouble,' Ronnie replied, annoyed at the way Guido was raising an eyebrow, as though the story was utterly improbable.

There was a long silence while Guido and Dave looked at each other meaningfully. It was eventually broken by Dave the Pave, returning to an earlier topic of conversation. 'Elvis practically invented rock'n'roll …' he pronounced, in a husky whisper. Dave's eyes slowly closed in mid-sentence. His features froze into immobility, his mouth slightly open. The only suggestion of movement came from Dave's eyeballs, which twitched beneath his eyelids, as if he'd launched into a dream. He reminded Ronnie of a dragonfly, hovering over a deep pond in the late summer heat.

'I saw Tommy Steele and the Cavemen live in 1956,' Guido said, intent on rolling a cigarette. His fingers crumbled tobacco into the paper with the care and precision of a craftsman, and he failed to notice Dave's lapse in concentration. 'At the Finsbury Park Empire. He was billed as *Britain's Answer to Elvis Presley*—'

'It probably scared those yobs off, when they saw me coming,' Ronnie said, trying to strike a bright and optimistic note. 'It would've been a lot worse if I hadn't shown up.'

'He was known as the Debs' Delight, Tommy Steele,' Guido continued, choosing to ignore Ronnie's comments.

'Dave can't hear you, he's gauched off,' Ronnie said, nodding towards the pavement artist. Dave's head slumped forward. He still held a fork in his right hand, with a wedge of cake and cream. They'd both been eating Rum Baba by the look of the plates.

Giving up on Dave, Guido turned to address Ronnie. 'Now that was a neat little con trick, wasn't it? How do you sell something in modern Britain? Combine two famous monsters in one horror story, like King Kong versus Godzilla. The working class teenage rocker meets the wild, aristocratic raver! The yob from Bermondsey shags the posh, debauched debutante! Overnight success. One minute Tommy's singing for a few bob a night, the next he's being chased down the street by screaming tarts.'

'Tommy Steele isn't what I'd call a yob, not like the guys who hammered the Sandman. They were real hard cases,' Ronnie said.

'Instant headlines: *Britain's Swinging Toffs …*' Guido's hands conjured up the square shape of a newspaper in the air. '*High Society Gets Hip; Debs Rock the Blues Away.*'

Guido was refusing to acknowledge the way he'd helped the Sandman, Ronnie thought. He felt increasingly annoyed at Guido's suspicion and mistrust, at his underlying snideyness. He said, 'That whole story was an invention, Guido. It was dreamed up by marketing men.'

'That's what I'm saying. It was a stroke of genius.' Guido swept some spilled tobacco off the table with the side of his hand and lit up.

Dave woke with a start, and continued where he'd left off, '... and *That's Alright Momma* was one of the greatest fucking records ever released. A real turning point, man.'

Ronnie had an uneasy feeling that neither Dave nor Guido believed his version of the attack on the Sandman. No one wanted to hear what he had to say. They preferred to witter on about Elvis. And he'd spent too many hours listening to Jack Fitt's record collection to let all this *King of Rock'n'Roll* shit go unchallenged. Dave and Guido knew fuck-all. He interrupted Dave to point out they were talking absolute bollocks, because there were Black musicians recording rock'n'roll in the late 1940s. Dave gauched off again, so the debate finished before it began. That was heroin for you. Very anti-social. None of the easy sociability of the boozer; the banter, the partying, the hearty laughter. More the hermit in his cave.

Ronnie turned to Guido and said, 'Big Mama Thornton made the original version of *Hound Dog*. And *That's Alright Momma* was by Arthur Big Boy Crudup, back in 1946.'

'I think you just made that name up,' Guido laughed.

'Big Boy Crudup? He's a blues singer from Mississippi.'

'Fizz, why do you specialise in singers that no one has ever heard of? Do you think it makes you into some kind of expert? If they were any good they'd be famous, like Elvis.'

Guido snapped his tobacco tin closed and placed it in his jacket pocket with a gesture of finality, as though there was nothing more to be said on the matter. He swept the window clear with his arm, so that he could see down Charlotte Place. Ronnie sensed that behind Guido's bluster, his appearance of supreme confidence, was a frightened man. He wondered how Guido would react to the news that a friend had been screwing his woman. Or did he know?

'Those guys were the originals,' Ronnie said. 'They couldn't get played on the White radio stations. Elvis copied their sound, and because he was White he made all the money.'

Guido shrugged and looked away. Ronnie persisted, 'And that Tommy Steele was never a real rock'n'roller, Guido. He was just a creation of the music industry. His *Rock with the Caveman* was a right load of old crap.'

A few moments' silence followed, and then Guido demanded to know whether Ronnie had given his doctor a new address yet. He addressed Ronnie while looking out of the window, watching three women in leather overcoats strolling up the alley. It was Graham's wife Pam and her new co-worker, a girl from the East End known as Miss Demeaner, together with the strange, fey beauty Ronnie had seen in the Duke, Mistress Elara. Spotting Guido, the three of them waved. Ronnie felt a jolt in his chest at the sight of Elara. He waved back, hoping to attract Elara's attention, but the three women had moved on.

Ronnie failed to register Guido's question. He wondered whether he could get Pam to introduce him to her new friend. If only he could get his script increased, he could offer to turn them all on; it would be worth a couple of jacks to get to know Elara. Or perhaps it would be better to warn her off junk? *Take my advice, don't touch the stuff. I wish I'd never started fixing.* That might go down well. Ronnie looked at his reflection in window, and sucked in his cheeks, so that he looked more like James Dean. *I'm really concerned about you. Stay off Horse.*

Still sucking his cheeks, he allowed his gaze to roam around the café. Bentwood chairs and coat-stand, like Lyons Corner House. Syrup-smeared plates, overloaded ashtrays. Greek newspapers on the tables. Must be like this in Nicosia? But red Formica tables; doubt if they have those in Cyprus? Or chocolate brown paint on the woodwork, and on the anaglypta paper beneath the Dado rail? Dark and sombre, but cream above, and on the ceiling. Used to see that in the Railway Hotel in Swindon, brown and cream. Great Western Railway livery; they had brown and cream coaches. And you sometimes got lime green walls in Swindon, like that cafe near the train station. Lime green and chocolate brown, with a print of the Monarch of the Glen hanging on the wall. Peculiarly depressing room. Was the green pigment made from arsenic? So many Victorians were poisoned by their own wallpaper.

'Have you given your doctor your new address?' Guido repeated his question more insistently.

'What are you talking about, man?'

Ronnie stared at an old placard above the counter, showing a meal of lamb chops, boiled potatoes and peas: *Heinz Tomato Ketchup Can Grace Any Table.* If you had a pen, you could alter that to *Disgrace.* Another placard, showing a rosy-cheeked mother and child: *We Speak for Milk.* And a sticker, *Fight Colds and Flu with MILK.* Could cross out *MILK*, and write *Strontium 90 (active ingredient).* Could draw wiggly lines coming off the mother, like radiation. We Speak for Nuclear Disasters. Radioactive milk.

'Your doctor, have you given him your new address yet? Or does he still think you're living at our place?' Guido drummed his matchbox on the table, as though this would speed Ronnie's response.

'I don't know. He likes to have a regular address. I can't put No Fixed Abode, it looks bad.'

'I don't want the Old Bill thinking you're staying with us, right? They'll be calling round to fucking check up on you. I think they've put the place under surveillance already.'

'You've been saying that for as long as I've known you.'

'Just get it changed!'

Guido's baleful eyes and distended nostrils filled Ronnie's field of vision. It was like sitting opposite an angry demon. Beelzebub and his 101 servitors, evoked to visible appearance. Ronnie wondered again what Guido would say about the affair with Samantha.

'Look,' Guido snarled, 'don't you know they're doing their nut about heroin at the moment? It's in all the papers. The number of junkies has increased to four hundred. One of the papers said heroin addiction is spreading like a social plague.' The muscles tensed in Guido's neck, and his eyes gleamed, as though he'd just thrown the first punch in a fight.

Ronnie moved to defend himself. 'Come on, Guido! Four hundred junkies in the entire British Isles? What's that as a percentage of the population? Bugger-all.'

'They reckon every junky at liberty is infecting two or three other people, and you should all be locked up.'

'No one's forcing people to use junk. No one "infected" me; I fix because I want to. Anyway, you'll find more junkies on any street corner in New York city. Britain doesn't have a junk problem. We don't even have a proper black market. No one imports heroin or cocaine, and that's because doctors are allowed to prescribe it.' Ronnie sat back, satisfied that he'd delivered the decisive blow in the fight.

'Well, don't count on that for much longer.' Guido seemed reluctant to concede the argument, and began hopping about on his seat. 'Not once the government gets involved. They're freaking out about youngsters like you being registered. There've been all these questions in Parliament—don't you ever read the papers? They're calling for another government inquiry. The Old Bill are fucking running round in circles. Anything to do with heroin is bad news right now. Do you think they want to be accused of doing nothing about teenage heroin addicts? That's why you're Public Enemy Number One. They're serious about taking you out, and I don't want to go down for assisting an escaped psychopath—'

'Haig!' Dave the Pave had opened his eyes.

'What?' Guido frowned.

'Haig, the acid bath murderer. He was a psychopath.'

'I've got to be off,' Guido announced abruptly, walking to the door.

'Tell Samantha I'm not an acid bath murderer,' Ronnie called after him.

Ronnie couldn't be sure that Guido wouldn't grass on him when he was in one of these moods. Guido wasn't really hip, or he wouldn't spend time and money on the horses. No one else on the scene spent afternoons in the betting shop, worrying about the form of runners at Haydon Park. It was uncool. And no one who was really hip would boast about seeing Tommy Steele. That was pathetic.

Ronnie called out, 'Hey, Dimitri: can I have a fried egg sandwich? And a cup of Rosy Lee?'

'What do you mean, "Hey Dimitri, can I have this, can I have that"? Didn't your momma teach you to say please and thank you?'

His mother: he pictured her serving Christmas dinner, carving the bird and giving him an extra big portion. Perhaps he should go home for a bit? It would be Christmas Eve tomorrow. Everything in the West End would close down on Christmas Day. He didn't want to be skippering, when everyone else was celebrating, living high on the hog. He could do with a bath, and a good meal. He needed an invite somewhere, but his options were running out. Everyone was pissed off with him. Moss kept complaining that he didn't wake him in the morning, when everyone knew it wasn't possible to wake Moss after he'd taken sleepers. Not that Moss had anywhere to go at Christmas. Nor had Dave the Pave, apart from his squat. And although Samantha would be pleased to see him, and she was a really brilliant cook, she lived with Guido, who didn't want him calling round. He wasn't sure he could trust Guido, if he just appeared at their door. All that talk about escaped psychopaths.

He could go home to Swindon, now that he had some money in his pocket. He wouldn't tell anyone on the scene where he was going; it would give the wrong impression. They might start calling him a country boy again. He wouldn't write to his Mum in advance, it would worry her. Best to just turn up on the doorstep. She'd be pleased to see him, to know he was all right, and he could explain to her why he'd done a runner. He'd only stay a couple of days. Maybe travel to Swindon tomorrow; see Samantha on Boxing Day, if she was at her parents'; and then come back. His plans made, he needed to get a Christmas present for his Mum. He decided to go in search of a gift, leaving Dave to doze over his half-eaten cake.

Steady rain started to fall as he stepped into the street. The Sandman was leaning against the wall of the Duke of York, with his head bowed, like a drunk. He had a graze under one eye, which was badly bruised.

'Sandman!' Ronnie called, 'What happened? What did the law do?'

'Fuck-all,' the Sandman replied, through swollen lips. 'They were just trying it on. I got a broken finger from those yobs.' He held up his left hand to show a splint and bandages. 'You were a fat lot of good!'

'What could I do, man? Be fair. There were too many of them.'

'You were supposed to be watching out for me. You could've told me they were coming, you fuck-pig!'

'How was I to know they would set on you? Be fair!'

The Sandman's lip curled in derision, as if fairness and compassion were the last things on his mind. He turned and limped away, soon becoming a diminutive figure in the distance, hunched over, with his bandaged hand held stiffly at his side. Ronnie knew the Sandman was feeling bitter, as usual. Life always dealt him a bad hand, and feckless people let him down. Ronnie's name would join the long list of those the Sandman condemned for their failings and inadequacies. For a moment, he considered running after the Sandman and apologising, but that would've been uncool.

Taking a bus to Dalston, Ronnie found a reasonably priced Indian brass coffee pot on a market stall. That would please his mother; she collected brass. The next day he went to his doctor's morning surgery, over in Chelsea. He knew from past experience that it would be difficult to fill a script for heroin in Swindon. The town's pharmacists didn't keep that much dia-morphine in stock, and they made a big song and dance about obtaining more. When he explained the problem, his doctor prescribed enough heroin for the Christmas break and, after collecting twenty grains at the local chemist's shop in the Fulham Road, he was able to set off.

He took the Tube out to Hammersmith and started hitchhiking along the A4. He was lucky with lifts, reaching Marlborough by lunchtime. The journey up to Swindon was a bit slower, but by three in the afternoon he was walking down the narrow road on the council estate, and into the front garden of his Mum's council house. It was a small terraced house that held few memories for him; she'd only moved here a year before he left home. She'd built a rockery in the garden since he was last here. It looked a bit odd, like a Christmas pudding, with lumps sticking out.

His mother opened the door slowly, peering through the gap. He heard her sharp intake of breath when she saw who it was, as though she'd been punched in the stomach.

'Hello Mum! Happy Christmas! Aren't you going to ask me in?'

Keep it cheerful, keep it upbeat. Get her in a good mood. Don't let's have any amateur dramatics. No weeping and wailing.

She stood aside so he could walk through the front door. He smelt her familiar perfume, *Evening in Paris*, the one she always wore when he was a boy. Her clothes had become rather drab, however. They seemed to hang from her body, as though she had no shape of her own. She seemed to have shrunken into herself.

'What are you doing here, Ronnie? I went to visit you at Devizes and they said you'd run away. The police have been looking for you everywhere.'

It looked as though it was a long time since she'd visited the hairdresser's. When her hair needed attention in the old days, she used to wrap a yellow tartan scarf around her head, and hide all her hair under a turban. Now she just looked ungroomed.

'I just couldn't stand it at Devizes, Mum. I had to get away.'

'I've been so worried about you.'

He was beginning to feel irritated by her distress. Careful now, keep it cheerful. Get her in a good mood.

'Yeah, well, sorry about that. There's nothing to worry about. Anyway, I thought we could have a nice day tomorrow. Here, I bought you a present. Happy Christmas.'

'You shouldn't have.'

She opened the package and seemed pleased with the coffee pot.

'It can go on the mantelpiece with all my other brass bits. I got you something as well.'

She placed the coffee pot in the centre of the mantelpiece, next to the framed photo of Ronnie as an eight-year-old boy that she always showed visitors. He was wearing a balaclava, and looked like a little urchin. There was a larger photo of him as a baby, sat upon her knee, and a studio portrait of her as a young woman, looking glamorous. This one had pride of place; it was how she liked to see herself.

She went out of the room and came back with a Harris tweed jacket which she held up against her body.

'I think you'll look nice in this, Ronnie. Something a bit respectable.'

He stared at it. It wasn't the kind of thing he ever saw himself wearing. Worse, it looked like a better quality version of the tweed jackets that patients wore in the Bin. If he ever went back, people would think he was wearing the uniform of a mental patient. Careful, don't say anything negative; she's smiling. She'll soon be in a good mood with him. He thanked her and said it must've cost a fortune.

'I got it from Mr Eldridge. On my club. I pay for it every week ... What are you going to do, Ronnie? Are you going to hand yourself in to the police? You've got to go back to Roundways.'

She was gripping the back of an armchair, as though she needed support in standing up. He noticed that she held on so tightly that her knuckles were white. She sounded terrified. This visit was a mistake; it wasn't going to work, unless he could find a way to divert her. He slipped up to the bathroom for a fix, but his mother pursued him up the stairs and talked through the bathroom door.

'I spoke to Mr Farr, the Mental Welfare Officer, last week, and he said I was to let him know if you turned up.'

He told her he would speak to the man after Christmas. He'd only been home an hour, and already she was treating him like a child. The best thing was to leave for London early on the day after Boxing Day, without giving her much warning. He sat on the toilet and used one of his old school ties as a tourniquet, gripping one end in his teeth and pulling it tightly around his left arm, while probing for a vein with the syringe in his right hand. Nothing was showing. He slapped his arm to encourage the veins to stand out.

'I told Mr Farr you're taking after your father. I hate to think you're going to turn out like Freddy.'

'What, become a senior policeman?'

'A blooming alcoholic!'

His mother had the ability to break through his carefully constructed composure, to find the words that would unsettle him. If all else failed, she would accuse him of taking after his father. It was so unfair. She must know they had nothing in common. His Dad was a cop, and he was an anarchist; his Dad believed in hard work, but he was a bum; his Dad was a heavy drinker, but he'd rejected alcohol and developed a heroin habit. As far as he was concerned, they were polar opposites, and he'd consciously eliminated any trace of his father's inheritance that could be found. And he'd adopted Jack Fitt as a substitute father. Far from being a cop, Jack argued that civil society should throw off the shackles of the State. And whereas his father had a fundamental dislike of women, Jack idealised them. Ruby was the centre of Jack's universe, and he held violent men in contempt. 'A man who would hit a woman is worse than a beast,' Jack would say. 'He's not a man. If a male friend ever raised a fist to a woman, I would never speak to him again. Well, I might stop to call him a *cunt*, but that would be all.'

Dark red blood showed in the syringe as Ronnie made a hit on the inner side of his elbow. Nice one. Good strong fix, like slipping into a warm bath. *Blue days, all of them gone, Nothing but blue skies, from now on.* His mother was still talking through the door.

'I just want to know why you do these things. Why? Why did you start taking drugs? Why? It's always mothers they blame!' Her anxiety was escalating.

'For fuck's sake, Mum, give it a rest!' he said to the closed door. She kept hammering away at a question to which there was no answer. He couldn't even identify the moment when his heroin use became an iron-clad habit, let alone identify the cause.

Through the door came the muffled sound of sobbing. Watch out, he thought, you're in for some amateur dramatics, a scene. Amateur dramatics: that's what his father called displays of strong emotion.

He remembered his mother ironing his Dad's spare uniform, years ago, bent over the ironing board in the kitchen. She was shaking and sobbing. Lifting the iron, she stared at its dull pewter face as if gazing into a mirror, and then spat on it, to test its heat. Ronnie felt she was spitting in his father's face. He asked what was wrong, but she just shook her head mutely, picked up the jacket and trousers, and carried them to the wardrobe, where she hung them carefully, making sure the trouser creases were straight. All this time, she kept her head turned to the wall.

On his way to the sitting room, Ronnie saw his father in his parent's bedroom, getting dressed. Father stood with a straight back, adjusting his cufflinks, not looking up. He set out, first, his keys, and then his spare change, on the dresser, in neat rows. He was getting ready for work, wearing his uniform trousers with their secret pocket for the truncheon. Sometimes Ronnie brought his friends into the bedroom, when his parents were out, and showed them the secret pocket in the trouser leg, so they would know where a policeman hid his cosh.

Freddy knew Ronnie was standing there, even though he hadn't looked round. 'Ever seen one of these?' he said, holding up a five pound note, but without turning to face his son.

On display was a large sheet of white paper, covered in copperplate writing, which looked quite unlike a pound note. Ronnie took it from his Dad, held it up for inspection, and tried to look suitably impressed.

'Go and tell your mother not to be so bleeding stupid,' his father said, taking back the note and putting it in his wallet. 'Bloody women and their amateur dramatics.'

That must have been 1955. Now, eight years later, Ronnie felt annoyed with himself for the way he'd adopted his father's terminology without realising it. In spite of all his efforts to eradicate his father's influence, some of it was still there beneath the surface, poisoning everything it touched.

'Why have you done this to me?' his mother cried.

'Let's talk about everything after Christmas, shall we Mum?' Ronnie called out. 'Let's just have a nice time now?'

Ronnie went to bed early and fell into an uneasy sleep. In his dream he was in an unlit passageway. In the darkness, he could just make out a menacing shape. He looked again and saw it was the comedian, Ted Ray. Ted was clutching a violin to his chest, just like he did in the comic, *Radio Fun*. He had a thin, sour smile.

'Here he is, the boy wonder! He was born on Halloween. I'm not saying he was a baby monster, but the only way his mother could stop him biting his nails was by replacing them with screws!'

Please, turn it off. There's no call for it. I don't want to hear him.

'When he was born he was covered in hair; he was a zombie baby. His mother said you take after your father. You have your father's eyes … in your fists behind your back!'

I'm no fan of yours, either. You're not welcome here.

The shadowy figure tucked the violin under its chin. It started to play *Following in Father's Footsteps*.

I know who you are, you bastard.

'What did they expect, he took after his parents? His mother was a werewolf, his father was a vampire. What do you get when you cross a werewolf and a vampire? A fur coat that fangs around your neck!'

Get out of my life!

'Come on, let's see you dance, young man. There you are, two left feet! What's worse than a zombie with two left feet? One with four left feet! And if you think that's bad, you haven't danced with my wife! I'm not saying my wife's a bad dancer, but when she takes to the floor they sound the air raid sirens!'

How can anyone laugh at him?

'She said, "I'll dance on your grave, Ted." I said, "I hope you do. I'm being buried at sea!" '

Oh back to back, belly to belly,
At the Zombie Jamboree!

'It's a cruel and heartless world, boys and girls, a cruel and heartless world.'

You're not welcome here!

'Not welcome? I'm your father, you bloody waste-of-space!'

The comedian stepped forward, out of the shadows. Ronnie recognised his father's features. His father was stooping slightly, as he always did, with his head held to one side, as though he had just asked a question and was waiting for an answer.

'He was always a mother's boy. He was tied to his mother's apron strings. Then one day she sent the apron to the laundry! So now you know why he always looks so washed out!'

Turn it off. No one's listening.

'You don't want to see your dear old Dad? I should've thrown you out the window when I had the chance.' His father was smiling angelically, but his voice was full of malice. 'When you were a bloody little zombie baby. A hairy zombie. You're no son of mine, you little rat. Just wait till I catch up with you. You can't keep running!'

Ronnie forced himself awake and reached for his syringe. He filled the barrel with some clean tap water, dropped in five jacks, and shook the works until the shit dissolved. Bad dreams meant you needed more shit. He made a hit inside his elbow and felt the junk smoothing out the wrinkles in his brain. Looking round for some reading material, he found a copy of an old comic, *Tales from the Crypt.* The African god Egungun had taken possession of a small Caribbean island at carnival. He tried to read, but his eyes drifted shut.

Now he was with Jack Fitt, running down the island's main street. Drums were beating faster and faster as a carnival procession wound its way up the crowded street towards them. It was first light. Everyone was assembling for Jump Up, the celebration of dawn on the first day of carnival. The djab-djab men were darting among the crowd. They were naked and coated in black motor oil, their heads were shaved except for two spikes of hair, twisted into horns. There were screams as young girls dived out of their way, desperate to evade the hug that would ruin their clothes. People were running in all directions. Jack Fitt had disappeared now, and Ronnie was on his own. He ran. The djab-djab had a filthy embrace that had to be avoided at all costs. They were heading towards him. He mustn't be caught. They surrounded him, but now they seemed to be in the street outside his mother's. The circle parted to let Egungun come dancing through. He glistened with black oil, and his face was painted blue. To touch him, even by accident, caused death.

Egungun bared his teeth, then shook a stick covered in red and white spots towards him. There was an odd, clattering sound and the spots flew through the air and covered his limbs. He realised he'd been naked in the crowd, like the djab-djab.

'A pox on you!' Egungun hissed, lifting a violin to his shoulder.

Ronnie woke with a start, and looked at the luminous clock face. It was 3 a.m. His heart was racing. The old fear in the night. For a moment he was back in his childhood bedroom, in his Gran's house. There was the old blackout curtain that hung over an alcove, turning it into a cupboard. After the night of his father's visit he would often wake in the night, convinced that something was hiding in the alcove. If he stared long enough, the blackness moved towards him. He had to light the candle before it reached him, otherwise his soul would die. He felt the old terror touch him, and decided he needed another fix, in order to calm down and get back to sleep.

He got up around ten, and Christmas morning passed amicably enough. His mother had cooked chicken and roast potatoes, which he loved. As usual, she'd overcooked the sprouts and carrots by boiling them for hours, but he never took more than a token amount of vegetables, so he hardly noticed. They left the table for a break before tackling the Christmas pudding, and she raised the subject of drug addiction, while he was trying to watch television. Mr Farr had told her that heroin was the worst drug in the world.

'He said it destroys people, body and soul.' She looked distraught, sat on the edge of her chair, with her legs twisted underneath, and a handkerchief screwed up in her fist.

The idea of an eternal soul was responsible for a lot of nameless terror, Ronnie thought. His Gran always lectured him about the danger of losing it, and recently his Mum had taken to hiding a Bible under his pillow whenever he visited. Trust this man Farr to play into her fears. She needed a good dose of rationalism, not more superstition. He said, 'That's a load of old bollocks. It's just a habit. What does he know?'

'He knows a lot about it. He said it was a disease of the will.'

'How can you have a disease of the will, Mum? The will isn't an organ of the body. That's just a load of old bollocks.'

He'd taken a big fix, and sat slumped in front of the coal fire, with the promise of an evening's undemanding telly. Heroin went with television, like fine wines went with gourmet food. Ronnie tried to curtail the discussion, and interest his mother in a Variety Special that had just started. The compere snatched a trumpet from a musician, threw it to the ground and jumped on it.

'Here, Mum, that man can play the trumpet, sing and tap-dance. All of it badly!'

Usually his mother would have responded to his invitation to evaluate a television performer, but she refused to be distracted, and launched into the question of why he took drugs. He changed the subject, asking if she'd heard how his father was doing. The mention of Freddy's name caused his mother to start.

'How should I know?' she said, crossly.

She seized the poker and raked the coals vigorously, as if assaulting her ex-husband. For several minutes she maintained a sullen silence, before relenting. 'His sister tells me he's doing very well. They've made him a Commander at Scotland Yard, in charge of the CID. Wicked old bugger! God only knows how he got promotion. He must've cultivated the right people. He could always turn on the charm. He could be very plausible.' After a pause, she added, 'A bit like you.'

Ronnie jumped up, and said that he must phone Samantha.

His mother called after him, 'I'm just worried you'll turn out like him, the way you're addicted to these drugs. He's a blooming alcoholic. He can't leave the drink alone.'

He hurried over the road to the phone box, shivering in the evening chill, but preferring discomfort to wearing the tweed jacket. Samantha was delighted to hear from him, and full of praise for his escape. Guido had told her nothing about meeting Ronnie, and banning him from their house. She arranged to call around the following day.

As he came back down the street, he was followed by a pack of five stray dogs. They were led by a big black Labrador cross. Despite missing a front leg, it seemed able to run as fast as the others. For some reason, the sight of the three-legged dog filled him with disgust, and he hurried to get behind the safety of his mother's front door. The dogs congregated outside his mother's gate and yelped.

***

On Boxing Day morning, he woke to the sound of Glen Miller. Struggling downstairs at eleven o'clock, he found his mother dancing around the sitting room.

'*In the Mood*', she said, nodding towards the radiogram. 'I used to dance to this during the war.'

'It's nice to see you smiling again,' he said, from the doorway. 'More like my old Mum. Life doesn't have to be full of problems and worries. Paint the town red, the way you used to do.'

'I wouldn't have to worry if you stopped taking drugs,' she snapped. 'There's been enough painting the town!'

She marched over to the radiogram and took off the record. To his relief, the doorbell rang and he didn't have to think of a response. He opened the door to see Samantha, wearing the shortest skirt he'd ever seen.

'Your face! Skirts are worn above the knee, Ronaldo. This is the Year of the Leg!'

'More like the year of the fanny!' he said, leading her into the kitchen, so they could talk without his mother overhearing.

'Are you a bit of a prude?' she asked in delight. 'That's not what I expect from a hipster. Where's all this metropolitan sophistication?'

A large kitchen cabinet, and a red Formica table, with four beech chairs, dominated the small kitchen, and there was not much space to walk around. He offered her a seat at the table and sat next to her. Removing a sliced white loaf and tub of marge from the table, he tossed them over her shoulder onto the enamelled shelf of the kitchen cabinet.

'I'm not prudish,' he said. 'It's just that I'm opposed to fashion. I mean, I think we should sabotage consumerism.'

'Is that why you painted red and black stripes on an old T-shirt?' she said, tilting her chin upwards like a street fighter issuing a challenge. 'And painted slogans all over the back of your combat jacket? All that Chinese writing? What was that supposed to be about?'

'It was an anti-fashion statement,' he said, reddening slightly.

She hooted with laughter. 'A Chinese friend of mine said it was the characters for water, agriculture and rice! Anyway, Levi's are a fashion, so are desert boots,' she said, pointing to his jeans and suede shoes. 'Long hair could become a fashion. Even grotty T-shirts covered in oil paint could become fashionable.'

'I'm just going over to the phone box,' his mother called from the front door. 'Hello Sam.'

'Hello Mrs Jarvis.'

His mother's eyes dropped to Samantha's hemline, and she frowned, but left without comment.

Samantha moved over to where he was sitting and sat on his lap. 'Now, are you going to start mixing it with me, or do I have to rape you?' she asked.

'You don't leave me much choice,' he smiled.

His mother was gone for about fifteen minutes. Samantha was sitting astride his lap when he heard his mother return and go into the front room. What had taken Mum so long? She hardly knew anyone with a telephone.

He kissed Samantha's cheek and inhaled her perfume, civet with black pepper, the scent of a mountain lion. He gazed into her deep, brown eyes, his hand slipping over her suspenders and onto the warm, smooth flesh beyond. Her eyes opened wide, but she was looking over his shoulder, at the opaque glass panel in the back door. Two blurred shapes in uniform blue stood outside. Ronnie jumped to his feet and ran through the house. As he threw the front door open, a uniformed police officer blocked his exit. A short man, looking like a racehorse owner in a tweed overcoat and trilby hat, held an identification card up to his face.

'Ronald William Jarvis? I am George Farr, Mental Welfare Officer, and I am taking you to Roundway Hospital, under Section 60 of the Mental Health Act, 1959.'

As the police seized his arms and snapped handcuffs over his wrists, Ronnie spun around to see Samantha cowering in the corner of the kitchen, frozen in horror. His mother watched from the doorway of the sitting room, her face wet with tears.

'You idiot!' he hissed. 'You grassed me up!'

'You've got to get the help you need, Ronnie,' his mother sobbed.

'You must be joking!'

'Don't worry, Mrs Jarvis,' Farr called out, 'he'll get good treatment in Roundway. It's one of the best mental hospitals in the country.'

As he looked at the policemen encircling him, Ronnie was reminded of his dream. There was no escape from the djab-djab men. He let them lead him towards the police cars, parked further down the street. Samantha came out to the garden gate and he turned to acknowledge her, but couldn't think of anything to say. His mother stood looking out of the sitting room window, wiping her eyes with her handkerchief.

Several dozen women lined the kerb opposite, watching him with solemn faces. One of his mother's neighbours was briefing the others.

'I feel sorry for her. That's her son. They're bringing him out now. They're going to take him to Devizes. He's a drug addict. She's ever such a nice woman as well.'

A police van pulled up behind the cars and a dog handler brought out his Alsatian on a leash. There were jeers from the surrounding police.

'What's all this, then? Where've you been?'

'It's all over now, Simon, you can take your dog back. We had to bite miladdo ourselves.'

'Simon—unless you want to put this character in the cage with your dog, and take him down to Devizes for us?'

The neighbourhood dogs had gathered to bark at the Alsatian, and it was straining at the leash and barking back. The dog-handler looked flustered.

'I'm not doing that, it would upset my dog,' he mumbled.

'Anything to get out of work, eh Simon?'

The police guided Ronnie onto the back seat of the first car, and the Mental Welfare Officer, Farr, moved in next to him. An ex-Army captain, who had served in the Wiltshire Regiment during the Second World War, Farr was a dapper dresser, with black, well-polished Oxford shoes, and clean, manicured fingernails. He had snow-white hair and a well-trimmed moustache, and his eyes were spaced well apart, and wide open, as though he was permanently surprised. The badge in his lapel showed he was a member of his regimental association.

The police driver paused, as he was about to get into the car, and called out to one of the neighbours, 'Any chance of a mince-pie for us, then?'

'What am I going to get in return?' she replied.

'I can think of something!'

'You go on! You'll get me in trouble with that girlfriend of yours, over in Gorse Hill!'

Ronnie felt intense irritation. The local police didn't seem to be taking him seriously. They were bloody yokels, Wiltshire bumpkins. The Flying Squad had kicked Guido's door down in London. They'd treated Ronnie like a *somebody*, a serious threat. Still, Farr had given up his Boxing Day to capture him. And all these neighbours who had turned out to watch his arrest—they must see him as a danger? Maybe his arrest would get him in the local paper? Front page of the *Evening Adver*? 'Swindon Man Was Slave to Heroin.' Or, maybe, 'Town in the Grip of the Deadly Drug'. He began to feel satisfied by the promise of notoriety.

Farr talked of the benefits of psychiatric care as they embarked on the twenty mile drive to the market town of Devizes.

'You're fortunate you're being taken back to Roundway Hospital, Ronald, because you're going to get some of the best psychiatric treatment that's available anywhere in Britain. And British psychiatry leads the world …'

Farr was the kind of man who would be intensely patriotic, Ronnie thought, who would've felt proud every time he saw those 1950s posters claiming *Britain Leads the World in Nuclear Power* and *Britain Leads the World in Jet Aviation.* When the nuclear reactors at Windscale caught fire and leaked radiation, and the Comet airliner began to fall out of the sky, it was a betrayal, a national humiliation. So Farr had found an area of medical science which was British, and could become a source of national pride.

'Our doctors aren't taken in by Freud or any of that nonsense,' Farr was saying. 'You won't get psychoanalysis or any of that malarkey in a British mental hospital. It was British doctors who were responsible for the discovery that General Paresis of the Insane was caused by syphilis. And that all the other mental illnesses have organic origins.'

Ronnie decided to ignore the man and look out the window, but Farr wasn't so easily discouraged.

'We lead the world in research into the organic basis of schizophrenia. And depression. And in our use of electric shock treatment, and insulin coma therapy.'

'I'm not having shock treatment. Fuck that!'

'There's no need for coarse language.' Farr removed his trilby hat and balanced it carefully on his knees before replying, in gentle, reassuring tones. 'I'm not saying you will have ECT, Ronald, though that will be for your doctors to decide. But they will understand that your addiction has a biological basis. That it's an illness. That you can't help yourself.'

'Burroughs says all that in *The Naked Lunch.* Junk alters your metabolism. It's like you develop this vegetative metabolism or something.' Ronnie knew that Farr would be horrified by this reference to *The Naked Lunch*, commonly regarded as a satanic text. Although the book was banned in England, Ronnie had read the version printed in Paris by Olympia Press. 'That's why I need to have heroin prescribed for me,' he continued. 'My metabolism has been permanently reconfigured.'

Farr looked at him as though he was a favourite nephew, who didn't see the error of his ways. 'No, no—you need total abstinence. You need to stop taking these drugs for ever, Ronald. And you'll understand why when you meet people from Alcoholics Anonymous, and they get a chance to explain the Twelve Steps to you.'

'Oh yeah?' Ronnie said. 'What's their remedy?'

'Well, essentially it's putting your life into the hands of God. God as you understand Him.'

Ronnie's eyes narrowed. Farr's voice had taken on a pious tone. 'I thought you just said addiction was a disease,' he said.

'It is a disease, but it's a disease of the will. That's why the cure is not something that a doctor does to you. It's something you do for yourself, Ronald. With God's help.'

The rain came down in dark sheets as they drove across the Marlborough Downs. They hurried past the Neolithic Long Barrows, and the sacred groves of trees on isolated hilltops.

'So—God gives everyone free will, but then he slips in a disease so some people are less free than others?' Ronnie said.

'I'm not going to debate this with you. You need to talk with people in Alcoholics Anonymous, who've gone through the same things you're going through—'

'No lush has gone through the things I'm going through.'

'Well, I'm not prepared to discuss it further.'

'Hey—it's not something that a doctor does to you, but I bet they claim the credit if you come off junk?'

'I know you're trying to catch me out!' Farr snapped. 'Well, you won't! I've dealt with your sort before. You're a clever lad, but you're a typical psychopath. You'll find they know how to deal with people like you at Roundway. You won't be the first case they've had.'

Ronnie allowed himself a broad smile. He'd pushed Farr deliberately, until the man abandoned his avuncular manner. It was all false, that friendliness. The old bugger thought he was dealing with a psychopath, and had tried to humour him. Ronnie said, 'I shan't be staying long at Roundway. They don't know nothing about heroin addiction. I'm going to be transferred to Weiss's unit in London, because he's a Home Office advisor. Not a country bumpkin.'

Both policeman looked round at this, and one of them caught Farr's eye and grinned. Farr rolled his eyes.

'The consultants might not want you in an alcoholism unit, have you ever thought of that?' Farr asked. 'You'd spend all your time undermining the other patients, trying to destroy their religious faith. It might be better for you to stay on Larch ward, even if it can't offer you specialist treatment. It would keep you out of harm's way, and stop other teenagers getting the idea that it's okay to use drugs.' There was a long pause, while Farr gazed out across the passing fields, and then he added, more for his own benefit, 'The greatest happiness of the greatest number, that's what mental health professionals should work towards.'

With the end of their conversation, fear entered Ronnie's mind, abruptly, like the first, sharp intake of breath on an icy morning. He wondered whether he faced another cold turkey. Why hadn't he made a run for it when he saw the uniforms outside the front door? They might not have caught him. He must react quicker next time. He might only get a split second to escape, and he had to be able to seize any opportunity. He imagined himself dodging the police outside his house, although he knew that, in reality, he would never run anywhere while he was on junk.

The cloud was so low it obscured the tops of the hills. As they descended into the Kennet river valley, the loudest sound was the thrashing of the windscreen wipers, and the drumming of rain on the roof of the car. The ancient avenue of standing stones at Avebury went unnoticed, as did the brooding presence of Silbury Hill, over-shadowing the flat fields like an Aztec pyramid. Ronnie paid little attention to the views, lost in his own thoughts.

Ronnie was furious with his mother for phoning the police. She'd grassed on him, after all the times he'd stood by her. She was stupid and naïve, believing all that rubbish Fry had fed her, about the evils of heroin, and the Looney Bin being the best place for her son. Ronnie thought of the last image he had of his mother, standing in the front window and crying, a handkerchief scrunched up in her fist, afraid to come into the street in front of the neighbours. Pathetic. Displays of strong emotion were so uncool. She would say she did it because of love, she always said that. If that was love, he was better off without it. Fry was trying to make out that he was a psychopath, but he had worked hard to free himself of passionate feelings, especially the fantasy that people called love. He'd had to toughen himself up, until he could watch a woman receive a beating with equanimity. You had to do that: it was a tough world out there.

The police car glided to a halt outside the yellow stone charnel-house near the back entrance to Roundway Hospital. Three sides of beef hung from hooks in the ceiling, and once again he noted a dark pool of ox blood on the sawdust-sprinkled floor. A male nurse led the party up the circular stairs to Larch ward. Somehow, Ronnie had never thought he would return. The gloomy day room was just as he remembered it, except now the two trees in the courtyard had lost all their leaves, and there were red, white and blue paper chains along the walls. The Ukrainian patient was pacing the length of the room, placing his heels down very deliberately, as though struggling to negotiate a slippery slope.

The escort asked the group to wait by the entrance to the ward while he went ahead and knocked on the office door. 'I've brought one back for you, Mr Butler. He liked Larch so much he can't stay away,' the escort said.

The charge nurse emerged as though stepping into the wrestling ring. He threw his shoulders back and stood with his legs apart, as though bracing himself for an attack. 'It's Old Matey! Our little psychopath, come to brighten up our days,' Butler said.

'Ronald Jarvis,' Farr announced. 'We've just picked him up from his mother's, in Swindon. He's back on heroin again.'

'Well, he'll have to wait until the duty doctor comes round to see what we do about that. But we'll have his clothes off him in the meantime, just in case he's got any ideas about running away again. And I suppose we ought to be billing him for damage to NHS property after his last little escapade, don't you?'

'A prime candidate for thump therapy, if you ask me!' Snakey Blakey appeared behind Butler in the office doorway.

'Get Wheeler to run him a bath and get those clothes off him,' Butler ordered his deputy. 'And make sure he isn't lousy before you stash his clothes away. We've got plenty of DDT.'

It took a little less than two hours for the new admission to be inspected for head, body and pubic lice, bathed in a solution of DDT as a precaution, dressed in pyjamas and a dressing gown, and allocated a bed in a single room. It took less than two minutes for him to receive a medical from the duty doctor. He was relieved to hear that his heroin would be withdrawn gradually, over a week. No cold turkey. But he was back in the Looney Bin. Back on Larch ward, which was a thousand times worse than being in prison. He had to escape, as soon as he could.

He had a sense that his life was beginning to go round in circles. Fix, get sick, fix again. Get busted, escape, get busted again. Meet the same old people on the same old Soho streets. It was like being trapped in a maze; you took a new turning and it led you right back to your starting point. He longed to break free, to be on an open road, walking along a straight highway into the future. He had to escape, and this time he had to find a way to stay at liberty.

Chapter Eight

Banging doors, rattling key chains and raucous shouting disturbed the afternoon calm. Ronnie came out of his room to see the return, after a day's labour, of the hospital work party, known as the Chain Gang, after a Sam Cooke song, popular two or three years before. One nurse stood guard on the door, while another counted the Gang members in, and a third nurse brought up the rear.

Two Gang members were engaged in a heated argument, one of them, Joe Long, insisting repeatedly that he knew what he was talking about. Snatching a billiard cue from the table, Long began waving it in the air. The gyrations of the cue became wilder and wilder, and swung closer and closer to his adversary. Joe was shouting at full volume now, and pausing between each word for emphasis: 'I-know-what-I'm-talking-about!'

There was something familiar about Joe's rage. His father had always known he was right. Without a sense of competence and intellectual certainty, you were less than a man. Confident, certain he was right, contemptuous of all opposition, his father would demonstrate his authority with his fists. Men who are right are men who will fight. Ronnie could still see his father standing over his mother's fallen body, that night when he'd betrayed her role in moving his bed, and ever since he'd despised men who resorted to violence.

An apprehensive silence settled over the ward, as patients looked worriedly at each other. Then Ronnie heard a loud wail, the cry of a wounded animal. Ben Wheeler and another nurse had grasped Long from behind and wrestled him to the ground. He was carried off to a side room to be sedated.

As the mood in the ward lightened, two nurses positioned themselves on either side of the patient who'd suffered meningitis as a child. Ronnie didn't really know the nurse on the left. His name was Mike Paxton, and he carried a large flat stone in the pocket of his white coat, to defend himself if a patient ever attacked him. Presumably, a stone could be thrown out of the window after use, and disposed of quickly. The nurse on the right was called George Alford. He had a round, moon-like face and a shock of black hair, which made him look honest and guileless. Alford's father had been an attendant at the asylum, and his father before him: 'Three generations of psychiatric nurses, Ronald, and over seventy years of service between us.' In rural districts, Ronnie thought, psychiatric nursing was an occupation which was handed down in the family, like being a ploughman.

Alford and Paxton leaned forward and muttered into the ears of the patient, who listened gravely, his gaze fixed on the floor, as though he was a priest hearing confession. A string of obscenities was presented for his attention: 'Shit, Bugger, Piss, Twat!' Every now and then, he would amuse his persecutors by clasping his hands to his ears in a vain attempt to shut out their whispers, or he would shout 'Language!' in horrified disapproval. Ronnie had often heard nurses say they needed a sense of humour to work on a locked ward, but for patients who were the butt of staff jokes it was a miserable existence.

Ronnie was taken back to the time he'd been bullied, as a new boy, in the toilets at secondary school. Because he hated milk, two fourth formers produced a warm, rancid bottle of the stuff, which they forced down his throat. Before he could throw up, they put his head down the lavatory and pulled the chain, then left him lying on the piss-soaked floor, water draining out of his hair. It was humiliating. He could've taken them on, and made them fight for their victory, but he always felt powerless in the face of physical violence. For years, watching his father dominate his mother, he'd lacked the courage to intervene. The same oppressive sense of inadequacy returned to haunt him now.

He wondered if he could make a formal complaint about the two nurses, but decided, after a moment's reflection, that there was no point. He was the psychopath, they were the respected members of a profession. Nothing he said would be believed. Just like his Grandfather hadn't been believed, all those years before, when he complained about his black eye.

As he walked towards Alford he wasn't sure what he was going to do. For one giddy moment, he visualised abandoning his own commitment to pacifism and punching Alford in the face, even though he knew that a violent act would result in swift retribution. And what if violence was used to justify cutting off his heroin? His courage failed. After a moment's confusion, he managed to say: 'I wonder how you'd feel if you had a child who'd suffered meningitis?'

'Ooh George, do you think we're being told off?' Paxton asked, putting one hand to his hair in a camp gesture, as though there was something impossibly effete about Ronnie's manner.

'What do you know about it?' Alford scowled. 'Have you had children? No. So don't talk about things you don't understand!'

'I just mean that he's someone's relative. Someone who would be upset to see this. And he can't help being mental. You shouldn't tease him.' The raw emotion that Ronnie was struggling to control began to gain the upper hand, and his voice shook as if he was on the brink of tears. 'It's just not fair!'

'It's just not fair, George!' Paxton wailed.

Alford's eyes narrowed. 'We're having a joke, do you mind? And we don't need interference from a lice-infested, addle-brained, teenage drug addict, who doesn't know when he's well off.'

Ronnie turned and walked away. The bastards had put him down, and he'd let them get away with it. No one else on the scene would allow a poxy mental nurse to speak to them like that. They would come straight back at Alford with wit and style. Deliver a put-down that ridiculed the nurse's grasp of professional ethics, or intellectual ability, or something. He'd failed, and he was ashamed of himself.

After this, Ronnie decided to stay in his room. It was a small cell, equipped with just an iron bed and an ashtray, but it was a refuge from the cacophony outside. He could lay on his bed in solitude, and smoke cigarettes. There were no comics, or newspapers, or books on the ward, so there was nothing else to do. For the first time in his life, he was living without reading material. Even the prison had supplied library books. Here, television was the only contact with the outside world, but it was switched on for only two hours a night, and the news was never watched. The hospital was cut off from the secular world, like a monastery.

As he lay stretched out on the bed, the door opened, and a dark form appeared, silhouetted against the window in the day room beyond.

'Everything all right in here?'

He could see Snakey Blakey's mouth twisted into a lop-sided arc, an unconvincing attempt at a smile.

'It was until you appeared, Blakey.'

'Ah, the rebel without a cause,' Snakey Blakey said, walking into the cell.

'I've got a cause, Blakey. It's called freedom.'

Snakey Blakey's hands, balled into fists, were thrust into the pockets of his white coat, as though this would mask his hostility. 'Excellent. You can join us down at the Conservative Club, one day.'

'No thanks, not your version of freedom. I'm an anarchist.'

'Now why doesn't that surprise me?'

A couple of years ago, Jack Fitt had taken Ronnie to the Freedom bookshop, in London's Red Lion Square, to stock up on anarchist literature. Ronnie remembered a little old lady, Lillian Wolfe, standing in a kitchen at the back of the shop and boiling up a large pan full of cabbage. Her husband had known Prince Kropotkin, when he'd lived in London as an exile, before the Russian Revolution. The shop smelt of cabbage and old newsprint.

'Set the people free by dismantling the power of the State,' Ronnie said. 'I'm going to send for some anarchist reading material: Kropotkin, Malatesta, Bakunin. I'll get your patients to read something that's a bit thought-provoking.'

'I don't think you'll have many takers, somehow.' Snakey Blakey's cold, stone-grey eyes flicked around the empty cell, as though he was searching for contraband, before scanning Ronnie's prostrate form. 'Would you mind taking your shoes off that bed?'

Ronnie moved the minimum distance, so that his feet hung over the end of the mattress. Snakey's eyes betrayed a complete absence of compassion, Ronnie decided; the man gazed on him as if engaged in the scientific study of a strange kind of insect, one that needed to be exterminated.

'The doctors are going to put you on Melleril, tomorrow,' Snakey Blakey said, with another lop-sided grin. 'That will calm you down a bit.'

'Kropotkin wrote about the incarceration of people in lunatic asylums. Kropotkin wrote, "The insane asylum is always a prison". Something like that. "The physicians' prison, the insane asylum, would be much worse than our present jails." He got that right, didn't he?'

'Not really. You've not in prison. You're here because you're not safe to go home. You're a drug addict, and a psychopath, and we have to stop you killing yourself. That's why you're locked up. You have a mental illness called psychopathy.'

Snakey reminded him of his old headmaster; the same self-righteous tone when he was listing the sins of other people. Ronnie ignored Snakey's views, and continued, 'This is the doctors' prison, like Kropotkin said. Every tyranny has its Bastille, Kropotkin said, its characteristic form of imprisonment. England's is Devizes, the doctors' prison. This is where you lock up people who challenge the system.'

'You ought to go back to Russia, then you'd see what tyranny really is.'

'Kropotkin knew a thing or two about prisons, and escaping from them. He was banged up by the French for years, and then imprisoned by the Czar in the Petropavlovsk Fortress, in St Petersburg. That's modern Leningrad.'

'Oh really?' Snakey Blakey's flat tones conveyed a complete lack of interest.

'The Czar tortured and killed the other rebels, but Kropotkin succeeded in breaking out. So did Mikhail Bakunin; he escaped from Siberia. He walked over a thousand miles to the eastern seaboard, and escaped on a ship to Japan.'

'Would I be right in thinking that you are contemplating escape? Because if you are, you should know that we reinforced all the windows, after your last little escapade, so you won't find it quite so easy to get out again.'

Ronnie had already decided that escape was going to be difficult. They watched him all the time. He'd have to adopt a disguise, like Jack Fitt, who'd walked through a cordon of British infantry dressed as a bride, during the Easter Uprising. He imagined telling Jack Fitt about the way he'd forced the window, and seeing him smile in approval. Jack would pat him on the back, like a modern-day Bakunin, and say something like: 'Escaping is your revolutionary duty, young man.'

Ronnie lit another cigarette. 'Not only are there no books round here, there's no music,' he said. 'How can people live without music?'

'Our patients aren't interested in these things. You have to remember they are all very sick people.'

'I need to hear some jazz, or a blast of rock'n'roll. Do you know, at one of the first rock'n'roll concerts in New York City, Black and White kids tore down the rope barrier that was supposed to keep the audience segregated, and danced together, until the cops arrived and stopped the concert?'

'The last thing our patients need is something to agitate them like that.'

'You see, that's why rock'n'roll was so controversial in the early 1950s. It was street music and it had the power to challenge the power structure, to set off a revolution. Just think what it would do to this sad, sick set-up?'

'Well, if you're keen on music, I'll see that your name is put down for the patient's dance, next Christmas.' A malicious smile flitted across Snakey Blakey's face. 'Who knows, it could be the first of many Christmas dances with us? Always a poor prognosis, psychopathy.' Snakey moved towards the door, and then looked back. 'When you're a bit fitter, I'll see if I can get you a job with the Chain Gang. On our farm. You can muck out the pigs. It'll be better than lying in your pit and wanking all day.'

Ronnie held two fingers up to the closing door.

Roundway Hospital held a dance for the patients every Christmas. Ronnie thought they were probably like the dances he used to attend at school. Every year at school, starting in October, they replaced gym with dance practise. The boys lined up on one side of the gym hall, the girls on the other. When the order came to 'take your partners for the *Dashing White Sergeant*' the boys advanced across the floor to claim a partner. There was a knack to it. If you were too quick, everyone took the piss out of you for fancying the girl. If you were too slow, you ended up with the Girl No One Wanted to Dance With. So you had to walk quickly to the centre of the hall and then slow down, so that you could pace yourself, and arrive just after the first three or four boys.

He could just see the male and female patients at Roundway, trudging round a hall, doing the Dashing White Sergeant or the waltz, when they should be having a bop. What a dismal thought. Was this going to be the highlight of his year, from now on? He would lead the patients in a revolt. He imagined himself as the compeer at a concert, putting his lips to the microphone, sending the asylum audience wild.

'Tonight we have Fats Domino! Chuck Berry! Wynonie Harris! Sugar Pie and Pee Wee!'

Prolonged cheering.

'And now let's have a big welcome for Little Willie Littlefield, who's going to sing his hit single, *Mistreated.*'

Little Willie bounded onstage and hit the piano keys. There was riotous applause in the old Corn Exchange. Patients jived in the aisles, while Longtown Lil slashed into the plush seats with a cut-throat razor, her ankle-length red dress sweeping the floor. Joe Long, his teeth clenched, swung a billiard cue over his head, and Alford and Paxton, who'd been trying to force the audience back to their seats, were knocked to the ground. Everyone was chanting *I've been mistreated too.* The doors barricaded, patients unfurled a red and black anarchist flag, while over the microphone, Ronnie proclaimed, *'Authority is absurd! Capitalism is the true madness! Seize control of the asylum!'*

Yes, that was what he'd do. There was no point trying to intervene over individual cases of cruelty. You should lead all the patients in an insurrection. Except he couldn't do that while he was waiting for a fix. Far from leading a revolt, he hadn't even been able to answer back. The reality was he couldn't lead the patients into anything. None of the bastards had any fight left in them. His mood collapsed. It had been well over four hours since his last fix and he was beginning to feel raw. He should've asked the duty doctor if he could have an interim fix on the first day, just to get settled in. Better have a cigarette, there was another two and a half hours to go. Two hours and 43 minutes, actually.

'And now Amos Milburn has a song for all you junkies out there who are feeling a bit strung out tonight: *When your medicine starts coming down.*'

Fuck it. When your medicine starts coming down, I want you to hug me tight.

In the absence of any further distractions, he spent several hours thinking about his next fix. When the time came, it was administered by intra-muscular injection in a ward downstairs, which seemed to be a sick bay. He soon found there was a negative side to gradual withdrawal. It was impossible to think of anything other than the next fix, which, when it came, was always a disappointment, because the dosage had been reduced. Sometimes, the charge nurse, Don Butler, told the staff to give him an injection of sterile water, believing his withdrawal symptoms would prove to be psychological. This produced a bitter anti-climax. Ronnie relaxed, waiting for the taste of heroin, but it never came. Instead, the withdrawal symptoms slowly increased in intensity, and the tension in his head became greater than ever.

Sometimes, the last injection of the day, which should have been at 5 p.m., was delayed. Butler had a meeting with his deputy at this time, and liked to leave the task for the night shift. The second time this happened, Ronnie parked himself on the office doorstep at 5.05 p.m., and demanded his fix every time the door opened. Twice Butler called out for him to stand away from the door. Eventually, Butler flew out of the office, his face contorted with rage.

'I've got a man with Huntingdon's chorea who's dying by degrees, and there's nothing I can do to alleviate his distress, and a fit young man like you is whining about an injection that he doesn't even need. Now do me a fucking favour and fucking shut up and give us all a fucking break!'

'If you gave me the fix I'm due, man, I wouldn't have to wait out here.'

The big man drew ominously close. His face was now about three inches away. 'Have you listened to a word I've fucking said? Now you'd better wise up, or you're going to end up somewhere a lot worse than this.'

'Oh yeah? Where's that? The lowest level of Hell?'

'A special hospital, that's where! Because you're showing me you're impossible to manage!'

'What, Broadmoor? Is that some kind of threat?'

At that the charge nurse turned his back and went back into his office, leaving the door ajar. Ronnie started to follow, but stopped, his hand on the doorknob. He could hear the deputy murmuring, 'I wouldn't waste your breath. Just get him shipped out.'

Through the gap, Ronnie saw Butler lean on the desk and lower his head, to stare mutely at the floor. 'Shipped out?' Butler repeated after a moment or two. 'Well, he is showing increasing signs of psychopathic behaviour. There was that incident you told me about.'

'When he had his visit?'

'You told me he made a young woman masturbate him in the dormitory?'

A shadow passed across Snakey Blakey's face, as though something troubled him about the memory, but then he smiled. 'I soon put a stop to that. Not exactly normal behaviour, is it?'

'We're not set up to deal with people like him,' Butler snapped in frustration. 'He needs to be in a more secure environment.'

'He has to be under constant surveillance because he's an escape threat. He's very cunning. If you ask me, he would still pose a risk after ECT.'

'That William Sargant down at St Thomas's reckons these drug addicts could be cured through psychosurgery,' Butler said, moving to the office window and staring out moodily. 'I know Fitzgerald's got this bee in his bonnet about viruses, but it's no good neglecting all the other approaches, especially when they're so effective—'

'The man's useless!' Snakey Blakey spat the words out. 'When's he going to think about making our job easier?'

'I mean, if we're going to keep Old Matey here, we might as well do something for him. He's the ideal candidate for psychosurgery. It's the only way to stop him using drugs. It's like a mania, he'll do anything to get them.'

'See, really, you could bring all these drug addicts in, and do the lot of them in one go,' Snakey said, thrusting his fists into the pockets of his white coat. He had a delighted smile on his face, as though he had just seen the solution to a particularly difficult puzzle. 'I'm surprised no one's thought of it. When you think of all the harm addicts do? It just needs the political will.'

'He's a very dangerous boy,' Butler said, turning back to his desk. 'I'm going to speak to Fitzgerald tomorrow. If they're not prepared to do something, they can ship him out.'

'Watch out,' said Snakey, nodding towards the open door.

Ronnie moved away, conscious that his situation was worse than he'd imagined. He didn't get his fix until the night staff came on duty. By then every nerve in his body was twitching, desperate for relief. He had to get away. Were they really planning to transfer him to Broadmoor? That was supposed to be for the criminally insane, wasn't it? How could they put him there? He hadn't done anything. They couldn't lock him up indefinitely for the possession of a small amount of opium, surely? They couldn't give him a lobotomy if he didn't want one? He decided he wouldn't wait to find out. He had to find a way out.

The next morning, Ronnie's injection was due to be reduced to twenty milligrams. When Ben Wheeler administered the injection, he had the habit of whistling jazz riffs. He was note-perfect, as if he was playing a cornet. In between bars of *Everybody Loves My Baby,* he said, 'We've got one of your oppos on Cedar ward.'

'What do you mean? Another junky?'

Wheeler swabbed Ronnie's left bicep with alcohol and jabbed the needle into the muscle. 'Yes, another addict. So we've got two of you on a withdrawal regime now. Tweedledum and Tweedledee.'

'Can I speak to him?' Ronnie asked, flexing his arm rapidly to speed up dispersal of the injection.

'Don't see why not, as long as you're quick.'

Wheeler took him along the corridor to a dormitory, where a middle-aged man with short, sandy-coloured hair and clean, freshly-ironed pyjamas lay in bed. The bed had been made immaculately, the starched white sheets tucked neatly around the man's chest. There was a little locker next to his bed, on top of which was a bowl of apples and a large jug of orange juice. Ronnie wondered why he didn't get orange juice on Larch ward.

'Hi man,' Ronnie called out, lifting his hand in a kind of minimal salute that people used on the scene—without lifting his arm, he turned his palm outwards, fingers pointing to the ceiling.

'Oh hello,' a man with a marked Birmingham accent replied. 'Who are you?'

'Ronnie Jarvis. Are you using?' Ronnie continued. 'Are you in for a Cure?'

'I'm a Pethidine addict, if that's what you mean.' The Brummie smiled in contentment.

Ronnie learned that the new admission was a lorry driver who had once been given Pethidine as an analgesic, after a road traffic accident. He'd liked it so much that he went to great lengths to recreate his initial experience. He would park his lorry on the outskirts of market towns like Devizes and rub fibreglass in his eyes, and then call an ambulance, saying he'd been injured in a crash. On arrival at a hospital accident and emergency department, he'd be administered Pethidine for pain relief, and would then 'confess' to being an addict. He was usually referred to the local psychiatric hospital for withdrawal, and was content to receive diminishing doses of Pethidine and bed rest. He knew nothing of the London junk scene. He'd never scored on the black market and didn't seem to realise he could find doctors prepared to prescribe narcotics. His ambition was simply to continue faking accidents all over the country.

'I'll be here for about three weeks, I expect,' the driver added, 'and then I'll have to get back to Birmingham. I don't like to be away from Brum too long. It's all arse-backwards down here, ain't it?'

Ronnie walked back to Larch ward slowly, with a profound sense of disappointment. Arse-backwards was about it. What he'd heard just didn't seem right.

'He became addicted through medical use?' Ronnie asked.

'Anyone can become addicted to opiates, can't they?' Wheeler said. 'If they take them long enough. It's biological, like having a brain disease.'

'Yeah, but the guy was uncool. He just didn't behave like a junky.'

Wheeler unlocked the door to Larch ward. Jim the Lobe was on his hands and knees in front of the door, with Alford sitting on his back.

'Come on, gee up, you soppy ha'porth!' Alford was saying. 'I want you to give me a ride. Come on, or I'll fart in your face!'

Alford looked directly at Ronnie as he was saying this, as if daring him to intervene. Then Alford sneered. Ronnie felt ashamed of himself. Alford could see that he lacked the courage to take him on. Alford's look said, you are complicit in all of this. You didn't defend anyone. You turned away. You can't criticise anyone now.

Ronnie went over to the window and gazed out on the trampled, sallow grass in the courtyard below. He could imagine the tormented souls of past inmates confined within the yellow stone walls. They were rising up out of the low earth, floating in the long shadows, enmeshed in the branches of the trees. But the hospital grounds could be glimpsed through a gap in the buildings opposite, and out there the distant lawns were enlivened by a burst of winter sun. He longed to be free to run out across the lawn, past the gatehouse, and up Pan's Lane beyond. Back to the modern world. He would run like Kropotkin when he escaped from the Fortress at St Petersburg. Kropotkin must've felt unfit after years of maltreatment, just like he felt now. But Kropotkin had the energy of desperation, and the guards at his heels were unable to prevent him hurling himself into a waiting carriage. You needed to be single-minded to escape, and then you could find the strength you needed.

'Come on, Dobbin,' Alford was shouting, 'you can go faster than this!'

Ronnie heard Jim shuffling down the ward on his hands and knees, carrying Alford on his back. He wouldn't turn round to look. Alford would be looking at him, wanting an audience.

A window cleaner, who'd been dragging his ladders around the courtyard, now drew level with the first floor window. Seeing Ronnie, the workman crossed his eyes, extended his tongue and mimicked idiocy. Ronnie was incredulous. He thinks I'm a nutter! This is how you get treated if people are told you're mad. No one listens to you any more. You lose all rights. Ronnie had been confident that any member of the public who saw him on Larch ward would regard him as someone who shouldn't really be there, a 'normal' person who'd ended up inside by an accident of the legal process. Now he had to accept that his identity had been deformed. He was seen as a mental patient. That's how it must have been for Jim the Lobe. One day Jim had been respected as one of the Few, a young and handsome Spitfire pilot; the next he'd had a segment of his brain cut through, and a buffoon like Alford was riding on his back.

They could do anything they liked to you, once you were under a court order. They could give you a lobotomy, and tell everyone it was humane, a blessed relief for a disordered personality. *We can shape people the way we want them.* What if they rounded up all the junkies, brought them to this godforsaken place, and then invited the American surgical team to perform the operation?

'This is the big one. The Grand Slam. We've got three hundred special patients for you. All junkies. All for the Big Chop. It will be a humanitarian mission, gentlemen.'

That night he dreamt that he went to the seaside with Samantha, and they were swimming in the Atlantic. The sea had a fierce undertow that sucked them both in, and then threw them bodily onto the stony beach. Ahead of them was a vast rubbish tip, a hill of smouldering rags and bones that towered above the beach. Gulls circled overhead. Several emaciated horses picked their way over the tip, scavenging for food. Then, along the shoreline, came a long line of blind men in single file, each carrying a staff, each with one hand on the shoulder of the man ahead. They were calling for alms over the noise of the surf. The Brummie lorry driver, smiling cheerfully, was the last man in the line. He called out, 'Hey, this is all right, ain't it? We've all had the Chop.'

Ronnie's dream, remembered at intervals throughout the next day, set the tone for all that followed. It was like a flavour that had once been tasted, and was never forgotten. The dream returned at regular intervals. At night, Ronnie was trapped on a lonely pebble beach at the end of the earth, behind a long line of blind beggars. In the daytime, he was trapped on Larch ward, with nurses who would find a way, through surgery, ECT or drugs, to take away his independence and break his spirit. He had to run away before it was too late. He vowed to escape, with renewed determination.

His opportunity did not come for another two weeks, and by this time his detox had been completed and his clothes returned. He was told he was being taken downstairs for a blood test.

'See if you've got syphilis,' said Butler. 'See if that's why you're so bloody gormless.'

Alford and Paxton were detailed as escorts, but they had another patient who also needed a blood test, and who walked with difficulty. Ronnie drew slightly ahead of them on the circular stone staircase, and then accelerated until he was out of sight. He hurried down the stairs, and emerged in the sick bay. Ahead, he knew there was a door leading into the courtyard, and he'd seen the key in the lock on several occasions. Yes—it was there. Speed was of the essence. Before anyone could react, he had turned the key and withdrawn a bolt at the top of the door. The door opened and he stepped into the courtyard. Staff lifting a bedridden patient turned their heads, and others started to move towards him. There must be no hesitation. He must run as fast as possible. He hurled himself forward and flew across the yard. An approaching ward orderly, carrying an armful of clean sheets, looked puzzled, but didn't try to tackle him.

Butler had told him that he'd been spotted in the village of Potterne on his first escape. A search party had been sent to recapture him, but had just missed him. There was no point in trying to cross the fields to Potterne again. They would anticipate that. Instead, he ran up Pan's Lane, in the direction of the town's busy market place. It was market day, and the wide square was packed with stalls, and enough of a crowd to make him difficult to spot.

He was not used to running, and had to stand holding on to the market cross while he gulped air down into his lungs. There was no time to wait until fully recovered. As soon as he could, he set off again. If anyone had seen the direction he'd taken, they could be as little as two minutes behind him. He had to find a bolt-hole. Maybe there would be a pub with a good view of the market square. As he crossed the square, he noticed a green and cream single-decker bus, waiting on the far side. He ran towards it. It was going to Swindon. He could take it as far as the London road, about eight miles away, and then hitchhike.

He made his way towards the rear of the bus, where a few seats remained, and sat down, next to a plump woman carrying a wicker basket, full of winter greens. Snakey Blakey, Wheeler, Alford and Paxton fanned out across the market place, walking in the general direction of the bus. Their long white coats marked them out from the shopping crowd. He might still evade them if the bus pulled out soon, but the driver showed no inclination to move. Ronnie bent down below the level of the windows, tying and retying his shoelaces. He didn't look conspicuous; he was wearing jeans and an Army surplus combat jacket, and none of the shoppers gave him a second glance. There was still a chance the nurses wouldn't see him, unless they boarded the bus.

His heart was thumping in his chest. The noise was so loud that he was convinced that others must be able to hear it. His pursuers must be about level with the bus now, but he daren't straighten up to look. A slight movement of the bus driver's shoulders and—yes!—he started the engine. Slowly, the bus pulled out into the road, but was then held up by traffic. They could still board the bus, as long as it was stationary, and if they did he would be trapped. He wished he'd chosen a hiding place with an escape route.

It seemed like an age before the traffic moved off and the driver engaged first gear. Ronnie waited for several seconds and then lifted his head to peep out of the rear window. Alford and Paxton were still in the centre of the square, standing on the steps of the old market cross and scanning the crowd, but Snakey Blakey and Ben Wheeler were standing next to the bus stop. Wheeler was looking straight at him, his mouth open, as if about to shout. He had been seen, there was no doubt.

Everything depended on whether Ronnie could hitch a lift before the search party caught up with him. They might think he was heading for Swindon, and simply send the police to his mother's. But if they had a car, they could follow the bus, and then they would see him as soon as he got off.

It was a risk he had to take. The bus crossed the main road near the hamlet of Beckhampton and, as it headed north, he decided the time had come to bail out. He made his way up the bus, hanging on to the seat backs as it swayed around on the winding country road, and asked the driver if he would pull in just ahead.

'Sorry, no-can-do,' the driver replied. 'Not an authorised bus stop.'

Ronnie stared at the man with contempt. There was something vaguely familiar about his face. His fair hair was plastered to his head with Brylcreem. There was an invisible meridian, about an inch above his ears, below which all hair had been shaved, and he wore glasses with clear plastic frames, which made him look bland and characterless. Maybe he had one of those anonymous faces that always reminded you of someone else?

He thought about grabbing the steering wheel and forcing the bus into the side of the road, but the driver would report any incident like that to the police.

'Look, I must have a piss! I'm sorry, but I'll just have to do it in your bus if you won't stop now.'

He fiddled with his flies, as if about to undo them. Watching from the rear of the bus, the plump woman called out, 'We don't want any of that! You put that away, you dirty boy!'

An old man, who sat with both hands propped on a walking stick, turned to face her. 'When you got to go, you got to go! You should know that, Mabel!'

'Ah, but not in public! He should spend a penny before he gets on the bus, like the rest of us.'

'It won't be the first one of those you've ever seen, our Mabel,' a young woman giggled.

'I've seen enough to know it'll be a lot of fuss about very little,' Mabel said, looking straight at the offender.

Ronnie began to blush, from the crown of his head down to his collar. They'd called his bluff. He couldn't go through with it. He'd lost. One last throw of the dice?

He addressed the driver again, 'I can't hold on much longer.'

The old man waved his stick in the general direction of the driver, 'You let the young man off. He's got to answer a *Call of Nature.*'

For some reason, the invocation of Nature proved decisive. Cursing, the driver pulled over, and Ronnie stumbled down the steps in his haste to get away.

'You're Florence Jarvis's boy,' the driver called after him. 'Florence Foxton as was. I knows your mother. I was at school with her. I shall ask her about your bladder problems.'

Fucking hell, just my luck. I'll never hear the end of this. I'll face an interrogation about it, next time I go home. Worse, if the Old Bill ask the driver, he'll know it was me, and he'll remember exactly where he dropped me. If I don't get a lift soon, they'll catch up with me. To be taken back to Larch ward again would be the end—of freedom, of happiness, of everything that made life worth living.

Crossing the lane, he started walking back towards the main road. Then, realising that his pursuers would spot him at the side of the road, he decided it would be safer to walk through the fields. He climbed a five bar gate and walked inside the hedge, arousing the curiosity of a herd of bullocks, who crowded around him, jostled him and refused to be waved away. As he watched the breath steaming from their nostrils in the frosty air, and felt the earth shake as they gadded around the field, he felt exhilarated. Every sense had come alive, was sharper than he could remember it, as if he had been reborn. He was on a natural high, an adrenaline rush, after his escape. They had been able to hold onto him for less than three weeks.

Life felt so good he could conceive of not returning to junk at all, just taking off and rambling from town to town, just like he had at fifteen. He hadn't run away from home, as his Mum said, he'd read the *Dharma Bums* and gone on the road. Leaving home was a joy—being a bum, being carefree, and never knowing how each day would unfold. He'd valued freedom above everything, even if it meant rejecting the security brought by money, employment and accommodation. It was better to live like a penniless hobo and be free, as Kerouac had found, than to have material comfort and be mentally dead.

Then, in the melancholy Bristol autumn, he discovered a refuge from his whole existence in heroin. He retreated from the burden of freedom, and accepted the constraints entailed by a heroin habit. Now he was trapped. He could not go back to his old way of life. If he went anywhere near most of his old haunts he would be arrested, and they could keep him in the Bin until he was an old man, like the patients on Larch ward, incarcerated for twenty years or more. The only way to stay at liberty was to live on the street, and to make out on the street he had to fix. It was logical enough, but it no longer felt like a free choice.

Chapter Nine

The day after leaving her husband, Florence Jarvis wrote to her mother, to arrange for the boy to be looked after in Swindon. She received a letter by return post, and later that morning took her son to Paddington railway station. As they emerged from the darkness of the London Underground, into the light and airy space underneath the glass vaulted roof, the boy quickened his step towards the locomotives. Squatting beside their platforms, they were like iron dragons trailing clouds of steam. She grabbed his shoulder and pulled him back. One hand seized his head in a vice-like grip, while the other raked through her handbag for a handkerchief. Soaking the hankie in copious amounts of spit, she scrubbed his face, leaving behind the smell he always identified with her; a warm, musky smell, with a faint floral note from her perfume. *Evening in Paris* it was called. He screwed his face up in protest.

'How do you get so dirty, you little so-and-so?' she asked. 'You've only been out five minutes. I'm not letting Granny see you like this.'

They stopped again by the ticket barrier. In case he failed to get off at the right station, she had written a label saying 'Put me off at SWINDON,' which she attached to the buttonhole in his jacket lapel.

She squatted on her heels, so they were eye-to-eye. 'If all goes well, I shall come and fetch you in a couple of weeks,' she said.

'What do you mean, if all goes well?'

'If Mummy and her new friend get on, and if we get somewhere to live, you can come and join us. But I need some time to myself first, to see if it will work out.'

She took a comb from her handbag, licked it, and scraped his hair into a parting.

He began crying. 'Why can't you see if it works out while I'm with you?' he wailed. 'I don't want to go away.' He was losing his mother, he thought, and leaving all his friends behind as well.

'Don't make this difficult for me,' she pleaded, tears coming into her eyes. 'Be a good boy. Try to understand.'

'Why can't you come to Swindon with me?' he sobbed.

'Because I have to spend some time with Georgie, my new friend. You want Mummy to be happy, don't you? It has to be this way. I have to have a life again. You'll understand, when you're older.'

His mother found him a window seat in a third class carriage, and put his suitcase in the rack above his head. Tears rolled down her cheeks when she hugged him goodbye. She turned and walked away quickly, handkerchief dabbing at her face, and he watched her slender back as it retreated into the distance. She had gone, and he felt alone in the world.

The journey took nearly two hours, on at a train that stopped at every station. He sat forward, raising and lowering the window on its leather strap, until a woman sitting opposite told him to leave it alone. He then breathed on the window and drew faces in the mist with his finger. He watched the steam from the engine rushing the full length of the train, sometimes blotting out the view, and made faces at his own reflection in the window. He tried to stick his tongue out so far that it touched his chin, but couldn't quite reach. The woman sitting opposite told the man next to her that the boy had some very nasty habits, and couldn't be trusted to travel alone. They both stared at him.

When the train finally pulled into Swindon station, his Mum's brother was waiting near the middle of the platform, with his hands thrust into his overall pockets, his chin jutting forward. He had a newspaper stuffed into the pocket of his old tweed jacket and his cap set on the back of his head. The boy got off quickly, in case his uncle came up to the carriage, and the woman got the chance to tell him about the nasty habits.

His uncle patted the boy's shoulder in an awkward demonstration of affection. He had the van outside, he said. As they walked through the station, his uncle said, 'You're getting into a big boy.' Ronnie was a bit puzzled by this, as he only came up to his uncle's breastbone, and was considered small for his age, but he said, 'Yes, I'm big.'

The back of his uncle's van was full of copper piping for a plumbing job, which clinked and rattled as they turned corners. They drove through a heavy downpour, water running down the hilly streets and collecting in deep puddles where the road dipped under low railway bridges. On one side of the main road was a high redbrick wall, which seemed to go on for ever. The words *No Nazi Army* were painted on it, in five-foot-high white letters.

'It's the Germans,' his uncle explained, noticing his interest. 'We don't want the buggers to rearm. Because if they do, they'll start another bloody world war.'

A siren went off behind the wall, and two tall gates opened in its side. There was a commotion, like hundreds of geese taking off from a lake. Out of the gap came a deluge, a grey tide of men, on bicycle and foot. They were all dressed identically, in fawn cloth caps and belted Macs. The traffic came to a standstill as the road filled with men on bikes, cycling five abreast. Most kept their gaze averted and had heavy, slow movements, although one or two cycled as if their lives depended on it, their knees pumping madly up and down to force their bikes forward through the rain.

'It's the hooter,' his uncle explained, as they crawled forwards behind a phalanx of bicycles. 'For lunch. The whole town can set its clock by that hooter. When it sounds again, at five past one, they have ten minutes to get back to work. If they're late they get a fine. Wouldn't do for me! Having my bloody life governed by a hooter? I'd rather be my own boss, out in the open air.'

Instinctively, as Ronnie watched the factory gates, he conceived a passionate hatred of the railway works, dominating the town like a prison. Above all, he hated the brutality of the workplace that had been responsible, Gran always said, for destroying his Grandfather's mind.

Standing in his Gran's hall, he heard his uncle say, 'If he gets to be a handful, you can send him over to us. One more won't make any difference.'

'He won't be a handful', his Gran said, 'or he'll get the sharp side of my tongue.'

As she spoke, Ronnie registered the smell of lavender floor polish, floating up from the encaustic tile floor, mingled with the scent of Michaelmas daisies, from a vase on the mahogany coat stand. Everything was polished, including the kitchen range. He hoped she wasn't going to be strict.

His Gran was strict, like his father, but unlike his father, who was often drunk by nightfall, she didn't miss much. On the first afternoon, when she was taking a nap, he found that he was locked out. He went to the rear of the property and climbed the drainpipe to the roof of the outside toilet, and then made the short climb up the slate roof to his bedroom window, on the first floor. He was able to open the clasp on the sash window with his penknife, but as he lifted the window it rattled and groaned. He had wriggled halfway over the windowsill when his blood froze. His Gran was stamping up the stairs.

'Is that you, our Ronnie? We're not having any of your London ways here!'

Gran made a ritual of taking him to bed, which he found comforting. 'Nighty night,' she would say, handing him the lighted candle in its white enamel holder. 'Up the little wooden hill.' A bit later she would come to check that he'd settled down: 'Have you got that candle on? Time to blow it out.'

A few days after he arrived, he was collecting the hot water bottles from the bedrooms, when he found a children's book from before the war, with a cut-away diagram of an airship, *The R100: the Future of Flight.* There was a photo of a cigar-shaped airship outside its hangar in East Yorkshire, and another of it over-flying St Paul's cathedral in London. In the future, giant airships would criss-cross the oceans of the world, uniting the countries of the British Empire. He went to look for his Gran, who was on her knees, black-leading the grate.

'Why don't we have airships in Swindon?' he asked. 'It says here British airships will rule the skies within twenty years.'

'Have you got your head in a book again?' his Gran answered. 'T'ain't never natural, a boy reading books all the time. You should be out in the fresh air. On the ground, mind, not climbing things all the time, like a ragamuffin.'

His Gran had fixed ideas on what were and were not natural pastimes for boys. On the question of reading books, she agreed with her son-in-law, Freddy: it was unwholesome. Ronnie tried to argue.

'In London, some boys have to stay in and read books all the time. They're not allowed out to play until they've finished swotting. They have to pass exams, and until they do their parents won't let them out.'

'We're not having any of your London ways here,' his Gran said firmly.

I don't see why not, he thought. London ways are better. That's obvious, because London's the capital. The capital has to be number one. And it's the biggest city in the whole world. Everything is more modern there. They have bathrooms, instead of old tin baths hanging out the back. And Londoners don't have toilets out the back, they have them indoors. And they have an underground railway called the Tube, and the lift at Hampstead Tube station is the fastest in the world. And London has airships, at least this book says it does. Instead of stupid locomotives, like Swindon.

It wasn't easy to play at being a giant airship. If you were flying a Spitfire you just had to stick your arms out at the side, like wings, but what did you do in an airship? He tried walking slowly, moving his upper body as little as possible and keeping his gaze fixed on the horizon, but it wasn't much fun. He returned to the book, after a token flight around the back garden. The next chapter had instructions on how to make a crystal set. There was no electricity upstairs in his Gran's house, but if he built a crystal set he wouldn't need electricity. And because a crystal set used headphones, Gran wouldn't be able to hear if he listened in bed.

He found a shop that sold second-hand and surplus radio parts, opposite the railway works in Rodbourne Road. Using several weeks' pocket money, he bought a pair of wartime headphones, a tuning coil and a germanium diode. The man told him that the germanium diode was the latest technology, and was replacing the cat's whisker. He strung his aerial thirty feet down the garden, attaching it to the post for the washing line. His earth wire went down to a copper rod in the garden. Not only could he get the BBC Light Programme and Home Service, but on a good night he could get Radio Luxembourg.

Luxembourg played records that were banned on the BBC, like *Garden of Eden*, which had been judged blasphemous. His teacher said blasphemy was when you hated God, but he couldn't see how a song could make God cross. Luxembourg also played popular music, like the mambo, and even rock'n'roll, which was never heard on the BBC. On his first night listening to the crystal set, he tuned in to Radio Luxembourg and heard Little Richard singing *Ready Teddy*. He sat up in bed and punched the air to keep time. 'When I grow up,' he promised himself, 'I'm going to be a Teddy Boy. And I'm going to dance to Little Richard all day long. And I won't ever bloody go to work!'

Later, he heard Little Richard's *Rip It Up*. Forgetting himself, he jumped out of bed to practise the jive. His Gran heard and called up the stairs, 'Is that you out of bed, our Ronnie? You get back before I have to come up to you.' He slipped back under the covers.

It was September, and daylight until eight o'clock. At dusk, he took off the headphones which, because of their weight, made his ears ache after a few minutes. Taking a break, he slipped out of bed to adjust the aerial, which came in under the bedroom window. As he did, he looked down on the back garden and there, like a pale ghost floating up the garden path, was his father, his lime green shirt glowing in the half-light. Ronnie's heart raced in terror. He called out, 'He's come! He's come! He's here now!'

By the time Gran climbed the stairs, he was in tears, and she had trouble understanding what he was saying. She looked out of the window. 'There's nobody out there,' she said. 'Just that Harry Greenaway doing his bonfire … Doesn't he stoop so? He's always got such a long face, that man.'

'He's out there!' the boy insisted.

'It was only the Sandman, come to help little boys back to sleep. Snuggle down in that bed.'

'My Dad's come for me!'

'Now, don't be a little worrit. If you're a good boy, and go back to sleep, I'll buy you a Tarzan comic in the morning.'

Later that evening, Ronnie awoke to hear raised voices at the front door.

'I just want to see my son!'

'You're not seeing nobody!'

'Where's Flo? Just tell me where she is and I'll go!'

'You're going all right, I'll see to that! And you're not speaking to your son nor nobody. Coming to respectable people's homes and making a racket at this time of night! Now get off my doorstep and be on your way, or I'll see that you do, policeman or no policeman!'

Without another word, Freddy turned and walked away. The next day, as Ronnie left the Rodbourne Road Junior School, Freddy was waiting, hiding behind the brick wall by the school gates. He grabbed the boy's shoulder and pinned him against the wall.

There was a strong smell of whisky on Freddy's breath. It was a familiar smell; when he'd lived with his parents, Ronnie would unscrew the stopper on a bottle of Scotch, hold it under his nose and inhale, deeply. Then he would drink a mouthful, longing for the day when he could swallow it without coughing. Drinking whisky was what you did when you were grown-up.

'Where is she? The bloody cow!'

'I don't know! I don't know! Let me go!' He struggled to get away, but Freddy tightened his grip. His father was unshaven, and the jacket of his double-breasted suit was creased. He looked wilder than Ronnie remembered, as though he'd been living on a campsite for a week or two.

'You wouldn't lie to your old Dad, would you? You'll get a good hiding if you do! Tell the truth!'

The boy remembered the time he had told the truth and been the cause of his mother getting a thrashing. He mustn't inform on her again. He shouted, 'I won't tell!'

His father's mouth fell open in surprise. He slapped Ronnie twice around the back of his head. The boy took the opportunity to tear himself away, and ran down the back alleys, until he came to a gap in a fence, which he squeezed through. He hid at the bottom of someone's garden for half an hour, until it was clear his father wasn't in pursuit.

Freddy caught up with his wife eventually. She came to Swindon on a Bank Holiday, to visit the boy. By chance, Freddy also travelled down, to see his sister. After weeks of fruitless searching, Freddy stepped out of his sister's front door in Stanley Street and there was his wife, just ahead of him, holding the boy's hand and walking past the workingmen's club. They started to run up the hill, but he caught up with them on the corner of Union Street and grabbed her by the hair. First, he punched her in the mouth. She cowered against a parked car, and tried to reason with him, but he answered every sentence with a punch. Ronnie stood in the middle of the street, watching in terror, and a group of local children gathered round. Every time Flo moved, her husband hit her around the head.

'I'm going to leave you with a black eye. You can go back to lover boy with a few beauty marks,' he hissed. 'Just like the whore that you are. You're going to beg me to take you back, by the time I've finished with you. No one will look at you. Tell lover boy I have a present for him as well!'

The watching children formed an excited ring around the car. The pupils in their eyes grew big and the boys balled their fists, just like they did when there was a fight in the playground. One boy was shadow boxing, practising uppercuts.

Freddy unleashed a flurry of punches, knocking her backwards against the car, and then sideways, until she fell on one knee. Finally, she broke free, and kicking off her high heels, she ran down the street towards her brother's house, blood streaming from her nose. Ronnie ran after her, and the children galloped after them, like sheriff's deputies, in a posse that was about to intercept a fugitive. Freddy remained standing by the parked car, breathing heavily from the exercise, a look of jubilation on his flushed face.

A year later, when Ronnie was eleven, Flo came back to Swindon to live. 'It didn't work out,' she explained to her son. They stayed at his Gran's for another year, until Flo was given a council house. It was on a new estate, being built on former farmland at Walcot. They moved at the beginning of September, and a few weeks later there was a knock on the front door. It was midnight, and Flo had just retired to bed. She darted out of her bedroom, onto the darkened landing, in time to stop Ronnie switching on the light or going downstairs.

'Someone's at the door,' he said, but she put her hand over his mouth to silence him.

'Shhh! It's *him,*' she whispered. 'He's found us. Don't go downstairs. Keep the lights out. He'll go away eventually.'

The blurred image of Freddy's face was peering through the ornamental glass in the front door. Then the letterbox opened, and they could sense his eyes swiveling to and fro, as he tried to see if there was anyone in the hall.

'Are you there, Flo?' Freddy called through the letter box, his speech slurred. 'I just want to talk to you, Flo. There's no sense in us carrying on like this, Flo, is there? Eh, Flo? *Oh, Blimey O'Bloody Riley!*' In trying to light his cigarette, Freddy had dropped all his matches. There was a scrabbling sound as he tried to pick them up. After a while he gave up, and opened the letterbox again. 'We can sort things out. Flo? You belong by my side, girl. We need each other. Flo? … Open this bloody door! Don't be a stupid bloody *cow!* You're bloody useless, you *cow!*'

At intervals over the next few months, Freddy would turn up, sometimes at the school gates but usually, in the dead of night, at the house. He would materialize when least expected, drunk, and often in a foul mood. Flo never opened the door at night. She would turn out any lights, to make it look as if nobody was home, and wait quietly upstairs, while he looked in all of the ground floor windows and tried the door handles.

One afternoon, when Ronnie was thirteen, his father gained entry. Ronnie came home from school to find the sitting room in disarray. His mother sat in the armchair, her lips swollen, a bruise on her cheek.

'One of his blooming visitations,' she explained. She held her head in her hands and cried, and he felt helpless, unable to say anything that would comfort her. 'I'll never go back with him,' she sobbed. 'I'd rather throw myself in the lake! Drown myself in Coate Water first!' Ronnie sat uneasily on the arm of the chair, watching her. He wished she could be stronger, like a man. Then she could defend herself and she could protect him. He was too little to be the adult in the family.

She took to staying in, the curtains drawn. Increasingly, the boy spent time away from home, at his Uncle's, or at his Gran's; anywhere, away from the heavy silence that settled over the darkened sitting room. He developed a fear of being pursued, a sense that he was the quarry to be hunted down. The only time he felt at ease was when he hitch-hiked from town to town, and stayed one step ahead of the shadows pursuing him.

Chapter Ten

It was three in the morning before Ronnie Jarvis arrived back in the centre of London, after a bad time hitching. He'd been dropped away from the main road, twice, and had ended up walking nearly ten miles. He decided to make straight for the lift-shaft. It was too late to be sure of scoring at Piccadilly, and, with any luck, Moss would be at home. If he could reach Moss before the barbiturates did, he might persuade him to repay his debts.

He turned into Eastcastle Street, and made for the garment factory. The fire exit was unlocked, as usual, and he slipped down the service stairs to the lift-shaft entrance. There was no sign of Moss, nor of his possessions. The newspapers had been removed from the floor. He found the milk bottle that Moss used for storing clean tap-water for fixing, still half-full, and, on a ledge in the corner, where Moss had stashed them, two clean hypodermic needles, a spare syringe and a box of matches. But no sign of Moss.

Ronnie awoke after a few hours' sleep, to the rattle of a milkman's float. He was hungry. Sneaking up the stairs, he slipped into the mews outside. There was hoar-frost underfoot. He lifted a milk bottle from the doorstep opposite. Full cream milk lined the stomach. It would keep him going until the cafes opened in an hour or so. Only about five bob left, but that would buy some breakfast and some fags.

After a leisurely breakfast of bacon, sausage, fried egg and beans, two cups of tea and a cigarette, he made his way down the Charing Cross Road and browsed in Zwemmer's bookshop, to kill time. Then, the pubs having opened, he headed back towards Charlotte Place, to see if anyone was in the Duke of York. In the space of two hours, a thick, yellow fog had descended, and as he reached Rathbone Place, he could just make out three dark figures walking towards him, in the middle of the road. As the trio came nearer, he could see Pam, in her black leather overcoat, strolling arm-in-arm with Guido. Pam's new colleague, Mistress Elara, came into view. She was also dressed in an expensive black leather outfit, and looked even more glamorous than he remembered.

He could hear them singing the Rufus Thomas song, *Walking the Dog.* They were exuberant and light-hearted. Pam stopped in the road to dance the Dog, her bottom thrust out behind her, grinding a circle, her tits shaking towards the ground. She pumped her fists up and down in the air. Passing cars hooted at them to get out of the road, but they responded by barking and yapping, like a chorus from the Battersea Dog's Home.

'Long-time-no-see, Ronnie Fizz!' Pam called out. 'Where've you been?'

'Out of town for a while,' Ronnie mumbled, not wanting to give Guido another excuse for moralising.

Guido beamed at him, however, with no trace of his former rancour. 'Relief, man! We thought you'd gone the same way as Tony Moss,' Guido replied. He was wearing a new Levi jacket and some kind of studded leather collar around his neck.

'Moss? Why? Where is he?'

'Haven't you heard? Moss is dead! He topped himself in Brixton prison,' said Pam.

Ronnie felt the solid ground dissolve beneath his feet. 'No, that's not possible!'

'They reckon he couldn't face another cold turkey,' Guido explained. 'Hanged himself with a belt, if you can believe that. I heard the screws did it to him. Made it look like suicide.'

Ronnie couldn't believe that Moss had died, by any human agency. Moss was indestructible. 'Oh fuck,' was all he could say. There was a cold feeling in the pit of his stomach.

'Yeah, he owed me four grains as well,' Pam said, misunderstanding the reason for his consternation.

'Oh fuck,' Ronnie repeated, still unable to comprehend the news.

'Dave the Pave's gone as well,' continued Guido, smiling as if relaying yet more good news. 'Gone to meet his Maker, that is. He O-Deed in the bogs at Piccadilly. They saw this pool of blood coming under the door.'

'The poor sod,' said Ronnie, still shocked by the news about Moss. He could see the stiff body hanging from the window bars, the face contorted, wine-red.

'You okay?' asked Elara. 'You look as though you ought to sit down. Would you like a coffee?'

'Come on, Fido,' Pam said to Guido, slipping her index finger through a ring on his collar. 'I shall have to get you a lead. See you later, folks.'

Three ten-year old girls, watching from the street corner, started laughing at the sight of Guido being towed along. Pam called over to them, '*Just a-walking her dog*,' and they looked delighted.

Elara slipped her hand through Ronnie's arm, as though she'd known him for years, and guided him towards the Greek. She had a deep, husky voice, and a mischievous, elfin face. Her eyes were bright blue, like sapphires. Thick black eye makeup, and dark lipstick, made her eyes seem even more striking. Two hard, sparkling sapphires, flung into the darkness. Sapphire blue, the colour of heaven.

She said, 'Did you know Tony Moss well?'

'We were skippering together. He used to say I was his apprentice.'

As they turned into Charlotte Place, dense fog reduced the visibility to ten yards. Someone on the street corner wanted to score coke. Ronnie shook his head angrily; the request was an intrusion.

'It's just that Moss was someone you couldn't kill,' Ronnie continued. 'He was like the undead, coming back to life after midnight, when he got his fix. He was indestructible. I can't imagine Piccadilly without him.'

'It's crap when something like this happens,' Elara said, looking thoughtful.

'It's like when I was a kid, I used to play with this boy, Lawrence McShane …' They reached the Greek, and Ronnie held the door open for Elara, remembering Pam's suggestion that he behave with courtesy. 'He could climb anything, break into any building in London. Then he joined the army. One day he gets leave and he's running along the roof of a train, jumping between the carriages …' The only free table was short of space, and Elara had to cram herself into a seat against the wall. He squeezed into the seat next to her, and felt her dress sliding up against her nylons as his thigh brushed against hers. '… And he got killed when the train went under a bridge. Just makes life seem pointless, somehow. Your heroes shouldn't get snuffed out.'

She raised her right hand in front of her face so that he would see, on her fourth finger, a silver death's head ring.

He said, 'What's that?'

'The skull and crossbones. In the midst of life—'

'It makes you look like a biker.'

Elara shrugged. She ordered two coffees from Dimitri, who seemed less resentful than usual. He even brought the coffees to the table, rather than leaving them on the counter to be collected.

'What's Guido doing with Pam?' Ronnie asked, as soon as the coffees arrived.

'He's moved in with her. He likes to have his bottom spanked.'

'Is he some kind of masochist? What happened to Samantha?'

Elara shrugged again. 'Still over Archway, I suppose. Pam booted Graham out and then Guido was looking for somewhere, so she let him move in. That Graham was a right lazy sod.'

He had it all wrong about Graham, he realized. He'd always understood that Graham was a successful pimp, a man who'd sent his wife out on the game so that he could live a life of comfort and ease. But it was clear that Graham had become the junior partner in the enterprise. And now he'd been dumped.

'So where are you kipping, Elara?'

'Mistress Elara's just my professional name. Like Madam Sterne is Pam's. My real name's Dawn. But you can call me Elara if you want.'

'Your professional name?'

He noticed that she bit her fingernails. She was expensively dressed, but the illusion was broken when you saw her grubby hands, with nails bitten to the quick; then she looked like an urchin.

'I'm an apprentice domme, just like you're an apprentice bum. Pam is showing me the ropes. Showing me how to be a proper dominatrix. I get to practise on some of her clients, and I help her out when she needs a second pair of hands.'

'What, flagellation?'

'She has this MP who likes to have two women humiliate him, so I oblige. Pam flogs him. I make him lay down in the bath and I piss on him; that sort of thing. He's a right slime-bag!'

A vivid image arose in Ronnie's mind. The young woman was standing astride a bath, and unloading the contents of her bladder on a prone, naked figure. A distinguished, middle-aged man cowered beneath her, his mouth open in supplication. Piss splattered down like heavy, yellow rain. It soaked his face, his hair. And then the same distinguished, middle-aged man stood in the House of Commons, to make a speech about the need for propriety in public life. Was the MP excited by the risk he was taking, the gamble that one disclosure would destroy his career?

Ronnie said: 'MP? Which party?'

'Labour, actually.'

'What's his name?'

'Now that would be telling. That would be unprofessional conduct, wouldn't it? We don't want another Profumo affair.' She smiled knowingly. 'Let's just say that if Labour win the election, I won't have to worry any more about the fuzz going through my ashtrays, looking for week-old roaches.'

'Bloody hell, Elara! You can tell me!'

'I ain't telling you nothing,' she said, 'because you'd go and flog the story round the newspapers. It's as confidential as the priesthood, this bloody job. That's why I make good money.'

'How much do you make?'

'Enough. Enough to afford my own pad in Berwick Street and a new wardrobe.'

'Stroll on!' A note of surprise and respect came into his voice.

Dimitri came up to their table and emptied the ashtray. 'Foggy old day,' he said to Elara. 'More coffee?' She nodded and he took the empty Pyrex cups away, bringing back two clean ones, filled with fresh coffee.

Elara ladled three spoonfuls of sugar into her cup. 'Maybe I'll have a Rum Baba,' she giggled. 'We've been smoking kif. It always makes me want to eat like a pig.'

Ronnie looked out the window and wondered whether he wasn't wasting time, when he could be out looking for a fix. She was gazing directly into his eyes and he tried to work out whether she fancied him. Every time he decided that she did, she said something that suggested the opposite. She was hard to read.

'Here,' she said, 'Pam knows that Christine Keeler.'

'The woman in the Profumo case?'

'They reckon she entertained a British Cabinet Minister and a Russian naval attaché in the same bed. And guess what? Pam had dinner with that Lord who wears nothing but a silk mask, and eats his food out of a dog's bowl.'

'He sounds a bundle of fun.'

'He's got a hairy arse … Are you picking up your script at the Dilly tonight, Ronnie Fizz?' Her bright blue eyes were studying him, her hand caressing his shoulder, as if he was already her lover.

Outside, the fog had grown so thick that Dimitri was obliged to switch on the lights, although it was only lunchtime. The temperature was falling fast; perhaps it would freeze.

'I need to get over to my doctor's in Chelsea this afternoon, fog or no fog,' Ronnie said, in an urgent rush. 'Get a week's scripts. I'm a bit strung out, actually. In a bit of a two-and-eight.' He tried to keep the whine out of his voice. All junkies ended up whining, even hard men like Moss.

'Really? I just might be able to help. I'm getting some morphine today from a GI down the Flamingo. Syrettes? Like a little toothpaste tube, with a needle at the end?' She drew the outline of a syrette in the air with her right forefinger.

He nodded. 'They're designed so you can give yourself a quick fix on the battlefield. The GIs nick them out their first aid kits.'

'This bloke's a nurse, or a medical orderly. Works in a military hospital. Anyway, you're welcome to a couple. I only skin pop them. Morphine's hard to mainline, ain't it?'

'It burns or tingles as it goes up your vein,' he said. His hope soared. There was just time to have a fix before finding his way to his doctor's. 'If you could loan me some, babe, I'll pay you back in Horse?'

As they stood up to go, he picked up her handbag, which she'd left on the table. He nearly dropped it.

'Christ! What have you got in here?' he said.

'Oh that!' she laughed. 'I carry a brick around in my bag, just in case I get trouble with a punter. You never know!'

As they stepped out of the cafe, the three little girls were skipping in the alleyway. They chanted:

Guido was a lapdog,
Guido was a hog,
Guido couldn't find his way,

Because of all the fog.
She made him put a lead on,
She made him scrub the floor,
She made him clean the baby's bum,
In 1964!

With Elara holding onto his arm, Ronnie made his way across Soho Square, and down Frith Street, before cutting through Shaftesbury Avenue to the southern end of Wardour Street. They could only just see across the street, and the traffic sounded muffled, as though the fog blotted out all sound. Ronnie could make out a couple of big American cars parked at the kerb, the kind that had long tail fins and masses of chrome. Five or six guys stood around a recessed doorway, under a small neon sign advertising the Flamingo Jazz Club. Most of the group were Black; there was one White guy, a thin man with a flat-top hairstyle and well-cut, Ivy League clothes.

Elara called out 'Shiner!' and the White guy turned and nodded in recognition. 'You were going to get me some M,' she whispered in his ear.

Shiner nodded again, but fixed his eyes on Ronnie's face, as if searching for a clue to a puzzle. Moving over to a red Buick, with six chromium-plated exhaust pipes, Shiner took out his car keys, paused and frowned.

'It's the Commie protester from Bird Drop Park! Hope you're not gonna do a dive on the sidewalk! Organise a sit-down protest or something?'

'Not unless you've got nuclear missiles hidden in there,' Ronnie said, gesturing towards the boot.

'I got everything you could ever want in here.'

Shiner slipped his arm around Elara's waist and, turning to face her as he opened the boot, pressed her up against his crotch. Ronnie could see that the boot was filled with LPs and bottles of Bourbon.

'You two know each other?' Elara asked.

'Customer of mine,' said Shiner. 'Least his Irish friend is. Used to buy records. Jazz, R&B. His friend uses morphine, too.'

So Jack Fitt had been scoring M in Swindon. Selfish bastard! Hadn't turned anyone on, had always been against fixing. The man was a hypocrite.

'Want any records?' Shiner said. 'Soul? Mose Allison, Booker T? Straight from the States; can't get them here. Liquor?'

'No sounds, no lush,' Ronnie said. 'Just the M.'

'I've got five syrettes for you,' Shiner said, addressing Elara. 'Best quality GI/M, courtesy of Uncle Sam.'

Elara beamed, put a hand on Shiner's shoulder, and gave him a gentle kiss on the cheek. Ronnie felt hollow, as if his life-force had drained away.

He turned away to hide his misery, and pretended to study a notice in the club doorway, but Elara was no longer aware of his presence. She could've told the man to take his hands off her, Ronnie thought, but she'd just smiled. She'd let Shiner rub himself up against her. There was a bounce to her step, as if Shiner made her feel good. Might as well leave now. Spare prick at a wedding. Except she was going to give him a fix. That was worth hanging around for. Forget the rest; he didn't rate her anyway.

Ronnie said little on the way to her flat, and the silence between them grew, until he felt there was no way it could be breached. Stretched out in front of Elara's gas fire, however, Ronnie relaxed, in anticipation of a fix. Her flat was comfortable yet staid. There were doilies on the chair backs, and matching bookcases on either side of the fireplace. Elara even had her own telephone, standing on a table in the hall.

'That's posh,' he said, as she walked through to the bedroom. 'Your own bloody phone … Where do you know that Yank from?'

She didn't reply, but returned carrying a large teddy bear, which she cradled to the side of her face while she waltzed around the room. He felt the stab of jealousy again, as though the bear was a stand-in for Shiner. He stood up and went over to her bookcase, seizing a bundle of comics from the top shelf and spreading them over the sofa with great care, as if they were valuable antiques.

'Classic Comics! I used to collect these, Elara, when I was a kid! *Call of the Wild*; I had that. *The Man In the Iron Mask*. *Moby Dick*.'

'What about number 72, *The Man Who Laughed*? Victor Hugo. That's hard to find.'

'I had that one. His face was all disfigured.'

'*Hamlet, Prince of Denmark*?'

'Brilliant art work. *When graveyards yawn—*'

'I knew you were well read.'

From the street below came the hoarse shouting of a costermonger; something was lovely, and a shilling a pound. Her windows looked down on the striped awnings of a busy street market. From above it looked like a tented city, floating in the fog. Never get a cop car along here in a hurry, he thought. Quite a safe place to live.

He emptied two syrettes into his syringe, and hit the vein inside his elbow. Elara was prepared to skin-pop, but he offered to help her mainline. He sterilized his needle with the flame of a match, and then stroked the veins in her arm, looking for the best candidate. She had good, plump veins and the syringe drew blood on the first attempt. Their eyes met, and it was an intimate moment, like a sexual penetration.

'Bit of a burn coming,' he warned as he pressed the plunger home.

She made a soft grunt as the morphine hit her back brain. It was a nice, calm sort of buzz, she said. Kneeling, she gazed at ten Tarot cards spread across the carpet to form a cross, while she scratched her face, rubbed her nose, and surrendered to morphine's embrace. The teddy bear lay discarded in a chair.

All the major arcana, she said, a thing to be feared. Five bridges to cross. A lonely child, an ocean of grief. The Charioteer, reversed: a terrible beauty is born.

Ronnie talked over her. The Tarot could tap into her intuition, but if she was saying it was some kind of supernatural thing, then he really didn't believe it. That was against his atheist principles.

'It still works, whether you believe in it or not.'

'Well, if you're saying it's supernatural, that's as bad as religion.'

The ruddy glow of the gas fire illuminated the sitting room. Beyond the window, the afternoon sun began to set, a red smear in the fog, like a wound bleeding into a dirty crepe bandage. In this strange, extraterrestrial light, Elara's face grew combative.

'That's because you're ruled by Mercury. You live in the head too much. You need to get back to the heart.' Her pupils had shrunk to small black dots, giving her blue eyes the faraway look of a hophead.

He could not believe what he was hearing. 'Ruled by Mercury? This is the 1960s, babe. That is so old-fashioned, that mystical stuff. Everyone knows we're entering a new era, an age of reason, protest and revolution.'

She rubbed her face with both hands, as though giving herself a sensuous massage. 'I thought you wanted to be one of the Beats, Mister Fizz? The Beats are about madness, not reason. The Beats are all poets and madmen. Holy Zen warriors.'

'Bollocks.' Ronnie could not allow a chick to lecture him on the Beat generation. She'd never even been on the road. He told her how the Beats were Dharma revolutionaries. Gary Snyder said you could smash the State using Zen shock tactics.

Her laughter rang out like the clatter of a pneumatic drill. 'Snyder wants free love, and no industry! A load of female craft workers shagging in the municipal park, that's his dream of socialism. Come on, Fizz, he's a fucking poet, not a revolutionary! And that Ginsberg's just as bad. All that stuff about people demanding instantaneous lobotomies.'

'Lobotomies?'

'I mean, *On the Road* is just a modern Don Quixote. The continual travels of two insane characters. The Beats are about madness and drunkenness and bumming around, not taking the system seriously, and trying to change it.'

He had fallen silent at the mention of lobotomy. Should he tell her about being in the Bin? The truth about lobotomy was a sad creature tormented by nurses, a war veteran reduced to a figure of fun. He decided he didn't know her well enough to confess to having been a mental patient. She might think he was a nutter.

'Must have a piss,' he announced. 'Where's the karzi?'

She stood up and led him into the hall. As she opened the toilet door, she said, 'Do you want me to hold it for you?'

He felt confused, bewilderment that carried an edge of raw panic. He wasn't sure, from her mischievous expression, whether she meant he was so helpless that he couldn't hold his own dick, or whether she wanted to watch him piss. Or was she offering to give him a J. Arthur Rank? He said, 'I can manage,' and then, when she walked away, he regretted not thinking of something witty.

'So, what do the cards foretell?' he asked on his return, looking over to where she had spread the cards over the sitting room carpet. He wanted to find a safe topic, after their difference of opinion.

Elara gazed down on the spread. 'The Charioteer is reversed. That shows a man who is irresolute, a dreamer, a drifter—'

'I think I've heard this sermon before,' he said, miming a yawn. 'You're going to tell me to give up junk in a minute?'

She smiled and reached for another card. 'And here are the Lovers: Perseus rescuing Andromeda from the Waters of Stagnation. Perseus is me, in this situation, and you are Andromeda. So that's me, and I'm going to fuck you!'

He turned to her in surprise as she leaned forward and kissed him full on the lips. His eyes opened wide. She placed a hand inside his shirt, covering his navel. 'There's not an ounce of spare flesh on your body,' she said approvingly.

He felt a surge of affection towards her. Elara was tough but gentle, shrewd but compassionate, an amalgam of male and female strengths. She was the embodiment of poise, confidence, passion: her presence seemed so dense and real that it might crush his own frail and insubstantial existence, yet the brush of her lips on his cheek was light and tender. He slipped a hand between her thighs, and upwards until he touched public hair.

'Can you get it up when you're fixing?' she asked, slipping her hand into his pants and stroking his cock.

'I can always get a hard-on', he said, as his dick stiffened, 'but I'm afraid I have a bit of trouble coming. I just grind on for hours.'

'Don't apologise,' she grinned, 'most women wouldn't find that a problem.'

'Do you want to fuck here, in front of the gas fire?' he asked, cautiously.

'Yes—with me on top and grinding!' she said, mimicking the hesitant way he'd spoken.

She smiled again as he attempted to hide his embarrassment. Gripping his shoulders, she pushed him back onto the floor. They embraced, kissing and biting each other's lips, and then pulled off each other's clothing, slowly, as if sleepwalking. The tempo was determined by morphine, rather than lust. He rolled on top of her, and sank his cock deep inside her, with several triumphant, hard thrusts. There was a sense of exhilaration. She rolled him over, mounted him and pounded her hips into his, as if trying to penetrate him with her clit. As she stooped to kiss him, their eyes met, and he glimpsed something strange, a face maddened and suffused with unholy delight, no longer a woman but a Gorgon's mask, shining and ecstatic in the firelight. A fear of women, and of their otherness, rushed into his mind. The Daughters of Grace. The female of the species. The Spider Goddess, descending from the sky to devour all men. There was a moment of blank terror, like being suspended above an abyss, and then a sense of letting go. He felt a thousand times lighter than he'd ever done before; he was floating above the earth. It was a moment of freedom.

After Elara came, she sunk her weight onto him, keeping his cock a prisoner within her body. Although the morphine had lessened the force of his own orgasm, he felt satiated, and the mound of flesh above his cock was bruised from the violence of their encounter. The only sound was the hissing of the gas fire. She climbed off, curled herself into a ball, and closed her eyes. He cuddled up to her, slipping a hand between her legs, so that he could feel the comforting wetness of her cunt.

He was fascinated by Elara. As he drifted off to sleep, he knew he wanted to be close to her. He began to wonder what life would be like if they were a team. She could stay on the game, perhaps, while he would be registered, and he'd get the doctor to put coke back on his script. Tell his doctor to stop fucking him around, treating him like a kid. Then, with a steady supply of H&C, they would be able to make out. It would be cool. He would be content, be in possession of everything that he could ever want in life. Falling asleep, he dreamt they were a domestic couple, holding hands. He woke with a start. The gas fire had gone out. Needed another shilling in the meter. The clock on the mantelpiece showed eight. Evening.

'Jesus, Elara, wake up! I've over-slept. My fucking doctor's surgery is closed.'

'Can't you go tomorrow?'

'Can I buggery!'

He struggled into his jeans, trying, in his panic, to force both feet into the same trouser leg, and falling backwards onto the sofa. He wasn't physically dependent, because he hadn't fixed for several weeks, but he could see no alternative to going to his doctor's house immediately, even though it was outside surgery hours. He'd done that before. His doctor wouldn't like it, but he'd understand. There would be no peace of mind until he had a script in his hand.

'Will you stay here tonight?' she asked.

He was delighted, although his brow remained furrowed, as if her invitation was a major problem.

'I've got a client at Pam's, at nine. If you wait in the Duke until I'm through ... You will come back, won't you?'

'Sure.'

'No sneaking off with a bunch of junkies and forgetting to pay me back?'

'No, of course not. What do you take me for? I'll be back by ten.'

'Here.' She handed him a scrap of paper, torn from an envelope. 'My telephone number, Gerard 4432. That's GER 4432, right? Phone me if you get held up.'

The fog had closed in, and the acrid smell of exhaust fumes, combined with sulphurous smoke from coal fires, penetrated closed windows and doors, even seeping into Underground stations. Trains were still running, and it took him less than half-an-hour by Tube from Oxford Street to Sloane Square, but nearly twice as long to walk the length of the King's Road. The streets were deserted. The only vehicle to pass him was a double-decker bus, driving on sidelights, managing ten miles an hour. Later, he saw that it had mounted the pavement, and the conductor was trying to guide the driver in reversing back onto the road.

When he arrived at his doctor's surgery, the house was dark. He mounted the short flight of steps to the front door and gave a long ring on the bell. No response. The man was out. He would have to wait. He began to fret. He was a devotee deprived of the sacrament, the central ritual in his life, his refuge.

It was just after midnight when a taxi drew up outside. He recognised his doctor, wearing a dinner jacket and white silk scarf, paying the driver. Seeing Ronnie's shape in the doorway, the doctor looked displeased. As he came up the steps, door key in hand, Ronnie explained that he was sick, and needed an immediate fix.

'You're flipping,' was the doctor's only response. Ronnie was shown into the surgery, but before he could launch into the spiel he'd prepared, the doctor cut him short.

'I understand you're on a Cure—'

'No, no, I'm not—'

'Now, you must give this a chance. Have you any idea how long it takes to get one of these beds? We've wanted to get you into hospital for ages.'

'Look, it's an appalling place. They mistreat all the patients. They get them to throw water at each other, and then—'

'I don't believe a word of it. I'm going to give you a script for one grain, just to last until you get back to hospital. I want you to go back in the morning.'

Without further argument, a prescription was written, placed in his hand, and he found himself outside the front door. One lousy fucking grain. He couldn't manage on that. He owed stuff to Elara. What would she think of him if he couldn't pay her back?

He looked at the writing. It specified one grain in letters, and there was also a figure one, with a circle around it. It occurred to him that the number one could be changed to a six, if only he could alter the 'one' in letters. He went into a nearby telephone booth and took out his pen. He made the figure one into a straight-backed six. That was okay, because his doctor used straight-backed sixes; there was a straight-backed six in the date. The capital letter O made a funny kind of S, but as the rest of the word was scrawled it wasn't too difficult to convert N and E into something like I and X. It wasn't bad, he persuaded himself. It now read *six* grains of dia-morphine hydrochloride.

He took the Tube to Oxford Street and made for John Bell and Croyden's, the all-night chemist in Wigmore Street. It was getting on for 1 a.m. There seemed to be no one in the queue ahead of him, except for two jazz musicians, private patients of Lady Frankau's. Sat with them, hunched up and perched on the edge of the seat, was the Sandman. He was waiting to score. Ronnie went to speak, but the Sandman gave a curt nod of his head, as though he wished to keep his distance, and Ronnie remembered they had not spoken since he'd failed to warn the Sandman about the yobs.

Then Ronnie heard a familiar voice from the far corner.

'Now here's a young man who knew me when I played with the Johnny Stiles band in Swindon.' Sitting opposite the musicians was Jack Fitt, who greeted him effusively.

The pharmacist seemed to stare at Ronnie's script for a second or two longer than usual, then asked him to take a seat. The door from the waiting room opened into a corridor, which led to the street door. Ronnie went over and sat by a large tank of tropical fish that filled the centre of the room, positioning himself so he could watch both the counter and the waiting room door. Through an opaque glass window on his left a screen lit up; the kind of thing doctors used for studying X-Rays. Were they studying the writing on his script, he wondered. Perhaps he should leave now? No, wait and see what happens. In about one more minute they should be handing over six grains of heroin. He could always do a runner if they sussed him.

Jack was ebullient. 'I had a gig yesterday, Ronnie. Recording a new Shirley Bassey LP, over at Decca.'

The jazz musicians looked unimpressed, even hostile. 'Where did you say you was recording?' asked the first musician.

'Decca.'

'That's funny—Shirley Bassey is with EMI!'

'Did I say Decca? *Did I say Decca?* I got half way to Decca when I realised my music was at EMI!'

'You always were a bit absent-minded, Jack,' Ronnie said. 'Tell them about the time you were supposed to be playing with Bird, and you forgot the name of the club. He had to ask a New York cop. The cop was Irish and a jazz fan, and told him the address of the venue straight away!'

The second musician smirked. He opened a copy of the Daily Mirror and tossed it down on the seat. The headline read *Shirley Bassey Returns in Triumph from Las Vegas.* The accompanying photo showed the singer waving as she descended the steps of a plane.

'Funny how you was recording with her yesterday, when she was on a plane over the Atlantic.'

It was cruel. Jack slumped in his seat.

'Sure you weren't over in Ireland, Jack, leading the unemployed in a charge on Dublin Castle?' asked the first musician. 'Or playing with Dizzy at Ronnie Scott's? He's someone you jam with, isn't he?'

'Fucking bull-shitters!' the Sandman said. 'Jarvis and Fitt: the two representatives of the Swindon junk scene. The anarchist contingent. Bull-shitters! The pair of them. Both full of shit!'

Ronnie stared at the Sandman in dismay. He was about to protest his innocence when the waiting room door opened, and two men walked straight towards him. The older man, who had a white moustache, and hair that was greying at the temples, did all the talking. The younger man was DC Andrews, who'd interviewed him over the opium bust. Andrews was dressed in a smart Italian suit with narrow lapels, his ginger hair greased back; he stood on the balls of his feet and stared at Ronnie as if he was ready to offer violence at the slightest excuse.

'Ronald William Jarvis? DI Meadows. I am arresting you for attempting to obtain dangerous drugs through fraudulent means.'

'What did I tell you?' he heard the Sandman saying, as the police hauled him to his feet. 'Even his bloody script is phoney.'

The police bundled him out of the pharmacy and across a fog-bound Oxford Street, and then through the back streets to Saville Row, and into the front entrance of West End Central. Before Ronnie had time to turn around, he found himself sitting on a wooden bench in a small cell. He was shocked at the speed of events. He went through his pockets searching for his last cigarette. As he lit up, the cell door banged open and DC Andrews put his head around the door, leaving one shoulder and one leg in the corridor, as if he was meant to be elsewhere.

'Is your doctor fucking you up the arse in exchange for drugs?'

'What?'

'You heard! Is he a ruddy shirt lifter?'

'No, he's just my doctor.'

'So who's selling you these drugs—apart from that poncey middle-class doctor of yours? Is it the Maltese?'

'No—they're just pimps aren't they?'

'Only, the last time you was interviewed, you tried to point the finger at the Mejlak brothers. Now you don't seem to know nothing about it. Sounds like a lot of old moody to me.'

'Well, the pushers are a bit foreign. Maybe they're Italian.'

'They're Italian now?' Andrews sneered, and smoothed his hair back with one hand.

'They could be Maltese, I suppose. I could find out if you like? If you're going to put in a word for me.' Ronnie was feeling agitated; things were on the point of going badly wrong. 'What sentence will I get?'

'Life, if I had my way.'

'Oh, thanks a lot! I can see you're not interested in nabbing Mr Big!'

'I'd lock you up and throw away the key, sunshine, but it's not up to me. Looks like they're not too keen on having you back at Devizes, so we're looking at vacancies in special hospitals. You'll probably get one day's imprisonment for this offence plus a transfer to Rampton under Section 60.'

Just when life was beginning to look up, everything was in danger of spirally out of control. He had to stop them sticking him in Rampton. If he had the choice, he'd rather finish his sentence in St Benedicts than disappear into a special hospital.

'No—look, I was supposed to go to St Benedicts in Southall,' he said. 'With Dr Weiss. He's a Home Office advisor. He's a world expert on addiction.'

'Like I say, it's nothing to do with me. And if it was, you'd be banged up for many years. To protect society. So you'd better think carefully about cooperating with us. You give me some serious information and I'll see what I can do.' Andrews fastened the middle button of his jacket and brushed his trousers with one hand, as though he was getting ready to go on public view.

'Look, what if I tell the truth about the Maltese? Would you phone St Benedicts for me? Find out what's happening about my bed there?'

Andrews gave a wolfish grin. 'You'll have to give us some kosher information this time, if you want any help. You're going to have to tell us everything you know about the drugs trade. Who's dealing what, and how, and where they're getting it.'

'Okay! Okay!' Ronnie began to pace up and down in the confined space. He needed more time to think. 'If I do that, could you drop this charge? Couldn't you just lose the evidence? Forget you've seen me? Let me go home? There's this bird I promised to see tonight and I really don't want to let her down.' Ronnie produced the scrap of paper with Elara's phone number and waved it in front of Andrews, as though it was important evidence.

'Cherchez la femme, eh? Wouldn't have thought you had it in you.'

'It's just that I only met her today, and I don't want to let her down.'

'Well, you're going to have to do a lot more than just give us a load of old cobblers. You're going to have to get yourself into a position where you can give us regular information.'

'You want me to become a grass?'

He'd informed on his mother's bed-moving activities, and she'd been beaten. That's why he refused to grass when his father caught him outside the junior school. He'd protected his mother on that occasion, and it had been the right thing to do, even if she repaid him by betraying him at Christmas. It was hard to forgive her; she should've shown loyalty. Nobody respected a grass, because they were loyal to no one.

'Doesn't look like you've got much choice. It's either that or say hello to Rampton.'

'Grasses usually end up being cut.'

'We'll look after you.'

Andrews couldn't even look after himself, Ronnie thought. There was a fresh round of knicks on Andrews chin, where a cut-throat razor had collided with his lumps and bumps and the alum pencil had been deployed to stop the bleeding.

'We'll get you into St Benedicts for a few months, and when you come out we'll get you a job down a club. And then,' said Andrews, leaning forward until his face was a few inches from Ronnie's, 'you can give us all the up-to-date intelligence we need to put these people behind bars.'

Just as life was on the up and up—a beautiful girlfriend with a smart pad, regular NHS prescriptions—the Old Bill had to ruin everything. There was no way round it, Ronnie thought: he would have to become a grass. If he refused, he could end up consigned to the back wards of a mental hospital. Maybe he would be able to string the bastards along, feed them some old moody? No, he *should* string them along, get Andrews to swallow the most ridiculous story possible, and then do a runner. Cause the maximum fucking embarrassment. He saw his Dad throwing that cheap plastic spaceman down on the bed, and telling him to spy on his Mum: stick it up your fucking arse!

'Okay. I'll do it,' Ronnie said, 'if you let me walk away from this. But I've got to get a message to this girl.'

‘Speak to the custody sergeant,’ said DC Andrews, as he closed the cell door and headed back down the corridor.

Chapter Eleven

The custody sergeant was unable to see Ronnie for several hours, and by that time they were too busy to let him out of his cell, so the phone call was never made. In the morning he appeared at Marlborough Street magistrates court and received a one-day prison sentence, as predicted. He'd been in custody overnight, so he was released immediately, to the care of an escort sent by St Benedicts hospital.

They took the Central line to Ealing Broadway, and then a bus. The escort, a gloomy ward orderly, was silent for the first fifteen minutes, and then started to talk compulsively. He was surprisingly frank about the hospital. St Benedicts had been the pauper asylum for Middlesex, he explained, an enlightened, caring establishment in 1840, pioneering the use of unlocked wards and occupational therapy. Now, it was just another over-populated, impoverished London mental hospital. Behind its dark Victorian walls, the inmates led what he described as a Spartan existence, in dormitories so crowded that beds could only be made if being shunted into the day room.

Two wards, one male and one female, had been set aside for the treatment of alcohol dependence, and here conditions were better. Ronnie was allocated a bed on Male Ward 20, in an ill-lit dormitory with a dark, well-polished, oak floor. While issuing a set of clean sheets, the charge nurse told Ronnie that Weiss, a distinguished-looking Viennese physician and Orthodox Jew, had fled Austria at the time of the Anschluss, and trained as a psychiatrist in England. He'd become the foremost British expert on alcohol dependence, and his unit had an international reputation.

Ronnie asked if he could make a phone call from the nurse's office, and took the opportunity to dial the Gerard number. There was no reply, which left him feeling rather empty.

The highlight of the day was the group meeting, in which the patients on Male Ward 20 were joined by those from Female Ward 18. Each patient told his or her life story. They were sad stories of drink-induced failure, humiliation, sickness and loss.

Today was Martin Keogh's turn. Keogh was an old Irishman who'd worked in the Print, a job that afforded him plenty of free time for drinking. He recounted a humiliating experience in which he'd gone on a three day bender, ended up in Guy's Hospital suffering from alcoholic poisoning, and missed his little girl's birthday party.

'That was when you hit rock-bottom?' asked Dr Weiss, stroking his moustache carefully with his index finger. He seemed deep in abstract thought, like Einstein considering a problem in theoretical physics.

Keogh nodded. 'It was then that I realised I was an alcoholic.'

Weiss nodded, 'An important insight.'

'I knew I was powerless to overcome my disease. I had to open my heart to a Higher Power.'

A murmur of assent went around the group. A man called Joe Calgon began to make a point, but Ronnie interrupted him, saying, 'Some of us don't believe in Higher Powers.'

No one spoke immediately. Then Joe Calgon smiled, and, in the manner of an adult explaining a complex story-line to a child, said: 'Ronald, we have all come to realise that we need a Higher Power in our lives. For me, that Power is the Lord Jesus, but everyone here has discovered the Higher Power for themselves.'

'You're talking about God?'

'We may have different ideas about what God is like, but we can all agree that there is a Higher Power.'

'Well, I'm with the Bishop of Woolwich on that one. If a bishop of the Church of England can come right out and say there is no God, who am I to disagree?'

A wizen old man called Mark McAuley, who turned out to be a former priest, gave Ronnie a venomous look. 'That is a gross distortion of the Bishop's position! He did not say there is no God!'

'All right, so it's my position. There is no God. No power higher than man. So bollocks to you!'

Weiss leaned forward. 'Language like that is unhelpful. I thought we'd agreed that. You can make your point, without being offensive.' Members of the group nodded in agreement, while Ronnie continued to look truculent.

'It is time for us to finish for today,' Weiss continued. He turned to Ronnie again. 'Perhaps you can give some more thought to your beliefs and tell us your own life story on Wednesday?'

Weiss left the day room hurriedly, already late for his next appointment, while the patients drifted out in twos and threes. As Ronnie wandered across the dining area, wondering if there was time to visit the art therapy department before lunch, a staff nurse entered the building. Behind him was a man wearing a dressing gown, walking with his head bowed, like a defeated boxer. When Ronnie saw who it was, he felt a surge of elation.

'Someone I already know,' said Jack Fitt, smiling uncertainly in Ronnie's direction.

'Jack, what's happening?' Ronnie called, as his friend waited outside the nurse's office.

'I'm the new admission,' Jack replied, with a shame-faced expression. 'I've been on de-tox, in the medical ward.'

'De-tox? But you've only been on junk for five minutes.'

'All right, that'll do,' interrupted the staff nurse, emerging from the office with a set of clean, starched bed sheets. 'Give the man a chance to settle in. He needs some peace and quiet.'

Later that evening, Ronnie popped his head around the door of the single room allocated to Jack. Shoes and socks off, his mentor lay on the bed, staring down at his naked feet, which were stretched out on the counterpane, like two slabs of dead white flesh.

'Am I glad to see you, Jack,' Ronnie said, hoping that Jack would react with his customary verve. 'I'll get some intelligent conversation again. Just wait till you hear some of the crap they talk here. It's all about God and Higher Powers. They reckon you have to give up your freedom and stop managing your own life.'

Jack nodded in a listless fashion. 'Man can only develop his individuality as a free being,' he said, in a hollow voice, as though repeating a verse learned by rote.

'We'll give them hell, eh Jack?' said Ronnie, relishing the prospect. 'Stand up for freedom! Smash the Church, smash the State!'

Jack flopped around on the bed. He was like a dying fish, left behind when the tide went out. Ronnie was about to leave when Jack said, 'I feel like I'm running out of options in life. There's no work for me in London, in the music business. Nothing regular. I can't pay my rent. I'm going to have to return to Swindon.'

'But you told me you were going to see Tubby Hayes.'

'He wasn't looking for anyone. And there's no more sessions work. I'm going to have to return to Swindon, but I don't know what I'll do there. I should never have resigned from the Post Office.'

Jack seemed to be talking himself into a low state of mind. Every statement he uttered took him one rung further down a ladder, at the bottom of which lurked a darkening abyss. Ronnie tried to reassure him, without success.

'You're coming off junk, Jack. It's bringing you down. You'll feel better, bye and bye.'

'I'm running out of options. It's like I've been funnelled into a cul-de-sac. I've reached a dead end in life.'

Ronnie was nonplussed. He'd never seen Jack in such a bleak mood. He left for the nurses' office, to see if he could phone Elara. This time he was in luck; he heard her husky voice on the other end of the line. His heart raced.

'Elara? Hi! It's Ronnie. Sorry about the other night—'

'Ronnie Fizz? Sorry, I've got a punter with me at the moment. Can't speak.'

There was a click as the receiver was replaced; she'd hung up. He was thrown into despair. Perhaps he'd just called at a bad time? But she'd sounded rather off-hand. Was she mad at him because of his disappearance? How could he explain if she wouldn't speak to him? She had to give him a chance. Perhaps he should write to her? Without further delay, he went to the nurse's office and requested a sheet of writing paper. Before lights-out, he'd written and posted a long letter, aimed at justifying himself.

When the group meeting commenced on Wednesday, Ronnie introduced himself in the customary way by saying, 'My name is Ronnie,' but he refused to repeat the formula 'and I am a drug addict.' Calgon and McAuley exchanged meaningful glances, signifying that this was an unpromising beginning.

There was a brief interruption as Jack Fitt hurried into the meeting room, a few minutes late, and looking the worse for wear. Ronnie felt encouraged when Jack took a vacant chair to his right. They could back each other up. Ronnie was aware of some hostility towards him in the room, possibly stoked up by Calgon, who seemed to be a militant Twelve Steps supporter.

Speaking without notes, Ronnie recounted the events since his arrest, focusing on the way he'd been treated in prison and hospital. He gave a detailed account of what he described as the abusive and degrading treatment of patients on the back wards of Roundway Hospital. Eventually, after looking around the group to see if anyone else was prepared to intervene, Joe Calgon spoke.

'Ronald, can you not see that your negative experiences in the Wiltshire mental hospital were the consequence of your drug-taking? That was why you had to be placed on a locked ward.'

'Why is it always my fault? It wasn't me that was ill-treating the patients, it was the bloody psychiatric nurses. They're a bunch of reprobates. That's why patients always get worse when they're sent to the nuthouse; it's no mystery!'

The charge nurse shifted in his seat and looked intensely irritated. 'Your perceptions were distorted by drug-taking.'

'Bollocks. They were not.'

'That's unhelpful,' said Weiss. 'I think we should move on to the rest of your life story. Could you start from the beginning, please? You've only talked about the last year, so far.'

Ronnie resumed his tale with his earliest memories of conflict between his parents, and of his father's violence, and the impact on those around him. His voice began to quiver, as if he was going to sob. The strength of feeling surprised him; it was hard to talk of his childhood without feeling overwhelmed, now that he was off heroin. It was as if he'd become much younger and more vulnerable overnight, and needed junk as a protective skin.

This time it was McAuley who intervened. 'Violence in the family is just an excuse. It's a way for you to avoid facing up to the disease of drug addiction, and the consequences of your own behaviour.'

'I don't agree! My father destroyed my mother's life. For years I was haunted by the threat of his arrival on the doorstep.'

He remembered how, when he was a child, every problem had been his own fault, even when he was bitten by his uncle Bert's Alsatian. His father had been so embarrassed, he'd apologised to Bert. Four years old, standing there with his cheek ripped open, and his father was apologising.

'My dog never bites,' said uncle Bert, despite the evidence to the contrary.

'He tried to stick his hand down the dog's throat,' his father said. 'Hasn't got the sense he was born with.'

'Do you want to take him down the hospital, or what?'

'There's no need for any fuss,' his father said. 'It's not the dog's fault.'

He pushed himself back in his chair, wanting to put as much distance between McAuley and himself as possible. The man was a poisonous toad. He debated whether he should spring to his feet and rush from the room.

'You see, you need to stop blaming everyone else in your life for your predicament,' said McAuley. 'Everyone and everything except your addiction. We've all been there.'

'I don't see it that way!' Ronnie said, his voice rising in anger.

'I think we all know that, by now. What you do and do not see!' McAuley's temper was also rising. 'You don't see it because you have trouble facing uncomfortable truths! You're in denial!'

'Jack, do you have anything you'd like to add?' asked the charge nurse. 'As someone who knew Ronald outside?'

All heads turned to Jack Fitt, who had yet to speak in the meeting.

'Well now, I've known this young man for quite a long time. I knew him before he became addicted to heroin, and I saw what it did to him. I have no doubt that he's in massive denial.'

A satisfied murmur went around the group. The charge nurse encouraged Dolly, one of the female patients, to speak next.

'I was a lot like you when I first came here,' she said to Ronnie, with the intensity of an evangelist at a revival meeting. 'I denied that I had any problems with alcohol. I thought my life was fine. Every party in my street, I wanted to join. Every chance of a drink, I wanted to take. But with the help of this group, and of Dr Weiss, I came to see how alcohol had ruined my life. Now I'm on the road to sobriety. I'm a recovering person, and I've found happiness at last.'

'It's not possible to have a proper debate with you lot, is it?' Ronnie sighed. 'If I don't agree with you, it's because there's something wrong with me. It's a load of bollocks.' He turned to Jack Fitt, his voice rising in anger again, 'And I'm surprised at you, Jack! Surprised you can't see the way it works. It's a way of controlling people!'

'I would not be a good friend to you if I supported you in these misperceptions,' Jack said, shaking his head sadly, and staring down at the carpet.

'Thank you for that,' said the charge nurse, smiling at Jack.

After the meeting, Ronnie went to lie on his bed in the dormitory. He practised throwing cigarettes at a spot on the wall, as though they were darts hitting a bull's-eye. When one of the cigarettes broke, he switched to flicking matches. Apart from Elara's morphine, he'd not had a fix for several weeks. He was free of physical dependence, but now he longed to shoot up. One fix, and then none of the buggers could bring him down.

'I hope you didn't feel got at, in there?' Joe Calgon was standing at the foot of his bed, smiling. 'Everyone here is very honest about what they feel. It's our way of combating all the dishonesty and self-deception involved in alcoholism.'

'I was being honest about what I feel. About all that religious crap.'

'We're not saying you have to be religious. I'm not religious, but I can still follow the Twelve Steps. You don't have to believe in God to take part in Alcoholics Anonymous. There are atheists and agnostics in AA.' Calgon produced a pamphlet out of his jacket pocket. 'This tells you what AA stands for. The Twelve Steps are on the back. To begin, you have to acknowledge—'

'What's this?

> Step Five. Admitted to God, to ourselves, and to another human being the exact nature of our wrongs.'

'It means we have to make a moral inventory, and—'

'Yes, but it says *God.* There. Quite clearly. You're saying it's not about *God.* Three of these Steps mention God, quite specifically. Look at this: Step Eleven.

> Sought through prayer and meditation to improve our contact with God, praying only for knowledge of His will for us, and the power to carry that out.

'That reads like the bloody catechism to me.'

He tossed the pamphlet back towards Calgon, but it landed on the floor. Calgon looked affronted, as if he'd witnessed an act of desecration. He retrieved the pamphlet and walked away, saying stiffly, 'I suspect you're too immature to benefit from rehab.'

Ronnie resumed targeting the spot on the wall. Martin Keogh had witnessed the conversation, and now came over and sat on the next bed. Keogh slapped his thigh as if he'd been told a good joke, and offered Ronnie a cigarette.

'You upset Mr Calgon there. He takes himself very seriously, Mr Calgon.'

'The worst type of person always does.'

'It all seems a bit strange?' Keogh said, with a merry twinkle in his eye. 'This talk of *Higher Power* and *recovering people* and being *in denial*?'

'Don't try and talk me round! You may believe it, but it's a load of old crap!'

Keogh looked discomfited. 'Some of us take the line of least resistance,' he said. 'We may appear to believe everything, but we keep our own counsel. Go through the motions. Don't make a fuss, don't stand out in the crowd, and get an early discharge. Get back to what you enjoy doing best. This is just a few weeks out of my life, that's my philosophy.'

'To be honest, it's like wandering into a strange church service,' Ronnie said. 'Like those freaks who handle snakes, in the American South.'

'You're not far wrong there,' Keogh chuckled. 'Some of them are freaks all right.'

Ronnie lay back on the bed and took a deep drag on the cigarette he'd been given, gathering strength to raise a topic that was troubling him. 'Martin, you've talked to Jack Fitt, the new admission? I've always wondered about his part in the Easter Uprising. Was he really one of the leaders, alongside Patrick Pearse?'

Jack had been on Ronnie's mind all morning, because of what he saw as an act of betrayal: Jack siding with the establishment, and adopting the language of oppression. His willingness to believe in Jack, to respect him as a heroic, larger-than-life figure, was being eroded. He needed to see Jack as a great revolutionary, as much as Jack needed to portray himself in that light. Now, he felt his trust had been abused; worse, people like the Sandman were regarding Ronnie and Jack as two of a kind, both lacking in integrity, both bullshit artists.

'Well now, I'm sure Mr Fitt would have been on the barricades, if he'd been old enough,' Keogh said. 'Right up there with the great men who fell. But I'm afraid he was a babe in arms at the time.'

Ronnie sat bolt upright on the bed. His sense of unease was growing by the minute. 'Are you sure? He escaped, didn't he, dressed in a bridal gown?'

'Well, he's fifty now, so that makes him about two-years-old in 1916, by my reckoning. Not that I'm the greatest mathematician, you understand, not by a long shot. But I make it two-years-old.'

'So why would he make it up?' Ronnie's body sagged, like a punctured balloon.

Martin Keogh shrugged; a slow, eloquent gesture which acknowledged all the mysteries of life which lay beyond man's understanding. 'He's a Dublin jackeen. His life story is an art form, a story made to be sung above the glass. It's not meant to be taken seriously.'

'Do you mean it's said for effect, and then forgotten?'

'It's gone with the morning light,' said Keogh, waving his hand, to signify mist being dispersed by the rising sun.

The charge nurse marched briskly through the dormitory, his heels clicking loudly on the wooden floor. He carried several starched, clean bedsheets in front of his chest, like a guardsman bearing a folded flag at a military funeral, after its removal from the coffin. Ronnie waited until he had gone before asking, 'So will Jack's conversion to the Twelve Steps be equally short-lived?'

'Well, that I wouldn't know. But I think most of the life histories we've heard here are stories. They're not like drinker's stories—they're said for a different kind of effect—but they're stories.'

Ronnie gave an exasperated sigh. He was surrounded by people who were incapable of living with the truth, who preferred romantic fiction to hard facts. Even Keogh seemed ambivalent about the truth. 'Martin,' he said, 'do you buy all this Twelve Steps stuff?'

Keogh looked around the dormitory, to check that there was no one within earshot. 'Put it this way, sometimes you're not doing people any favours by exposing falsehood. What they call the Twelve Steps are not doing them any harm, in fact they may be saving life, in one or two cases. So does it matter whether it's true?'

'But do you accept all that stuff they were on about in the meeting, about giving up freedom, giving up any attempt to manage your own life? You're a Catholic, aren't you, Martin? Is that what the Catholic Church teaches?'

'As a lapsed Catholic, I'm not the best person to ask about the Church.'

'But do Catholics believe in the Twelve Steps?'

'It's not actually against the teaching of the Church. But Alcoholics Anonymous has never really taken root in any Catholic countries, apart from Ireland. It's a Protestant thing. It was born out of the Protestant Mid-west of America.'

Ronnie looked blank.

'You see, AA's an adaptation of the teachings of the Oxford Movement,' Keogh said, lowering his voice as if imparting secret information. 'The founders of AA were members of the Oxford Movement.'

'What's that when it's at home?'

'It was a kind of cult that was popular before the war. They argued that if dictators like Herr Hitler could be converted to the true religion, they would become a force for good. The Reich would become the dictatorship of God. The Almighty would use Hitler to realize his plan for mankind. Hitler would be a bulwark against Bolshevism, that sort of thing. After the war, it was renamed Moral Rearmament. Anyway, all this emphasis on group discussion and confession and repentance comes from the Oxford Movement.'

'A bit like the snake handlers' cult, then?'

'So it is,' Keogh laughed. 'But don't go round here saying that, if you want to live to a ripe old age!'

'So how did it become so influential?'

'It's the power of film.'

'Film? Why?'

'From the 1930s onwards, all the big Hollywood studios had AA advisors on the set, every time they made a film about drinking problems, to make sure that they got the story right. That they showed problem drinking to be the result of a disease, called *alcohol-ism*. To make sure the studios showed Alcoholics Anonymous as the cure.'

'I've seen some of those films: *Lost Weekend*, *Days of Wine and Roses*?'

'Hollywood made hundreds of films about drink; some of the biggest films of their day. That's how AA got their ideas publicised. As a result, the man in the street is familiar with the concept of alcoholism. And everyone has heard that abstinence, through AA, is the only salvation. It's a powerful thing, film. It's resulted in hundreds of alcoholism clinics, all over America, all promoting the Twelve Steps. It's a million dollar industry. You wouldn't want to get on the wrong side of them.'

There was something about Keogh's air of quiet reflection, of wisdom tinged with melancholy, that made Ronnie want to trust him. He said, 'Martin, I think I may come off junk this time. Because I've met this girl, and I think we've got something special. Well, we could have.' He stopped, aware that he needed to speak to Elara again, to know whether there was any reality to his dream.

'You wouldn't be the first young man to achieve sobriety by that route. *Some woman's yellow hair has maddened every mother's son.*'

'I can give up fixing. But I have to do it my own way, Martin. I'm not going to be dishonest and reject everything I've ever believed in. I'm not going to give up the battle for freedom, like Jack Fitt.'

'Well, do you mind if I give you a little bit of advice? You'll have an easier time here if you just keep your head down. Don't take them all on. Let them think you're considering it all, that you might be converted.'

Ronnie couldn't bear to fake a conversion to the Twelve Steps. Was this was the only way to get an early discharge? Before he could ask Keogh, he noticed the charge nurse heading back to his office. On impulse, he raced over, to ask if he could make a quick phone call. He dialled Elara's number. He couldn't wait for her to get his letter, and then endure a further delay while she wrote back.

'Hi Elara?' he said brightly, when her voice came on the line.

'Fuck off, right?' Again, the receiver slammed down.

He could not believe her response. He'd had such a good understanding with her, it couldn't just end like this. If only he could see her again, he would be able to explain, he would make it all right. He went to sleep that night determined to leave St Benedicts.

The next morning's group saw Joe Calgon telling everyone about a low period in his life, when he'd been drinking more than a bottle of vodka a day, and had beaten his wife so badly that she'd been hospitalised, with a compound fracture to her skull. Calgon had made amends to her, when he became abstinent, although by then they were divorced.

Ronnie said, 'You vicious bastard!'

'We are not judgmental here,' said Weiss, sternly.

'I beg your pardon?' said Calgon, addressing himself to Ronnie. 'I thought I'd just explained that this violence was the result of drinking. I had a disease. Alcoholism robs you of your free will. But I was able to make restitution to my ex-wife, when I became a recovering person.'

'You say that; my father was violent whether he was drinking or not.' Ronnie said. 'What do you think, Jack? Nothing excuses violence to women, does it?'

Jack Fitt had been gazing at the floor, without participating in the discussion. Now he frowned, as if considering the question for the first time. 'Well now, from what I've heard, alcoholics are not themselves when they do these things,' he said. 'You see, the disease of alcoholism is what you might call the primary problem. Deal with that and you deal with the violence.'

'That's very clear,' said Weiss.

'Exactly,' said the charge nurse, nodding in approval.

Ronnie was incredulous. Jack seemed to have abandoned a position on violence that he'd held for as long as they'd been friends. Before he could comment, a frail little woman called Maisie spoke up.

'Well, my husband was violent to me, and there's nothing he could do now that would make amends. I agree with this young man; nothing excuses it.'

'We're talking about the way alcoholism destroys relationships here,' frowned the charge nurse.

Another woman joined in. 'Drink doesn't cause people to be violent. However drunk my man was, he knew the times he could get away with thumping me, and the times he couldn't. And he knew how to hit me without leaving marks. He wasn't out of control. He was a cunning bastard.'

'The fact remains that alcohol is the primary problem,' insisted the charge nurse. 'Achieve sobriety and the violence will stop.'

'My husband was still violent to me when he was in recovery,' Maisie persisted.

'Then he wasn't working through the Twelve Steps properly!' snapped the charge nurse.

Dr Weiss intervened at this point. 'I'm afraid that is all we have time for, today. But I would like to ask you all not to lose sight of the fact that alcohol is central to your problems—or heroin, in the case of the two drug addicts. Thank you.'

The morning arrived when Jack Fitt was due to deliver his life story to the group. Ronnie wondered whether Jack would be able to get through the session without indulging in romance. Jack surprised him, however. He began by saying his name was Jack, and that he was a drug addict. He'd been born in Dublin, the youngest of seven children, and had gone to a Christian Brothers' school. When he was thirteen, his parents had moved to Hitchen, in Hertfordshire, where he joined the sea cadets, and learned to play the cornet. On leaving school at fifteen, he signed up for the merchant navy, and travelled all over North and South America, and the Caribbean. He'd seen many great jazz musicians while on shore leave, which gave him a great love for swing and be-bop, and this had inspired him to practise the trumpet. He left the merchant navy, started to get sessions work in London, and eventually secured a job with a dance band. He'd tried heroin while a sessions musician, but hadn't developed a problem until recently, when he'd attempted to get back into the music business, after working as a postman for many years.

Jack added that he knew now that he would be an addict for the rest of his life, and the only hope for him was abstinence. The Twelve Steps had saved his life; he would've killed himself if there had been no alternative to the miserable life he was leading. And he wanted everyone to know what a relief it was to tell the truth about his life, without embellishment. He was sick of the lies, deceit and confabulation to which addiction had reduced him. He felt he had been reborn as an honest man.

Ronnie knew that Jack's history as a teller of fabulous tales preceded his brief period of heroin addiction. And while he could appreciate the brave step Jack had taken, in telling a less than glamorous story about himself, he could not believe that he was being honest about his conversion to the Twelve Steps. After the meeting, he cornered Jack.

'Jack, you seem to have turned your back on everything you ever believed. What the hell's wrong with you?'

'We're never free of illusion in a Floating World,' Jack said, smiling vaguely.

'What the fuck's that supposed to mean? You were wrong about anarchism and atheism and everything? What?'

'It means I've done an honest assessment of my life, and I can see how misguided I've been.'

'How can you say you're being honest, Jack? You know all that Twelve Steps stuff is so much bollocks. How can you be honest if you're basing your life on a lie?'

Jack looked perplexed. 'I built my life on foundations of sand,' he said. 'Now I've discovered a rock.'

'Jack, this goes against everything you've ever believed. How can you describe that load of dishonest mumbo-jumbo as a rock?'

'I've begun the process of recovery. I wish I could say the same for you. You'll never be free of drugs unless you change. Open your heart to our Saviour, Jesus Christ.'

Ronnie was speechless. Within days, Jack seemed to have abandoned his humanist convictions, and embraced the Twelve Steps. He was not the strong character that Ronnie had assumed. He was casting around for security, and found it in the approval and support of the group.

'I've got a visitor for you,' the charge nurse called out later that evening, as Ronnie joined several bored-looking patients in the television room, to watch *Juke Box Jury*. 'In the sun lounge.'

'For me?' Ronnie said. 'Who's that?'

The charge nurse had already moved on, and didn't hear. Ronnie made his way to the sun lounge, wondering whether Elara had managed to visit. The lights were off. Pushing the door open with his fingertips, he saw the back view of a dark, brooding figure, gazing through the French Windows at the setting sun.

'What are you doing here?' Ronnie said. 'Who asked you to come?'

'How are you, son? How they been treating you?'

'I haven't got anything to say to you. You made my mother's life a misery.'

'I still care about what happens to you, Ronnie. You're my son. I want to see you fit and well again.'

'You tormented my mother.'

Freddy turned to face him, and moved to within striking distance. He'd put on weight since Ronnie had seen him last, and now had pronounced jowls, and thinning hair. His suit was expensive, well tailored, and without a crease out of place; he looked like a successful businessman, or perhaps a bailiff.

'Don't you think she drove me to it?' Freddy said. 'All that lying and deceit? Carrying on with other men? It was like a knife going in, every time I realised how much she'd lied.'

Freddy started to say something, but Ronnie talked over him: 'The only reason she lied was to protect herself from you. You were always drunk, always unreasonable, always liable to fly off the handle—'

'Listen!' his father said, raising his voice, '*Listen!* What do you know? What do you think it does to you, risking your life every day? Do you know how many commendations I've received? For bravery? It all comes at a cost! That's why coppers drink. It's the price we bloody pay!'

The sun lounge was a long, narrow room, like a wide corridor, with windows ranged along one side. The armchairs, arranged in two long rows, faced each other. Ronnie sat down, in a chair that looked towards the windows. It felt less confrontational than standing. He was scared his father might slap him, but his reply was anything but placatory: 'You found a job that would put up with your boozing. That's the only reason you're not in a place like this.'

Freddy's face darkened, and for a moment it looked as if he was on the verge of hitting out. Then he lowered his voice and spoke in a controlled, menacing tone that Ronnie could remember from childhood. 'What do you know? I sacrificed my personal life for the job. That's the reality. I served the community. Put away the thieves, the murderers, while people like you sat around on their backsides. You've never done a day's work in your life.'

'Hallelujah, I'm a bum!'

It was now nearly dark in the unlit room, but he could see that Freddy's face was the colour of a ripe plum. In case his father hadn't got the message, he added, 'I'm proud of never soiling my hands with work.'

Freddy stared at him for several seconds, before replying. 'I can see that! If I had my way, you'd all be conscripted. The army would sort you out: you and all the Teddy Boys, the Beatniks, the spivs. God help this nation if the Russians ever invade! Your generation wouldn't hold out for two minutes. No backbone! A nation has to stay fighting fit if it's going to survive. Keep up its standards.'

'What do you call keeping up standards? Hanging and flogging?'

'Moral standards! You wouldn't know anything about them.'

'I know it's all changing. Ding-dong! Wake up, the war's over! The future doesn't belong to people like you. It's unbuttoned; it's a big fat spliff and shagging in the afternoon. A speedball at the cocktail hour.'

Along the icy path in front of the French Windows, three patients struggled to tow a heavy trailer loaded with dustbins. The work party wore big, unlaced boots and shabby, over-sized greatcoats. Freddy contemplated their progress in the fading light. 'What are they, spastics?' he asked. 'Imbeciles or something?'

'They're mental defectives,' Ronnie said. 'They do a lot of the work here.'

'Should've been strangled at birth!' His father spat the words out.

'That,' Ronnie said, with an air of resignation, 'is what the Nazis did. Killed them at birth.'

'Not everything the Nazis did was wrong,' his father replied.

Ronnie leaned back and looked at the ceiling. 'You know, you sound more and more like a fascist.'

'Fascism's just love of your country. A lot of coppers supported the Blackshirts before the war. You've got to remember the Jews were very interbred …'

Ronnie experienced a wave of revulsion, an awareness that he had nothing in common with his father whatsoever. He felt immense sadness. They were not just strangers; that was bad enough. They were enemies. His father stood for everything he hated. He avoided looking at him directly, addressing the corner of the room. 'You'd better not say that in front of my psychiatrist. He had to escape from Nazi Germany.'

Freddy snorted. There was silence for a few moments, while they regarded each other with bitterness. Freddy spoke first: 'You had no reason to turn to drugs. No reason, except idleness. And the chance of shaming me. I've done some bad things in my time, but I never stooped to taking heroin.'

'It's just a habit. You smoke cigarettes don't you? What's the difference?'

'Moral degradation.' Freddy pronounced the words clearly and with emphasis, as though standing in the pulpit and announcing the theme of a sermon. His father always spoke with great authority on matters of morality.

'You're chained to fags, and for much less reward than I get from Horse,' Ronnie said. 'So why make all this moralistic fuss about heroin, when you're happy about them promoting tobacco? I'll tell you what, tobacco kills more of its users than heroin does. Any day of the week.'

'I make a moralistic fuss because heroin turns people into mindless zombies, like you.' Freddy's smile looked more like a snarl. He moved away from the window and allowed his body to drop heavily into a leather armchair opposite, producing the sound of a loud slap. Then, as he faced his son, his expression softened. 'Let's start again. I want you to give this unit a chance, son. Get off drugs. Rebuild your life. I'm your Dad, for Christ's sake. I love you.'

'You know what you can do, don't you?'

There was a minute's silence, and then Freddy sighed, 'You're your own worst enemy, you know that? But I haven't come all the way out here to argue the toss with you. I've come to tell you what you're going to do. How the future's going to be. You see, now that I've been promoted to Commander, I'm in line for one of the top jobs, and I mean top. I don't want silly rumours flying around the police canteen about me having a criminal son. They had you in Devizes and they were doing their best to help you, but you did a runner. I heard all about it. I even had the Sweeny out looking for you. So now you're going to stay here, until you've stopped wanting to take drugs. You'll do everything they tell you, no ifs and no buts. I know they've got you on Section 60, and if I hear that you're out on the street again, I'll make sure you're picked up and taken to a place where you can't commit any more mischief. For your own good. Do I make myself clear?'

Ronnie grunted. 'Visiting time ended ten minutes ago.'

'Do I make myself clear?'

'Sure. Can you see yourself out?'

After his father left, Ronnie paced around the sun lounge, unable to sleep. He remembered the times when his father turned up at the school gates, or on the doorstep, and the old feeling of dread returned. He had to move on. The ultimatum issued by his father made him determined to leave St Benedicts as soon as possible. He had to be *free*. And he had to find Elara, and get her to see sense. He knew Weiss was unlikely to agree an early discharge, when he'd been so critical of the treatment programme, but there was one possibility. Perhaps Andrews would have some influence with the hospital? What if he could persuade Andrews that he should be released, because some big job was coming off? It might all go wrong if his father heard, but it was worth a try.

The next day, he asked the charge nurse if he could make one more local call. He got the number of West End Central from directory enquiries, and asked for DC Andrews. To his surprise, Andrews came on the line almost immediately.

'I'm a bit busy right now. Is it anything that can wait?'

Ronnie had heard of a big deal coming off; lot of heroin coming into the country. He wondered whether Andrews could arrange for him to leave hospital a little bit early; he could be in position, relaying information.

'I'll speak to Weiss and see if he'll discharge you next Monday,' Andrews said. 'From what I hear, he won't be sorry to see the back of you. Seems like you're not very well-motivated?' Andrews made every question sound like an accusation.

‘It’s just that I don’t see eye-to-eye with the older alcoholics here,’ Ronnie said. ‘It’s a generation-gap-thing. Lushes don’t have anything in common with junkies. Otherwise, everything’s fine. I’ve learnt a lot.’

‘Well, you need to find the motivation to leave drugs alone, and do what I tell you. Then everything will be hunky-dory. And if you don’t, you’ll understand what deep pain I can inflict on you. I’ll make you wish you’d never been born.’

Chapter Twelve

It was a fresh spring morning when DC Andrews picked up his potential informant at the hospital gates. They looked ill-matched. Andrews was wearing a new Italian suit, a white shirt with a cut-away collar, and a knitted tie, fastened carefully with a Windsor knot. Ronnie had on his old combat jacket and jeans. His hair was beginning to grow out, and flopped over his forehead in a Beatles fringe.

They drove to Old Compton Street, in London's Soho, and Andrews spent the time lecturing Ronnie about his responsibilities towards the person who had secured his release.

'Think of it as like being on parole,' Andrews said, while they were waiting at traffic lights. 'You're out for as long as you behave yourself. If you fuck up, I'll send you back. To St Benedicts, or to somewhere more secure—and you know what that means. So all you've got to do is be a good boy, behave yourself, and supply me with the information I need.' Andrews smiled menacingly. 'Let me tell you about the sort of copper I am, so there's no misunderstanding between us. I always uphold the law. I will not bend the rules for anyone, especially for a slime-bag like you.'

Andrews paused, as if something had just occurred to him. 'Jarvis … Jarvis? Have you got any relatives in the Force?'

Ronnie shook his head in a determined fashion. 'No.'

'Uncle, anything like that?'

'Nope.'

'I know a Jarvis at the Yard.'

'You've got a low opinion of him, then, if you think he's related to a slime-bag?'

They rang the doorbell to the Medusa club, and followed the doorman up steep stairs to a long, narrow bar. The manager was leaning on the counter, two hands cradling an early morning Scotch, which he called an 'eye-opener'. His eyes looked as if they needed assistance to stay open. They were bleary and unfocused.

'Monty?' said Andrews. 'The young man I was telling you about.'

Monty looked dubiously at the boy's scruffy appearance. 'I know I agreed to offer this boy a job, John, but he looks like a liability.' He slid a bunch of keys along the bar towards the bouncer, asked him to fetch some more soda water from the cellar, and knocked back the Scotch. 'You ever done this work before, young man?'

Ronnie decided Monty was Jewish, and thought he knew how to reassure him. 'I used to wash-up for a firm doing weddings and barmitzvahs. I understand about keeping everything kosher. Two sinks and that. The milk and the meat.'

'Kosher?' Monty sounded irritated. 'What do you think this is, the Jewish Ex-Serviceman's Club? I'm the rabbi round here: you don't need to worry about kosher. Just keep yourself clean and tidy. Here!' He threw two five pound notes on the counter. 'Get yourself some decent clothes. A white shirt and some black trousers. You can start tonight. I want you here at six every evening. You knock off whenever we finish, usually about 4 a.m. I'll give you a couple of quid a night. If you don't show, you don't get paid. Two no-shows and you're out … John, do you want a drink?'

Andrews stood up, and motioned with his head for Ronnie to follow. 'No, I've got to work. Thanks all the same, Monty. Are you well?'

'Do I look bleeding well? I've got an abscess under my front tooth. I've got an ulcer. I'm not supposed to drink. It's only the bleeding drink that keeps me going!'

They moved towards the stairs, and Andrews called over his shoulder. 'Don't worry, Monty. You'll still be going strong when I'm in my box.'

'That may not be so difficult,' Monty called after him. 'I wouldn't like to say what your life expectancy is.'

As they stepped into the street, Andrews grabbed Ronnie's lapel, and pulled him up against a shop front. 'Remember, if you do what I tell you, you'll be okay. If you don't, you'll find I can be utterly ruthless. I shall steel myself to be utterly ruthless, remorseless and implacable. If you try to give me the slip, I'll root you out. There is only one thing I care about, and that's cleaning up this city, turning back this tide of filth. And I should warn you, I will succeed. I have the best record of any copper at West End Central. I get results. And if someone like you gets in the way, they can expect to suffer.'

Andrews stood with his jaw thrust forward, glaring at the first prostitutes and touts to venture forth in the thin morning light. Ronnie decided that the man must be some kind of puritan. A Roundhead from Warwickshire. Surrounded by the denizens of Soho, Andrews burned with zeal. His sense of conviction would not have been out of place in one of Cromwell's more militant supporters.

Leaving the detective constable on the corner of Old Compton Street, Ronnie hurried over to Elara's flat, determined to try to put things right. He bumped into her before he'd gone a hundred yards; she was coming down Brewer Street carrying a bag of groceries. She wore false eyelashes, and her hair was swept back in a French Pleat, with a few strands of blue-black hair hanging down to frame her face. Ronnie felt overwhelmed by her beauty and grace.

'Are we still friends?' she called out. 'Sorry I was a bit short with you the other night.' She covered her mouth with her hand, as if in apology for something she had said. 'Thanks for your letter. It made me laugh.'

'Well, you know what fun we have in the nuthouse,' Ronnie said dryly. 'It's a laugh a minute.'

'What're you doing out? I was coming to see you tonight!'

'I'm out,' he said. 'It's a long story. The Old Bill have me over a barrel. They got me out of hospital, and they've given me a job in a club, but they want the earth in return. Am I pleased to see you, Elara.'

They kissed. He settled in for a long embrace, but she broke off to say, 'What do you mean, they want the earth?'

'They think I'm going to shop all the dealers in London. Get inside information.'

'Are you mad?'

'They think I'm going to tell them who's behind the importation of heroin. Who's responsible for the increase in heroin addiction. There isn't anyone, of course. The only black market is whatever junkies can spare from their prescriptions, but they believe there's a Mr Big.'

'Are you mad? If people even think you're a grass, you'll get done!'

'But I'm not a grass. I'm just spinning them a yarn. No one's going to get put in the frame by me. I'm just using the Old Bill to get what I want.'

'Sometimes your brain goes on holiday! Hello, is there anybody there?' She tapped his forehead. 'Come back to my flat. I need to give you a good seeing-to.'

Returning to the flat in Berwick Street, they spent the rest of the afternoon in bed. Elara argued that he'd got himself into a tight corner and needed rescuing, but Ronnie said she was over-reacting. He had Andrews sussed out.

At five, Ronnie popped out to Oxford Street and bought a shirt and a pair of trousers, and at six he presented himself at his place of employment. The Medusa was a drinking club popular with villains. The Mejlak brothers often drank there, as did Slim Wallace and, on occasions, Albert Dimes. Ronnie's duties included washing up and clearing tables, and keeping the bar supplied with bottled beers and soft drinks.

The barman briefed Ronnie about the clientele. 'That's Frank Scalesi over there: Italian Frank. See the big bloke standing next to him? Tommy Bolt. Well, you've heard of the towpath murders? Tommy chopped the bodies up, and Italian Frank tipped all the bits into sacks, and put them in the canal. And you see that geezer at the end? Nick Barratt. Don't upset him. He took the top off someone's head with a shotgun, just for looking at him funny.'

If the club wasn't busy, the barman would ask Ronnie to sit behind the bar for short periods, while he had a break. In this way, Ronnie got to chat to some of the regulars, like Slim Wallace. Ronnie didn't bother seeking information on heroin dealing; he knew there was no large-scale trafficking. The only problem was Andrews, expecting him to come up with names, dates and times.

A few weeks went by, with Andrews contacting him every few days. Ronnie found it difficult to fob him off, so he started avoiding him. Eventually, Andrews was waiting for him when he arrived at work.

'Right, no more messing about, sunshine. What've you got for us?'

'There's going to be a shipment.'

'Yes?'

'A shipment of heroin. That's what you want to know, ain't it?'

'Well, I could've worked that much out for myself. Now, how much? Where and when? Who's involved? Stop pissing us about, or you're going to end up banged away in the Loony Bin, which is where you belong!'

'It's …' Ronnie paused to take a deep breath. 'It's going to be delivered to the Uranus bookshop, in Lisle Street.' Uranüs was the only shop name that Ronnie could remember, and that was because he'd assumed it specialised in astrology, until he'd looked in the window. 'At about one in the morning, on Wednesday. Can't tell you how much. I mean, it's several thousand quid's worth.'

'At last, we're getting somewhere! Are the Mejlak brothers going to be there?'

'I'm not sure if they'll actually be there. I mean they are behind it all, as you know. There's a chance they'll be there.'

'Well? How will it get there?'

'A Bedford van. Green Bedford. It'll turn up at the Uranus, at one in the morning, next Wednesday. That's it really. It's Turkish heroin. That's it.'

'You better be on the level, sunshine, or you're going to wish you hadn't been born.'

'Be fair. I can only tell you what I hear.'

Ronnie was gambling for high stakes. He'd invented the story of the van outside Uranus Books, but he would have to move fast when his deception was discovered. He would persuade Andrews that the venue had changed—convince him that he should raid somewhere a bit more prestigious. Then, with the DC's reputation for competence dented, Ronnie would disappear for a while. Leave the dishwashing job, and stop taking his scripts to central London pharmacies.

***

Andrews obtained a search warrant on the following day, and began to assemble his team. The bookshop in Lisle Street was staked out on the

Wednesday night, with Andrews and a colleague, Chalky White, in an unmarked police car. Three other officers were hidden in a van, and two others positioned up the street. The appointed time came and went, with no sign of the drop.

'A black van's pulled in over there, John,' said Chalky. 'A Bedford. Do you think he was wrong about the colour?'

'It's got to be the one,' Andrews said. 'It's 1.40. There's nothing else in sight.'

They watched as the van driver began ferrying six large cardboard boxes, and one smaller one, across the road, into Uranus Books.

'Let's go!' said Andrews.

The van driver and shop manager looked confused as the street door was forced open, and DC White held up the warrant. Andrews opened the first of the larger boxes. It was packed with copies of a Scandinavian magazine called *Anal Delight*. The second box contained *Bum Suckers*. The remaining four large boxes contained more of the same. He ripped open the smallest box. It contained about two hundred purple hearts, hardly enough amphetamine to supply the Mods in a club like the *Flamingo* for one night.

'Book them,' said Andrews. 'It's probably amphetamine. Doesn't look like there's any heroin, but we'll keep looking.'

The next morning, when Andrews passed Detective Chief Superintendent Milbright in the corridor at West End Central, he apologised. 'Sorry about that, guvnor. There was no heroin. My snout's got some explaining to do.'

'No apologies needed, John. Forensics found the heroin. Apparently, it was hidden in the bodywork of the van.'

A smile spread slowly across Andrews' face. 'Excellent! Well, I did the young man an injustice. We've got a result.'

'Yes, we'll have them for amphetamine and heroin.'

'And the pornography. Don't forget all those dirty books. It's about time some of these Soho bookshops were closed down.'

Milbright frowned. Before Andrews could pursue the matter, Chalky White called down the corridor, 'John? Someone from the Obscene Publications Squad would like a word.'

'Obscene Publications? What do they want? I hope this isn't turning into a turf war. This is our case.'

He walked quickly to his office and saw a detective inspector from Scotland Yard looking surreptitiously at the papers on his desk. The man spun on his heel and extended a hand for him to shake.

'Hello, John Andrews? DI George Underwood, C1. I hear congratulations are in order.'

'What, for the Uranus arrests? Thanks. We've got both the Mejlak brothers in the cells downstairs. Hope you don't think we're poaching, sir. We're primarily interested in the drugs.'

DI George Underwood took a brown envelope from his coat pocket and laid it carefully on the desk in front of DC Andrews.

'A little something for your lady wife, John. On account,' he said, moving to the window and looking down on the street.

DC Andrews ripped opened the envelope. Inside, he saw several hundred pounds in used banknotes.

'I hope this doesn't mean what I think it means. I don't take bribes.'

'Bribes? Don't insult me, John! That's not a bribe. It's a donation, a whip-round from the lads. To pay any additional expenses you might incur, when you're initiated into our lodge.'

'Well, you can save yourselves some dough, because I've no intention of being initiated,' Andrews replied, handing him back the envelope. 'Into Freemasonry or anything else. My intention is to clean up this manor. And I've got a snout on the inside, so it's only a matter of time before I start pulling them all in. The drug traffickers, the pornographers, and all the other riff-raff! You can take that message back to your boss.'

'Don't take that tone with me, John. We're all interested in cleaning things up. We're all good coppers, doing our best to pull them in.'

***

At 3.15 that afternoon, Commander Freddy Jarvis received a phone call from two business associates, requesting an urgent meeting at the Capers Club in Mayfair. Frank Scalesi and Benny Mejlak were sat in a dimly lit corner, as far away as possible from the stage, a makeshift construction that had once been part of a boxing ring in a boy's club. Several would-be strippers were about to be auditioned onstage.

'What's the panic?' Freddy said, moving a chair so that it wasn't in such close proximity to the two seated men, and perching on it with his hands still thrust into his overcoat pockets.

'This drugs raid. We want all charges dropped,' Scalesi said, waving to the barman to bring Freddy his usual Scotch.

'Sorry, Frank. No can do,' Freddy said. 'This is politics. You'll have to bite the bullet on this one.'

Benny Mejlak's face flushed with indignation. 'It's a fucking liberty, Freddy!' His Maltese accent was more pronounced than usual. 'They're going to prosecute Uranus Books for porn! What are we fucking paying George Underwood for?'

'What do you want, a refund?' said Freddy, downing his drink, and pushing the glass towards Scalesi for a refill. 'Don't make out you're hard done by, Benny. I hear you've just bought yourself a flaming yacht.'

The stage curtain billowed out into the room, and a young woman wearing stilettos, fishnet stockings and a large feather boa made her entrance. There was a loud blast of music, as one of the staff put Dean Martin's *Return to Me* on the record player, and joined in the chorus, '… Cara mia ti amo …' The dancer tripped on a loose board and fell backwards, pulling the stage curtain down with her. Scalesi rose from his seat and waved his hands dismissively, shooing away the unsuccessful candidate. He drew a heavy finger across his throat, for the sound to be turned off. It was turned down, until it was barely audible.

Turning back to the table, Scalesi sighed with exasperation. 'Freddy, we can't do business on this basis! George Underwood's had five grand to sort this, and now we hear there's nothing doing!' He slumped back into his seat, muttering, 'Fucking sue him for non-compliance! We had a contract!' Taking out a biro, Scalesi began to doodle on the back of a cigarette packet, a five petalled daisy that grew darker and darker as he went over the outline again and again.

'Get me another bloody drink!' Freddy said, irritated that he'd had to ask. 'You needn't worry about the porn charges. They'll disappear. But you have to let your driver put his hands up to this drugs thing. You look after him while he's inside, and we'll make it up to you.'

'And what about this DC Andrews?' Scalesi said. He waved to the barman, and made a circular motion with his hand to indicate drinks all round. 'Underwood was supposed to straighten him. Now we hear that Andrews won't take a bung. He's been watching too many episodes of the *Untouchables*! He'll be going round with a bloody axe next, whacking barrels of beer! He's got to be pulled into line.'

The barman arrived with the drinks on a tray, and the group fell silent.

'You'll have to leave that one with me, for now,' Freddy said as the barman left.

'Okay Freddy, but the grass has to go,' said Benny Mejlak, leaning forward in an earnest manner.

Freddy looked down at Mejlak's hands, and noticed that the man's tremor was getting worse. Mejlak had some kind of rare disease, which meant that a build-up of copper in his body slowly poisoned him. He was often admitted to a private hospital in an emergency, leaving his younger brother to run the business. Pity the doctors didn't just let him die, Freddy thought; behind Mejlak's watery eyes was a vicious, calculating brain. Typical ponce. Would cheat his own mother out of her life savings. Freddy didn't trust Scalesi, either. Italian Frank: he was born over here. He'd been one of Darby Sabini's boys before the War. Been had up for murder, after doing a Brighton bookmaker, but he got off on a technicality. Make the bastards pay for any help over this.

Mejlak smiled in an ingratiating way. 'There was none of this grassing in the old days, now everyone's at it. It's got to stop. It's bad for business if people get the idea they can grass on whoever they like. This grass has got to be *hit*. We want to take him out. That's the deal.' He tapped the table with a shaky forefinger, to indicate that this was his sticking point.

'That's over and above our regular deal. That's a lot of extra work.'

'It'll be a traffic accident, as agreed,' Scalesi said. 'No guns, no violence.' He had coloured the daisy black, and now began to surround it with a garland of black flowers, like a strange funeral wreath.

'I'll need a bung for my troubles,' Freddy said. 'It's a lot of extra work. A lot of people have to be straightened. I'll need five grand.'

The music had gradually increased in volume, so that it was now nearly as loud as before. A teenage girl was stripping to the Booker T and the MGs hit, *Green Onions*. Freddy moved his chair so he could see better.

'Fucking Madonna!' Scalesi threw his pen down on the table and looked around the room in annoyance. 'That's a total of ten grand, for something that's been planted on us. It's bleeding daylight robbery!'

'Okay Freddy, here's the deal,' Mejlak said. 'You get your bung. The porn charges are dropped. Andrews starts behaving himself. Our driver goes down for drugs, but the informant bends over and kisses his arse goodbye.'

Freddy said, 'Five grand by tomorrow night?'

Scalesi and Mejlak exchanged a glance, and then nodded.

Freddy shook hands with each of them in turn. 'There you are,' he said, 'that wasn't so bad. We're one big happy family again.' He waved for another round of drinks. 'Look at the tits on that,' he said, pointing to the teenager, who had just finished her set and was being helped offstage.

***

The following morning, Andrews had a court appearance, and didn't get back to the nick until 11.30 a.m. The desk sergeant had an urgent message for him.

'John? DCS Milbright wants to see you, pronto. He's got Commander Jarvis with him.'

'What's it about?'

'No idea, John.'

'If there was money riding on it?'

'It's either going to be about Tanky Challenor's trial or this drug trafficking case?'

'Might be Challenor. I was brought in to replace one of his men.'

Tanky Challenor's team at West End Central had planted evidence on a group of protestors at the state visit of the Queen of Greece, the year before. Forensic evidence had disproved the police case, and now Detective Sergeant Challenor and colleagues were being prosecuted for conspiring to pervert the course of justice.

Andrews knocked on Milbright's door and, after a long pause, was called in. Freddy Jarvis was sitting behind Milbright's desk, and Milbright stood behind him, his back to the wall. Both men appeared to be relaxed and in good humour. Andrews disliked Jarvis on sight. He looked typical of the old-style, unprincipled senior officers who had achieved high rank through some mysterious process that was patently unrelated to ability.

'Andrews?' said Jarvis. 'Sit ye down. I was just explaining to DCS Milbright about some developments in relation to dangerous drugs. Now you're here, I can tell the whole story.'

'Sir?'

'As you may know, Andrews, the government are under pressure from the Americans over heroin. The Yanks don't just want us to stop prescribing the stuff to addicts, they want it outlawed. Banned from medical use. You know our puritan cousins. Ever since they failed to prohibit alcohol, they've had this bee in their bonnet about prohibiting opium and heroin. Apparently, they have a God-given mission to lead the world to sobriety, and we're all standing in the way.'

Jarvis looked to Milbright for a response, and Milbright rolled his eyes to the heavens.

'Anyway, a ban on heroin is not something we could ever get past the medical profession in this country, or the Ministry of Health for that matter. So the government is looking for an initiative, something that will show how seriously we take all this drug dealing. Show that we're getting tough. A big arrest, maximum publicity. Quite frankly, this case of yours is our first ray of hope. We want you to pursue it. But we don't want you to waste your time on porn. Pornography is like the poor: it's always with us. It's heroin trafficking we want to hear about.'

Andrews didn't like the way the discussion was going. He was convinced that someone of senior rank was protecting the Soho vice kings, and it could be Jarvis. He was determined to confront the issue. He said, 'I have to say, sir, I think there may be an element of police corruption in relation to pornography.'

There was a long pause while Freddy Jarvis stared at Andrews in amazement. 'I hope you've got evidence before you start making accusations like that! I needn't remind you that the Met are facing a difficult time with all this fuss over Tanky Challenor. The last thing we want is more unfounded accusations of police malpractice. Now, get back to your informant, and get us some useful information. And because this is a high-profile operation, I want DCS Milbright to take overall responsibility for the case. Let's round up these drug dealers! And leave pornography to the specialists at the Yard. Oh, and Andrews: I see you've had a commendation already? Excellent work! Keep it up!'

After Andrews left there was a long silence. It was broken by the Commander: 'What's wrong with him, Brian?'

'Andrews? He's a swede-basher, sir. He transferred from Warwickshire. Doesn't fit in round here. Everyone's on the square and he's a swede-basher, who lives by the rulebook. Doesn't understand what a tough world London is, thinks everything should be done by the book, like in ruddy rural Warwickshire. They tell me he grew up as a Salvationist, so maybe he still thinks he's in the Sally Ann.'

'Oh, God help us! Does he know you slipped that heroin into the van?'

'No, he thinks Forensics uncovered it.'

'You're going to have to mark his card, Brian. And send someone over to the lock-up at Holborn, and get hold of that load of porn that he snatched. We'll recycle it. It'll be worth a couple of bob.'

'Sir.'

'And then the porn charges can be dropped, because of loss of evidence. We'll proceed on the drugs charges; the van driver's going to take the rap. The Mejlaks will look after his family while he's inside. Everything's been sorted. The Home Office are going to be pleased with this one, Brian.'

There was a pause while Brian Milbright, who was looking out of the window, seemed to search for a way to raise an issue that was on his mind. 'Fred, you and me go back a long way. I remember when you made it as sergeant in Hampstead. I remember your son as a babe-in-arms. I was sorry to hear about the problems he's got himself into.'

'Not as sorry as I am, Brian.'

'If there's anything I can ever do—'

'Thanks Brian. He's gone off the rails, but he's still my son. At least he's somewhere where he can receive help at present. How did you hear, if you don't mind me asking?'

'It was when I was at that conference the other day.'

'Well, I'd appreciate it if you kept it under your hat for now. You know how people talk.' Freddy Jarvis scowled at Milbright's back. 'And I want you to neutralize that ponce Andrews, before he starts upsetting everyone.'

***

As news began to filter out that one of the Mejlaks' drivers had been nicked, Elara took counsel from her friends. She called at Miss

Demeaner's flat, just around the corner in Noel Street. Miss Demeaner sat on the karzi with the door open, so she could chat. Elara told her that Ronnie had put himself in a dangerous position.

'He doesn't want to get mixed up with the law round here,' Demeaner said. 'He'll end up getting slashed, like Jack Spot. Why doesn't he do a runner?'

'He'd have to disappear totally. Go and live in the sticks or something. Maybe Swindon, but he doesn't want to go there. Anyway, I want him with me. He's my new man.' Elara wandered into the bedroom. 'Bloody hell, Demeaner. This is an absolute tip.' The room looked as though it had been hit by a typhoon. Blankets, eiderdown, newspapers and dirty underwear were strewn across the floor. She wondered how Demeaner could live in such a mess. Elara's own flat was always tidy; she needed to feel her life was well-organised.

'You can clean it for me, if you like,' Demeaner replied. 'Does he want to stay in town so he can carrying on fixing?'

'He won't be living with me if he does. I don't mind using H occasionally, but junkies are losers. They're always trouble. Besides, I want him to do something with his life. He's got such a lot of potential.' Elara was examining an SS uniform she could see on a hanger. 'What's this, Demeaner?'

'That? It's my new SS uniform, for role-plays with the punters. I had it made-to-measure, with a mini skirt. I wear it with black fishnets. Do you like it?'

Elara shrugged. 'Nazi regalia gives me the creeps, actually. I'm thinking of getting out of the S&M business.'

Demeaner pulled the lavatory chain. 'What for? You don't want to go back to stripping do you?' She romped into the hall like a playful kitten, coming to an abrupt halt in front of her friend. She had combined an old, dingy bra with new lacy knickers. 'Here, do you like my knickers? Italian. I got them from a new boutique called *Fundies*. Fun-undies?'

Elara nodded in acknowledgement of Demeaner's fashion sense, then said, 'No, I'm not going back to stripping. I need a new career. I want to develop my spiritual side …' She hesitated, not sure if Demeaner would understand her aspirations. 'I'm thinking of setting myself up as a Tarot card reader.'

'You'll be Madame Elara. You'll have a little booth down at Brighton, and a long queue along the pier? All those old men with hankies on their heads? Eating jellied eels and having their palms read?'

'No thanks, I'll go for the top end of the market, the rich and famous. Eating caviar and using the services of a psychic. I think I'll bill myself as Madame Elara, prophetess and seer. Let Madame Elara gaze into your soul.'

Both women threw themselves on the sofa and sat facing each other, with their feet up.

'There's more money in spanking men's bums,' Demeaner said.

'It's not about money,' Elara said, resting her chin on her knees. 'I'm like Ronnie, not into material things. I'm more interested in the mystical side of life—'

'Sounds like you're keen on him?'

'I'm rather taken with him,' Elara said, looking up with a broad smile. She began to pin a loose strand of hair into her French Pleat, then changed her mind, and let her hair down over her shoulders. 'He's not fixed for several weeks now, and he's a much nicer person.'

'I never think of you as being mystical, Elara. You're so practical. Much more practical than me; I can't even boil an egg! It's Ronnie that I think of as mystical. He's a dreamer. He's somewhere else most of the time.'

'Don't tell him that. He thinks of himself as a rationalist.'

'Men always think they're rational, even when they're over the bloody rainbow. Elara, why don't you speak to that punter of yours? The one at the Home Office? Ask him how Ronnie can get off the hook?'

***

While Elara was phoning her contact in the Home Office, Guido Roberts sat in the Greek, with a London evening paper spread out across the table in front of him. He'd just rolled a cigarette and now he brushed the loose tobacco off the page, and scanned the news section with a frown. He settled down to read a story about the new Labour Cabinet, filleting it for information with the patience and close attention to detail that he usually reserved for the form of runners at Newmarket.

Guido looked up as two well-known faces joined him at the table. Frank Scalesi wore a pork-pie hat pulled low over his eyes. Tommy Bolt, his minder, was battle-scarred and pugilistic, with a glass eye, which he sometimes removed for a joke. Bolt liked to drop his eye into someone's pint of bitter, so they noticed an eye staring up at them when they neared the end of their drink. Both were regulars at the Medusa Club, where Ronnie was working, although they didn't know him by name.

'Hello Guido, old son,' said Scalesi. 'How's tricks?'

'Hi. How you doing, Frank? Tommy?' Guido's lumpy face assumed the colour and texture of fresh putty.

'Still selling the wacky baccy? Still stashing away the loot? Making all that big money out of my manor?'

'I'm getting by, Frank. Making a living. There's no money in pot.'

'You'll be retiring early, I hear,' Scalesi scoffed.

Guido gathered his paper together, pocketed his tobacco tin, and made to leave.

'You know the drug scene, Gweeda,' said Bolt, placing a restraining hand on Guido's arm. 'Who's this Ronnie Fizz character?'

'*Guido*. My name's *Guido*. Fizz is just a junky. Why?'

'A junky? Who's he working for?

'No one. He's just a kid. He don't work for no one. He's a nutter; he's been in the Bin. Why?

'We've got word from our friends in the Met that he's been stirring up a lot of trouble for us,' said Scalesi. 'He's trying to fit us up. What's his game?'

'Well, like I said, he ain't got no game. Pam calls him the apprentice bum. He follows the other bums around, learning the business. He wouldn't know how to fit you up if he wanted to, Frank.'

Scalesi's eyes narrowed: 'Is he a mate of yours?'

Guido's throat felt very dry; he drank his tea in one long gulp. He said, 'Not exactly a mate. I know him. I see him around … Look, do you want to know the truth? He's a wrong 'un. No morals. I mean, there's certain rules in life and you have to keep them. He tried it on with my Samantha once, when I was putting him up. Tried to get his leg over.'

Scalesi laughed. 'Like that Mickey Marshall when you was in Parkhurst, Tommy.'

'Marshall didn't try it on with anyone else, after I came out, did he?' Bolt said, with an angelic smile. 'He didn't have any equipment left to fuck around with.'

'Frank, do you want me to have a word with Fizz?' Guido said.

'It's gone too far for that, Guido. Like you said, he's a wrong 'un. A fucking grass. A prize prat, who's stirred up a real hornet's nest. There's a lot at stake here, Guido. This is business. We want you to deal with it—Tommy?'

'It's quite simple, Gweeda,' Bolt announced, his voice dropping to a low murmur. 'You just wait in a motor till this grass is coming down the street and then you drive into him. Crash-Bang-Wallop! And then away. One more road traffic fatality. No one ever susses anything. Hit and Run. Only make sure the bastard's dead before you have it away on your toes. If necessary, reverse back over the body, just to make sure.'

Bolt's final words were drowned out by the loud hiss of steam escaping from the coffee machine. He looked round at Dimitri in disapproval, before repeating, in a loud voice, 'Reverse back over the body.'

'Don't worry, Guido,' Scalesi added, 'we'll make sure our people at West End Central are the first ones on the scene. They'll tidy everything up.'

'Sorry, I can't do it,' said Guido. He looked around the cafe, searching for a pretext to break off the conversation, but no one would catch his eye. Dimitri was busying himself dismantling and cleaning the coffee machine.

Scalesi frowned. 'I don't think you understand the nature of the request we're making, old son. You don't have no choice. We're calling in a favour. That time we got you out of trouble with the bookies?'

'No, you see, I can't—'

'Look, nothing personal, Guido, but if you don't do as you're told, Tommy here is going to shoot your bollocks off. Then he'll cut off your thin and thick. And then you'll sit down to piss for the rest of your life!'

Tommy Bolt nodded and smiled benignly. 'Nothing personal you understand, Gweeda.'

'Sounds pretty personal to me,' Guido replied.

'So you'd better say yes,' said Scalesi.

There was a blast of cold night air as the cafe door opened. A young woman known as Tin Lizzie hurried in and made straight for their table. As thin as a skeleton, her translucent skin was sprayed over her bones rather than resting on flesh.

'Guido!' she called, in a thin nasal whine. 'Where's Dave the Pave?'

'He's dead,' Guido said, without any attempt to soften the blow. 'OD.'

He looked away, as if a beggar had tried to stop him in the street, and he was avoiding eye contact.

'Oh no!' Tin Lizzie wailed loudly, as though she'd just discovered Dave's body; every head in the cafe turned to look at her. 'Oh, please God! Mary mother of Jesus!'

Scalesi threw his hat down on the table and looked at Guido impatiently.

'Have you got any smack?' Tin Lizzie continued, in a high-pitched voice. Dimitri came out from behind the counter and moved towards her.

'I don't use the stuff,' Guido said, his gaze averted.

'Hop it!' Bolt ordered, pointing to the door.

'I've got to score!' Her dark eyes filled with tears.

'Can't help you,' Guido said, as Tin Lizzie walked away with an odd, stiff-legged gait. She stumbled on the doorstep, and then slammed the door as she went out.

'Fucking stick insect!' Guido said.

'So Guido, you'll do it?' asked Scalesi.

'No!' Guido said, turning back to Scalesi, 'I can't do it—'

Scalesi raised his eyebrows.

'—I mean I don't actually know how to drive,' Guido concluded.

There was a long silence. 'He doesn't bloody drive!' Scalesi said wearily. 'He doesn't bloody drive, Tommy, you *pillock*! Who was it said he would be all right? Who brought him in on this? You, *you berk!*'

Tommy Bolt looked embarrassed. 'I'll give Gweeda a shooter, and then he can do him,' he offered.

'No! I told you the coppers don't want no shooting, Tommy. They don't want any silly questions about gun crime. It's got to be an accident, that's the deal.' Scalesi sat gazing at the nicotine-yellow ceiling for a long minute. 'Okay: Tommy, you're going to have to drive the motor. Guido here will be with you to identify the grass.' Scalesi stopped and stared at Guido. 'What the fuck are you wearing that studded dog collar round your neck for?'

'It's a fashion.'

'Fashion?'

'Yeah, like winklepickers.'

'Winklepickers? Look, you better not fuck up on this, Guido, otherwise there really will be some radical surgery in store for you. Winkle choppers. Do you understand?'

Guido gazed into his empty teacup and didn't reply.

Chapter Thirteen

Tony Talbot, Minister of State at the Home Office, was in a quandary. He was due to vote in an important division in the House, when he'd received a phone call from Mistress Elara, instructing him to drop everything and attend on her. After agonising over his decision for several minutes, he told his secretary to pass on his excuses to the government Whips, and took a taxi to Soho. Now, he was on his hands and knees, because Elara had insisted that he could not walk into her presence, but had to crawl out of the room, and then crawl back in.

'I'm going to punish you, slave,' she said, swishing a cane through the air, 'because you haven't been in touch with me.'

Talbot bowed his head, while Elara administered thirty strokes of the cane across his bare buttocks. He began to sob, 'You didn't ask me to get in touch with you.'

'You'll get another six for arguing. You shouldn't need to be asked to maintain contact. Look up!' she commanded. 'I need your help on something. Something called Section 60 of the Mental Health Act.'

'Please Mistress, mental health is the responsibility of the Ministry of Health.'

Elara was aware that she was finding it hard to keep up the pretence. Her heart wasn't in it any more. But if she lost enthusiasm for acting the dominatrix, she would begin to lose business. Even this client, one of her most loyal and devoted slaves, could desert her. She didn't want to lose him before he'd been of use to her, so she made an effort to rise to the challenge of the role. She pulled his hair until his neck strained back as far as it would go, and whispered in his ear.

'You can find out about Section 60, or your civil servants can. A young man has been told he can be recalled to a mental hospital at any time.' Another tug on the hair, to keep his attention. 'What do we have to do to get him off their books? I want him discharged. I want to know what you can do to help.'

'I'll go back to the office and find out, Mistress. I'll ring you as soon as I can.'

'You'd better.'

A little after 4 p.m., Elara received the call from Talbot. He had found the papers on the case, and his civil servants had drafted an answer for her, which he summarised over the phone. It wasn't true that the person concerned could be recalled at any time. Dr Weiss had discharged him from Section 60. He was, therefore, a free agent. If anyone wanted to send him to hospital against his will, it would be necessary now to make a committal under another section of the Act. Unless he committed another offence, drug addiction would not be a sufficient cause; he would need to be seriously ill, perhaps psychotic.

'Thank you, slave,' she said. 'Your Mistress is very pleased with you.'

***

Monty was not a happy man. Ronnie had not shown up at the Medusa for several days. Now, with no explanation, he'd re-appeared. Monty came into the kitchen, where Ronnie was about to tackle a backlog of dirty plates, and threw five pound notes down on the table.

'That's what I owe you,' Monty said. 'You're fired. I told you what would happen if you took time off, so sling your hook!'

Ronnie pocketed the cash and left without further delay. He was not sorry to lose his job, because Andrews had been able to find him at the club. As he turned the notes over in his hand, it occurred to him that he could afford to score a couple of grains of Horse. He was planning to stay off junk, but he could do with a fix right now. Help him to think straight. On the other hand, he was putting himself at risk if Andrews saw him in any of the usual junky haunts, like the Dilly. He decided to go and find Elara, who was meeting Pam in the Duke, and tell her about losing the job. He might just score afterwards, if there were any faces around Goodge Street.

He caught up with Elara in Rathbone Street. She was walking slowly, arm-in-arm with Miss Demeaner, on the opposite side of the street. He called for them to wait. Both women stepped into the road, intending to cross. He waved at them to stay put and walked towards them. As he reached the middle of the road, they all heard a car engine being gunned. A maroon Rover jumped away from the kerb, like a racing car flying out of a pit stop. It hurtled towards them. Next to the driver, they could see the white face of Guido Roberts, an expression of sheer terror frozen across his features.

What happened next seemed to take place in slow motion: Ronnie stepped backwards, while Elara raised her left arm, and her brick-laden handbag flew towards the windscreen. The Rover was only yards away when the windscreen exploded in a shower of glass. The motor veered sharply to the left, mounted the pavement and crashed into a cast iron lamppost. The bonnet of the Rover concertinaed into a space less than four feet long, and petrol began to leak over the tarmac. The chassis twisted as if it had been made of cardboard; the boot sprang open. One front wheel, still spinning, managed to point skywards, while diamond-shaped fragments of glass spread out across the road, forcing oncoming cars to screech to a halt.

Elara ran towards the wreck, glass crunching underfoot. Tommy Bolt had taken the full force of the projectile, before being catapulted forwards by the crash. His face was lacerated, his neck broken. His lifeless body had fallen across both front seats, and Guido struggled to extricate himself from beneath the corpse. Elara pulled open the passenger door and helped Guido to his feet.

'He's dead,' she said. 'Tommy Bolt, he's dead … Can you hear me, Guido?'

'My face is cut …' Guido looked like a little boy, about to burst into tears. 'I'm bleeding, Elara.'

The Duke of York emptied: people came to stare at the wrecked car, most still holding their beer glasses. Further down the street, a crowd from the Newman Arms congregated around the wreck. Everyone was studying the corpse on the front seat, the spreading petrol stain, and shards of glass.

'Guido, you silly, silly prick!' said Elara, helping him to the side of the road. 'What've you got yourself into?'

'Not my fault,' Guido said, his eyes unfocussed.

An onlooker asked if he wanted a brandy, and Guido nodded.

'Listen …' Elara spoke slowly and precisely, as if she was addressing someone who relied on lip reading: 'If you want to stay in Pam's good books, you'd better start behaving yourself. Is this Italian Frank's work? Tommy Bolt worked for Frank Scalesi, didn't he?'

Guido sat on the kerb, gazing into the gutter, and then covered his eyes with his hand. 'They both work for the Maltese brothers.'

They were now surrounded by a ring of spectators, all discussing what had happened. There were several eye-witnesses, although only one woman claimed to have seen it all. It wasn't an accident; she'd seen some geezer shoot the driver. Taking a packet of Woodbines from her coat pocket, the woman placed a fag between her lips, and produced a gold cigarette lighter from her handbag. Then, looking down at the petrol beneath her feet, she thought better of it, and stuck the fag behind her ear.

'I was forced to go along with it,' Guido mumbled. 'They can get very nasty.'

One of the onlookers arrived with a double brandy, which he thrust into Guido's hand, and everyone watched while he knocked it back. Elara looked across at Ronnie. 'Somebody wants you out the way,' she said.

Ronnie was unsure what he really felt, like an actor who can't remember his lines and looks around desperately for a prompt that never comes. He nudged Guido with his foot, thinking that maybe he should kick him into the road.

'Fucking could've killed me,' Ronnie said, in a matter-of-fact way, as if he was ordering fish and chips. 'I can't believe you'd treat a friend like this.'

'Friend?' Guido said. 'You're a grass. A devious little shit! You were carrying on with Samantha behind my back.'

So Guido knew all along. Ronnie adopted an outraged tone of voice. 'Do you believe any old slander, or what? I never grassed on anyone, you ginger cunt!'

'You were carrying on with Samantha, behind my back. When I gave you somewhere to stay.'

The onlooker took the glass back from Guido and asked Demeaner if she needed a drink. She beamed.

'Guido, this ain't the time for all that!' Elara said. 'Now listen: you don't want to tell Scalesi that a woman did this, do you? Tell him that Tommy was hit by the Francome Mob from Camden Town. That you think they're behind this. Ronnie wasn't even the grass. You were set up by the Francome Mob, get it? They shot at the car.'

A police patrol car appeared at the top of the street, and then stopped for several seconds, as its occupants struggled to make sense of the scene. It drove towards them at a walking pace. The Bill looked as though they didn't know what to do. Elara strode over to the police car.

'What're you waiting for? A car crash—get an ambulance.'

The two policemen exchanged worried looks. Elara turned back to Ronnie, now standing beside Demeaner, who was chewing gum with an expressionless face.

'Let's scarper,' Demeaner said, 'before the Old Bill wake up and start asking for witness statements.'

'I'd better take Guido up the Middlesex Hospital,' Elara said. 'He might be concussed or something. I'm not leaving him here with Plod.'

'After what he's done?' Ronnie said, his numbness replaced by anger. 'Jesus Christ! He just tried to bloody kill me!'

'Guido's as much a victim as you are, Ronnie.'

'Victim? He's a failed executioner!'

'He was forced into it! Anyway, if you hadn't got mixed up with the fuzz, this would never have happened. You've only got yourself to blame.'

The onlooker arrived with a double brandy for Demeaner, which she accepted with a gracious smile.

'I might've guessed it would be my fault!' Ronnie snapped. 'Okay. Fine. Do what you like. We'll be in the Duke when you finish your mission of mercy.'

Elara was being a bitch, spending time with Guido when the idiot had tried to kill him. Guido had taken part in an attempted execution. *You've only got yourself to blame!* What was she thinking of? That was what his mother always said. Whatever bad things happened in life were always your own fault, especially catching a cold. That was always culpable. Murdered? Serves you right. Now perhaps you'll listen to what your mother tells you.

Ronnie sat with Demeaner at a corner table until closing time, but no users showed up and he was unable to score. Elara had not shown, so he suggested they went down the all-night café in Frith Street. 'Might be able to score there, Demeaner, if you fancy a fix,' he said. 'I mean, after all the upset you've had.'

Demeaner shrugged, as though she wasn't particularly distressed. 'Why don't you go down the Dilly if you want to score?'

'I can't go there right now. Do you want to come down Frith Street or not?'

She shrugged again. 'Yeah, all right.'

Demeaner walked fast, with short steps—two for every one of his. Her round buttocks swung and bounced with every step. As they crossed Soho Square, men stopped and stared, or turned to watch her bum proceed down the street. It was the opening scene in *The Girl Can't Help It*, where Jayne Mansfield turned the milkman's head, and the milk boiled out of the bottle in his hand. Little Richard at the piano: *If she winks an eye, the bread slice turn to toast.* That was Demeaner. A hip wiggler, like Mansfield.

Demeaner talked and chewed gum incessantly, but there was a kind of purity about her. It was as if her mind never slowed to dwell on complexity. It was a fast-flowing stream, always seeking out new territory. Her conversation ranged from ballet to sex: punters she hated and the occasional one who turned her on.

'If I can't stand them, I just sit on their faces,' she said. 'At least it shuts them up. If they're all right, I'll shag them. I get paid either way.'

In her uncomplicated lust, she reminded him of a girl he once snogged in a village bus shelter. 'I just like fucking,' the girl had said, blowing a gum bubble.

He was happy to let Demeaner talk. It was a distraction, an alternative to worrying about the attempt on his life. He knew he had to sit down at some point and think about what had happened, but for now he just wanted to get stoned and recover his composure.

As they neared the cafe, Demeaner took his arm. 'Don't want any hassle when we go in,' she explained. 'Pretend we're a couple.'

He pushed open the door to the cafe. Billy McGuinness, the self-styled King of the Gypsies, was holding forth in the middle of the floor, a Spanish Flamenco hat perched on the back of his head.

'The matrimonial couple,' McGuinness announced as they entered. 'What a gorgeous bride! Let me be your sidetrack till your mainline comes

… No, no, that's just a joke, mein leibling; the King of the Gypsies is spoken for. Better play *Here Comes the Bride* …'

Demeaner rewarded McGuinness with a dazzling smile. At the rear of the cafe Ronnie spotted Gypsy Dave, and they slid into the seats opposite him. All that Ronnie knew of Dave's background was that he was from Essex; he had no idea whether he was really a gypsy. Dave was tall and wiry, with long, thin teeth, which resembled a horse's. He bared them when he smiled, and showed the whites of his eyes, like a horse about to bolt. His hair had been cropped short with a pair of scissors, crudely, as though he'd received treatment for head lice, but otherwise he took great care over his appearance. He wore a paisley neck-scarf and a blue fisherman's jumper, its heavy, oiled, wool woven into a sinuous pattern, like a Celtic knot.

'Can we score off you, Dave?' Ronnie asked.

Dave gave the slightest of nods, almost imperceptible. 'I can let you have two grains. It'll have to be two quid, I'm afraid. No loans, no discounts, no birthday-present-in-advance; I'm skint. I need cash for my doctor tomorrow.'

'Why do they call you Gypsy Dave?' asked Demeaner.

'It's just the gypsy in my soul,' Dave said, clenching his teeth in a smile.

'Well, you look like a sailor in that jumper,' Demeaner said, stroking Dave's sleeve. 'And there's something about a sailor …'

Dave smiled even more broadly at this obvious ploy. 'It's still two quid: I can't go any lower than that … My jumper's from Whitby. Every fishing port has its own design. It helps identify drowned fishermen.'

'You'll be the first fisherman to drown in Soho,' said Ronnie, placing two pound notes into Dave's out-stretched hand.

'You could be a jockey, except you're a bit too tall,' Demeaner said.

Dave grinned, showing all his teeth, as if they were clenched in pain. Under the table, he counted twelve tablets of heroin into the palm of his hand.

'You must be psychic or something. My family are all jockeys,' Dave said. 'My uncle's a jockey in Malton, my cousin at Lambourne Down.' He accepted a cigarette from Ronnie and lit up. 'Frankau's a leech, a blood-sucker. She's bleeding me dry. She wants the thirty guineas I owe her by tomorrow, or she's going to cut me off. I'm just five quid short. Here, you don't want to score in advance? Give us a fiver, and I'll give you seven grains of smack tomorrow afternoon.'

Ronnie shook his head slowly: they both knew he'd never see the shit if he parted with money today. It was a half-hearted blag; there was already an air of defeat about Dave.

Ronnie placed the H in his matchbox and they left without buying coffee. Demeaner said her gaff was not far away, and they could go back and shoot up. As they turned up Dean Street, he was aware that she kept looking at him, quick glances that searched for eye contact. He felt nervous. Finally he was unable to avoid her gaze any longer.

'Would you like to lick my clit?' she asked, in the casual way she might proffer a cigarette.

'Your what?'

'Suck my cunt.'

'Jesus, Demeaner! I need to fix. I've had people trying to kill me tonight. I can't think of anything else right now.'

'Are you a virgin?'

'Course not. Where do you get a stupid idea like that?'

'How many girls have you slept with?'

'I don't know. Loads.'

'Later, then. We can do a 69.' She slipped her arm around his waist, reached up and kissed his cheek.

He realised that Demeaner took it for granted that she could find comfort in a caress, in physicality, in another's body. When he was a child, he'd climbed on his mother's lap, and buried his face in her breast. A cuddle had soothed him, taken the sting out of life. But that was years ago. Now, junk was his only source of comfort. Well, there had been one time when Samantha sucked his dick, and he had leaned back and felt that the world was a warm and benevolent place. That was about twelve months ago; since then his body only felt at ease when stoned, and he'd become indifferent to sex.

Sitting on Demeaner's unmade bed, he took two jacks to make his fix. It'd been a while since he'd used, and his tolerance had reduced. Two jacks felt more like four. He began to gauche off before he'd helped Demeaner find a vein. She managed by herself, and shot up one jack. For the first time that evening, her talking ceased.

They lay back on her bed, and drifted in and out of sleep. He awoke with a start to see Elara standing over him, hands on her hips.

She was incandescent: 'What the *fuck* is going on?'

Her anger surrounded her like a halo of flame, burning everything she touched. He moved further away, aware that he was wearing nothing but his Y-fronts and his socks, although he couldn't remember undressing. His works was standing in a glass of water by the bed. The water was rosy pink, where he'd begun to flush the syringe clean, before falling asleep.

'We're just having a fix,' Demeaner said. At some point, she'd removed all her clothes, apart from her bra and knickers. Her discarded garments were in a pile on the floor, by the bedroom door.

'Fuck off, Demeaner! What's he doing in your bed?' Elara shouted, the veins standing out on her neck. '*You were shagging!*'

'What are you getting so upset about, babe?' Ronnie said. 'Have a fix. Stay cool.'

'You toe-rag! I'm out the way for a few hours and you're sleeping with my best friend.'

'No babe, you got it wrong.'

'He was just turning me on, Elara.'

'Fuck off, Demeaner! I know the sort of tricks you get up to. Well you can keep him. He's not coming back with me!'

'Babe, you got this all wrong—'

'I'll bring your clothes round tomorrow, toe-rag. Don't bother calling me. And next time you decide to shag someone else's fellow,' Elara said to Demeaner, 'do it to someone who hasn't got your spare door key, so they can't walk in and catch you at it!'

'Don't be such an idiot, Elara. You know there's nothing going on,' Demeaner said.

But Elara had gone, slamming the front door behind her. They listened to the man downstairs, shouting after her, 'Why don't you fucking shut-up? It's two in the morning, for Christ's sake! One day I'll call the police! Turning the place into a ruddy brothel!'

Demeaner said, 'Don't let it bring you down, Fizz. We can do a 69.'

Ronnie's eyes closed. He allowed himself to gauche off.

Around noon the next day, Demeaner woke him with a cup of tea. 'I ain't got any food in. I don't usually eat breakfast.'

She lit a fag and offered him one, as he pulled on his jeans.

He said, 'What was all that bollocks last night? Elara taking Guido up the Middlesex, when the bastard was trying to kill me.'

'Elara felt sorry for him. He looked so woe-begone.'

'Woe-begone? He looked like a jerk. Sitting on the pavement, crying about a cut on his face. Thought he was supposed to be a masochist. They like pain don't they?'

'Guido's what you call a switch. Sometimes he dominates, sometimes he submits. I call him a Wobbly Joe, because he wobbles from one kink to another. Any old how, Elara always has a soft spot for the under-dog, and Guido was the one what got hurt. Apart from Tommy Bolt, of course, but he's beyond caring.'

'And all that effing and blinding last night, about us sleeping together? She was like a flame thrower.'

'She got a bit upset, didn't she? Daft cow. By the way, she sorted out that business about you being recalled to hospital. You ain't under a Section no more. You're free. They can't take you to Broadmoor or wherever.'

He was struck by how beautiful Demeaner looked when she smiled.

'Thanks, Dem. I'll tell you something: being free is the most important thing in the world. There's nothing more precious to me than freedom. Brilliant news. I think I'll go over to Chelsea to see my doctor. Get registered again. I'll see you this evening.'

'You can't stay here tonight, Fizz. Sorry. I'm working. Maybe some other time.'

Demeaner's dazzling smile lit up her face.

***

Brian Milbright was planning to leave work early when the door to his office was flung open. The bulky shape of Freddy Jarvis appeared in the doorway.

'What the bloody hell's going on, Brian? I thought I'd left this in capable hands! Everyone's telling me that it's mayhem on the streets of Soho. We're going back to the days of gang warfare!'

'Calm down, Freddy. A few bookshops have been attacked, that's all. A few brawls in the street, nothing more.'

'I hear it started when the Mejlaks tried to bump off a police informer who was something to do with Johnny Francome, and that someone set them up! Is this Andrews' doing? Blimey O'Bloody Riley, Brian!'

'Calm down. It's Andrews' informer. No one else has met him. I've no idea who he is, or what Andrews is doing about it.'

'Well you should know! I told you to neutralize Andrews! He's creating bloody chaos. He's got a bee in his bonnet about pornography, and about the Mejlaks. I want to see him, now.'

Milbright went to the door and asked his secretary to find DC Andrews. A few minutes later the detective appeared in the doorway, looking from Milbright to Jarvis for some clue as to why he'd been summoned.

'Take a seat, Andrews,' said Jarvis. 'What's happened to your informer on the Uranus case?'

'I'm waiting to hear, sir.'

'I understand an attempt has been made on his life.'

'All I know is that one of the Mejlak firm was killed in a car crash. I've no idea whether my snout was involved or not. Not until I catch up with him.'

'What protection have you organized for him?'

'If we provided protection for every snout in the West End, sir, you'd need to double our budget.'

'So none is the answer?'

'I didn't think it necessary.'

'And what's the link between your informer and Johnny Francome?'

'None whatsoever, as far as I'm aware.'

'I'm going to read you the lead story in tonight's *Evening News*. The headline is *Crime out of control*. "In the middle of the capital's greatest ever crime wave …" Are you listening, Andrews?'

'Sir!'

'I've not come to see you for the sake of my health! You're in serious trouble!

> In the middle of the capital's greatest ever crime wave, a gangland feud has broken out. Police are linking a betting shop that was bombed in Camden Town to a number of Soho book shops that burned down on Tuesday night. The shops are believed to be owned by rival gangs.

'Blah, blah, Francome mob, blah, blah. And then we get this:

> West End Central is the police station at the centre of allegations of police corruption, being made at the trial of Detective Sergeant Harry Challenor and colleagues. Police sources …

'Police sources? Is that you Andrews?'

'No sir!'

'Frankly, I'm disappointed in you, Andrews. The whole manor is going up in flames. It's bloody mayhem out there. You were supposed to nip all this drug dealing in bud, not start bleeding World War Three!'

'With respect, I think that's a bit unfair, sir. A number of arrests are imminent. I have information on pornography which will lead to further arrests. I've got the Mejlak brothers bang to rights this time.'

'Well, you can pass your information over to the Obscene Publications Squad. They'll handle it from here. You're going to be transferred. You're going to be at YF Division from next Monday, so you can go and clear your desk.'

'Yankee Foxtrot?'

'That's right, Andrews, Ponders End!'

'Ponders End?'

'Yes, you can do something about all those thefts from allotment sheds they're having up there. And be thankful that I'm not asking you to resign.'

***

Ronnie took the Northern Line to Archway, having collected a new prescription for heroin and cocaine, and fixed up in a public karzi on the Fulham Road. Got the script without too much trouble. His doctor was all right really. Wouldn't give more than three grains of Horse, on the grounds that his tolerance couldn't be so high after a lay-off. That would be a problem, inside a month or so. On the other hand, the man agreed to prescribe cocaine, if Ronnie promised to consider going in for a Cure.

Quite a good rush from the coke. Nothing hits harder than mainline coke. Snorting coke's a waste of time and money, you need a speedball. H&C. Flash-bulbs go off inside your skull. Bastard when it wears off, though. Not so rosy then. Face facts: no girlfriend, nowhere to live, no cash. Bet Elara's screwing Guido. That's why she took the idiot up the hospital. Bitch. Then she called round Demeaner's so she'd have an excuse to dump him. It was all planned. And Demeaner couldn't wait to boot him out this morning. Cow. She was from Tottenham, she said, not the East End. The Sweet Maid of Tottenham: *She was as full of lechery as letters in a book*. Slags, both of them. Can't trust women, that's what his father reckoned.

He wasn't going to get caught out like that again. He'd changed all his plans. Instead of looking for Elara, he made for Samantha's address off the Archway Road. At least she wouldn't let him down.

Samantha's new gaff was a three storey Victorian town house, which had been condemned but was available on a short lease. He noticed that someone had painted the slogan *Keep Britain White* on her garden wall. He hammered on the heavy cast iron knocker, and heard the noise reverberate around what sounded like an empty property. He stood waiting and listening, one hand in his jacket pocket, jiggling together his bottles of H & C. At last he heard a light footstep, skipping swiftly down the uncarpeted stairs.

'Oh, it's you!'

Samantha seemed taken aback, as though he was the last person she was expecting. She was wearing a mini-dress in a purple and yellow zigzag print, and a white trenchcoat, as though she was just going out.

'Hi babe. Going to ask me in?'

She kissed his cheek. 'To what do I owe the pleasure?

'I've just got registered again. Any chance of kipping here for a few nights?'

He walked into the front room. It was unfurnished except for an old sofa, covered in an exotic West African fabric. Other fabrics covered the walls, in dramatic colours and strange, compelling patterns.

'It's for my work,' Samantha said, seeing the direction of his gaze. 'I told you, I've gone into the fashion business. I'm using traditional African designs and materials, but putting them into a space age context.'

'What's wrong with black?'

'I forgot, you don't approve of fashionable things, like new fabrics and bright colours.' She took a joint off the mantel-shelf. 'Fancy a smoke?'

'So is it okay to kip here?' he asked.

'Okay if you're going to share my bed,' she said, lighting the joint.

He moved in. At first, she seemed happy. He watched her cutting cloth, and pinning together dresses. They spent the evenings talking, in front of the sitting room fire, discussing her ideas for the future. As the days passed, however, she became withdrawn and disconsolate. She made several attempts to draw him into a serious discussion about his own plans. She wanted him to make a commitment to being junk-free.

'You're not so sexy when you fix,' she said.

'Don't try to change me, babe! Why can't you just live in the present?'

Every discussion about the future ended in angry exchanges, with one of them walking out of the room. After a while, she stopped trying to engage him in conversation, and began playing the same record over and over again: *You'll Lose a Good Thing* by Barbara Lynn. He wondered if she was waiting for him to get the message.

It was true that he had a good thing with Samantha. She was someone he could rely on. He felt a measure of safety in their relationship, although he was aware that security always came at a cost. He was trading-in his freedom, losing the unpredictable, random element in life. Although it was painful, he knew he would have to sacrifice domestic comfort, in order to become a free spirit once again. One evening, going through his pockets looking for some cigarette papers, he found Elara's phone number. On the spur of the moment, he went out to the neighbourhood callbox and dialled her number. She seemed delighted to hear from him. They had a long, animated conversation, only stopping when his cash ran out.

He felt torn between the security he felt with Samantha and the excitement generated by Elara. For the next two weeks he sat alone in the bedroom, shooting up junk. By his side was an airgun he'd found in the attic. He took pot-shots at a nude calendar he'd pinned to the wall, until it was peppered with holes.

'You want to shoot women?' Samantha asked, looking in the open door.

'No—it's just cheese. It's full of holes, see? I'm taking apart the illusion. The bullshit. It's like, I'm taking down the Floating World.'

'It's like, you're nuts.'

The next day he walked out. He'd decided to go back to Elara. He told Samantha that Elara was someone who wouldn't judge him, who would allow him to be himself, to be free.

'Don't start going on about freedom,' Samantha said. 'You don't know the meaning of the word.'

'I'm going to live how I choose, without anyone restricting me.'

She stood in the doorway of the front room, watching while he rooted through the bookshelves, looking for his spare syringe.

'Freedom isn't doing whatever you feel like,' she said. 'You've been doing that for a couple of years now, and look where it's got you. Hooked on junk.'

He rolled his eyes in exasperation. 'Have you seen my works?' he asked.

She shook her head. 'You can't be free when your life is governed by having to shoot up every four hours. Freedom is exercising free will, being independent. Not being a slave to junk. It's like a big security blanket to you. You've actually chosen security, not freedom.'

He gave up on his missing syringe and pushed past her into the hallway. As he opened the front door, he turned and said, 'Living here was safe and secure, but I was dying inside. I have to be creative, to live on the edge. Unlike you, I don't want to know what I'm going to be doing tomorrow, and the day after.'

She threw a heavy dinner plate at him, but it missed and shattered against the wall.

'You haven't got a clue about women!' she shouted after him. 'You stupid, ineffectual prick!'

Trains on the Northern Line were delayed, and the journey from Archway to Tottenham Court Road took more than an hour. At one point, the train was stationary in the tunnel for ten minutes and he felt intensely irritated, brought down by the lack of progress, the things Samantha had said, and the loss of his spare works. His sense of misfortune increased when he reached Elara's flat in Berwick Street, and found that her name had disappeared from the doorbell. It now read Mistress Sadie. There was another girl in occupancy.

'Elara don't live here no more,' said the new tenant. 'You a punter?'

She'd left no forwarding address. He hurried around the corner to Miss Demeaner's, to see if he could find out more. Demeaner came to the door in a silk dressing gown, with her hair wrapped in a white towel, like a turban. Without speaking, she left the door open and went back to her living room, her head held on one side as she massaged her wet hair, her bum wiggling from side to side. He followed her.

'She's pushed off, Elara. With that Shiner,' Demeaner said. 'He's her new man.'

Ronnie felt a dull pain, a sick feeling in his stomach.

'Yeah, he left the American air force. Got some kind of discharge. He's gone legit with his bootleg record business—got a shop or stall over in Camden Town. Her name's Dawn now, she don't call herself Elara no more. She's given up hustling. They're going to be a record company.'

'But what about her mysticism?' He was bewildered by the turn of events, and couldn't hide his dismay. 'She was going to be a fortune teller.'

'She's a bread-head now. She reckons that with the Beatles and the Stones and that, a lot of kids have joined groups and are looking for recording contracts. There's a lot of money to be made.'

'It's so uncool. Everyone's chasing bread.' He heard a note of desolation creep into his voice.

Demeaner jumped to her feet and tidied away some cushions. Ronnie noticed that the flat looked clean and uncluttered, the first time he'd seen it without Demeaner's dirty laundry scattered across the floor.

'They're all bread-heads now,' she said. 'The whole scene's changing. No one's scruffy no more, everyone's dressing sharp like Rod the Mod.' She lit two cigarettes and passed him one. 'He's just made a record, Rod the Mod,' she continued. 'He's a singer with a group now. The world's gone mad since they sent Chris Keeler to prison. It's all the publicity. I'm turning business away; I'm run off my feet. At this rate the punters will be queuing round the block.'

'Did Elara say anything about me?' He was aware after he said it that he'd given the game away. He sounded like a little boy, and he could see from the way she paused that she had noticed a vulnerable side to him for the first time. He wished he'd been less direct.

'She reckoned you had to go back to Swindon and come off junk, or you wouldn't make old bones.'

'Well, she's wrong!' He made an effort to sound tough and assertive. 'I'm going to do what I want with my own life. I'm an anarcho-individualist.'

'The real mystics are Guido and Pam. They've got religion.'

'You are joking? I can't imagine Guido opening *Hymns Ancient and Modern*. Not unless he was looking for the name of a nag.'

'It's not C of E, it's witchcraft. They've joined a coven in Notting Hill. They're dead serious about it. Guido's going to be a high priest of Wicca, Pam told me. That's what they call it, Wic-cah. Pam's gone all la-di-dah.' Demeaner put on a posh accent: 'When you're in Wic-cah, like us.'

'No one believes in witchcraft any more, surely?'

'Did you see Guido's photo in the *Sunday Pic*? Bollock naked, with a big loving cup positioned *here*.' She placed a hand in front of her crotch. 'Pam's the goddess apparently. They had one of Pam with her tits hanging out. She was holding up this dagger called a thingamebob. Athame. About to thrust it into Guido's sodding love cup. I kid you not! They got fifty guineas.'

'Guido's a fucking moron. He'll do anything for bread. That's why he spent half his life flogging ten bob deals. Then lost all the loot down the bookies.'

They both heard the front door open and close.

'That'll be Dave,' said Demeaner.

Gypsy Dave ambled into the room. He seemed to be at home, switching on the telly, and throwing himself down on the couch.

'All right man?' Dave said. 'Just been to see the lady of the manor, to get a week's scripts. Lady Frankau. Isabella Frankau-stein, the demon duchess of Wimpole Street!' Dave laughed for a long time at his own joke. 'Any chance of a cup of tea, doll?' Dave looked at Ronnie enquiringly, 'You want one?'

Ronnie shook his head. Demeaner kissed Dave on the forehead as she went out to the kitchen. It was a surprisingly domestic scene, and Ronnie felt excluded. He realised, for the first time, that he was lonely. He could not go back to Samantha, and he'd lost Elara.

Watch with Mother came on the telly. They turned away from each other and faced the screen. It was a puppet show about two men made from flowerpots. Dave said, 'Perfect viewing for junkies, the *Flowerpot Men.* No bloody effort. And it's got a character called Weed.'

'So Frankau didn't cut you off?' Ronnie said.

'Dem gave us the bread to settle my account. I don't owe Frankau nothing no more. She's as nice as pie these days.' Dave paused to treat his face to a prolonged scratch, before continuing, 'Some geezer's been looking for you down Piccadilly.'

'What did he want?'

'Just asked if anyone had seen you.' Dave's eyes remained glued to the screen. 'Reckoned you'd grassed up the Mejlak brothers. You never said nothing about that before?'

'Because it's a load of bollocks.'

'Well, I'd stay away from the Dilly if I was you. A lot of people reckon you're some kind of grass.'

'He's not!' Demeaner called out from the kitchen. 'Blooming Guido started that rumour.'

'I'm not,' Ronnie confirmed. 'Guido lives in a fucking fantasy world. That's why he claims he's found witches in Notting Hill. I would never grass on anyone, man—not even to save my life.'

'Well, some people have got the hump with you. I'd lay low for a while, if I was you.'

Although it was only two hours since his last fix, Ronnie felt miserable. Leaving Demeaner's flat, he walked the short distance along Poland Street towards Oxford Street. Crap, crap, crap: that's how things were turning out. Life was fucking toxic. He put his hand in his jacket pocket and felt for his bottle of H. Even the knowledge that several grains of pure heroin lay in the palm of his hand didn't comfort him anymore. He didn't feel high, he was just fixing to stay straight. His habit was dragging him down.

Before this moment, he'd never cared whether he had a girlfriend or not. He hadn't needed other people, as long as he had a regular supply of junk. His family and friends had been minor characters in his life story, at the core of which was his relationship with Horse. Now, there was something missing. He wanted to be with Elara, or even reliable old Samantha. He wanted to become flesh and blood, not a grey ghost, haunting the midnight chemists, depending on a prescription for his vitality.

The way forward was almost unthinkable: stop using. It wasn't just the discomfort of withdrawal. Without fixing he wouldn't know what to do with his time, how to be with people. Being a junky was his identity, it was *who he was*. Without his habit, he'd be a nobody, a straight person whose exciting days were behind him, like those soldiers who'd had a good war and couldn't settle down in civvy street.

Still, life couldn't be any worse. He had to come off junk, to get Elara back. Or Samantha: she was all right really, and she'd take him back. He would go to his doctor first thing tomorrow, and ask for a Cure. There was this new unit down at Cane Hill in Surrey, he'd ask for a place. Tell his doctor he wanted a bed immediately. They had loads of vacancies, they'd be only too pleased to get another patient. Now that he'd made the decision, he felt at peace, confident that he had taken charge of his own life. Tomorrow would be the first day of a new, junk-free life.

As he turned into Oxford Street, the Blonde Widow was about one hundred yards away, lurking in the crowds. She was still wearing the black suit, and the hat adorned with a pink orchid, and she still had a veil covering most of her face. First sighting for quite a while. She was back on his tail. But maybe she wasn't the law? Maybe she just wanted to meet up? Perhaps she wanted a fix-for-a-fuck? Maybe it was that simple? The Widow didn't know where to score, but she'd figured out he was on junk, so she wanted to approach him. This time he wouldn't try to give her the slip; perhaps he would give her a present of his remaining junk. He walked slowly, wondering whether she might catch up with him and speak. She seemed to maintain her distance, but she had a bad limp, so perhaps he was just outpacing her.

He turned off Eastcastle Street into the mews, and let himself into the emergency exit. Home at last. Squatting in the corner of the lift-shaft, he prepared a big fix, conscious that this would be the last time he would ever go through the old, familiar ritual. He tied a belt around his left arm to act as a tourniquet, and made a hit on the inside of his elbow. As his blood blossomed into the syringe, he heard her footstep on the stair, tap-tapping. He listened to her limp along the corridor towards him, one leg dragged behind the other. At last he would meet the old cow, face-to-face.

The door to the corridor opened so slowly that at times it seemed stationary; it was thirty seconds before Ronnie could see the person on the threshold. Standing in the shadows, his hat pulled low over his face, was Frank Scalesi. He gestured to Ronnie to stand up. Ronnie pulled the needle from his vein—slowly, because it was blunt, with a burr on the tip, which made the blood vessel bleed copiously.

'I know you from the Medusa,' Ronnie said. He felt a rush from the Horse, and his awareness turned away from the external world, and settled deep within his own flesh. He felt complete indifference towards his visitor, and the reason for his visit.

Scalesi stepped forward into the dim light of the 40 watt service lamp. He produced a Walther PPK pistol from his coat pocket, and pointed it at Ronnie, jerking it upwards to indicate that he must stand.

'No … a mistake,' Ronnie said. 'Listen, I am not …' Ronnie loosened the tourniquet, and struggled to his feet, his fingers compressed over the wound left by the blunt spike. Blood dripped onto the concrete floor. 'It's a load of old bollocks about—'

'Fucking face the wall!'

Ronnie turned towards the wall. Scalesi brought the gun up to the back of the boy's head and pulled the trigger twice.

She is in the churchyard when he finds her, standing with her back against an ancient yew tree. In the dense, dark green shade, he brushes his hand up against her flat stomach, and feels the ridges of her corset, a pink whalebone corset like his mother used to wear. He tries to loosen its elastic bonds, but his fingers aren't nimble enough. Lichen on granite, moss on slate. Her eyes are as deep as two pools of brown bog water, peaty and brackish. He is still unable to see behind the veil with any clarity, but he is aware of her direct gaze, her dark eyes staring out at him, and her voluptuous tits, and the demure chrysanthemums scattered over the grass. He brings his hand up between her legs and touches the smooth skin at the top of her stockings, one of her legs noticeably thinner than the other, withered. He places his open hand over her moist cunt, while he leans forward to kiss her lips. Her face is blurred, like a picture out of focus, but he can smell her sweet breath, like meadow hay. Rye grass, corn cockle, poppies waving in the breeze. As soon as you pick the poppy, its petals fall.

***

Freddy made his way from his office at Scotland Yard along the Embankment, as far as Hungerford Bridge. He walked at a slow pace, almost a shuffle. It was three in the morning, and a thick mist hung over the river and the road; he could see the lights along the river, and the bulk of nearby lamp stands, modelled as dolphins, and the outline of trees about fifteen yards ahead, but that was it. Whisky swirled around his brain, but whenever there was a moment of clarity he could see his son's body again, stretched out on the floor of the lift-shaft, blood and brains splattered over one wall. Like that Wehrmacht officer in the Pas de Calais, all those years ago. Except it was his own flesh and blood this time.

The officers at the scene had been right to call him out. He needed to know. He'd identified the body. Made some preliminary arrangements. After the inquest there would have to be a funeral. People would have to be invited. He circled around the pain, and came back at it from another direction. Had the murder been anything to do with Benny Mejlak, and the deal they'd struck at the Capers Club?

He crossed the road to the all-night coffee stall outside Embankment Tube station, and bought a cup of tea. A group of deadbeats, with bedrolls or guitars slung over their shoulders, stood huddled in a semi-circle, drinking coffee. They were doing their best to ignore Billy McGuinness, the King of the Gypsies, who paced up and down in front of them, like a shaman conducting a spirit dance. 'Drifters!' McGuinness ranted. 'Just flotsom and jetsom in the river of life ...'

Freddy turned away. Flotsom and jetsom. Dead cuttlefish, whelk's eggs, limpet shells, tar. Driftwood. Drowned bodies floating on the Spring tide: sleepwalkers making their slow progress out to sea. The corpse: Freddy's thoughts always came back to his son's corpse.

He carried his tea over the road to the river, and gazed down on the brown water. He fancied he could smell the sea at Tilbury in the damp air, and a thousand cargoes being carried up and down the shrouded river, and all the wharfs and piers in between. The scent of molasses and pine, of a damp pile of wheat infested with rats.

It was all the fault of that rat, Andrews. The Warwickshire Salvationist. He had no business arranging the boy's release, when Freddy was keeping him out of harm's way. No business concealing his informant's identity, putting the boy at risk. Had the satisfaction of wiping the smile off the little Salvationist's face, though. Andrews had a new career, pursuing sinners in the outer reaches of Ponder's End.

Had to face the fact that the Mejlak firm had killed the boy, with his agreement. He'd put it about that it was a drugs-related murder. Couldn't have people investigating the Mejlaks, they would uncover his own role. In the fullness of time he would exact his revenge on Benny Mejlak. Dirty little syphilitic ponce.

Freddy had travelled down to Swindon to tell Flo. The silly cow had tried to shut the door in his face. Had to force his way into the house to speak to her. No easy way to break the news, of course. Had to come straight out with it. Told her that the boy had been killed in a quarrel over drugs. She started howling, like a beast. Absolutely hysterical: punching and kicking him. Had to slap her around the face to bring some sense. She virtually accused him of murder. Everything bad in their lives was supposed to be his fault. Good job she didn't know the truth ... His mind edged up to the central horror: he had taken a bribe in exchange for his own son's life. But how could he have known? He thought the boy was safely locked away in the nuthouse. No one would blame him, surely? He had to live with the knowledge, that was punishment enough.

He'd devoted his life to justice, but in reality there was none. No goddess with a sword and scales, anyway: no cosmic justice. There was just a pile of gold in a precision weighing balance. You either amassed gold or lost it. And where did that get you? He had one of the top jobs now, and a personal fortune, but it was all empty. There was no person in the world he was close to; hardly anyone he spoke to, outside of work. The money wasn't much use to him. He came alive through his work. He had no home life, but he had his public role, his duty. He would make his mark on the world through the policies that he would force through over the next few years. He would shape the future, not die without a trace, like so many happier men. He was not flotsom, nor was his boy. Ronnie would have a monument.

***

'He was a devoted father.'

DCS Brian Milbright produced a bottle and two tumblers from the lower left hand drawer of his desk and poured two generous measures of Scotch, passing one to George Meadows.

'That's not my understanding,' said Meadows, nodding his thanks.

'He split up with his wife a number of years ago, but he always tried to keep in touch with his son,' Milbright continued, replacing the bottle in his drawer. 'She made it impossible. Bit of a depressive. A nervous sort of woman—'

'He was a bit handy with his fists, I heard.'

Milbright frowned at the interruption, but seemed to decide against defending the reputation of Freddy Jarvis, a man known for his foul temper. Instead, he brought the bottle out of the drawer again, placed it between them, and continued, 'Then some bastard got the boy hooked on heroin, and it was downhill all the way. Another *chota peg*, George?'

'Why not?' Meadows said, pushing his glass across the desk. This time Milbright filled both glasses brim-full. It was one of the better quality blended whiskies, Meadows noticed. Higher proportion of malt to grain whisky than most. No cheap rubbish for Milbright, even if he drank it by the bottle rather than the tot.

'The boy had the best treatment available in England—they had him in a mental hospital under the best psychiatrists and everything—but it was no good,' Milbright said. 'Once they get on that stuff, they're finished. Slow suicide.'

'So much more sensible to just drink yourself to death.'

There was a long pause while Milbright considered the remark. When he finally spoke, he seemed muddled and a little ponderous. 'At least we've paid our dues to society, George. We've earned the right to piss it up the wall … Booze doesn't destroy people like addictive drugs. It's legal.' He fell silent and stared morosely at the floor. After a while, he recharged their glasses and resumed, 'Anyway, that was why Freddy started all this fuss about drugs. He wants to make sure that no other kid dies like that. Drugs-related murder. Head blown off at the bottom of a lift-shaft: not very nice. Freddy forced himself to go to the inquest, of course. Sat through all the evidence. Post mortem. Spoke with the officer who found the body. I thought it was going to drive him mad.'

'Freddy was never far off it. Madness, I mean.' Meadows felt the whisky make his gums slightly numb. He was beginning to get drunk, to become more candid than was wise.

Milbright held up the front page of the *Evening News*. The headline was *Curb Heroin—Top Cop's Get Tough Call.*

'Have you read it?' Milbright asked.

'I haven't seen an evening paper yet.'

Milbright read aloud:

> Scotland Yard's new Assistant Commissioner Frederick Jarvis has called for a curb on the right of doctors to prescribe heroin and cocaine. "It's time to get tough," Jarvis said yesterday. "The number of addicts has doubled in recent years. Family doctors should no longer be involved in the treatment of addicts, because they have over-prescribed. Because of their failure, Britain now has 400 drug addicts. There need to be special clinics or prisons where these people can be treated, and there should be a major police campaign against drug peddlers. In future, the police should lead the fight against drug use."

'That'll be as successful as our fight against prostitution, I suppose?' said Meadows.

'Were you always a cynic, George?'

'It comes with working here.'

Milbright read on:

> In response to questions in Parliament, Home Office junior minister Tony Talbot said that the Government had already announced an Inquiry to look at these issues. "It may be that there

> is a case for specialist drug clinics, and for restrictions on prescribing, but this is one of the questions the Inquiry will consider."

'Why does my heart sink every time they announce a new Inquiry?' said Meadows.

Milbright rose from his desk and walked to the window. Although his view was limited to a nearby office block, he stood there for several minutes. Meadows remembered that his boss had been the sublieutenant on a corvette during the War: Milbright was still on the bridge of the ship, surveying the distant horizon of the North Atlantic.

'Freddy reckons this business of treating drug addicts like ruddy invalids hasn't worked.' Milbright said. 'Stop them prescribing heroin, get Mr Big behind bars and smash the black market! He says if we crack down now, we can get rid of the problem within five years.'

'Sounds like the first step down the road to criminalising drug addiction, like in the States.'

'We can learn from the Americans. Set up proper, dedicated Drug Squads. Start undercover work. Make proper use of informers—'

Meadows shook his head in disbelief. 'We've only got a few hundred heroin addicts, Brian. This is the first drugs murder we've had. The Yanks have got hundreds of thousands of addicts. They have drugs killings every day of the week. Why copy them? Let our doctors continue prescribing heroin, and then there's no real black market, no need for crime to feed a drugs habit, no need for any murders. You used to agree with me on this, Brian. So did Freddy.'

'That's the soft option, George. The government wants to stop all this moral degeneracy.' Milbright warmed to his theme. 'The Met are going to wipe out the drugs trade in London. Starting with heroin, and then purple hearts, and then hemp: the bloody lot! In five years' time, you won't even be able to buy a Smarty on the black market. And Fred Jarvis is just the man for the job!' Milbright leaned forward confidentially. 'He wants to stamp out drug addiction. It will be his son's memorial.'

Other books from Year Zero authors

Year Zero is a group of writers, all of whom believe passionately in the direct relationship between writers and their readers. As writers, we are committed to giving you our words unfiltered by market tastes or trends. And we're committed to listening to what you have to say in return. We are not a publisher.

In addition to *Glimpses of a Floating World* by Larry Harrison, the following books are available from Year Zero writers:

Brief Objects of Beauty and Despair is a sampler of some of today's most exciting contemporary fiction. Featuring 13 pieces by Year Zero writers, it's free to browse or download on http://yearzerowriters.wordpress.com

Benny Platonov by Oliver Johns. A refugee from the former East Germany believes he can save the homeless of Hong Kong. If only he didn't have writer's block.

Songs from the Other Side of the Wall by Dan Holloway. A teenage girl growing up in Post-Communist Hungary faces a heartbreaking choice between past and future.

Year Zero writers include Mary Banks, Simon Betterton, Marcella O'Connor, Larry Harrison, Heikki Hietala, Dan Holloway, Oliver Johns, Annia Lekka, Anna Le Pard, Karine Levecque, Anne Lyken-Garner, Sarah E. Melville and Julia Sutton. Many of their books will appear in the months and years to come. Follow their progress at:
www.yearzerowriters.wordpress.com

www.ingramcontent.com/pod-product-compliance
Ingram Content Group UK Ltd.
Pitfield, Milton Keynes, MK11 3LW, UK
UKHW041946190726
13854UKWH00004B/1824